WAVE OF TERROR

WAVE OF TERROR

Theodore Odrach

Translated from Ukrainian by Erma Odrach

Introduction by T. F. Rigelhof

An Anita Miller Book

Academy Chicago Publishers

Published in 2008 by
Academy Chicago Publishers
363 W. Erie Street
Chicago, Illinois 60610

© 2007 by Erma Odrach

Printed in the USA.

Library of Congress Cataloging-in-Publication Data

Odrach, Fedir.
  [Voshchad. English]
  Wave of terror / Theodore Odrach ; translated from Ukrainian by Erma
Odrach.
     p. cm.
  ISBN 978-0-89733-562-1 (pbk.)
  I. Odrach, Erma. II. Title.

PG3979.O3V6713 2008
891.7'9334—dc22

2007027777

To Klara, the author's wife,
and his granddaughters
Tania, Claire and Christina.

THEODORE ODRACH: AN INTRODUCTION

Theodore Odrach's life as a writer was brief, prolific, and extraordinary. In the span of eleven years between 1953 and his death in 1964, he wrote four novels, two collections of short stories, a memoir, an historical account of the land from which he sprang, and numerous essays. He wrote during whatever hours he could spend away from his wife and young family at the end of his working day in a Toronto printing shop. To Erma, the daughter who has become his translator, he was doting, loving, and involved, but also unlike the fathers of her friends. He was not only more domestic—he did the dishes and regular housework — but he was also strange and shadowy. The sound of his typewriter filled the evenings of her childhood and posed a mystery she only began to untangle through the close reading of his writings that transport readers into a complex and difficult world, but one that's observed with gentle humor and genuine humanity.

Open the pages of *Wave of Terror* and you're immediately an eyewitness to some of the more casual brutalities of the twentieth century—the topsy-turvy world of the Ukrainian-Belorussian borderlands as farms, villages, towns, cities, and their peoples pass from Polish to Soviet rule. Odrach's fictional rendering of the ancient town of Pinsk, the village of Hlaby, and the rustic inhabitants of the Pinsk Marshes feels as the everyday world must have felt for ordinary people living through those bizarre times of fraudulent faiths and false hopes. As Headmaster Kulik, who is the eyes, ears, and heart of much of the novel, gazes out the classroom window in the opening paragraphs, the thoughts that weave through his mind raise a question that many ponder but few risk asking: "A person rises, then falls; the earth swallows up his flesh and within time he is forgotten. For example just yesterday . . . there was a regime, and today there is another. Yesterday's was swept away, just like that."

Kulik isn't Odrach, but their lives are parallel in an important way: both went to university, studied the past attentively and learned from historical precedent that when the world is in the grip of ideological hysteria, it is the diffident man, the civil although uncertain man, who is far happier than any other. And that makes them masters of their own lives despite all that befall them.

Like his protagonist, Theodore Odrach lived an eventful life. A child of the marshlands, Odrach was born Theodore Sholomitsky in Misiatichy on the outskirts of Pinsk, Belarus on February 13, 1912. At the age of nine, he was taken from his family and sent to reform school in Vilno for minor acts of delinquency. After his release as a teenager, he worked at odd handyman jobs while he put himself through school, graduating with a degree in ancient history and philosophy from the Stefan Batory University (now the University of Vilno). Following the Soviet invasion of 1939, he fled Vilno and returned to the Pinsk Marshes where he taught school in an unusually remote village.

Actively pursued by the Bolsheviks, he moved to Ukraine where he edited and circulated underground newspapers in collaboration with the Ukrainian Insurgent Army as it resisted the Soviets on one front and the Germans on the other. Forced to flee from house to house at the fringes of the forest, setting up and dismantling his presses on the run (a part of his life briefly but memorably sketched in the poignant short story "The Night Before Christmas" included in *The Penguin Book of Christmas Stories*, 2005, edited by Alberto Manguel), Odrach ultimately managed to escape across the Carpathian Mountains into Czechoslovakia. At war's end, he made his way first to Germany and then to England where he lived for five years before emigrating to Canada in 1953. Settling in Toronto, he dedicated himself to putting on paper a record of the everyday lives he had witnessed, shaken by fear, betrayed by cowardice, humiliated, persecuted, imprisoned, tortured, slain or permanently displaced as the larger world they inhabited was turned upside down thrice over.

Wave of Terror (originally published in Ukrainian as *Voshchad* in 1972) was a work-in-progress when Theodore Odrach's writing life ended. It forms the first volume of a projected trilogy that would have dealt with the situation in the borderlands during the Soviet takeover, the German occupation, and the aftermath of World War II. Like Alexander Solzhenitsyn, Odrach learned to survive the horrors he witnessed by remembering precisely what happened to those around him and turning their lives into stories and himself into a writer who is a rigorous investigative reporter as well as a consummate storyteller. Keeping these tales to himself and hidden from the world as he moved from refugee group to refugee group until he found a refuge of his own in Canada, they emerged from his typewriter as short stories and novels in intense bursts of creativity. Long gestation and quick composition give his work unforced urgency. Odrach's individual gift as a recorder of a lost world—the thing that sets him apart from his Cold War contemporaries and draws him closer to George Orwell and D.H. Lawrence—is the range of his emotional sympathies and, specifically, his unromantic, anti-sentimental, matter-of-fact approach to the sensual lives of girls and women. Odrach has much to tell us that hasn't been reported in this way by anyone else about how the coming of the Soviets affected the sexual identities of women along the outer edges of the USSR as the Kremlin, through the agency of the NKVD (People's Commisariat of Internal Affairs), elevated psychopaths and sociopaths to positions of petty tyranny and abusive power, including their domination of women:

> Marusia, looking through the open window of her living room, was happy to feel the warmth of spring upon her face. Watching

flocks of geese soaring high above the treetops and small red squirrels scrambling from tree limb to tree limb, she thought suddenly of Sobakin. His heavy face, with dark puches under his eyes, haunted her night and day. . . . Marusia felt as if his eyes were always on her. Her only consolation was in knowing that almost always, he was detained in the Zovty Prison. What exactly he did there she did not know, or rather, she did not want to know, but the one thing she knew for certain was that each time he passed her house he searched her windows.

Odrach's most obvious literary debts are to Anton Chekhov and Isaac Babel. He uses irony and humor in similar ways as he captures the internal drama of his characters with psychological concision. The subjects may be difficult, but the writing isn't. Odrach tells his tales in clean, clear prose that conceals rather than reveals its own artistry. *Wave of Terror* is compelling and compulsive as it portrays tumult in the daily lives and shifts in political perspectives among a wide range of residents of Pinsk and its backward marshland villages as the intimidating Red Army arrives and is duly followed by Bolshevik agitators who muscle their way into every nook and cranny of Hlaby with shrill propaganda, endless meetings, public confessions, deportations of Polish sympathizers, and a doctrinaire redistribution of wealth and power that refuses to recognize its own ignorance and folly.

Unlike so many others who were reduced to silence by the weight of their experiences and the indifference of postwar North America to their stories, Theodore Odrach found his voice despite an audience that began with his wife and extended only as far as fellow expatriates. For those of us who lost both ancestral languages and whole branches of our family trees in Stalin's purges and Hitler's wars, *Wave of Terror* is an eloquent and important reminder of lives for which there can never be happy endings, but it is equally a testament to the beauty of the idea of the pursuit of happiness and open to all readers. As V.S. Naipaul writes in "Our Universal Civilization" in *The Writer and the World* (Knopf 2002):

The idea of the pursuit of happiness. . . . is an elastic idea; it fits all men. It implies a certain kind of society, a certain kind of awakened spirit. . . . So much is contained in it: the idea of the individual, responsibility, choice, the life of the intellect, the idea of vocation and perfectibility and achievement. It is an immense human idea. It cannot be reduced to a fixed system. It cannot generate fanaticism. But it is known to exist; and because of that, other more rigid systems in the end blow away.

Long after the crimes of Kovzalo, the Village Chairman, and Leyzarov, the Representative of the District Committee of Pinsk, and even those of Sobakin of the NKVD, fade from memory, Headmaster Kulik remains vivid as a man of great sorrows, bitter tears, and unbearable uncertainties who nevertheless keeps moving, staying one step ahead of the secret police, constantly pursued but pursuing with even greater tenacity the unquenchable spirit that rises up in him at the sound of running water and the sight of the ascending sun.

The Pinsk Marshes, the setting for *Wave of Terror*, is Europe's last great wetland—a vast tract of dense forest intermingled with swamps, moors, ponds and streams that cover southern Belarus and northwestern Ukraine. Its earliest settlements can be traced back at least two thousand years. In 1939, its villages were connected to Pinsk by rough roads and trails that were difficult to negotiate even in dry weather. Frequently cut off from outside visitors, the villagers were regarded as very much in need of enlightenment by the Soviet invaders. The marshes suffered greatly not only from the events Theodore Odrach recounts but also, a half century later, from the nuclear catastrophe at Chernobyl. The Zovty Prison which features prominently in the lives of Odrach's characters is now a cancer hospital where the original bars have not yet been removed from all the windows.

T.F. RIGELHOF
MONTREAL, DECEMBER 2007

TRANSLATOR'S NOTE

My father was an enigma to me, always in the shadows, always at a distance. He was tall, dark-haired, with deep-set eyes that were forever lost in another world. I would watch him come and go as if he wasn't really my father but rather a stranger in the house. I would listen to his footsteps, to the sound of his typewriter, hear him talking quietly to my mother late into the night as I slept in an adjoining room. Mostly he remained in his office at the front of our house, at his typewriter, sitting there every free moment he could find. What was he doing in there for hours on end, and why was he filling pages up with words written in the Cyrillic alphabet? Sometimes with my sister I would spy on him through the front window to try and figure things out, to see what he was up to. But it was always the same; he was sitting at his desk typing away. Then one day the sound of the typewriter stopped and the house fell silent. My father was there one day and the next day he was gone. I cried and cried and thought God was playing a joke on me. But it wasn't a joke, my father was dead.

It wasn't until later, perhaps when I was ten or eleven, that I realized what my father had indeed been doing those long hours in the front room: he had been working on manuscripts and sending them out to publishing houses in Buenos Aires, New York, Toronto, and they were coming back in book form. There were novels, collections of short stories, and a memoir.

Growing up, my father's books always graced the top shelf of the bookcase in our living room. What sort of writer he was or what he wrote about were all a mystery to me. Although I spoke Ukrainian, reading Ukrainian at a literary level was a completely different matter—it was virtually incomprehensible. In my teens and later in my early twenties I made several attempts to decipher his works but without much luck. Forever curious, at last, armed with a Ukrainian-English dictionary, I was determined to learn about his world no matter what it took. And slowly but surely the pages started to come to life. There were people living inside them, there were great panoramas, history was in the making, and I soon found myself completely absorbed. Then one day I picked up a pen and started to play around with words, wondering what it all might sound like in English. And before I knew it, I was on my way to becoming his translator.

My father never really completed *Wave of Terror*, at least not to the extent that he would have liked. He left behind countless corrections and revisions in the margins of his original manuscript and various drafts, and these were never considered for the final Ukrainian text, published posthumously in 1972. I've drawn on his extensive notes and alterations, and have incorporated them into the translation to provide a broader and more comprehensive representation of his work.

ERMA ODRACH
SEPTEMBER 2007

ACKNOWLEDGEMENTS

I'd like to express a heartfelt thanks to several people who have helped me along to the way: to Klara Odrach who acted as the voice of my father, to Tania Odrach for reading the draft of the translation and making invaluable suggestions, to Michael Mychaluk for his never-ending devotion to my father's work, to Jane Wilson for her insightful comments regarding particular chapters, to T.F. Rigelhof for his encouragement and support, and to Anita Miller for artfully shaping my father's work and bringing it to its final stage.

CHAPTER I

O n the edge of the village of Hlaby stood a large school surrounded by an old run-down fence and facing a road filled with puddles from a heavy rain.

Ivan Kulik, the headmaster, stood at the classroom window, gazing at a sprawling lilac bush brushing up against the pane. Hundreds of drops had collected on its branches; one drop was larger than the others. A gust of wind from the east swept the drop to the ground.

Kulik thought, "A person rises, then falls; the earth swallows him up and in time he is forgotten. Just yesterday there was a regime, and today there is another. Yesterday's was swept away just like that drop. And today's? Will it too fall and vanish one day?"

The rain intensified and began to hit the window like the fine seeds from a poppy. Dark autumn clouds loomed overhead, painting the sky a heavy leaden gray.

To the right of the school stood a small, shabby wooden cottage with a sloping straw roof and a fair-sized garden plot that ran parallel to the road. Grandfather Cemen, in his drab peasant overcoat buckled at the waist, paced back and forth there. A long white beard reached past his chest, and from time to time, as he stared at the sky, his eyes filled with tears.

Kulik watched from his window and muttered under his breath, "There is no more hope, old man. The weather reflects the new regime. It's as if God has turned his back on us. There's no place

1

for the sun; there are only clouds—clouds in the sky, clouds over the earth, clouds in our souls."

The old man hobbled over to the gate and stared for a long time to the east where the road shot in a straight line to Pinsk; in fact, lately all the villagers had fallen into the same habit. Everyone knew that evil came from the east. This was a time in history filled with danger and uncertainty. Too many strangers had taken an interest in Hlaby.

Suddenly a rumbling came from the road. With great determination two mangy horses were pulling a wagon filled with men toward the village center. The wheels and sideboards were splattered with mud and the floorboards were cold and soggy. After laboring past the school, the wagon wound its way behind a neighboring supply shed and disappeared.

"More trouble." Kulik shook his head. For a brief moment he looked at the ruts in the road and thought about the new regime: "First the Red Army is sent in to intimidate the villagers, then bands of agitators follow, with their black shoulder bags, dark riding breeches and sagging leather boots. They give shrill propaganda speeches, calling themselves long-awaited liberators. Like swarms of locusts, they seep through the smallest of cracks and infest the villages and settlements. They wear forage caps, with visors that partially hide their faces. They shout out to passersby, 'We are honest and sincere. Only a true Bolshevik can look you straight in the eye!'" Kulik stepped back from the window. "The wagon has probably made it to the Lenin Clubhouse by now. There's going to be another meeting."

Dusk began to set in. The rain continued to hit against the window. As Kulik turned into the adjoining room that acted as his office and switched on the light, the rain became a violent downpour, rattling the panes, while fierce thunder exploded overhead. He couldn't help but feel restless and irritable. Ever since he had been appointed headmaster of School Number Seven, a few weeks earlier, an intense dreariness had set in. He felt miserable in this out-of-the-way place, as if his mind was being buried alive. And the surrounding countryside of bog and marsh that seemed to go on forever only heightened his feelings of isolation and loneliness.

At that moment he heard footsteps on the porch stairs. There was an abrupt knock on the door and a young man of about nineteen appeared on the threshold. He was quite good-looking: tall, with cropped yellow hair, and wore a dark brown student's jacket from some now-defunct Polish *gymnasium*.

"Good evening, Director." The visitor smiled politely and offered his hand. "Allow me to introduce myself. My name's Sergei Stepanovich. I'd like to welcome you to our village."

"Please, have a seat." Kulik pointed to one of two comfortable-looking armchairs standing against the wall.

"I live in a small cottage on the other side of the school," the young man said. "My 'castle,' so to speak. I had to secure it with support beams this past summer because the porch was starting to sag. My grandfather built the cottage when he was just twenty years old. If you look outside your kitchen window you can probably catch the tip of my rooftop." Then, curiously, "Excuse my asking, but are you from Hvador? That's what I've heard."

A barely perceptible smile touched Kulik's lips. "Yes, that's correct, but I haven't been there for quite some time."

The two men chatted and soon felt comfortable with each other. There was only a few years' difference in age between them, and they both tended to be even-tempered and easy-going.

After about half an hour of friendly talk, noises erupted from the corridor. Someone coughed and from a neighboring yard a sharp whistle blew. The front door banged open and shut, and before long young voices surfaced. Girls giggled and boys shouted.

"Hurry up, get going!"

"Leave me alone, don't push!"

For several minutes, the stamping of feet and slamming of doors grew louder. Eventually everything quieted down, only to start up again.

"It sounds like there's going to be another meeting tonight," Sergei observed. "What do you think of these meetings?"

"Well, if anything, I find them rather amusing." Kulik went to the door and peered outside. "I had better go and turn on the lights before something gets broken."

He was walking down the corridor, when, to his surprise, two men suddenly emerged from one of the side doors along the left wall. They pushed past him, directly into his office. One was Cornelius Kovzalo, the recently elected Village Chairman; the other, Iofe Nicel Leyzarov, Representative of the District Committee of the Pinsk Region.

Cornelius, short and fat with beady black eyes, was the first to speak. "Comrade Kulik, greetings. We have come on official state business. Tonight, by orders of the Party, we will be holding a meeting. Comrade Leyzarov has been instructed to give a speech to the people."

"Uh, excuse me, Cornelius," Leyzarov interrupted, with a condescending nod. "You've got it all wrong. The Party issued no orders of that kind. Perhaps you misunderstood. The people *themselves* have expressed a desire to hear me speak. It's what the *people* want, and not what the Party wants. Is that clear?"

Cornelius's face turned red. "Of course, yes, you're right, quite right. How stupid of me to have made such a mistake."

Leyzarov continued his reprimand. "Where the Party is concerned, one must always be mindful of what one says. The Party first and foremost is here to guide and protect us. It has no tolerance for subversive or empty-headed remarks. Understood?"

Cornelius fidgeted, and noticed Sergei standing by the window. Looking him over, he said derisively, "Sergei, what in the devil's name brought you to the school? Don't you have anything better to do with your time? Are you trying to get on good terms with our new headmaster, is that it?"

Sergei scowled at him. "What if I am? It's none of your business, but if you really must know, I am here to become acquainted with our new headmaster. I find it refreshing to be in the company of someone intelligent for a change. As the old saying goes, it's better to lose something with someone smart than to find it with an idiot."

Cornelius took this as a personal affront. "What are you imply-ing? You really know how to wag your tongue, Sergei. This time you've gone too far. One of these days you'll find yourself cor-nered. You'll see . . . you'll . . . you'll . . ." He suddenly fell into a fit of coughing. In a desperate attempt to save face before the Repre-sentative of the District Committee, he changed the subject.

"Comrade," he said to Leyzarov, "this is the way things stand in our village. We're thankful and thrilled that our Russian broth-ers emancipated us from Polish occupation and made us a part of the Belorussian S.S.R. Olivinski, the bourgeois landowner, enjoyed the comforts of the great manor house on the hill, while the rest of us lived like swine in slop. Olivinski was a real bastard and treated the villagers like dirt. When he went hunting with his hounds and came across women picking berries along the river, he would beat them black and blue and steal their buckets. And if he found some poor soul carrying a bundle of brushwood out of the forest he would thrash him with his whip and then burn everything."

Pleased by the sound of his own voice, feeling rather confident, curling the tips of his waxed moustache with his fingertips, he con-tinued at length. "The forest, just look at it. It has no beginning and no end; the trees are thick and plentiful. What crime is there in picking berries or gathering brushwood? All winter we sat and froze to death in our little shacks while Olivinski chopped down our trees and sold them for firewood to the Jews in the Pinsk mar-ketplace. And for what . . ."

Cornelius broke off when he noticed Leyzarov glaring at him. Shifting uncomfortably, he tried to think what it was he could just have said to upset the Representative again.

"Well, well, Cornelius." Leyzarov tapped his foot. "What you said about Olivinski is quite true. He was oppressive and corrupt, a true villain and an enemy of the people. But what concerns me is your use of the word *Jew*. Didn't you know it is completely against all Communist principles? You must stop calling fellow-comrades *Jews* because that is very offensive to them. We, the people of the

Soviet Union, have adopted a new and more progressive term—
Israelis. Yes, *Israelis*. Do you understand, Cornelius?"

"Yes, I understand. You're quite right. Forgive me."

Cornelius bobbed his head obsequiously to acknowledge his
error, but took the liberty of starting up again. "As I was saying
about that forest. It begins in Hvador and extends well beyond the
Stryy River, all the way past Hrivkovich. There are so many trees,
as far as the eye can see, which leads me to think: did that Polish
son-of-a-bitch plant those trees? Did he water them? Did he fertil-
ize them? Just think about it. What right did he have to that forest?
Isn't it God's creation, after all?"

Leyzarov's eyes narrowed. Cornelius's babbling was pushing
him over the edge. "Cornelius, this 'God' of yours, as we all very
well know, doesn't exist. 'God' is just an ordinary bourgeois fabrication. How can 'God' set about planting trees, or watering them
for that matter? It's ridiculous. Just think about it."

"Yes, of course." Cornelius's shoulders drooped. "Sometimes I
don't think before I speak. We live in the dark here in the Pinsk
Marshes, we're ignorant of what's going on in the outside world.
That's why so many of us have a tendency to go on about nothing."

Leyzarov, trying to control himself, gestured to Cornelius to follow him as he stepped out into the corridor and made for the grade
three classroom. Kulik and Sergei followed close behind them.

The classroom was full. In the first two rows sat the older villagers; the schoolchildren stood against the back wall along with
several teenagers. Leyzarov seated himself behind the teacher's
desk and began to flip through several sheets of paper filled with
notes. He was looking over the speech he was about to give. The
people gradually quieted down, although there was still some bustle in the back rows.

Leyzarov put down his notes and stared piercingly at the crowd.
"Comrades! I am pleased that you have all come to tonight's meeting. I look at you and my heart beats with joy. You show such
excitement, such fervor, such emotion. I see in your faces a profound appreciation and love for your beloved Russian blood broth-

ers, who have more than generously extended their helping hand to you. You can now celebrate the historic day of September seventeenth, the day the Red Army freed you from Polish oppression. Under the command of our glorious leader, Joseph Vissarionovich Stalin, our endless line of tanks and our tireless infantry units moved in over this vast land of yours and brought you freedom. On this great day, brutal servitude came to an end. Comrades, let us show our eternal gratitude to our great genius teacher and father of the proletarian movement, Joseph Vissarionovich. Let us give him a huge round of applause."

The crowd roared and cheered.

The first speaker was called to the stand, a man by the name of Voznitsin. He was of average height, in his mid-thirties, miserably dressed, with distinct Russian features—a broad, flat face, a snub nose and small, slanted eyes. Although he spoke Belorussian, he did so poorly and with a thick Russian accent. His speech was barely intelligible.

"It's a great honor and a great pleasure to be a part of the new Belorussian Soviet Socialist Republic. The people of Belorussia are good, faithful, honest citizens. The evil capitalist forces have finally met their doom. There's nothing left to fear. Our Russian law is an established one, set on solid ground. Yes, comrades, the united nations of the USSR are destined to tread upon happy and prosperous roads, led by the most brilliant leader of all time, Comrade Joseph Vissarionovich. And upon this road, hand-in-hand with the Bolshevik Party, will go Belorussia. What a privilege it is for you to join the great family of Soviet nations! You, my dear Belorussian comrades, have survived terrible persecution. A new age has arrived. Now at last you will have your own Belorussian schools, your own Belorussian language, and your own Belorussian culture. But most importantly, under the protection of the Bolshevik party, you will walk hand-in-hand with mighty Mother Russia."

When he finally came to the end of his speech, he yelled out a few standard Party slogans, and then saluted a picture of Stalin that hung on the wall. Some people applauded and cheered, while others looked around in utter confusion. They wondered, how was it that the Russians had annexed the Pinsk Marshes to Belorussia rather than Ukraine? Wasn't the Marsh region clearly Ukrainian? And didn't the majority of the people speak Ukrainian while very few spoke Belorussian? To most of them, the annexation to Belorussia made little, if any, sense. The question of nationality in this half-wet, half-dry world was a complex and puzzling one, to say the least.

A rather haggard middle-aged woman with large eyes and a protruding jaw, stood up from her seat. Her graying brown hair was caught up in a loose knot behind her head. She was of genuine peasant stock. It was Timushka, wife of the local butcher. Gesticulating with her large hands, she hastened to say what was on her mind. "If we're Belorussian, as that comrade tells us, then why do we speak a language different from his? The local people here are Orthodox Christians and speak Ukrainian. We lead simple, peaceful lives. Why doesn't everyone just leave us alone? We only want to remain the simple *moujiks* that we are."

Cornelius, who was sitting a few seats behind her, lost his temper, and leapt up. "Shut up, old woman! You're too stupid to voice an opinion on complicated matters. You think all *moujiks* want to be kept in the dark? No! Unlike yourself, some of us want to be enlightened." He turned to face the crowd. "About language, it's true we speak differently from our government comrades. We're now part of the Belorussian Republic, but we don't speak Belorussian. It appears we're not Polish or Russian either. The fact is we're Ukrainian. Yes, that's right, Ukrainian. And how do I know this? Because when I visited the city of Lvov the people there, although they ate delicate white rolls and fancy pastries and put cream in their coffee, spoke the way we speak here, in Ukrainian. So there you have it. Since they call themselves Ukrainians, then we must be Ukrainian, too. And furthermore, when the late Father Dyukov, may his soul rest in peace, became angry with us at Sunday mass, what did he call us? Yes, that's right, a pack of lazy, good-for-nothing *moujiks*. And who do Russians call *moujiks*? Only Ukrainians! So, what more proof do you need? We are Ukrainian through and through, no doubt about it." Cornelius had barely finished his last word, when a loud and steady voice rose above the crowd. All eyes fell on Sergei, who was standing in the middle of the room looking very serious and shaking his head.

"I think Timushka's right." Sergei looked at Leyzarov. "Don't you think it's rather odd that our Soviet brothers have annexed this region to Belorussia instead of Ukraine? Truly, what kind of Belorussians can we be when we don't even speak the same language? We're grateful to you for liberating us, but why not let us remain who we are?"

The crowd began to stir.

"People! People!" Leyzarov clapped his hands. "Quiet down! This is too complicated an issue and one that we're not at liberty to discuss. It will be settled by the national congress of deputies who are already in Bialystock. I hereby put forth a motion to end all further discussion on the topic of language."

The people reluctantly agreed and when things finally began to settle down, Cornelius took it upon himself to address the crowd again. The people in the front rows started to laugh, while those at the back joked and nudged each other playfully. It was clear that he was about to make a fool of himself again.

"Citizens!" Cornelius yelled at the top of his voice, "You see how things have progressed. In the past our eyes were focused on the West, but now times have changed. Even my old lady is starting to see the light. For example, early one morning during harvest, she went outside and hollered through the window to me, 'Corny, Corny, get out of bed! Come look how big and bright the rising sun is. It's going to be a fine day today. The rye by the Sishno Creek has to be bundled!' So I got up, put on my trousers, and went outside. All the while I thought to myself: This sun my wife speaks of is rubbish compared to the sun in the Kremlin. Our smart Vissarionovich Stalin sits in his office and shines bigger and brighter than any sun in the sky. He worries constantly about us *moujiks*, because who are we, after all? Who are we, I ask you? Well, I'll tell you. We are as dark as coal, we are like pigs that roll around in the mud and have seen nothing of the world. But everything will change now. And I don't lie when I say that the new regime will put knowledge into our heads. They will not only build schools and factories but also modernize our farms. They will teach us how to live, as befits true fighters of the working class revolution. And furthermore . . ."

But Cornelius could not think of what to say next. Finally he managed to blurt out, "Glory to—" but before he could finish, to his great dismay, the people began to boo and hiss and stamp their feet. One young man called out, "Hey, Corny, you talk too much. You should stick to things you do best, like laying down manure. Leave the politics to us!"

The catcalls came one after the other, like blows to his head. Humiliated and enraged, he felt as though his body was on fire. He returned to his seat, and sat cursing and muttering under his breath.

The meeting was over and everyone started to leave the school. When Cornelius was in the yard, Leyzarov caught up to him. Patting him on the back, he said, "Well, Cornelius, you're a driveling idiot, no doubt about it. But not to worry, I still have faith in you. You'll get the hang of things yet."

CHAPTER 2

The classroom was now empty. Only Kulik and Sergei remained. The rain had long since stopped; the faint sound of thunder could be heard rumbling in the distance. There was mud on the floor everywhere and a thick cloud of tobacco smoke clung to the ceiling. Kulik disappeared into the supply room and soon returned with a bucket of hot, soapy water and a mop.

"What a mess." He shook his head and looked around. "Only more work for me. By day the school headmaster, by night, the janitor." Then to Sergei, who was standing near the door, "Would you mind giving me a hand with this?"

"No, not at all . . . Why don't we move all the desks to one side, then it'll be easier to sweep." When the desks were all piled together, he turned to Kulik. "I see Cornelius hasn't assigned a cleaning woman for the school yet."

"No, he hasn't."

"Well, he will, eventually." He dropped his voice and leaned forward. "About Cornelius. Just watch your backside. I have a feeling he'll be going out of his way to make things difficult for you here."

"Yes, I think you're right about that. There's something about him I didn't like from the very start. He seems on the shifty side. I suppose I'll just have to find a way to get around him."

Sergei's blue eyes darkened. "A word of advice: be firm, use physical force if you have to. It's true he holds the local power in his hands, but as you've seen tonight, he's an idiot. He's failed at almost everything he's tried. And his dealings have always been shady at best. He's been badly beaten more than once and has even had bones broken. One day a few years ago he was spotted by villagers crawling back to his house on all fours with his face battered and his legs all twisted up. He was barely alive."

"Was it because he was a nationalist?"

"A nationalist?" Sergei laughed. "No, nothing like that. No politics here. He was nothing more than a common horse thief. Late into the night he would sneak into some stable, and lead out the finest horses, then vanish into thin air. He did business with the gypsies. One night he got caught and the police took him to the station and interrogated him till all hours of the night. They gave him a brutal beating and threw him into a cell, and he couldn't move for three weeks. Then came a trial in Pinsk, then two years in the Bereza Prison. Now, as you've seen for yourself tonight, the Kremlin sun has made him see the light. From the gutter he's managed to crawl up to the ladder's first rung. What have you got to say about all of this?"

Kulik narrowed his eyes and looked troubled. He knew very well that times were far from certain, and with danger looming around every corner, it was best to keep one's mouth shut. After a moment he said, "I think you're being too candid for your own good, Sergei."

The two men resumed cleaning. The mud had already settled on the floor and had become hard as rock. Sergei filled up another bucket and wet the floor with a large rag to soften the small mounds. Kulik then got down on his hands and knees and scrubbed. They kept changing the water every so often, and in a short time the room was orderly once more.

This joint effort strengthened their friendship. When the floor had been dried and everything returned to the supply room, Kulik invited Sergei to his office for a cup of coffee. Kulik had a small canister of Colombian beans he had purchased in a shop in Vilno, where he had lived and worked before taking the position of headmaster. He had been saving the coffee for a special occasion.

Sergei wasted no time making himself comfortable in one of the armchairs. He noticed that plaster on the far wall was starting to crack and crumble, exposing bare lathes. "Before us," he said, "we have a contradiction: a run-down school and at the same time all this lavish furniture. Do you know where most of it came from? Yes, from the Olivinski manor house. The Russians had just barely ousted the Poles, when Cornelius turned up at the Olivinski estate and laid claim to all the furniture. The first thing he saw was a beautiful hand-carved cherry-wood table. He dragged that table to his miserable little shanty by the river and tried every way to fit it through the door. The entire village could hear him huffing and puffing, working up a sweat. But the table wouldn't go through. He got so mad, he even kicked the legs several times. The villagers watched, laughing. He lost face from that and couldn't bring himself to take anything else, not even these wonderful armchairs. The villagers suggested they be donated to the school. And now, as you can see, the benefit is ours."

"Yes, I was told in Pinsk by the People's Commissariat of Education that all the office furniture had come from the Olivinski manor house. It's very impressive."

"Yes, these two armchairs, the desk, those end tables, and this bookcase have all seen better days. *Pani* Olivinski, who escaped somewhere across the border, undoubtedly agonizes over her lost wealth. And of course, she must mourn her husband terribly."

"I heard he was shot."

"Actually, he was beaten to death. The peasants finally caught up with him somewhere on the edge of a cornfield near Morozovich, along one of the farm roads. He had been trying to get to the Polish border. He was dragged from his *britzka* and struck over the head with a club. They said his skull split open like a ripe watermelon." Sergei pointed to a large, crudely made cabinet in the corner. "That cabinet, of course, is not from the Olivinski estate. It belonged to the former headmaster and his wife—a pleasant enough couple. They planned to spend the rest of their lives here; they believed their Polish domain would flourish until the end of time. But of course we all know what happened. When the Bolsheviks invaded he was killed somewhere on the village outskirts; she fled to Poznan to be with relatives."

There was a brief silence. Kulik propped his chin on his fist and gave himself up to thoughts that had been causing him great uneasiness. For many years, during his stay in Vilno, he had yearned to return to the Pinsk Marshes where he was born. But now that he was back, things were not as he had expected. Everything had changed, and he was surrounded by strangers. Take for example Cornelius—not only was he very unpleasant but he seemed always to have some kind of scheme in mind—surely there were others just like him. What had happened to the people he had once known? They had all become servile, more than willing to submit to a ruling power from beyond their border. They were even being charged up with a new kind of nationalism that was foreign to them.

He wondered whether he would come to understand his own people and whether they would come to understand him. Would they grow closer to the Soviet occupiers than to each other? Would he find himself walking a fine line? As he flipped through a pile of assigned papers on his desk still to be graded, he felt overcome by gloom. Looking at Sergei, he said softly, "I'm rather troubled about the local inhabitants. I'm afraid . . . Actually, I don't know exactly what I'm afraid of. You and I seem to understand each other, we seem to see things in the same light. But the villagers? When worse comes to worse, they'll side with the new regime and we'll be left out in the cold."

Sergei gave Kulik a sidelong glance. "You have to try and understand the mentality of the people here. They're rather simpleminded and most are illiterate. They are content to be kept in the dark, and they have little if any understanding of the outside world. As long as they have enough to eat and drink they're happy." Pausing a moment, he went on, "But then on the other hand, it's true many are being stirred up by the annexation of the Pinsk Marshes to Belorussia instead of to Ukraine. They think we should be part of the Ukrainian Soviet Socialist Republic." His face hardened. "It's downright criminal to have a foreign language imposed on us. Did you hear how that comrade at the meeting went on in his broken Belorussian? Imagine how confusing it will be, especially for the elders, not to mention the children. We'll end up with a kind of chaos."

"Yes, that's true. Our region is predominantly Ukrainian, but it's being annexed to Belorussia. Belorussian is being promoted everywhere, but the fact of the matter is, what the government really wants is Russification. I agree things couldn't be more confusing. One thing's certain, however, and that's that in the end the Russian language will prevail, and the villagers will come to favor Russian ways over their own. Even now, they're being made to believe it's the way of the future. I hate to see it happening all around us. But mastering the Russian language is proving quite an ordeal even for the best of them."

Sergei got up, walked over to the window that was partially hidden behind muslin curtains, and glanced outside. "Yes, no doubt about it, we're now in the early stages of mass Russification. And it's not just happening in the villages; it's happening in the cities too. You should meet my aunt Efrosinia, who lives in Pinsk, on Luninetska Street. She's managed to transform herself into quite the Russian lady. Although she speaks striking Ukrainian, she goes out of her way to mix in Russian words wherever she can. She even cooks *shtchi* and boiled beef with potatoes twice a week. Her family acts grateful and asks for second helpings, but secretly what they really want to do is spit it all out.

"When I attended the *gymnasium* in Pinsk I lived in my aunt's house. She pronounced my name half in Ukrainian, half in Russian: 'Syerhey.' I said to her, 'Auntie, if you're trying to pronounce my name in Russian, why don't you at least say it properly?' She got angry and defensive, 'What do you mean 'properly'?' Then my cousin, Marusia used my diminutive. 'Mother, Seryoza is right. You're mixing his name up horribly. When you talk like that you sound like such a *moujik*.' My aunt could never stand to be corrected; she turned red in the face and the two of them got into a terrible argument.

"When my aunt finally left the room, Marusia turned on me. 'Seryoza,' she said, 'you're such a *moujik*, and so stubborn. It's really quite embarrassing to be seen with you. People stare at us. What kind of *gymnasium* graduate are you when you go on like that? Why don't you at least try speaking Russian? I know you can, and very well at that.'

"I've tried to explain to Marusia that by denigrating her language she's betraying herself and her people. I've recited to her the poetry of Taras Shevchenko, I've even tried to introduce her to our great novelists Kotsyubinsky and Stefanik, but she only rolls her eyes and yawns. Once I even tried to sing 'Why am I not a falcon? Why can I not fly?' But she just broke into giggles." Sergei looked curiously at Kulik. "Do you sing?"

"A little. I sang baritone with the university choir. But let me warn you, I'm not very good when it comes to sentimental songs."

"One of these days I'll take you over to my aunt's house. She has a piano. You can sing to Marusia, maybe a song about the Cossacks. Some of our '*moujik*' ways just might find their way back into her heart." He paused and his face lit up. "Ivan, you've got to meet her. My cousin, that is. She's so absolutely lovely."

For a brief moment Kulik imagined what she might look like: delicate features, a slim build, pretty eyes. And what kind of person might she be? Headstrong, arrogant, opportunistic. . . .

Sergei stood up. He seemed very excited; there was something else on his mind. "I almost forgot to tell you. There's big news in the village, very big news. The new teacher for Morozovich has just arrived and her name is Dounia Avdeevna. And believe me, there are no words to describe her. She's the daughter of a Pinsk cab driver and a local housemaid. She used to haul bricks for some construction company and after that she sold schmaltz herring at the marketplace. Her barrels of herring used to stand at the far end by the Pina River, and when people passed by she would wave one in the air by its tail and shout out to them: 'You can eat it with potatoes or you can eat it on its own—it will calm your nerves and regulate your bowels, but most importantly it will awaken your libido. Buy your schmaltz herring here!'

"Now Dounia Avdeevna has decided to become a teacher. In fact, just the other day Cornelius stood before the Clubhouse, and boasted to a crowd of people how he had welcomed to our region the most cultured and qualified teacher, and one who came from the city. Lord help us!"

Sergei went on to talk about how the children of Morozovich had greeted Dounia on the first day of school. "Just before she came in, on the outside door they drew a fat woman standing beside a barrel overflowing with herring. One fish was between her teeth, another was jumping out of her ear. Under the picture they wrote in big black letters, 'Get away, Dounia Avdeevna, you illiterate! Go back to your schmaltz herring!'

"You can't even begin to imagine Dounia's reaction to this. The children had expected her to go into a fit of rage, but they were surprised to see her collapse into a fit of laughter. She laughed so loud and hard her belly heaved and there were tears in her eyes. 'Hah, hah, hah! This is so funny, I'm about to burst at the seams!' When a crowd formed around her, she called out to them, 'You people wallow in ignorance. You live in a dark and isolated place and don't know anything about life. Do you have a problem with herring? Do you consider them to be the same as a pile of shit? Herring, I'll have you know, are not the mere chickens or pigs you're used to, shut up in small coops or pens; no, herring are children of the open seas. They're free, they've traveled the world over. They're caught with enormous nets thrown from the sides of big fishing vessels. And the seas are very dangerous places. When the winds blow, the waves swell up as high as mountains. I advise you not to make fun of herring, I find no humor in that. I'm proud and honored that I sold them.'

"While Dounia was carrying on like that, you could see that she was enjoying herself and feeling self-important. She believed

that her new position as schoolteacher was a great mission to educate the poor illiterate peasant children of the marsh, to show
them the light.

"Right after her little speech, Cornelius broke through of the
crowd and rushed up to her. He rummaged through his pockets
and pulled out a large silver key tied with a red ribbon. 'Dounia
Avdeevna, I present you with a key to the Morozovich school.'"

Kulik listened to Sergei's account, dumbfounded and disturbed.
What would the level of education be like for the children with a
teacher like Dounia? Her appointment by the Party was a complete
farce, and as far as he could see, its aim could only be to destroy
the existing culture and widen the tide of Russification. He found
it too painful to think about, so he tried to change the subject.

"I believe you mentioned you have had some form of higher
education?" he said to Sergei.

"Yes, I graduated from a *gymnasium* in Pinsk just over two years
ago."

"Have you ever thought of teaching? As it happens, we're short
a couple of teachers. Three classrooms in the left wing are still
empty and they'll most likely be assigned to higher grades, probably grades five and six. What do you think, would you like to try
your hand at it? To tell the truth, our working together will make
life a little more bearable here. Please say you'll consider it."

Sergei paused, but not for long. He smiled broadly.

"Actually, I have a confession to make—the reason I came to see
you tonight was to ask you about this very thing."

"Well, then it's settled." Kulik was very pleased.

Glancing at his watch, he noticed it was well past midnight. The
two men shook hands and bade each other goodnight.

CHAPTER 3

Beyond the village, at the top of a steep hill, camouflaged by dense fog, was a large manor house. It was three stories of whitish gray stone with an expansive veranda and a galvanized iron cornice. The tall arched windows on the first level were boarded up with sheets of scrap wood, and the front and back doors were nailed shut by crisscross wooden beams. There were two huge wooden signs in the yard reading KEEP OUT. Next to the house on the left stood a barn with goats, sheep, bulls and milking cows. Farther down on the slope of the hill beneath an elderberry bush was a chicken coop, and attached to it, a makeshift tumbledown turkey roost. Thick chestnut trees encircled the property and lined the driveway, and their branches, already bare, snapped and creaked in the cold autumn breeze.

Yesterday Olivinski was the owner of the large house on the hill, its lord and master, and today he was gone. With one heavy blow the new regime destroyed his little paradise, turning it to smoke and dust. Everything had been transformed and all its past glory abruptly ended.

It was an unparalleled time in history. Revolution had changed the destiny of so many, so suddenly, and so decisively: the farmlands were being ripped away from the bourgeoisie and given to the peasants, *kolkhozes* were popping up everywhere, and in the cities, the factories and government offices had become the property of the new regime. Nothing like it had ever been seen before. The poor, the hungry, and the oppressed would now, for the first time ever, enjoy happiness and plenty, and all thanks to their new Russian liberators.

To the right of the manor house, in a garden patch overgrown with milkweed and wild grasses, there appeared a large, strange bird, foreign to these parts. It was a peacock, whose wide, resplendent train was on full display as he strutted through the garden, wailing like a screech owl. His long, drawn-out cries rose above the fields and traveled into the heart of the village, to come back as a muted echo.

As the sun rose, the fog lifted and the morning countryside was brought into full view. Almost all the villagers had gathered before the broad wooden gates of the manor house. The new regime had promised them that the big house on the hill was no longer a symbol of misery and repression: it was now a bastion of hope.

Everyone knew that the Olivinski manor was home to a superior breed of cattle imported from Holland, to the finest pigs, and the best roosting chickens to be found anywhere. The poorest peasants huddled together, carrying empty sacks and baskets, some even came with rickety old wheelbarrows and broken-down handcarts. They were awaiting Iofe Nicel Leyzarov, who yesterday had made the following announcement:

"Comrades, in the name of Stalin and the Bolshevik Party, the riches of the Olivinski estate will be handed out to the people. We will first distribute it among the poorest of the poor. As you all know, Olivinski was a very rich and powerful man and stopped at nothing to get what he wanted. And how do you suppose he got that way? By the toil and sweat of the masses. You have suffered enough, people. Today marks the beginning of the end, and by this time tomorrow everything that was his will be yours. And the poorest will benefit the most. They will have so many eggs they won't know what to do with them all, they'll be up to their elbows in sausages and backfat, and there will be enough milk to feed an army. Tomorrow, dear people, is your day of reckoning! Remember, a pledge given by a Bolshevik is as solid as the written law itself."

When Leyzarov's speech ended, there were such outbursts of joyful, hysterical cheering that the ground shook as if from an earthquake.

———

That morning a woman banged on Kulik's door. She was in her early thirties with a very pale, almost glassy complexion, hollow cheeks and dark-ringed eyes. Her name was Paraska Braskovia, and she was the new school cleaning woman finally assigned by Cornelius. Her shabby overcoat and oversized worn leather boots made her poverty evident at once.

"Director! Director!" she cried at the top of her voice. "Get up! You've got to help me! Come to the manor house with me. Please get up before everything is given away. I beg you!"

Kulik had been sound asleep; he flipped over onto his side and threw his pillow over his head to muffle the sound of her voice. He called out, "Do you know what time it is? It's barely six o'clock. Just go to the meeting and find a spot near the front gates. You've got nothing to worry about, you'll get what you deserve."

But Paraska only banged harder. "Director, don't go back to sleep, I need your help. I can't get through. I've already tried and the crowd is too big. Oh, I'm completely beside myself! Please, you've got to help me."

As Paraska's voice grew louder and more insistent, Kulik rolled over and reluctantly pulled himself out of bed. Rubbing his eyes, he shouted, "Give me a couple of minutes. I'll be right with you." Then under his breath, "Oh, that insufferable woman!"

Hardly giving him time to button his shirt and put on his trousers, she banged again. "Hurry, Director, hurry! When the mob sees you at my side, they'll make way for me. Just one word from the headmaster of the school, and the Representative of the District Committee will present me with the finest milking cow. Just you wait and see!"

Paraska was convinced that the headmaster's position in the village could really help her case. He would explain to the officials her desperate situation and how she barely had enough to make ends meet. He would tell them how miserable and hopeless her life was, that her husband was deathly ill, probably on the brink of death, that she had no money or possessions, and that her five small children were barefoot and hungry most of the time.

Opening the door at last, Kulik, avoiding her eyes, agreed to accompany her to the manor house. They made their way out of the cold, gray village. The road, completely deserted, was one long stretch of mud, barely passable. From time to time the silence was broken by vague noises from the surrounding fields.

Paraska, clutching a crochet shawl around her head, fell into a chatty mood as they walked. Kulik felt irritated and resentful. Why was he going to the Olivinski manor and at this ungodly hour? Did Paraska have to babble on and on? And why had he allowed her to talk him into doing something he didn't want to do? After all, she was a stranger to him and her problems were no business of his. And besides, it was not a good idea to get involved in other people's affairs, especially now. He had a strong inclination to turn back, and began to do it, but when he saw how hopeless and stricken she looked, his heart melted. This poor, desperate woman, in her endless struggle with poverty, wanted only to help her children. How could he be so selfish and so cruel?

Paraska had only one purpose in mind: to get to the manor house as quickly as possible and lay claim to some of the riches, maybe a cow, possibly even an ox. She complained, "This cursed road. It's so muddy it's impossible to get through it. I'm sinking up to my ankles. Maybe it's drier over there." Stepping over potholes and great puddles of water, pulling up her cheap brown skirt, already splattered and soaked to the knees, she tried to reach the other side of the road. But it was just as bad there, if not worse.

"We're almost there, Director," she called out, pointing to a big, noisy crowd of people.

Kulik expected her to natter on, but she fell silent. He was surprised to hear her sobbing and murmuring, "Oh, my children, my poor children. They came into this world like innocent little lambs. Olivinski was up to his ears in money, and for my little ones I couldn't even find a drop of milk. Every night they go to bed hungry, crying for a crust of bread. Where's the fairness in that? Their eyes are like precious gems, I'd give them the world if I could, but all we have in our lives are misfortune and poverty. I drag myself from one place to another; I work myself to the bone just to keep them alive."

She added something in a trembling voice, but Kulik was unable to make out her words. He could see that strain and exertion were getting the better of her. After several minutes, she straightened her back and seemed to recover. Turning to him, her eyes shining, she clasped her hands together and said with passion, "Now at last there is hope, the new regime has promised to help us. Finally we'll be able to lead better lives."

Kulik pulled up his coat collar to keep out the autumn chill.

Paraska, ahead of Kulik by a few paces, stopped abruptly and turned to wait for him in the middle of the road. Her malnourished, almost skeletal, frame wrapped in rags, looked as if it were about to be blown away. Suddenly all her feelings of hope and promise seemed to have vanished. Her voice faltered, then broke. "It's all rather strange. These new officials who've been coming around—even though they're full of promises, there's something not quite right about them. Somehow I don't trust them. It all sounds too good to be true. And the way they praise Stalin—it's hard to believe that such a fine and charitable human being can be found anywhere in the world."

At the Olivinski manor, there was a dense crowd of peasants and a tremendous uproar. Besides folks from Hlaby, there were those from Lopatina, Morozovich, Krive Selo, even from villages and settlements beyond the Stryy River. People were swarming everywhere, in front of the main gate, against the fence, along the road, even up in surrounding trees. They were all staring at the manor, where Iofe Nicel Leyzarov was just emerging from a side door.

He stood before the wide wooden staircase that led to the veranda, holding a sheet of paper with a list of names typed neatly in three even columns. After studying it for several minutes, when he looked up, although he was smiling, it was with an air of derision that even the most trusting villagers caught at once. As he began to speak, suddenly the manor peacock, which had been all the while strutting in and around the garden, let out a long, ear-splitting cry. All heads turned and everyone started talking, shouting and pointing at the bird. Then a single sarcastic voice shot out across the yard:

"Oh, that poor, miserable bird, he must miss his master terribly! He was his most prized possession. In his wildest dreams Olivinski never would have imagined we the people would be walking off with his fortunes!"

Then someone else shouted, "He had the world at his feet and now he's deep in the cold, cold ground, he's no longer around. He pampered that stupid peacock only to be struck on the head with a club. The bastard!" The shouter was Zachary Buhai, a former captain in the Czar's navy. For some reason, no one knew exactly why, whenever he could manage it, he spoke in rhyme.

The crowd grew more and more rowdy.

"Settle down! Settle down!" Leyzarov clapped his hands. He turned to his list and quickly called out the first name.

"Ostap Pavlovich Bubon! Please step forward!"

A stooped man, well over seventy, emerged from the crowd and hobbled into the yard leaning on a cane. He had on bast shoes wrapped in lamb's wool to keep his feet warm and was dressed in a shabby peasant overcoat two sizes too small for him.

"Ostap Pavlovich Bubon!" repeated Leyzarov, feigning a sincere smile. "I present you with this cow. Take good care of her, she's yours."

Bubon, who was almost blind, strained to get a look at his new possession. He wanted to see her head, her spine, her tail, but no matter how hard he tried, all he could make out was a vaguely distinguishable blob. Nevertheless, he felt privileged to be receiving a cow, and even though he was unable to see her clearly, he was confident she was one of the best milk producers the farm had to offer.

Fumbling for the rope around her neck, he managed to grab hold of the end and yank her toward him. He could feel her give a slight tug and moo faintly. With his head held high, happily and proudly he escorted his new possession through the crowd, pausing now and then to pay homage to the new regime. At last he found his way past the gates and onto the main road. There he bent forward to run the tips of his fingers up and down her teats, then along her sack. He was stunned to find that her udder was completely dried up and felt hard and cold, like an empty leather sack. He slipped his hand along her spine. Nothing but skin and bones. Stooping to look her in the eye, he exclaimed: "Hah, may the Devil take you; I bet you're older than I am!"

Back in the Olivinski yard, as Leyzarov was about to call out the next name on his list, he was interrupted again by the cry of the peacock. The bird now had its train lowered and folded and stood by the fence, shoving its pointed head between the planks, looking to the left, then to the right, as if waiting for something to happen.

"Look!" Cornelius pointed. "The peacock's searching for his master. When I catch that son-of-a-bitch I'll pluck him until he's as smooth as a board. That'll put an end to his misery once and for all. Hah! Hah! Hah!"

He had hardly uttered these words when a group of teenagers, laughing and shouting, hopped the fence and raced each other into the garden after the peacock, trying to corner it at the far end. The bird, squealing and flapping its wings, managed to escape into the depths of a raspberry patch.

Leyzarov, in an effort to calm everybody, resumed calling out the names. Calves were led out of the barn, two one-year-old bulls, numerous steers and several billy goats. The animals were handed over to those in greatest need. The crowd cheered and praised the benevolence of the new regime.

Paraska, followed by Kulik, elbowed her way eagerly to the main gates. She was pleased she had not come too late and that her name had not yet been called. She knew that there were at least twenty Holstein-Friesien cows with large, full udders still in the barn, and she was certain one of them had been assigned especially to her. It was just a matter of time before lofe Nicel Leyzarov would call out her name. Certainly she was a prime contender and she was feeling very confident about her prospects. Waiting patiently, she watched Leyzarov's every move. But to her dismay when she caught his eye, it was as though he didn't even recognize her. Ten minutes went by, then another ten, and still no mention of her name. She wrung her hands in anxiety and distress. Then all at once Leyzarov seemed to become distracted by something in the barn, and shoving the list into his trouser pocket, looking very exasperated, shouted for Kirilo the farmhand.

"Kirilo! The animals are getting out of hand in there! Come here at once! Go see what the problem is."

A small man with a puffy pink face emerged from a nearby storage shed, holding a thick, coiled rope. He hastened toward Leyzarov with a serious look on his face. For many years Kirilo had worked on the Olivinski manor, tending the animals. Almost every day, he, together with the collies, had herded the cattle out to the lushest pasturelands on the far side of the Stryy. If anyone knew anything about farm animals, it was Kirilo.

"Kirilo," Leyzarov said brusquely, "bring me that black bull with the large curled horns, the one that's causing all the trouble in the barn."

"You mean Caesar?"

"Caesar?" Leyzarov gave a sidelong glance. "Is that what you call him? What kind of name is that for a bull?" Then with authority, "Bring him to me."

Kirilo obeyed immediately. He had barely disappeared behind the barn doors, when Leyzarov called out, "Cornelius Kovzalo! The black bull is yours."

At the sound of these words a voice broke frantically from the crowd. "No!" It belonged to Timushka, who was violently shaking her head. "Don't give the bull to Cornelius. Tell me it isn't so! That bull's a prizewinner. You can't waste such a fine animal on a worthless scoundrel like Cornelius. How will he ever take care of him? A bull needs a lot of attention, not to mention a proper diet. What's a *moujik* going to do with a bull like that? Give Cornelius a chicken instead!"

Zachary Buhai, who had been standing behind Timushka, snarled at her, gritting his teeth. "Do you have a problem with *moujiks*? Do you think we're just a pile of dirt? You're ignorant and stupid. Don't you realize that now we live in a time of equality and that the new regime is fair to all, even to us *moujiks*?"

"Hey, Timushka!" another voice picked up. "What the devil brought you out here today, anyway? You're better off than most. Don't you have enough?"

Timushka turned red with rage. She placed her hands on her hips and took a step forward. "Are you suggesting I came here to beg? I worked hard all my life and at least now I have something to show for it, not like the rest of you lazy good-for-nothings."

"Look!" A man's voice ripped across the yard. Everyone looked to where he pointed. A broad, muscular animal as black as coal with short stumpy legs and a prominent hump, was being led out of the barn.

Timushka kept it up. "Don't give the bull to Corny! What's he going to do with such a fine specimen? Give it to someone else. Why not to—to—Buhai? If anyone deserves it, it's Buhai. Yes, give it to Buhai. Better Buhai than Cornelius."

Someone else responded, "What a good idea! Buhai and Caesar, those two were made for each other. The bull's horns stick out of the sides of his head just like Buhai's ears. And look how he kicks up his heels. Just like Buhai! Hah! Hah! Hah! Give the bull to Buhai!"

"Quiet everyone, quiet!" Leyzarov shouted. He looked at the bull and turned to the crowd. "People, before us stands Caesar, a fine bull of the best lineage. But Caesar? What kind of name is Caesar? I will tell you what kind of name Caesar is, it's a totally unacceptable one. It is a bourgeois name given him by a bourgeois master. I hereby rename him Striker."

Almost at once there was an outbreak of cheering. Caps were hurled into the air and whistling came from all sides as the bull's new name was chanted over and over. "Striker! Striker!"

There was so much racket that Caesar became confused and agitated, and swung his massive body from side to side. Soon he started snorting and kicking up his heels. Tensing his strong neck muscles and panting wildly, he aimed his horns and made for the mob. People panicked, screaming and shouting and running in all directions. At that moment Kirilo jumped in and, skillfully catching hold of the rope around the bull's neck, managed to restrain the animal. The crowd breathed a sigh of relief.

"And why are you still swishing your tail around and kicking up your heels, Striker?" Kirilo looked the bull in the eye and stroked his nose. "What's wrong, you can tell me." But the bull only flicked his head and grunted. Kirilo turned to Leyzarov. "Excuse me, comrade, but as you can see the bull is restless. He doesn't understand when I call him Striker. I don't think he likes his new name."

Leyzarov frowned, considerably irritated. He avoided looking at Kirilo and, acting as though he didn't hear him, focused his attention on Cornelius who was now standing beside him. Placing his hand on Cornelius's shoulder, Leyzarov addressed the crowd, his voice filled with emotion.

"People, I have an announcement to make. This man standing next to me here has been most devoted to the worker's cause and has suffered greatly under Polish oppression. As a result, I hereby proclaim Cornelius Kovzalo, our loyal Village Chairman, the new owner of Striker."

Taking hold of the animal's rope, with great formality, he handed it to Cornelius and said, "Cornelius Kovzalo, Striker is yours."

"No, no!" Timushka couldn't accept this. "What did Corny ever do to deserve such a fine bull? Why, he's nothing more than a common horse thief. The bull should go to Buhai! Better Buhai should get the bull than Corny. Look, Buhai's standing right over there!"

"Shut up, you old busybody," Buhai snarled at her. "Stop sticking your nose where it doesn't belong. What do you know about bulls anyway? You should keep your big mouth shut. You should stay in the kitchen where you belong."

The truth of the matter was that Buhai wanted to keep as far away from the bull as possible. He knew it was not just an ordinary bull but a fighting bull, and fighting bulls were known to be short-tempered and quick to charge. To own an animal like that would be nothing but trouble, and trouble was something Buhai did not need. He spouted a few more choice words at Timushka but stopped short when Leyzarov addressed the crowd again.

"People, allow me to say a few words about Cornelius Kovzalo, our Village Chairman. Cornelius Kovzalo, as you all know, has shown signs of great courage. He has never hesitated to defend our glorious Soviet Empire, even while under the oppressive Polish occupiers. How he has suffered! The Poles put him in prison and punished him for defending our great national cause. For two years he sat in the Bereza Prison, cold and hungry, and never gave up hope. Now the reign of terror has come to an end and before you stands Cornelius Kovzalo, a true hero!"

"You mean horse thief!" Timushka's voice rang out.

"Don't you ever shut up, you old *baba*!" Buhai was at the end of his rope. What he feared most was that with her mindless babble, Leyzarov might be persuaded to change his mind and grant Caesar to him instead of to Cornelius. And that was something he wanted to avoid at all costs. He was determined to put a stop to her right then and there. Coming from behind and grabbing her by the neck, he pushed her through the crowd and kicked her into the road. Timushka fought back, screaming at the top of her lungs. But Buhai wouldn't let up. With great force he twisted her arms and drove her into a roadside ditch, where she landed headfirst in the mud. Lifting herself up almost immediately, she turned on a group of men standing nearby, "You call yourselves men! Men, hah! You ought to be ashamed of yourselves, all of you, letting that ruffian get away with such brutality! He used to be a respectable seaman and now look what's become of him, nothing more than a woman beater. Cowards, all of you!"

All the while Cornelius, who stood in the yard facing Caesar, seemed not to notice what was going on in the road. He had his own problems to think about. Never had he expected the regime to grant him such a formidable specimen. The truth of the matter was, he was not familiar with farm animals, especially bulls, and he wondered if his shed would be big enough or strong enough to hold this one. Somehow he didn't think it would be. Striker was enormous; he most definitely exceeded eight hundred kilograms. He could easily ram his horns through the door or into the walls and knock everything down. How could he manage him? Everyone in the village knew that Striker was a difficult beast with a mind of his own and listened only to Kirilo. Cornelius was growing more and more uneasy.

"Take him by the horns and show him who's boss!" someone shouted, laughing, from over the fence. "Take him home, Corny, you'll have enough meat for two winters!" Then, "Look, Corny's shaking. He's white as a ghost! He's scared."

Cornelius turned angrily on the crowd. "I'm not scared. I've had more in life to deal with than the likes of this stupid bull. I, Cornelius Kovzalo, I'll have you know, have been through hell and high water. And now I'm being rewarded with this very fine bull. But people, I don't want you to forget the real issue at hand here. Our wonderful new regime is giving away all the riches of the land to the working masses. If it weren't for our heroic blood brothers, Olivinski would still be slashing our backs with his horsewhip and digging his boot heels into our shins. We should all bow down to our great ruler, Joseph Stalin, to show our thanks. Hurrah to our new leader, our liberator!"

He turned to Leyzarov. "And I'm most grateful to you, Comrade Iofe Nicel for presenting me with this grand bull. I'm going to tie him to a beam in my shed and when a cow comes into season, he'll more than prove his worth. That's the way I see it. This bull is mine, but at the same time he's not mine. He'll generate life and prosperity for the whole village. As you all know, our livestock is weak and meager, but Striker is an exceptional animal; his great virility will create a revolution on our farms. Our bulls will become broad and healthy and our cows will not only produce an abundance of milk but they'll bear an endless stream of strong, healthy calves. So you see, citizens, profits from this one bull will be never-ending, thanks only to our new family in Moscow. We must always remember to show our loyalty. May I be afflicted with cholera and suffer instant death if I ever say or do anything to betray our new regime in even the slightest way. I detest all landowners, and let a boil jump out where the sun doesn't shine if I don't wring the neck of every bourgeois pig that comes my way!"

Listening closely to him, the crowd was growing more and more agitated. All eyes were on the bull and it was not long before the catcalls began again.

"Hey, Corny, let the bullfighting begin!"

"Make sure he doesn't gore you!"

"Corny, swing your red cape!"

The people stood counting the minutes for the face-off to begin. And sure enough, at that very moment Striker started digging his heels into the ground and kicking up his feet. He released several long ear-splitting yelps, and then, with his eyes gleaming fiercely, charged after Cornelius. Cornelius took to his heels and fled; blood rushed to his head and sweat poured down his back. Coming to the barn and pressing himself up against the wall, holding his arms out in self-defense, he cried, "Down, boy, down! I'm not your enemy! Come on, let me take you home!"

But the bull only became more enraged. The black hairs on his back stood on end and he snorted wildly. Cornelius braced himself for the fight of his life.

The crowd waited in suspense. Cornelius dared not move a muscle, and flicking his eyes left and right, quickly considered his options. Should he try again to calm Striker, or should he make a run for it? Finally he made a decision, and as fast as his legs could carry him, fled toward the garden fence.

Panting heavily, aiming his horns, the bull took after him in full force. The distance between them lessened with each second and Cornelius could feel the bull's hot breath on his neck. The bull almost took him down with his horns, but with a stroke of luck, somehow Cornelius managed to scramble up and over the fence to safety. Striker shook with rage and foamed at the mouth.

"Hah! Hah!" Cornelius laughed, peering victoriously through the paling. "I've outsmarted you, you bourgeois bastard! You tried to pin me with your horns, and I outdid you." Then boastfully to the crowd, "Cornelius Kovzalo, Village Chairman, has been through hell and high water! And today all he had to do was jump the fence to win the game! Hah, hah, hah!"

Sniffing the fence for a moment or two, Striker began to grunt and snort and swing his enormous body. Growing increasingly agitated, he seemed determined to get to the other side. Aiming his horns, he rammed them into the half-rotted planks, stabbing at each one as if with a knife. It was not long before the entire fence collapsed, and the bull once again took after Cornelius, who ran like the wind. But which way should he go? The fence connecting the garden to the outlying pasture was much too far, he'd never make it, and the crowd was even farther away. Cornelius ran in a zigzag and made his way into the orchard. Not knowing which way to go, he spotted a young *antonivka* and dashed toward it. Grabbing hold of a limb, he scrambled up the trunk and balanced himself on a branch halfway up. By the time the bull reached the tree, Cornelius was already safely out of reach. Shaking like a leaf, he called out to the crowd:

"Someone, quick, throw me up a revolver!"

But the bull wouldn't let up. Taking a step backward, his body in full swing, with all his might, he rammed his head into the tree. The young *antonivka* shook as if in a terrible storm. Rotted apples dropped to the ground and branches crackled. The bull banged the tree again and again.

"Help! Help!" cried Cornelius desperately.

The people roared with laughter and clapped their hands.

At that moment Kirilo emerged from the barn, and cautiously approached the bull. In his right hand he carried a large clump of hay. He called out softly: "Caesar, hey, Caesar, come here. Why don't you leave that idiot up in the tree, let him spend the night up there if he wants to. Come on, boy, I brought you some hay."

The bull, hearing Kirilo's voice, calmed down almost instantly. Giving a slight toss to his head and lowering his eyes, he began to swish his tail back and forth. Kirilo lifted the rope that was tied around his neck and stroked him gently behind the ears. The bull stuck out his thick, prickly tongue and affectionately licked his hand.

The crowd cheered. Kirilo became an instant hero.

In the meantime, Cornelius could not find the courage to climb down from the tree. It was not until he saw Kirilo lead the bull into the barn and shut the door behind him, that he slipped down. All eyes were on him and he saw everyone laughing.

"Well, Corny." Leyzarov walked up to him and patted him on the back. "You're very good at jumping fences and scrambling up trees. I must hand it to you, you put on quite a show for us today, yes, you really outdid yourself. Now go on home and rest up."

Cornelius, his head lowered and his pride bitterly wounded, made for the village road. He had been so humiliated that he felt no better than a dirty old dishrag. Hurrying to get out of sight, he was soon lost behind a dense stand of trees.

Leyzarov returned to his list. He called out at last:

"Paraska Braskovia!"

When Paraska heard her name, her eyes lit up. Finally it was her turn and she would get what she had come for. She squeezed through the crowd, her eyes fixed on the barn door, when to her dismay, something entirely unexpected happened. Instead of a milking cow, a wretched little goat with a short tail and stunted horns was being led toward her. As it walked it swayed from side to side, kicking feebly.

Leyzarov turned to Paraska with great ceremony. "Take this goat, Paraska, she's yours. Don't worry that she's a little on the thin side. Soon she'll be bearing young ones and before you know it, you'll have yourself a whole family." Then, frowning, he asked, "What's wrong, Paraska, why are you upset?"

Paraska stood dumbstruck for a moment. Then she sank to the ground and wept in despair. Is this why she had come? Is this why she had gone to the trouble of dragging the headmaster with her? To take home a useless goat? Raising her tear-stained face and wiping her eyes with her hands, she stared first at Kulik, then at Leyzarov.

"I never thought I'd live to see the day," she began. "I'm being given a goat, a pitiful goat and on its last legs. Just look at it!" Grasping Kulik's arm, she became almost hysterical. "Director, tell Comrade Leyzarov how destitute I am! Tell him about my children! Tell him, please!"

Kulik shifted awkwardly as the eyes of the crowd fell upon him. He didn't know how to react. Everyone stood waiting for something to happen. Suddenly an uncontrollable rage broke inside him, and looking at the crowd, he wanted to shout, "Help Paraska? Why should I help her, why should I help any of you? You all stand there knocking into one another and bobbing your heads, hoping for the new regime to grant you a small piece of the Olivinski estate. Can't you see the hypocrisy of it all? They invade your land, and then act like your benefactors. Beg them for a fraction of what rightfully belongs to you, and then be grateful! You're better off bashing your heads against the wall!"

But he knew he couldn't say this; he could barely even dare to think it. It could cost him his life. Everything that was happening was entirely new and sudden; he found it strange and awful. He wanted nothing more than to return to his quarters, bury his head in his pillow and forget about everything.

Paraska tugged frantically at his sleeve, beside herself . "Director, Director! Tell the Party Representative how poor I am. Tell him how much I need a milking cow! Tell him about my children!"

Kulik turned to Leyzarov and spoke carefully. "Paraska Braskovia, our new cleaning woman, feels she has been slighted and thinks she ought to get a milking cow. A milking cow will help feed her children, who are terribly undernourished. This goat that you want to give her looks rather mangy and I can't see how she can benefit from it. It will only consume hay and that will be very expensive, something Paraska cannot afford. You must understand, Paraska has five small children at home, yes, five, and she needs to feed them."

Leyzarov stepped back and looked Paraska over. Stroking his chin as if considering Kulik's every word, he seemed to agree. "Hmm . . . five children you say? Yes, and from what I can see, she's still quite a young woman and could easily bear another five. Hmm . . . I think you're right. Paraska Braskovia can certainly use a milking cow."

Kulik wasted no time in picking up on Leyzarov's benevolence. "We really must encourage women like Paraska. Her little ones need milk to grow big and strong, and the Soviet regime, as we all know, cares very much about the welfare of its children, especially the children of its workers. I beg you, comrade, give Paraska a milking cow. I understand you have at least twenty in the barn."

Leyzarov tightened his lips. "No, I'm afraid that's impossible. All the milking cows are to remain here. I have strict orders."

"Well, then, maybe you can find something else for her?" Kulik was struck by his own boldness.

"Something else for Paraska? Let me see. How about a pregnant heifer? In a month's time she will be with young and producing milk. Well, Paraska, what do you say about that?"

Paraska's eyes opened wide. "Oh, thank you, comrade, thank you. That would be wonderful." She grasped his hands and her face beamed with gratitude. She could scarcely believe her good fortune. "Is she really with young?"

"She certainly is." Leyzarov turned sharply around and shouted, "Kirilo! Bring out the pregnant cow, the black-and-white spotted one at the back of the barn."

In no time, Kirilo appeared with a rather heavy animal with broad shoulders and a strong horned head. Leyzarov forced a smile and with great formality handed her over to Paraska.

Paraska quickly took hold of the rope and, looking into the animal's big round yellow eyes, immediately named her Rohula. She did not go directly home, but walked out into the road and proudly paraded the cow back and forth for all the villagers to see.

CHAPTER 4

The first snow fell over Hlaby. Like the soft down from a pillow, it piled in the yards and walkways of the small wooden cottages and collected high on their rooftops. A cold, harsh wind blew in from the north and hurled the flakes up into the air and over the vast frozen mudlands beyond. Before a newly erected building, home of the Lenin Clubhouse, there was a pile of snow twice the size of any other. The clubhouse had shot up several weeks ago, like a mushroom after a rainfall, on a site where had once stood a one-story barrack that housed the Olivinski farmhands. The clubhouse, now the heart of the village, bustled with activity. There were meetings almost every night and people, some known and some not, rushed in and out at all hours.

A few weeks before Christmas, something rather unexpected happened, to which all the villagers reacted with surprise and confusion. A large black-and-white poster was erected in front of the clubhouse, showing a Red Army soldier in full uniform embracing a poorly dressed peasant who held a hoe in one hand and a sickle in the other. The peasant stood gazing up at the soldier in adoration, smiling, almost teary-eyed. On the bottom of the poster was printed: LONG LIVE THE RED ARMY OF WORKERS AND PEASANTS! LONG LIVE THE REVOLUTION!

Although Bolshevism had manifested itself in almost all areas of the Pinsk Marshes, with such images popping up in towns and villages everywhere, for Hlaby at least, a display like this was a novelty. The first to take interest in it was Timushka. Standing on the frost-covered walkway, huddled in her brown frayed overcoat, she stared fixedly at it, trying to grasp its full meaning. Before long, she turned to call out to passersby and even rushed to bang on the doors of several nearby houses:

"People! People! Come see for yourselves! You won't believe it! There's a huge picture in front of the Lenin Clubhouse. It's a Russian Army man and he's embracing one of our very own. Yes, believe it or not, he's embracing Cornelius Kovzalo! They're standing like true brothers and out in the open for everyone to see! The soldier has a pink smooth face, and our horse thief is hiding behind his moustache. As if he hasn't caused enough trouble already!"

This news did not take long to reach Grandfather Cemen. At first the old man could not believe that this could be possible—a man from the marshes and a Soviet together in an embrace? He decided he must see this spectacle for himself. Wrapped in his worn sheepskin, his woolen hat pulled over his ears, he leaned heavily on his walking stick and hobbled over the frozen mudland toward the clubhouse. The wind howled, cutting into his face like a knife while the frost collected on his brows and lashes. He labored painfully through the deep snow, pausing now and then, until he reached the marketplace, where he descended rather easily along a cleared path to the clubhouse entrance. A crowd had already gathered by the main door and the old man strained to get a look. People were knocking into one another, and pointing excitedly.

"Let me through! Let me through!" the old man cried, waving his cane. "I want to see!" When finally he faced the poster, he studied it for the longest time and from different angles, screwing up his mouth. The icy wind, now blowing even harder, made his eyes water, and the image became blurred. When he wiped his eyes with his coat cuffs, he was able to see what he feared most. The man whom the Red Army soldier was embracing was indeed Cornelius Kovzalo.

"Last night I dreamed of a black dog," he shouted, "and a black dog is the sign of the Devil. Satan has embraced Satan. One of our very own has brought dishonor and shame to our village. And now

God is punishing us with this brutal cold. And it won't end here. When spring comes, the Stryy and the Pripyat rivers will overrun their banks like never before and drown all the sinners. The waves will pound against the shores and flood not only our fields but also our towns and villages. The Lenin Clubhouse will collapse and be carried off downriver in a thousand pieces."

The crowd listened to the old man with strained attention. He had presented his dream so vividly that no matter how hard they tried, they couldn't get rid of it. A gloomy silence followed that lasted several minutes.

With his pale lips quivering, the old man turned to go. As he made his way back to his house, he forgot about Kovzalo. He mumbled to himself and wept: "My poor Philip. Will he live to see tomorrow? Do they think they own him? Why do they chase him out into the woods and work him senseless? He can barely stand anymore, his head pounds day and night. And why did he have to marry Paraska? I told him over and over: 'Son, find yourself a useful wife.' But he didn't listen to me. Those are the sons of today, they don't listen."

Reaching the steps of his house and climbing onto the porch, he paused a moment to catch his breath. With his back against the wall, looking up at the sky, he was able to enjoy, at least for a moment, the warmth of a white wintry sun breaking through the clouds. He took off his gloves, loosened his coat collar, and began to dust the snow from his arms and shoulders and then from his beard. The sound of children singing was coming from across the street, from one of the school windows. As it happened, Sergei was giving music lessons. Whenever someone hit a flat note, the singing stopped, then after a few seconds started up again more loudly and the lyrics reached the old man's ears. The words he was hearing filled him with such anger and disgust he could hardly catch his breath. He couldn't believe it. He hurried down the porch stairs as fast as his old legs would carry him, forgetting even his cane, made for the school and banged the classroom door open.

"Stop this singing at once!" he demanded. "It's nothing but sacrilege. The children should not be singing ballads this time of year; they should be singing carols. Christmas is barely a week away." Then he sang hoarsely and off-key, "Christ is born on Christmas day . . . on Christmas . . ." He fell into a fit of coughing.

"Hey, Grandfather!" a pupil jeered from the back row. "With a voice like that you should have been a church cantor!"

The children turned red with laughter and banged their desks. Little Tolik sitting in the third row stuck out his tongue, as did Ohrimko, who sat next to him.

"Tolik! Ohrimko! Both of you, come here!" Sergei barked at them.

Tolik, his head hanging, rose reluctantly from his seat, and shuffled slowly to the teacher's desk. Ohrimko sat looking defiant.

Sergei tapped his ruler against the palm of his hand. "Tolik, I saw what you did. It was very disrespectful. I want you to tell Grandfather Cemen that you're sorry."

The boy turned scarlet. Edging his way toward the old man, he timidly kissed his hand and sputtered out an apology.

"You may return to your seat, Tolik. Ohrimko, your turn."

Ohrimko refused to budge. "Why should I apologize? I didn't do anything wrong."

Sergei gave him a stern look.

The boy stood his ground.

The old man hobbled over to Ohrimko. Squinting at him, he exclaimed, "Why, it's you, you little hooligan! You're the one who threw snowballs at me the other day. Is that what they teach you in school these days, to disrespect your elders? What you need is a good thrashing."

"Ohrimko, come here!" Losing patience, Sergei pointed to a chalk line in front of his desk, where he wanted the boy to stand.

At that moment, Kulik, having heard the commotion from his office, came through the door. The children jumped instantly to their feet and said together, loudly and clearly, "Good morning, Director Kulik."

Frowning, Kulik stood at the head of the class, his hands behind his back, and looked around. "What, may I ask, is going on here?"

Looking first at Ohrimko, then at the old man, it did not take him long to understand the situation. Sergei was quick to fill him in on the details.

Kulik took a moment to think. Although he was headmaster and had control of the school, he had to act in accordance with the new regime. Thoughts whirled through his head as he tried to find a way out. It was true, Ohrimko had stepped out of line and ought to be punished for it. On the other hand, the old man had no business barging into the school in the first place. Kulik was on the verge of reprimanding them both, when he changed his mind. If he were to scold Ohrimko, he would not only be condoning the old man's intrusion into the school, but, worse yet, condoning his outburst, which, under the new laws of the land, was clearly antagonistic and subversive. And if he were to turn on the old man, the children would become ruder and more abusive. As he struggled with these thoughts, he became less certain of what to do. He looked at Sergei, and came to a decision. "Why don't you go ahead and dismiss the children for the rest of the day?"

Quickly and silently, the children pulled their satchels from under their desks and as fast as they could, scrambled outside. Ohrimko was first out the door.

The old man scowled. "Is this how you release the children, like a pack of sheep and with no prayer?" He looked along the walls for an icon. "And where are your icons? I see they've been ripped from the walls. Is nothing sacred anymore?"

"What you say has some truth to it, Grandfather." Kulik leaned forward and spoke softly. He was aware the slightest slip could seriously compromise his position. "Atheism has become the new way of life and unfortunately there's not much you or I can do about it."

The old man pushed on. "At one time things were much different. In Kiev I used to go to the Lavra Pecherska monastery and pray, and I did it openly. But today God has been replaced by the Devil. Evil has triumphed."

Kulik listened patiently to the old man's ramblings, and finally invited him into his office for a cup of tea. Taking him by the arm, he escorted him down the corridor. Sergei had packed up his belongings and gone home.

Grandfather Cemen settled in one of the leather armchairs. Resting his head against the back, he closed his eyes and almost at once drifted off. The chair was so very soft and comfortable, unlike any he had ever sat in, and he thought how having such a chair would help ease his arthritis. If only he could take it back to his shack and set it before the tile stove, he would feel better in no time. Falling into a deeper slumber, he didn't notice that a tray of food had been set on a small table before him.

"Wake up, Grandfather." Kulik nudged him lightly on the arm. "Paraska made us a bite to eat. Help yourself. I know it's hard to eat without teeth, but if you soak the rolls in your tea, it'll be easier to swallow. Here's a spoon and some milk." Then turning toward the door leading into the kitchen, he called, "Paraska, could you please bring us a few lumps of sugar?"

Barely a minute later Paraska appeared in the doorway. When she saw the old man, her pale cheeks flushed and she looked distressed. Quietly, like a cat, she slipped behind Kulik and complained in his ear.

"How did *he* get in here? I can't seem to get away from him. I've had more of him than I can take. He's tearing me apart with his constant grumbling. Every day he finds something new to say about me: I'm a sinner, I'm lazy, I don't care for Philip properly, I'm no good. Everything I do is wrong. There's no end to it. He's sucking the blood out of me. And now to make matters worse, he's senile!"

Seeing Paraska whispering to Kulik, Grandfather Cemen, now wide awake, shifted to the edge of his seat and strained to hear what she was saying. Not being able to make out a word, he spoke haughtily and contemptuously, as if Paraska were not in the room.

"You must keep that girl on a short rope, Director. Teach her some discipline. My Philip spoiled her rotten and now she brings him no profit. And she's an unfit mother; her children are like wild animals, dirty and ragged. I said to my son, 'Philip, why didn't you take Anna Novak for your wife, she would have made a very good housekeeper and mother to your children. She's well-organized and hard-working and has respect for the elderly.' But my son didn't listen. He said his heart was with Paraska."

Pausing to take some tea, after a moment he started up again. "Oh, the heart of a young man, it's like the spring rain, it will pour for about a month, then by summer everything will dry up. And so it goes. Their household has fallen apart completely and now poverty has consumed them like fleas on a dog. Everything Paraska touches turns to smoke and dust. That's the kind of daughter-in-law I have, as useless as an old shoe."

Paraska burst into tears, and fled the room, banging the door behind her. She could be heard sobbing in the hallway.

Kulik responded to this little domestic scene with amazement and sorrow. Finding himself confronted with the complexities of other people's lives always caused him to feel awkward and embarrassed. But his heart went out to Paraska. Her life was hard enough without the old man breathing down her neck at every turn. Kulik felt she did a more than adequate job tidying the classrooms and preparing his meals. She was always punctual and efficient and never left until her work was finished. Not knowing what to do, Kulik said nothing, hoping that the old man would stop his bitter harangue and go home. But he went on for another hour, describing each private interlude in detail and coming to lengthy, tiresome conclusions. Kulik only half listened, trying without success to think of ways to change the subject.

As the clock struck three, the old man finally prepared to take his leave. Kulik helped him out of the chair, and taking him by the arm, accompanied him to the door. The old man stopped to look Kulik in the face.

"I can tell by your eyes you've had a good upbringing and you're a decent man. But I can also see you're too much on the soft side." In the yard, turning around, he called out as if in warning, "About my daughter-in-law, don't forget what I told you. She's neglectful and irresponsible and doesn't care about anything. May you live a hundred years for the delicious rolls and tea. God bless you!"

Kulik watched the old man hobble along the narrow, snow-beaten path to his house. Back inside the school, Kulik did not return to his office, but headed for the grade one classroom, where he noticed the light had been turned on. He was delighted to find it spotless and in perfect order: the floor had been scrubbed, the desks washed, and the blackboards and slates wiped clean. Obviously while he had entertained his visitor, Paraska had busied herself tidying up. When he retired to his quarters, he was startled to find her there, slouched on a footstool, throwing logs into the tile stove. Her face was red and swollen and she sat lost in meditation, as if hypnotized by the fire's glow. When she noticed Kulik standing over her, she buried her head in her hands, and broke into a fit of weeping.

"I don't know how much more of this I can take. That old man probably went on and on about me. He doesn't give me a moment's rest. I'm sick and tired of him. I'm just grateful I can get away from him when I'm at the school."

She stoked the logs every so often, while she sobbed.

"My life is so wretched. Nothing turned out the way it was supposed to. When I was young I wanted to be free and travel the world, but instead I married and bore my children. That's when things really started to go bad. Something crept into my heart and tore away at it. Now my children cry all night and I can't get any sleep. Then the old man starts in on me. And that's only part of my troubles. Bad luck has settled in all around me and there's no escape."

Kulik looked sympathetically at her. "Is there anything I can do to help?"

Paraska shook her head. "It's my husband, Philip. He's terribly sick. He's dying. When he was sent to work in the forest he became gravely ill. Some kind of lump appeared on his head and now there's another one. He's suffering. Cornelius and that bastard Leyzarov, may they both rot in hell, chased him into the forest and worked him to the bone until he collapsed. It's nothing but slave labor. With other men he hauled wood from Hvador to Pinsk, then past Pinsk all the way to the Bugsy-Dnieprovsky Canal. From anywhere and everywhere our men are chased into the forest to cut down trees and haul them to that damned canal. They want to open it up for ships by springtime. It'll be the new gateway to Moscow, they say. Our so-called saviors are just working our men to death."

Holding back her tears, the anguish in her eyes deepened into fear. "And now there's talk about war. Everything's pointing to it."

"There's not going to be any war, Paraska. People are always talking." Kulik tried to console her, but he had trouble believing his own words.

A brief silence followed. Lowering his voice and looking directly at her, he said earnestly, "Let me give you a word of advice. You mustn't speak so openly. It's a very dangerous thing to do and it can only lead to a bad end. The eyes of the Party are everywhere."

Paraska said timidly, "But I only say these sorts of things to you, Director, because I know you're one of us. About my Philip, I'm at a complete loss. I don't know what to do or think anymore. Those lumps on his head won't heal and they're getting bigger. His head throbs night and day and he screams from pain. He wants to go to Pinsk to the doctor but Cornelius won't issue him a pass. The bastard only laughs and accuses Philip of being lazy and trying to wangle his way out of working."

As Paraska went on, all at once there was a scratching on the window which was so thick with frost it was impossible to see who was out there. Someone could be heard calling from the other side. The voice called again, and it soon became evident it was Grandfather Cemen.

"Paraska! Paraska!" he shouted. "Go home, Philip needs you!"

Jumping to her feet, already halfway out the door, she turned to look at Kulik, and cried desperately, "Please, Director, I beg you, don't dismiss me from the school. I don't know what would become of my children. I'm all they've got!"

CHAPTER 5

That night Kulik tossed and turned into the early morning hours and did not get a moment's rest. When six o'clock finally struck he rolled out of bed, went to the washbasin and splattered his face with water. Immediately he felt revived. He puttered around the kitchen, put on the kettle, and sat down to a breakfast of buttered black bread and boiled eggs. To his great relief today was a special day; he did not have to hurry to his office and he was able to enjoy a second cup of coffee. Yesterday the children had been dismissed for the winter holidays and he did not have to prepare lessons and organize the day's activities. This break in the monotony of school life was a most welcome change.

At a quarter past nine he began unpacking his trunk and suitcases and organizing his rooms, something he had not yet found time to do since arriving in Hlaby. In the evening Paraska appeared, refilled the tile stove in the kitchen and prepared him a meal of unground buckwheat with small chunks of stewed beef. The windows were heavily covered with frost and a north wind rushing in from over the frozen fields made the panes rattle. Outside, the land was cold and desolate. The sub-zero temperature cut straight to the bone and the slightest breath froze in the air. The residents of Hlaby could not remember such a brutal winter. But in his quarters Kulik felt warm and snug, as if he were in a cocoon; his thoughts drifted. Suddenly he was startled by a loud, shrill bird-like cry coming from somewhere outside. After a few minutes it came again. Where had he heard that sound before? Then silence. He waited for the cry to start up once more but it never did and he decided that it was just the wind.

He began to think about Pinsk. In two days' time he would be attending a regional teachers' conference there, along with teachers from the surrounding towns and villages. The aim of the conference was to initiate a political re-education of all those in the profession. Although he was not particularly keen on making the trip or of spending countless hours in some lecture hall listening to long, drawn-out speeches, he was interested in change and change was something Pinsk had to offer.

He tried to focus on something more pleasant, more inspiring, and almost at once he thought of Marusia, Sergei's cousin. Was she really as beautiful as Sergei had said? He had described her as fair-haired and lovely, with soft green eyes and a full mouth. She was well-educated, almost always good-humored, and gracious. But Sergei had gone on to say she could be arrogant and obstinate and ready to flaunt her newly acquired Russified ways. In fact, she was typical of the residents of the small provincial town where she lived, looking upon peasants with utter disdain and poking fun at old men in bast shoes. Kulik felt he understood her only too well. To scorn your own kind and embrace foreign attitudes was definitely a sign of the times, and Marusia was apparently caught up in it.

Kulik was beginning to feel hostile to her and to all those like her. Not too long ago, under Polish occupation, the people of Pinsk had embraced the Polish language and customs. They spoke Polish in schools, in towns and villages, even in the churches. And now with the coming of the Bolsheviks, they strove to speak only in Russian. They had changed almost overnight, from one to the other, having long ago forgotten their own way of life.

These thoughts streamed through Kulik's mind and jangled his nerves. He tried to focus on something else, something more positive. Springtime was several months away, and that time of year always inspired change and he thought that perhaps he could make plans. But today was only the twenty-third of December and how could he go about making plans when the land was still buried in snow, and more was coming, judging from the dark clouds looming overhead? And what would spring bring anyway?

Then again from behind the window came that same shrill, bird-like cry. Kulik raised his head and listened. But now he heard another kind of noise, this time voices, men's voices, and they appeared to be inside the school, in the grade one classroom. One voice rose above the others but was completely unintelligible. Then more sounds: howling, knocking, wailing. After about five minutes everything quieted and there came a rush of feet, then the shuffling of benches and desks, the banging of doors. How could there be so much disruption in the school at this late hour and with all the classes cancelled? Feeling somewhat unsettled, he quickly rose to his feet and in the dark groped his way along the corridor to check out the first grade classroom. Opening the door he was startled to find it empty. Striking up a match, he noticed the teacher's desk stood exactly where it always stood and the benches and desks had not been disturbed; rather, everything was in perfect order, precisely the way Paraska had left it the evening before.

"How strange," he muttered to himself, "I could have sworn I heard noises."

He returned to his bedroom, stopping now and then to listen. Once he thought he heard a woman scream, then he was certain he heard a tapping on the wall. He went to his door, straining for several minutes to hear even the slightest murmur; but there was only silence.

When the clock struck midnight, he put on his pajamas and sank into bed. He lay on his back, wide awake, thinking of nothing. Two hours went by, then another two, and though he was exhausted, he could not fall asleep. Finally he saw dawn approaching. With each minute his room grew lighter. He felt the sense of relief that comes when the invisible becomes visible. His eyes wandered across the ceiling. It was painted a blue-gray, like slate, and it was filled with cracks and peeling plaster, and over the door there was a big yellow water stain. At the far right corner, a dark smudge no more than a few centimeters long, caught his attention. He was surprised to see it move. He realized it was not a smudge, but a spider weaving a web. This struck him as strange. A spider weaving a web in the dead of winter when there is nothing for it to trap? Although he was not superstitious, this made him uneasy; he could not help but feel it was a bad omen. Something was about to happen, he could feel it with all his heart and soul, something terrible. But what? He was paralyzed by a sudden knock on the door.

Three men barged into his room. They wore dark gray overcoats and high leather boots; rifles were strapped over their shoulders. Kulik recognized two of them: Iofe Nicel Leyzarov and Leon Kuzikov. The third he had never seen before, but the insignia on his arm made clear that he was a lieutenant in the NKVD. Leyzarov and Kuzikov scanned the room hurriedly. Leyzarov said to Kulik, "Well, *da*, we're here to inform you that we will be occupying the school for the next two hours."

At that moment there was a great bustle outside the door; people could be heard tramping up and down the hallway. Voices rose and fell; and there appeared to be great confusion. There was crying and wailing that grew louder and louder. Then came the sound of a woman screaming, barely coherently: "Where are they taking us? Why is this happening? Oh, Lord, what have we done?"

Kulik recognized the voice of Timushka. Soon from outside came the clatter of horses. Peering out the window, he saw there were about ten of them, all hitched to large wooden sleighs lined up along the road. Something gripped his heart; he felt rooted to the spot. What was happening? Why all the sleighs? And why did these armed NKVD men push their way into the school?

Kuzikov turned to him and said with a sly grin, "Not to worry, comrade, we're merely filtering through trash, if you know what I mean. We'll be done in no time."

Kulik grew more anxious and distressed. He did not utter a word but kept his eyes fixed on the men, waiting for what would come next. They retreated to a corner and talked in low voices. As the lieutenant paused to loosen his overcoat, Kulik caught sight of a pistol at his waist.

It was precisely at that moment that Paraska flew into the room. She was pale and breathless and her lips quivered uncontrollably.

The presence of the three officials alarmed her, even though she had seen them enter the school from the window of the storage room where she had been scrubbing the floor. She stared at them with wide eyes, wringing her hands.

The lieutenant turned to Kulik. "Yes, comrade, we'll be through in no time. We've just about cleared the school of all the trash."

"Trash?" Paraska cut in. "What trash are you talking about? There's no trash in the school. Why, just yesterday I gave it a thorough cleaning."

The lieutenant gave a hearty laugh. He said ironically, "Yes, I'm sure you did. Not to worry, we have everything under control. You'll understand soon enough."

Out in the hallway there were more footsteps. Some were heavier than others, and then there were those that were barely audible. There followed a flurry of sounds: whimpering, crying, sniffling, sobbing. Men, women and children were making these sounds, all at the same time, sounds so strained and unnatural it was almost as if they weren't even human.

Kulik stood horror-stricken, barely able to take in what was happening. There was a pounding in his chest. Through a crack in the window he could see about twenty villagers being prodded outside by armed soldiers and packed into the waiting sleighs. What was going on? Why were they being taken away? And where were they being taken to? And for how long? Leyzarov, adjusting his rifle, stepped to the door and signaled with his head for his men to follow him. They moved into the hallway and in single file made for the grade one classroom.

Kulik and Paraska glanced at each other, too frightened to speak. Kulik followed the men down the hallway.

The classroom was packed with people. Most were from the immediate area, although there were also some from Morozovich and Lopatina. Some wept, while others looked around helplessly, shaking with fear. Like wooden statues, armed Bolshevik soldiers stood against the walls and windows and blocked the doorway.

More people were shoved through the door. The air was thick with sweat and heavy clouds of tobacco smoke floated beneath the ceiling. The people did not understand why they had been brought here or what was going to happen to them, but they knew that there was no escape and that no one was going to help them. Never before, not under the Czar or under Polish occupation, had they ever been through anything like this. Yesterday they had peacefully farmed their land and tended to their animals and today the future was shutting down on them and fast; their past had just been destroyed.

Timushka, who sat on a bench near the back of the room, rocked back and forth, heaving deep, bitter sighs. Her daughter, Olena, who was to have married the shoemaker's son in the spring, sat at her side, and on her other side was her little granddaughter, Claudia. Her three sons huddled in a corner, while her husband nervously paced the floor. The entire family had fallen victim to the new reality gripping the nation.

In front of Timushka sat a small-framed, rather pretty woman not much over thirty, with her two young daughters, Adriana and Oksana. Adriana, who looked like her mother, was ten years old and a pupil of Kulik's. She was lightly dressed in a tattered gray frock, and a thick long braid of chestnut hair hung over her left shoulder. Tears streamed down her cheeks; grasping her mother's arm, she asked her over and over, "Why are we here? Who are those men and what do they want from us? What's going to happen to us?" Oksana, who was not yet two and bundled in rags, cried at the top of her voice, begging her mother to take her in her arms.

Then from somewhere in the crowd a girl of no more than seventeen sprang to her feet. She too was shabbily dressed in torn shoes with no stockings and her thin overcoat had been patched and mended at the elbows. Her eyes on fire, she pushed her way to the lieutenant and threw him a cold, hateful look. She said to him, "Do you think I'm going to cry too, like that baby over there? You're mistaken! You're vile and contemptible, you filthy bastard!" Taking a step forward, she spat directly in his face.

The lieutenant shook with rage. He pulled a handkerchief from his jacket pocket, and wiping himself clean, called to his soldiers, "Men, take her away!"

Two NKVD men jumped from behind and grabbed the girl's arms. She kicked and cried as they dragged her across the floor and into the hallway. A few minutes passed. Then from the window a roaring wind slammed up against the panes. It was soon drowned out by howling and screaming. There were more sounds, some wailing, some clattering, and several minutes later, silence.

The lieutenant tried to contain his fury. For the longest time he stared into the crowd without saying a word. When he saw Kulik standing by the door, he walked over to him and asked as if nothing had happened, "Are you from this village?"

Kulik, hardly able to answer, said, "No, I'm pretty much a stranger to these parts. I've been in Hlaby only a few weeks."

"Do you know any of the people here?"

"No, in fact, I hardly know anybody, although some I recognize as the parents of my pupils."

The lieutenant continued in much the same nonchalant manner. "See that woman over there, the one with the two young girls? She's the widow of a forest guard who worked for the Poles. In other words, she's from the antagonistic class, a subversive. And her children are no better." Then, pointing across the room, laughing, "And see that short, stumpy bastard in the corner? He keeps moving around as if he has ants in his pants. It seems he just can't wait to take to the road. Hah! Hah! Hah!"

As the lieutenant was about to go on, Paraska flew into the room looking more flustered than ever. "Director, Director," she cried. "You're being summoned outside. Please, come quickly."

Excusing himself, Kulik walked out of the school and into the schoolyard. The cold wind whipped at his face and he could feel his hands go numb. There he came upon Kirilo, the former Olivinski farmhand, who was standing in line with about ten other men. They were all lightly dressed with no hats and their hands and feet were bound by thick rope. Kirilo was shivering.

"They came and took everything," he mumbled. "They took my wife, my children. What does anything matter anymore? They say I'm subverting and weakening the Soviet system because I worked as a farmhand on the Olivinski estate. What does all that mean? Nothing makes sense anymore." Then shrugging and waving his hand, "If it's off to a slave labor camp, then it's off to a slave labor camp. And in slave labor camps they say life is so unbearable that death is a relief. We'll see. I wanted to say goodbye to you personally. You're a good man, Director Kulik. May God be with you."

Kulik didn't know what to do with himself. His heart was still throbbing. Quickly he made his way to his living quarters, and slamming the door shut, fell onto his bed. He was dizzy and a tide of nausea was rising inside him. There was no escaping the horror; with each passing minute it was moving closer and closer. He tried to keep from thinking of the insanity just steps away. But suddenly he was overcome with uncontrollable rage. If he had a machine gun in his hands he would shoot them all and watch them drop like flies, one after the other. He would sink his boot heels into their faces and wipe off those smug and arrogant smirks once and for all.

A cold damp draft came from the window and penetrated his whole body. He began to shake. Drawing a blanket over himself and burying his head in his pillow, he cried and cried and could not stop. Then he heard noise coming from his office. At first he thought he was imagining it, but when it became louder and more pronounced, he realized there was something going on in there. People were talking, shouting, shoving boxes around, banging drawers, opening and closing doors. Straining his ears to listen, it was not long before he recognized the voices of Sergei and Hrisko Suchok, father of little Ohrimko. Suchok was yelling at the top of his voice; he seemed completely beside himself. "What is there left to do? Nothing can be done, absolutely nothing."

Kulik got up and walked to his office. He stood in the doorway several minutes in total bewilderment. There was chaos everywhere; the entire room had been turned upside down. When Sergei saw Kulik, he pointed to a big pile of clothing in the corner. "We've managed to collect a few things—a couple of jackets, some boot liners, scarves, mittens, hats, and three wool blankets. We tried to give them to the villagers for their journey, but those bastards won't allow it. They say it isn't necessary."

Suchok asked, "Director, how about you, do you have any suggestions?"

Kulik stood a while in thought. "Hmm . . . We have to find a way to tame the wild beast. Nothing else will work."

"And how does one go about taming a beast gone wild beyond control?" Sergei screwed up his mouth ironically. "Maybe we should prepare a feast?"

"A feast!" Kulik repeated. "That's it, Sergei! What a brilliant idea! We'll prepare a feast, and maybe that will distract them. Now quickly, we don't have a moment to lose. Let's add up what we've got. I have two liters of vodka stashed in the bottom of my dresser drawer, and if I'm not mistaken, there are a couple of bottles of wine in the kitchen cabinet."

Sergei scowled. "And I hope they're all tainted with arsenic."

Kulik narrowed his eyes. "I don't think we're looking to find ourselves before a firing squad. We won't be of any use to anybody that way."

Sergei threw up his hands. "Maybe you're right. This plan of yours, crazy as it sounds, just might work. I have at least ten eggs and some cheese in the cold cellar. I'll be back in a few minutes."

"And I've got a tub of lard," offered Suchok, "and half a loaf of bread."

Paraska appeared in the doorway. At first she looked around in utter confusion, then realizing what the men were up to, she was quick to contribute. "I've got some boiled *kasha* and a pot of beans. With everything combined, that should be enough to fill the table." She turned to leave, cursing under her breath. "May those bastards be stricken with cholera and die. May they all rot in hell."

Several minutes passed. Paraska was the first to return with a basket under her arm, followed almost immediately by Hrisko and then Sergei. When all the provisions were arranged neatly on the table and the tile stove filled and lit, Kulik headed to the grade one classroom. The lieutenant was sitting behind the teacher's desk flipping through some papers. Kulik made an effort to strike up a conversation. "I was just outside," he started, "and it's freezing out there. I swear it must be at least minus thirty degrees celsius."

"Minus thirty degrees, is that all?" Without looking up, the lieutenant gave a prolonged laugh. "For two years I was stationed in Arkhangelsk, near the White Sea, and believe me, I know the true meaning of winter! This is like springtime. Hah! Hah! Hah!"

"Is that where these people are being taken? To Arkhangelsk?" Kulik turned white and numb at hearing his own words.

The lieutenant looked up, frowning. "I strongly advise you not to interfere in matters that don't concern you. Too many questions will only lead to a bad end. Understand?"

Returning to his papers, the lieutenant jotted something down in his ledger book. Noticing Kulik still standing near the desk, he snapped, "Comrade Kulik, do you want something? Can't you see I'm busy?"

Kulik tried to keep his anger out of his voice. "I was simply commenting on the weather. It's quite nasty out there today. As a matter of fact, I wanted to offer you and your men food and drink before you take to the road. Paraska, our school matron, has taken it upon herself to prepare a feast."

The lieutenant raised his head and his eyes lit up. He struck the desk with his fist. "A feast, you say? Now that's what I want to hear!" Rising from his seat, he took Kulik's hand and shook it vigorously. "You're very thoughtful, comrade."

The NKVD men hurried into the kitchen. The table held bowls of borscht with sour cream, and trays filled with scrambled eggs, chunks of backfat, bread, and boiled beef. Kulik poured the vodka.

"Pretty girls and vodka, what more can a man ask for?" The lieutenant settled in one of the chairs and eyed Paraska, who stood quietly by the door. Smacking his lips, he downed his first glass.

When he was drinking his third, he called out, "Come here, Paraska. Come over to me, don't be shy."

Stumbling to his feet, he reached out and grabbed hold of her skirt.

Paraska let out a little shriek and jumped back.

"You stupid girl, what are you so scared of? Do you think NKVD men don't know how to treat a woman? Come here, let me show you."

All the color drained from Paraska's face and her heart beat wildly. She couldn't have found the lieutenant more repulsive.

"Uh, Lieutenant." Kulik rushed to break things up, not really knowing what to do or say. "You must be patient with Paraska. She's a bit on the timid side."

Kuzikov leapt up, swinging a bottle in the air. The drink had gone completely to his head. "Those goddamn capitalist pigs! They don't give a damn about women or women's rights. Here in our socialist motherland a woman is equal to a man and she walks with him arm in arm. Why, just look at our construction industry, some of our best bricklayers are women! And it's the women not the men who are building our cities, making our factories prosper. Where in the world will you find anything like that?"

Kuzikov belched several times, then started in on female emancipation, then went on about equality of the sexes, until at last he lost himself completely.

"Hey, Paraska!" The lieutenant poured more drinks. "Come over here and join me. I've drunk too much. Damn the vodka!"

Kulik kept his eyes on the lieutenant. He had to find a way to get Paraska out of there before it was too late. But how? Finally, all he could come up with was, "Paraska, we're out of water. Would you be so kind as to go to the well and bring us a fresh pitcher?"

Exchanging glances with Kulik, Paraska took to her heels and fled out the door.

The lieutenant was now very drunk and his speech was slurred. He patted Kulik on the back. "You're a wonderful host, Comrade Director. Obviously you're from the working class."

"Yes, I'm the son of poor peasants."

"Excellent! Excellent! I believe I forgot to formally introduce myself. My name is Sobakin. Simon Stepanovich Sobakin. Yes, I agree, Sobakin is a most unfortunate name. It's downright degrading. My great-great-grandfather passed it down to me and there's not much I can do about it. Some bourgeois bastard back then decided my great-great-grandfather was no better than a dog, so he called him Sobakin. Yes, Sobakin comes from the word *sobaka*, which, of course, as we all know, means dog. And what does a dog do? He barks and slobbers and licks your feet, and to the bourgeoisie that's what we are, just a pack of dogs. What do you think about that?" Sinking back in his seat, he mumbled, "Yes, Sobakin's my name. Sobakin it was and Sobakin it remains. Even today, in this great time of revolution, we're all still living testimony of our oppressive past."

"Here, here!" The NKVD men raised their glasses in a toast.

"What are you men up to over there?" The lieutenant poured himself another drink. He looked severely at them. "Do you think I look like a dog? That I'm a son-of-a-bitch? Hah, may you all burn in hell!"

Grabbing hold of a wine bottle, he looked to the door and shouted, "Hey, Paraska, why aren't you back yet? I'm waiting for you!"

Leyzarov sprang from his seat as if suddenly sober. He raised his glass. "Paraska! Let's give a toast to Paraska, a true woman of our times! She has five children, all still very young. One day they will grow up and become loyal and dedicated proletarians. We need more women like Paraska to guarantee our future generations! Three cheers for Paraska!".

Sobakin looked around. "Paraska, Paraska, where are you?" Then to the men, "She's quite a woman, I agree. Still young enough and not bad-looking either. Five children, you say? Another toast to Paraska!"

At that moment Sergei hurried to the table with a message. "Uh, excuse me, Lieutenant, sir, but Paraska it appears had to go and feed her children. She apologizes and promises to be back as soon as she puts her youngest to bed. In the meantime, however, she asks if you might consider doing her a little favor. . . . "

"A favor? For Paraska?" The lieutenant could now barely sit up. His face was flushed and his eyes rolled. "Tell me. For Paraska, anything. Just name it and it's as good as done."

"Well, comrade, see that pile of clothing over there? She asks that you distribute it among the villagers before they take to the road."

"What?" Sobakin's head swam and he seemed to have trouble understanding what Sergei was saying. He shouted nonetheless, "For Paraska, it's as good as done. Whatever she wants. Damn that woman!"

Kulik and Sergei hurried to gather up the clothes, and followed the NKVD men into the grade one classroom. The lieutenant somehow managed to stumble to the teacher's desk, and teetering before the crowd, shouted out to them, "Counterrevolutionaries, renegades, all of you. Listen to what I have to say! The great Soviet regime never makes mistakes. A Bolshevik can spot an enemy of the people even with his eyes closed. I'm not the swine you think I am. I'm a man of honor and great conscience. I'm passing on to you this pile of clothing. Take them, use them as you see fit."

The people looked on in bewilderment. Those most scantily dressed were the first to bundle up, followed by the children and the elderly. When the pile finally disappeared, the doors were opened wide and everyone was herded outside where the sleighs awaited them. They now understood what was going on. They were being taken away, first to Pinsk, to the train station; from there they would be packed into boxcars and sent straight north to Arkhangelsk. Women and children were loaded up first, followed by the men. They all knew that what was happening to them was terrible and irreversible.

On one of the sleighs sat Timushka with her family. Between her feet were two small bundles containing some personal items she had managed to snatch up before being forced out of her house, including a down pillow and a small embroidered cloth, both of which she had set aside for her daughter's dowry. Timushka's husband sat on her left and waved his cap to the small group of onlookers who had come to bid farewell. He called out to them, "Merry Christmas to you all! Remember us in a good way!"

A whistle hooted. The sleds inched forward and the bells jangled. The teams of horses labored through the deep snow, neighing as if protesting the heavy loads, slowly moving into the distance past the outlying houses, with the falling snow thickening. A dead silence hung in the air, broken only by the sound of the wind. Almost half the village was gone.

Paraska stood with her husband Philip and watched the sleds. Philip's face was pale and thin and a thick white bandage was wrapped around his head. Supported by his wife, he panted and coughed, and every few minutes spat out a thick mucus. He stared fixedly at the road and said nothing.

Grandfather Cemen paced to and fro, rubbing his hands and breathing heavily. No matter how much he moved, he could not get warm. His heart was torn with anguish. All at once he spoke loudly and clearly. Everyone, including Sobakin, turned to listen.

"At one time the sinners sent Christ to Golgotha where they crucified him. Your road, my children, is a road to Golgotha. Go with God. Let your hearts be at peace, because one day soon Satan will perish and Christ will triumph once again. Angels will sing Hosanna, and when they do, these warmongers, these Satanists, will drop like flies and the ravenous crows overhead will peck at their rotting flesh."

As the old man spoke, Sobakin's face crimsoned and he flew into a rage. "Why, you senile old bastard!"

He pulled out his revolver, and said derisively, "Well, well, it looks like I've found myself another subversive!"

Everyone in the crowd froze and waited for the sound of gunfire. But there was no gunfire. Instead, Sobakin, with as much strength as he could muster, slammed the butt end of his revolver into the old man's head. Blood trickled out of his skull in a thin stream. He fell to the ground without so much as a twitch.

"He's dead!" someone cried out. "Grandfather Cemen is dead!"

Sobakin turned on the crowd. "Get out of here, all of you!"

Slipping his revolver back into its holster and rubbing his hands together as if to wash them clean, he turned and trudged back into the school. The minute he disappeared, several young men jumped over the fence and ran to the old man. Covering him with a blanket, they carried him into his house and laid him on a small cot in the kitchen. A few villagers followed to the door. Philip knelt and wept at his father's side, saying the Lord's Prayer. Paraska, also kneeling and weeping, kissed the old man's hands and wailed, "They murdered you, they murdered you in cold blood! Dear God, dear God!"

Kulik headed back to the school and walked into the kitchen. It was hot and stuffy and stank of *makhorka* cigarettes and stale liquor. A shudder passed over him as he replayed the day's events in his mind: the armed NKVD men, the pile of clothing on the kitchen floor, the looks of hopelessness and despair on the faces of the peasants. Fear had so rapidly swept over the region and death was everywhere.

He felt such bitter hatred and anger that he lost control. Clenching both fists, he banged the wall. Catching sight of the table where the emptied plates and trays with leftover food were piled up, his stomach turned as he thought of the NKVD men laughing, drinking and stuffing their mouths. The room became hotter and more unbearable. He tried to calm himself, but the more he tried, the more he felt himself falling apart. Then all at once he seized a broom from behind the tile stove, and raising it in the air, struck the top of the table and sent everything crashing to the floor. Plates went flying, glasses, cups, bowls, everything, smashed to pieces. Then flinging himself around, he aimed the broom at the lamp hanging over his head. He wanted to destroy the windows, the chairs, the walls, he wanted to destroy everything in sight. But instead he dropped to his knees and wept feverishly, like a child. What happened today was a sign of things to come. The people in this small, out-of-the-way place were falling victim to a huge, complex organization they couldn't even begin to understand. They knew only that something terrible was happening to them. If this was the beginning, what would life be like tomorrow, after tomorrow?

After several minutes, he wandered into his bedroom, unaware that he was still holding the broom. Dull lamplight burned on his night table, casting huge eerie shadows on the wall. Looking up, he saw the grayish-black smudge in the corner of the ceiling.

He cursed aloud. Then raising the broom over his head, with one heavy stroke he knocked the spider to the floor and crushed it with his foot.

CHAPTER 6

The teachers' conference in Pinsk was held at the former Holzman Theater. The teachers who had arrived early sat in the front rows, while those arriving later, among whom were Kulik and Sergei, had to find seating at the back, beneath the gallery. On stage, where only last summer there had been performances of Ibsen's *Hedda Gabler* and Molière's *The School for Husbands*, sat a presidium of high-ranking officials, carefully selected by Moscow. The head of the conference was Yeliseyenko, chief of the People's Commissariat of Education. He was about forty-five years old, short and thickset, with a broad nose and wide face. Dressed in a gray wool suit of fair quality and black patent leather shoes that looked imported, he flipped through a stack of papers, occasionally looking up through horn-rimmed glasses. To his right sat a delegate from the National Committee from Minsk by the name of Melnik, with very small features, pencil-thin brows and a receding hairline. Next to him was Litovsky, secretary of the regional committee of the Party and behind him, almost in the corner, was Iofe Nicel Leyzarov.

Leyzarov's presence baffled Kulik; he wondered how he had managed to come to the conference and even to have found a seat on the presidium. Leyzarov was not a teacher or an educator of any sort, but a government official, a representative from the district committee of Pinsk, to be exact, and he really had no business there.

Sergei leaned over and whispered in Kulik's ear, "Ivan, do you see that woman on stage, the oversized one beside Leyzarov?"

61

Kulik craned his neck. "You mean the one in the gray dress?"

"Yes. That's Dounia Avdeevna. Do you remember I mentioned her to you the other day? She's the fishmonger, the one who had a stall in the marketplace and sold schmaltz herring."

Her formidable size and coarse features made an immediate impression on Kulik. With her arms folded over her more than ample belly, she reminded him of a Buddha. She seemed to him to be saying to the crowd, "Look at me, people! Look how important I am! I no longer sell schmaltz herring. I'm a teacher now!"

On the wall at the back of the stage behind the presidium hung two large posters, one of Lenin and the other of Stalin. Vladimir Ilich, in a dark three-piece suit, was reaching his arms toward the masses with a tender smile. Joseph Vissarionovich, in his customary high-collared jacket and black leather boots, wore a benevolent expression. The posters were adorned with red flags and ribbons and nailed to the wall between them was a hammer and sickle. Suspended across the stage was a bright red banner with bold white letters: "Welcome to the First Teachers' Conference of Western Belorussia."

Although somewhat apprehensive, Kulik was relieved to be at the conference. Since taking up his teaching position in Hlaby, he had been hoping in some way to break free from there. He was glad to be in Pinsk, the small but busy provincial port city, where he could meet with fellow teachers, exchange ideas, perhaps even have a few interesting conversations.

Yeliseyenko stood up and clapped his hands.

"Attention, teachers! Welcome to the first teachers' conference of the Pinsk region. In the next couple of weeks our aim is to get to know one another and to familiarize ourselves with the new Soviet system of education. We will come to understand and appreciate the political transformation of our schools, from ones that were selective and bourgeois to ones that are now free and accessible to all. The day has come for the oppressed working-class masses to enter a place never before imagined. Everyone will now have the equal right to an education. And your responsibility as teachers will be to guide your students accordingly, using our great Soviet plan. The first speaker I would like to introduce today is Comrade Melnik, a distinguished delegate from the National Committee in Minsk. Welcome, Comrade Melnik!"

Rising from his seat, Melnik, a slightly built man with bowlegs and a curved spine, carefully placed his papers upon the table, and fumbled in his jacket pocket for his reading glasses. He spoke in a resonant voice with impressive emphasis. Unfortunately, his speech was in Belorussian and as a result many did not understand what he was saying while others grasped only parts of it. But what he was saying was nothing new. He merely expounded upon the usual Soviet platitudes, denouncing the ousted "oppressive bourgeois Polish regime," and the "suffering endured by the Belorussian brotherhood." After about fifteen minutes he ended with, "To freedom! To liberty! Three cheers for the liberating Red Army!"

There was a round of loud applause, and when it finally died down, Yeliseyenko addressed the crowd.

"Our next speaker is Comrade Isaac Abramovich, an esteemed teacher of mathematics and sciences and a graduate of Moscow University, now posted here in Pinsk. Welcome, Comrade Abramovich!"

A handsome giant of a man, with a head full of curly black hair and a nose shaped like a pickle, was the next one to rise. He appeared calm and self-assured and had a good-humored and friendly air. With his hands buried in his trouser pockets, he spoke in a clear Russian without the trace of an accent and without notes. His voice was low and had a mechanical ring.

"Welcome, comrades. We have found ourselves in very fortunate times. A wonderful life awaits us, one free of oppression and poverty, where the poor and the hungry will, for the first time ever, enjoy happiness and plenty. We will all not only thrive under the sun of Stalin's constitution but more importantly we will promote Communism worldwide."

It was not long before it became evident to everyone that his speech was carefully scripted and had been delivered many times before and on many different occasions. When finally he ended, he threw up both arms and shouted, "History is being rewritten before our very eyes! We are witnessing first-hand the birth of the working class revolution! Hurrah to Stalin!" After bowing to loud applause and looking very satisfied with himself, he took his seat once more.

As Yeliseyenko was about to announce the next speaker, a man at the back of the hall suddenly raised his hand, and got up. He turned out to be a Pole by the name of Zaleski, a teacher from Krive Selo. He squeezed his way timidly and awkwardly through the crowd. He spoke softly in a clear Ukrainian, the language he had adopted during his long stay in the marshes.

"My fellow comrades," he coughed slightly to clear his throat, "the question of language in our schools is a matter of great importance. We have already heard from delegate Melnik, who informs us that we are to have Belorussian schools. This is indeed, in my opinion, a frightening proposition. I myself am a Pole and for nearly fifteen years have taught the local children in Polish. I am the first to admit that nothing ever came of it. The majority of inhabitants here are Ukrainian and it is my belief that it is best to teach the children in Ukrainian. What do you think it will be like if overnight they are told to forget what they've already managed to learn in Polish, to forget their native Ukrainian, and to start learning Belorussian? I guarantee you the result will be catastrophic. The result is, the local inhabitants of the area don't speak or understand Belorussian, and it appears to me neither do most of the teachers. As a result, wouldn't it make more sense to bring Ukrainian schools into the region?"

Another voice hastened to pick up the point. "I agree completely. I've taught in the marshes for nearly three decades. I know the locals are predominantly Ukrainian, and they want their children to be taught in Ukrainian. If Belorussian schools are brought in, the people will literally be crippled. My vote is to institute Ukrainian schools."

Looking agitated and trying to remain calm, Yeliseyenko quickly rose to respond. "The question of language is not a matter to be voted on. I've already heard more than enough. Before we continue, let me make one thing clear: it's not for us to decide in what language we are to teach the children. The regime has already made up its mind and the decision is final."

Glancing down at his papers, Yeliseyenko then started calling out names from his long list.

As the hours passed. speaker after speaker came to the stage and, one after the other, elaborated upon various themes, for the most part praising Stalin and glorifying the new regime. Kulik listened attentively at first, and then eventually began to block out what was being said; everything he heard was a rehash of everything that had already been said a million times before.

Growing more and more restless and irritable, with everything grating on his nerves, he raised his hand without thinking of the possible consequences. When Yeliseyenko called upon him and he stepped up to the stage, the words came pouring out, not about language or the new regime, but about the history of Ukraine. "Even as far back as the seventeenth century, Bohdan Hmelnytsky, the greatest *hetman* of Ukraine, proudly wanted to unite his people with Mother Russia. Our ties go back a long way." He praised Hmelnytsky in a way the Soviets wanted to hear. "He led an unprecedented uprising of the oppressed working-class masses and it was through him that Ukraine became permanently unified with Russia. Yes, till this day we enjoy a historic link."

Mention of the "historic link" caught the attention of Melnik, Yeliseyenko and Leyzarov. They knew nothing about Hmelnytsky or about Ukrainian history, for that matter, but they liked what they were hearing about the "historic link." When they nodded, Kulik felt a pang. Now was his chance to say what he had really set out to say. His hands trembled as he forced out his conclusion. "I believe the Soviet brotherhood, given our interrelated history, will not draw boundaries when it comes to the Pinsk Marshes. I have utmost faith that the new regime will attach us not to the Belorussian S.S.R., but to the Ukrainian S.S.R."

At this, Yeliseyenko looked very long and hard at Kulik; he frowned and it was clear that he was furious. Kulik's imprudent remark had hit him like a thunderbolt; it was obvious that he would not soon forget it. A few people applauded Kulik, but most could not care less about Ukraine or, for that matter, its connection to the Pinsk Marshes. The audience was made up predominantly of Poles, Jews, Belorussians and Russians, for whom Ukrainian was a crude, backward language spoken only by a mob of illiterate peasants. To them, Ukrainian was as vital as last year's snow.

As Kulik stepped down from the stage and made his way back to his seat, a shabbily dressed man with a sparse yellow beard leapt up and rushed to the stage. Obviously outraged, he shouted, "Good day, comrades, my name is Kopitsia and I must admit I'm completely beside myself. Kulik has no understanding whatsoever of what's at stake here. He talks about the Pinsk Marshes and how historically they are tied to Ukraine. But how can this be when at one time we weren't even referred to as Ukrainians, but as little Russians? Through culture and language, we have always enjoyed a very close relationship with Mother Russia, and at heart we have always been a part of Russia. I take great pride in telling you we should not be called Ukrainians or Belorussians or Little Russians, or even Russians, but rather, True Russians. I'm sure our great new regime will correct this error. We must," he cried, "protect our great new regime at all costs. There are those of you who see Russia as an imperial presence, and I call you all traitors!"

Few understood Kopitsia's point, and no one applauded him except Dounia Avdeevna, who was half asleep. Yeliseyenko, looking very perturbed, ordered Kopitsia to sit down but Kopitsia ignored him and went on.

"And now about Kulik. His suggestion to bring in Ukrainian schools is the most ridiculous thing I've ever heard. He would rather have our children taught in a crude, uncivilized language than in the wonderful Russian tongue. Obviously he wants us to remain in the dark, which brings me to my next point. Why Belorussian schools? This is an extremely bad idea. Belorussian is a language that is just as crude and uncivilized as Ukrainian. What we need in our marshes are Russian schools and only Russian schools. Russian is our window to the future! To the world!"

Kopitsia talked on, in circles, repeating himself.

Sergei nudged Kulik. "You see what we're up against?"

Yeliseyenko, who had by now reached the end of his rope, rushed up to Kopitsia, grabbed his arm and pushed him off the stage. Then he turned angrily on the crowd. "This meeting's gone far enough. I'm extremely disappointed in you all. Let me get one thing straight about Party policies: we are all equal members of the great Soviet Empire and there is no such thing as an inferior or superior language. Everyone here is free and on the same footing." Then to Melnik apologetically, "I'm sorry Comrade Kopitsia is so ill-informed about our history and that he insulted your Belorussian language. Eventually he will come to understand that all languages in our great new empire deserve honor and respect. To freedom! To liberty! To Stalin!"

With these last words, loud applause erupted, followed by the stamping of feet. Yeliseyenko grinned broadly and it was evident that he was congratulating himself for having at the last moment set the conference back on track.

CHAPTER 7

After the first day of the conference, Sergei invited Kulik to call on his cousin, Marusia, an invitation Kulik readily accepted. Marusia lived with her parents in a spacious two-story house on Luninetska Street in Karalyn, a nearby suburb. The two men walked down several narrow streets and wooden gangways, and turned into a small, fenced-in yard planted with shrubs and a gnarled old chestnut tree. Rather than entering through the front door, they made for the side of the house and mounted a set of stairs leading into the kitchen. As they were about to knock on the door, they stopped short at the sound of loud voices coming from inside. Soon shouting was followed by screaming and cursing. The men exchanged glances. Sergei's aunt and uncle were obviously in the middle of a quarrel, something, according to Sergei, they did quite often. His aunt's voice drowned out his uncle's and with each second grew louder and more intense.

"How can anyone live with you?" This was his aunt. "You're impossible. I've asked you time and time again to fix that damn sofa. The front leg has almost completely fallen off. And you still haven't even looked at it. Are you waiting for the whole thing to collapse? The squeaking gets on my nerves. Oh, life with you is impossible! And that beard of yours! Why don't you shave it off? It makes you look like an old goat!"

A voice crooned back. "Talk all you want, old woman. Yes, yes, it'll do you good to get it out of your system."

When the visitors knocked on the door, the old couple, startled by the intrusion, abruptly stopped their argument. As they entered, Sergei's aunt glared at them, while his uncle, emitting a sigh of relief, greeted his nephew with open arms. "Sergei, my boy! I was just thinking about you the other day. So glad to see you! You couldn't have come at a more opportune time. And who's your friend?"

"Ivan Kulik, headmaster of School Number Seven. Ivan, I'd like you to meet my uncle, Valentyn Bohdanovich."

"A pleasure, an absolute pleasure! Welcome to our home. And this is my wife, Efrosinia." Then, with a wink, "At least that's what it says on our marriage certificate." He escorted his guests into the living room, and invited them to sit down. "We can talk here. Have you any news? There's so much going on these days. There's such upheaval everywhere."

As the young men moved toward the sofa, Efrosinia stepped in front of them. "Don't sit there, the whole thing will go crashing if you do. The front leg is loose." Then swinging around, she shouted through an open door and up the staircase, "Marusia! Can you come down please! We have guests! And bring some chairs with you!"

Throwing her husband a hostile glance, she grasped Kulik's arm, and looked him in the face as if she had something she wanted to say. "Young man, you seem level-headed enough to me. May I ask you a simple question? When something, say, a door or a window gets broken, what would you do about it? Or if a chair gets damaged, or a table becomes wobbly, or if the foot of a sofa becomes loose? What would you do?"

"Well," Kulik shrugged awkwardly and took a step back. "I suppose I would try and fix whatever needed repair."

"Aha!" Efrosinia clapped her hands. "There you have it! Did you hear that, old man? Did you hear what he just said?" Pushing Kulik toward her husband, she breathed deeply. "What you say makes perfect sense, young man, and I agree with you totally. If something breaks, then it ought to get fixed. It's as simple as that. If I say to the old man 'Fix the sofa, it's broken,' he always says, 'Aha, hm, well, um . . .' And then he walks off into another room and shuts the door behind him. A hammer and a nail, a couple of bangs, and the problem would be solved!"

Valentyn, who usually paid little attention to his wife, suddenly pricked up his ears. "A hammer and nail? Hah! Old woman, you don't know what you're talking about. Do you think fixing a sofa is as simple as that? To do it properly takes time, you need a chisel, a drill, and some glue—and not just any ordinary glue, but good carpenter's glue! Hammer and nail, hah!"

Efrosinia glared at him. Choice words were at the tip of her tongue and in another second, she would shower him with abuse. But by a stroke of luck, at that very moment Marusia entered the room, dragging two rather large chairs behind her. She seemed to be bored by the chore. Sergei hurried to help her. Her demeanor was cool and aloof, radiating a sort of frigid insolence. Although she greeted her cousin with real affection and even kissed him on the cheek, she seemed quite indifferent to Kulik. When she started back toward the kitchen, Sergei called out, "Marusia, don't go! I would like to introduce you to my good friend, Ivan Kulik."

A strained pause followed, and in an attempt to break the ice, Kulik said, "Marusia, finally I get to meet you. I've heard some very nice things about you."

The girl smiled a little and blushed. "Oh, that Seryoza." Marusia was always careful to use Sergei's diminutive. "I don't really deserve half the credit he gives me."

"Well, perhaps you're right, perhaps you don't." Kulik could not believe what had just come out of his mouth. Why was he being so rude and to someone he had just met? Shifting uncomfortably, for a brief moment he reproached himself for his insolence, but when he saw the haughty expression on her face, he decided to press on. "I believe the more beautiful a woman is the more dangerous she becomes."

Marusia, though clearly annoyed at first by his words, burst suddenly into a fit of laughter, and cried, "Now I get it! Oh, now I understand you! I understand you perfectly! This is going to be great fun!"

Kulik raised his brows, puzzled. "I don't get it. What's so funny? Maybe you misunderstood what I said. It wasn't meant as a joke."

Efrosinia joined in her daughter's laughter. She hastened to explain. "It's not what you said, young man, that's so funny, but how you said it. The truth of the matter is you are an aberration, a true aberration, and it's all so unexpected. You look like a sophisticated city dweller, but when you open your mouth, you talk like a *moujik*. We all assumed you would go on in Russian, but what did you go and do? You spoke in Ukrainian."

Then scrutinizing him more closely, she looked bewildered. "It's strange, even though you speak in Ukrainian, somehow your words sound unusually smooth, they sound, rather, well, rather nice, even cultured. It's almost as if you weren't talking Ukrainian at all. Why, you could have almost been speaking Russian! You're a very odd young man, and pardon my frankness, but a bit on the stubborn side."

Kulik took a deep breath. He couldn't hide his anger. "On the stubborn side?" he burst out. "Why? Because I speak Ukrainian and not Russian? Because I haven't sold out to the occupiers the way you have? Is that what's so funny?" Then, deliberately insulting her, "And you, *Pani* Bohdanovich, with your broken Russian, where do you come from? Moscow, perhaps?"

After he said this, he felt ashamed of himself for having lost his temper. But he did not apologize; he went on being sarcastic. "In what language do you propose I speak? German? *Sehr gut, dann können wir deutsch sprechen.*"

"You speak German?" Marusia's eyes widened; she was completely taken aback. She had never before heard a *moujik* speak anything but Ukrainian. Now she decided this young man was worth further investigation. Who was he? And how strange that he spoke German, and so well! She tried to figure him out, but without much luck. He seemed, at least in a general way, amiable enough and well-disposed, and he wasn't bad-looking either: she rather liked his deep-set gray eyes and his mop of thick black hair. But still there was an impudence about him that really irritated her. She sat on the edge of the sofa and looked quizzically at him.

"I know some German myself," she said. "Why, just last year in school we studied German literature, you know, Nietzsche, Goethe, Anzangruber . . . It was most absorbing and stimulating. Later we studied French. Of course, Russian is absolutely the best . . ."

"Enough about language already!" Sergei stamped his foot. He had no intention of letting things get out of hand again. Trying to lighten the situation, he said, "About language, I've got the perfect solution. Why don't we just start communicating in sign language?"

Everybody laughed, and the atmosphere became more friendly. They chatted into the late evening hours. Kulik spoke only Ukrainian, while Marusia went on in Russian, though poorly. Efrosinia spoke predominantly Russian, throwing in Ukrainian words and phrases and sometimes even Polish ones; Valentyn for the most part kept to Ukrainian, now and then using odd Russian expressions for added emphasis; Sergei too spoke only Ukrainian, and did not mix it with Russian or Polish, in both of which he was fluent.

When Efrosinia disappeared into the kitchen to put on tea and prepare a snack, Kulik turned to the girl, resolved to set her off again.

"May I call you Marika?"

"Marika?" She leaned back. The sofa let out a screech.

"Yes, Marika is a lovely name, more appealing than Marusia, wouldn't you agree?"

Marusia stared at him. "I don't agree with you at all," she said. "Marika is not a nicer name than Marusia. In fact, I find it rather plain, too commonplace." Then with her eyes narrowing, "Uh . . . what did you say your name was again, Ivan was it?"

"Yes, Ivan. Ivan Kulik."

"Ivan?" The girl rolled her eyes and grimaced.

"Yes, it's a very ordinary name, I agree, but there's not much I can do about it."

Marusia wanted to even the score. "Well, actually there is. Why don't you use your Russian diminutive? Vanya. There, that sounds much better."

Kulik gave her a harsh look. He felt like scolding her, but held himself back, and came at her from another angle. "I would say that your newly adopted language has somehow lost its power to form diminutives, Vanya included."

As he spoke, he found it increasingly difficult to focus on what he was saying. Her mouth had an extraordinary fullness, and there was an unexpected tenderness in her eyes that affected him deeply. Still, he felt compelled to strike back at her. "The Russians take Ivan and make Vanya out of it, that's the same as taking Maria and forming Marusia. In Ukrainian, which you've clearly denounced, everything has a natural order. Maria becomes Marika, Ivan becomes Ivasik, Vasil becomes Vasilik. We don't take Ivan and transform it into Vanya, or Vladimir into Vova."

The girl threw back her head and laughed. She found the point he was trying to make exaggerated and unreasonable. In the end it had no effect on her at all.

Busy in the kitchen, Efrosinia strained to listen to what the young people were saying. But her daughter went on too rapidly and excitedly, and Kulik spoke so softly, she had trouble catching even the slightest word. And, save for a few monosyllables here and there, it was as if Sergei wasn't in the room at all.

When she returned to the living room and set the tray of food on a side table by the sofa, she had lost interest in the young people's chatter. She seemed to be distracted by something, and looked a little distressed. Her head bent and her eyes welling with tears, she settled next to Kulik, and said to him, "What do you say, young man, will I see my Lonia again? Sergei's probably mentioned him to you."

"That's your son, isn't it? I'm sure you'll see him again, and soon."

"Yes, soon." She wrung her hands. "He's my only son. So, you really think I'll see him again?"

Valentyn, who stood by the window smoking a pipe, remarked, "Lonia is studying engineering in Lvov. But now that war's broken out . . . there's so much uncertainty everywhere . . . We've been waiting to hear from him . . . But . . ."

His voice suddenly broke off and he began to examine his hands; first looking at his thumbs, then his index fingers, then his palms. "My hands," he said, "how would we ever have got by without them? They've done everything. If not for these hands, Lonia would never have gone to university. Marusia would not have had tutors. That's how precious my hands are!"

"My old man's a cabinet maker," Efrosinia volunteered. "His hands are truly made of gold, or at least they used to be. Now, as you can see, they're gnarled and arthritic. They're certainly not what they used to be." Then working herself up again, "He can't even repair the sofa. And now, to make matters worse, he's gone deaf. He doesn't hear a word I say."

"Oh, Mother, please!" Marusia cut in. "What a thing to say, and in front of guests!"

"Tell me, *Pan* Bohdanovich." Kulik quickly turned to the old man to ward off another scene. "What sort of things did you build?"

"A little bit of this, a little bit of that. But mostly coffins."

As the old man spoke, his eyes twinkled and his chest puffed up. "The summer before the war, business boomed. In that one summer alone, more people died than at any other time, and not just your average citizens, but dignitaries as well. First the representative for urban affairs died, then the assistant to the director of public works, then the district representative. They all dropped like flies. And when our distinguished mayor died, I built him the most exquisite coffin and out of the best ebony I could find. I even made carvings of birds and leaves along the edges, as requested by his widow. I built almost all the coffins in Pinsk. No one in this town is or was capable of building a better coffin than I. And that's the truth. I selected the finest wood, I measured my corners with the greatest precision, I sanded down the boards until they were as smooth as silk. I also built in elevated headrests to ensure the corpses were propped up for suitable viewing. I must say, the mortician did a fine job on the district representative's head, but without my headrest, everything would have gone to waste. You see how precious my hands are!"

"Father!" Marusia's face flushed a deep crimson. "Must you go on?"

Valentyn glared at his daughter. "Are you ashamed of my trade? Didn't I provide you with all the comforts of life? Would you be wearing that pretty satin dress or those Italian pumps if not for those coffins?"

The girl tightened her lips.

Valentyn went on. "Yes, my hands have created wonders. And the police commissioner who drowned in the Karalyn River, who do you think built his coffin? I made him a palatial resting spot for all eternity, and his widow showed her appreciation by paying me one hundred *zlotys*. The commissioner looked like a general! No, a king! He had a funeral like no other. Why, practically the whole of Pinsk came. Oh, what wonderful hands I have!"

Efrosinia frowned. "Don't get too carried away, old man. What was, has already happened. Bragging won't bring our Lonia back." She told Kulik, "I write Lonia regularly but he doesn't answer my letters, and he doesn't come home either. Day in and day out I sit by the window and watch for him. And now just yesterday I found out that Lonia is ill and in hospital, with consumption. Oh, this is a mother's curse! What am I to do? What am I to do?" Clutching her head, she burst into tears. "What bitter agony! Is my Lonia suffering? Is he even conscious? My poor baby!"

In her anguish and grief, she was not aware that she had begun speaking Ukrainian, clearly and concisely, without a single Russian word. "How brilliantly he studied at the *gymnasium*. He even received a medal of excellence for having the highest grade in his final year. Then he left for Lvov to study at the university . . ." She reached for Kulik's hand and squeezed it tightly. "He's about your age and so full of promise. And he's about your size too, only his hair is fair like Marusia's and his eyes are blue. Marusia was our second-born. We only have two children."

"We had two others," Valentyn corrected her, "but sadly they died. One day they were with us and the next day they were gone. A boy and a girl. They died of consumption. As I built their little coffins, I wept and kissed each board."

Efrosinia snapped at him. "Have you no shame, old man? You even use the death of our children to go on about your damned coffins." Throwing up her arms and swallowing her tears, she stormed out of the room.

A quiet tension settled over the room. Valentyn turned apologetically to his visitors. "As you can see, my Efrosinia is on the excitable side. It's now nine-thirty. She always does this sort of thing around this time. In about an hour she'll settle down and go off to bed. Then at last we'll have some peace and quiet."

Looking at his nephew, he said almost cheerfully, "And what about you, Sergei? I understand you've become a teacher. Not too long ago you were a pupil yourself and now you teach. A noble profession, I admit, but why don't you consider something more stimulating, like engineering, like our Lonia?"

"One day I still might, Uncle, but for now I want to teach. Everything has its time and place."

When the clock struck ten-thirty, Valentyn tiptoed to the door and poked his head into the hallway. "Didn't I tell you? Just as I predicted, Efrosinia is sound asleep. The more she hollers and screams, the better she sleeps. Now, if you'll excuse me, I think I'll retreat into the kitchen and finish reading my newspaper."

When Valentyn closed the door behind him, the young people began to chat. All were in high spirits, and even Marusia laughed from time to time.

In the quiet kitchen, Valentyn was finally able to relax. He settled comfortably in an armchair by the tile stove and put his feet up. Taking a deep breath and striking a match to light his pipe, he reflected on the events of the day. How wonderful it was to see his nephew again and how nice that he should bring along a friend.

True, his wife had been a nuisance, but now at least she was fast asleep. Why, he thought, he could probably dance the *hopak* and howl at the top of his lungs and it wouldn't wake her.

Suddenly he heard a loud thump, then a heavy knock against the wall. Someone was standing on the other side of the door, turning the knob vigorously. The door banged open, and to his horror in flew Efrosinia.

"I see you've found the perfect spot for yourself, like a lazy old cat." She waved her fists, and by the look on her face, it was clear she was really going to let him have it. "There's a vicious frost outside and all you can do is sit by the fire and warm those brittle old bones of yours. That's what you do best, sit and relax, day in and day out, not a care in the world. And that unsightly beard of yours, you still haven't shaved it off! And what about Lonia? Well, I'm here to tell you how it's going to be. After tossing and turning in bed, I've come to a decision. Somehow I'm going to scrape together the money to buy a train ticket and I'm going to send you off to Lvov. You'll bring our son home once and for all. And I'm warning you, don't try and get out of it, because I won't rest until I see Lonia."

Valentyn tensed and sat up. "I can't just pick up and leave, it's not that simple. Going to Lvov is a very serious matter and we must think it over carefully." Then, trying to reason with her, "It's very difficult to come to any sort of agreement with you, Efrosinia. All you ever do is curse and holler, and you even do it in front of company. And as far as Lvov is concerned, do you realize it's over five hundred kilometers away?"

"Five hundred kilometers!" Efrosinia couldn't contain herself. "Don't tell me you're scared of a measly five hundred kilometers!"

The violence of their shouting escalated and the young people in the living room began having trouble hearing each other. With every outburst Kulik found himself more shocked, while Sergei, shrugging and lowering his head in embarrassment, muttered, "After a while one gets used to it." Marusia seemed not to be affected in the least; she began to fuss with her hair.

As the shouting intensified and became obscene, Kulik found it unbearable. He got up, gathered his things and bade a quick farewell. As he was heading for the door, he heard Valentyn's voice shoot across the room, "Louder, old woman, why don't you scream louder. Go on, wake up the entire neighborhood!"

"Why, you old bull!" she shot back. "You moan and groan for half the day and the other half you sleep. What, pray God, did I ever do to deserve a husband like you?"

Then came more outbursts and Efrosinia started to call her husband every foul name she could think of. Dishes went crashing to the floor, there was a heavy thud, then a loud bang.

Marusia had seemed oblivious to what was going on. Now, without uttering a word, she pulled herself up from the sofa, and walked a little unsteadily across the room to the kitchen door. Opening it a crack, she called out quietly, "Mother, you must calm yourself, please. Your valerian drops are in the top dresser drawer by your bed. Shall I go and get them for you?" Then to Kulik and Sergei, "Poor Mother, she has a heart condition. I do worry about her so."

CHAPTER 8

During his two-week stay in Pinsk, Kulik rented a small garret in a house on Zaliznitsa Street. It was cold and drafty, with a low, musty ceiling and faded, water-stained walls. The furniture was in keeping with the room: a cot covered with worn but clean linen, a painted chest of drawers, and, by the door, an old wooden chair. The one window, not much bigger than a small picture frame, overlooked the busy street, the sounds of which filled the room night and day. Heavy armored trucks rolled by one after the other, and every few minutes one could hear the clamoring of *troikas*. People shouted nonstop. It felt as if the room existed in the middle of a train station at some busy crossroads.

Standing by the window, Kulik found himself thinking of Marusia, Sergei's green-eyed cousin. Her beauty was truly startling, and it was difficult for him to imagine how such a lovely creature could be found in a drab provincial town like Pinsk. Her poise and grace could rival that of any woman in Vienna or Berlin.

But she had a cold and capricious personality, and seemed to treat people, especially men, with a certain disrespect. She had a classic Ukrainian face, high cheekbones, deep-set eyes, an upturned nose, but her soul was foreign. She had clearly lost any sense of her own self and all too readily accepted the ways of an aggressive alien culture. She spoke only Russian, frequented only Russian cinemas, and read only Russian books and newspapers. She had slipped so far away from her own people that she showed contempt for them when they were mentioned.

Kulik felt uneasy, and questions gnawed away at him. How could he have allowed himself to become helplessly attracted to a girl so misguided and so aloof? He felt almost as if some spell had been cast over him, one he could not fight.

And he wondered about Pinsk. What had it become? Where did its glory go? It had so readily succumbed to a brutal, insatiable power, bowing and bobbing to its every whim. He thought of Cornelius, Efrosinia, Valentyn, Marusia. . . . They all want Ukraine to become part of the USSR, he thought, and all Ukrainians to become Russians. An unredeemable strain of weakness runs through their veins and they are heading for a cataclysmic end. Don't they see they are being systematically destroyed, so that in the end it will be easier to declare them all part of a single Russian people?

A light snow was falling, dusting the streets where a procession of tanks and trucks were passing directly beneath him, all in the same direction. He thought in anguish, Pinsk, you have become a lost city. It's as if you have landed at the bottom of a raging inferno. The deeper Kulik delved into these thoughts, the thicker the air in the room became. He felt dizzy, stumbled over to the chair by the door and sat down, his head dropped between his shoulders like a limp cabbage. After five or ten minutes, taking several long, deep breaths, he began to feel revitalized. He got up slowly, and put on his overcoat and cap.

He set out for the city center. The roads were full of potholes, and the small wooden houses lining either side showed signs of decay, even abandonment. On occasion, dim light from oil lamps glowed through tiny curtained windows, where faint, barely perceptible movement could be detected.

Further along, coming upon the old Jewish quarter, he passed several inns, all stucco, two stories high and built in the shape of matchboxes. Peasants traveling to Pinsk from surrounding villages to sell their wares in the marketplace often came here to spend the night in exchange for eggs, grains and other products. These inns, always bustling with life and activity, were now silenced. The window panes were knocked out, the walls had become cracked and stained, in some places even showing bare laths, and over the doors, boarded and padlocked, the respective signs had been torn down. The extent of destruction was evident everywhere, and it had a profoundly upsetting effect on Kulik. As he continued down the road, everywhere he looked he saw more of the same.

After crossing several intersections, he finally reached the city center. Turning left, he entered Lahishenska Street, a lovely, broad, tree-lined avenue with shops, restaurants and government buildings. He remembered coming as a young boy to Lahishenska with his father, strolling up and down its walkways and lanes, admiring the fine architecture and enjoying the hustle and bustle of city life. Passersby had greeted each other amicably. Kulik had always loved his visits here; they were a welcome escape from the dreariness of village life.

But now Lahishenska was overrun with army trucks, armored cars and tank units. They roared non-stop in both directions over the rough surface of the reddish cobblestones, their blinding head-lights tearing into the night. Kulik stood back and watched, angry and astonished. The entire city had become transformed. Militia-men in long gray overcoats with satchels under their arms whirled past him, small groups of rank-and-file workers rushed in and out of buildings, chattering urgently, pulling large bundles behind them, and there were shabbily dressed laborers going to work in nearby shipbuilding yards or metal-working factories, carrying lunches wrapped in newspapers. Everywhere, on building walls, on fences, in entranceways, were pictures of Stalin.

Kulik walked over the dirty snow, his head down, overhearing snatches of conversation, all in Russian. No one paid any attention to him; he felt like a stranger among strangers in a strange city, one that had once been dear to him. Almost overnight Pinsk, the beau-tiful ancient port city, had undergone a complete transformation.

After walking to the end of Lahishenska, Kulik turned right onto Market Square, where there was a magnificent stone church in the baroque style, its elaborate tower twisted into curves. The intricate plasterwork on the numerous arches glowed like exquisite, exotic jewels. Kulik did not know the entire history of this church, but he did know that it had housed Polish Jesuits, and before that, prior to the 1914 war, it had been in the hands of the Ukrainian Orthodox Church.

He had come to the square with his father for the first time when he was about six or seven. He remembered being mesmerized by the tower that seemed to go on forever; it radiated vibrantly and majestically against the cloudless blue sky. At the top of its onion-shaped dome, covered in sheets of galvanized iron, a golden cross shimmered in the bright afternoon sun. He had never seen anything so splendid.

And now this magnificent tower was in ruins. A bomb had ripped off the east wall and damaged the others beyond repair. Mounds of dirt and rubble lay on the ground, littered with scraps of paper and empty whisky bottles. What was left of the church was boarded up. In its front yard was a huge sign: "Future Home of the Regional Military Commissariat."

Back in the city center, with his coat collar pulled up to his ears, Kulik wandered about. He found himself in Sovietskaya, this time in front of one of Pinsk's most revered landmarks, St. Barbara's Orthodox Church. Built in the Byzantine style, it had a dome and large arched windows. Incredibly, it stood undamaged. Kulik decided to go inside. He passed through the half-open door, making the sign of the cross.

Though the church was dimly lit, he could see that it was richly decorated with mosaics, frescoes, stone carvings and icons. A priest stood between golden altars and chanted the service in Russian. Swinging his brass censer, he filled the church with the smell of incense. The worshippers, about twenty of them, knelt with their heads bowed and their hands clasped in prayer. A cantor chanted along with the priest, in a heavy, almost unintelligible accent.

Kulik stopped to pray before an icon of the Virgin; but he stepped back, shocked by the expression he saw on its face. The lips were parted in a malignant smile and there was a strange look of cunning about the eyes. The cold and damp penetrated his

bones; he began to shiver. The church suddenly fell silent; a silence
that seemed somehow threatening and sinister. He looked at the
priest. Who was he? Was he really a man of the cloth or was he
an informer? And those women kneeling by the icon—were they
here to pray or were they looking for their next victim? He felt
sick. How could he possibly have thought of praying in a church
that wasn't a church anymore? Everywhere he looked, he saw contempt for God and everything sacred.

He reached the exit doors just as a woman was entering. She
was tall and dark-haired and wore a gray overcoat; a red shawl
was thrown over her head. Her eyes moved with a sort of nervous impatience along the aisles, then paused briefly to study a
group of men gathered beneath an icon on the east wall. When
the priest emerged from the sanctuary, she stared at him and then
turned her head toward the center. She did not make the sign of
the cross, nor did she lower her head in prayer. Who was this tall,
dark, mysterious creature? What was she up to? Kulik watched her
for a few minutes and then quite unexpectedly her eyes met his.
After a second, she turned and started toward the door. Why had
she come to the church? Clearly not to pray. What could she possibly be looking for? The priest's Russian filled the church again,
followed by the chanting of the cantor. Kulik wanted to shout at
them, "Blasphemers! Imposters!" And now this woman, whose
black eyes seemed to radiate a passion—a passion from Hell?

Kulik followed her out of the church, watching as she buttoned
her coat and wrapped the shawl tightly around her head, and began
to walk with a slight swing to her hips. He stayed behind her until
she reached a large, three-story building and disappeared inside.

There was a sign over the building doors: *Oblispolkom: Executive
Committee of a Regional Soviet of People's Deputies. Government person-
nel only.*

CHAPTER 9

Kulik stood before the mirror and shaved. Tomorrow would be the start of a new year: 1940. It was now seven o'clock and the New Year's Eve dance was about to begin on former Leshchinska Street, in the assembly hall of School Number Nineteen. The thought of a celebration raised his spirits; he always looked forward to meeting with friends and making new acquaintances. He remembered his student days in Vilno—especially New Year's Eve! The dancing, the singing, the boozing. Fiddles played, drums boomed, couples flew madly across the floor, and at the stroke of midnight hundreds of colorful paper garlands were hurled up into the air. How he missed those carefree, happy days of his youth!

For a brief moment, as he drew the razor across his face, he tried to forget where he was. He thought about being in another part of the world, perhaps Prague or Bucharest, and in another profession—maybe a newspaper editor or a doctor. But the truth of the matter was, he was a teacher and a village teacher at that, destined to spend his life in an out-of-the-way, backward community. Yet at the same time, he had to admit that he couldn't have found himself in a better place; he knew he should really count himself lucky. In the village he was far from the probing Soviet eye. Emissaries were already swarming into towns and big cities like Minsk, Lvov and Kiev and arresting people, mostly the educated, for resisting, or even questioning, the new authority. History had not yet caught up with the remote areas. In the village he could still buy himself time. He knew if he learned to sit tight and somehow prove himself a faithful servant, he might just be allowed to survive.

As he was dabbing on some cologne, there was a knock on the door and Sergei entered. He looked rather dapper in a black suit with broad lapels, but he seemed to be in a bad mood. "It looks like we're out of luck tonight, my friend," he said. "I invited Marusia to join us but she declined. In fact, she flatly refused. And do you know why? Because she doesn't want to be seen in our company. She considers us *moujiks*, and we embarrass her."

Kulik shrugged. "Well, it seems there's not much we can do about it. Don't worry, we'll manage perfectly well without her."

As the clock struck eight, Kulik threw on his overcoat, wrapped a scarf around his neck, and cap in hand, started for the door. "Marusia's stubborn as a mule," Sergei went on as they descended the stairs. "When I invited her she laughed right in my face. Can you imagine? Then she made up all sorts of excuses: she was too busy, she had to visit a friend, she had to check on her mother. How unfortunate for us. She has a white evening dress and looks absolutely radiant in it—like a flower. Every man at the party would have been green with envy. And she's quite the dancer. Without her, the evening is ruined."

Sergei continued to mope, but not for very long. He was suddenly struck with an idea. "Maybe if we visit her together, we'll be able to persuade her to change her mind. What do you say? Come on, let's give it a try."

This idea didn't appeal to Kulik; he couldn't imagine his presence giving the girl any sort of incentive. It was obvious she disliked him. But, on the other hand, if it would please his friend, it was certainly worth a try, and he had nothing to lose. "All right, but first let's stop off on Leshchinska to see how the party's coming along."

The sky was heavy and dark; large snowflakes were falling. The wind howled and whipped at their backs, making it feel even colder than it was. Tonight the city was a dead place, blacker and more impenetrable than ever.

They entered through the main doors of School Number Nineteen. The hall was thronged with people, mostly in their twenties. Up on the stage a band was playing; it consisted of four men and a girl of about eighteen at the piano. Some couples were dancing, others sat close to the walls, sipping wine and tapping their feet to the music. When the musicians struck up a polka-mazurka, there was a flurry of excitement and almost everyone took to his or her heels and began spinning around at breakneck speeds. They were having great fun.

It was not long before Sergei got into the spirit of things. He said excitedly, "The Pinsk Orchestra is fabulous, isn't it? They play all over town and for every occasion: for weddings, in Zaliznichy Park—practically all the festivals. As you can see, they're extremely versatile."

Kulik watched the scene in silence. Everything had been transformed. Polish signs and the Polish *Lot* of yesterday had been replaced by Russian banners, huge posters of Stalin, and red flags. People were dressed differently, too; Western influences had all but disappeared: the men wore long shirts belted at the waist over trousers and the women's dresses were cheap and shapeless, with high necks and big, flat bows at the back. Everyone was speaking Russian, swept up in the new mood of the day, a thing that Kulik would never have expected.

Couples twirled and spun past him, men whispering into women's ears; women tossing back their heads and laughing.

Sergei poked his friend in the arm and said, "Well, what do you say, shall we go see Marusia now and give it our best shot?"

Kulik agreed. Just as they were about to step outside, a loud, high-pitched voice rang out from somewhere on the dance floor.

"Yoo hoo! Citizens! Over here!"

It was Dounia Avdeevna. She was waving at them, elbowing her way through the crowd. On her fleshy face was a broad smile that revealed a gold molar. "How nice that you could come. It's a wonderful party, isn't it? The band is absolutely lovely." Then she pouted, "But there's no one for me to dance with. There simply aren't enough men to go around. You two aren't thinking of deserting me, are you?"

Kulik tried to think of a way to get away from her. He said, "Excuse me, but I don't think we've been introduced."

"Nonsense, my dear man. I know who you are, you're the headmaster from Hlaby. Why, we're practically neighbors. I teach in Morozovich, a few kilometers away." Then to Sergei, "And you also teach in Hlaby. Your name is Seryoza, if I'm not mistaken."

Sergei forced a smile. "If you don't mind, I don't normally go by my diminutive." Then, not to appear rude, he added, "And what is your name?"

"Dounia Avdeevna Zemlankova." Fanning her flushed face with her handkerchief, she said, "Why, gentleman, you still have your coats on. Don't be shy. The cloak room is over there to the right."

As she spoke, Kulik held his breath, repelled by her penetrating scent of garlic. He said quickly, "Thank you, but we only popped in for a minute. We still have something to tend to in the city."

Dounia's smile faded. "Well, all right, but hurry back. As you can see, my feet are itching to dance. And, of course, I want to put my new dress to good use." Looking down at her cotton gown, she took the opportunity to flatter herself. "You know, this dress was made especially for me by my seamstress, Marfa Fedorovna. Marfa said to me, 'Dounia, you are a full-figured girl. A classic cut with a wide crinoline would do your body justice. It will not only accentuate your curves but tone down your plump thighs.' Marfa Fedorovna even gave me some practical advice. She said, 'And if you ever find yourself in hard times, you'll be all the richer because out of a gown like this, you'll be able to cut at least three dresses out of it!'"

When the men finally managed to get away, she called after them, "I'll have you know I'm a superb dancer—the tango, the foxtrot, the shimmy. Whatever step works with our new Soviet music, I'm ready for it. Hurry back! I'll be waiting!"

Outside, a little ice fog hung over the street and a slight wind was blowing in from the east. Walking twenty or thirty paces,

Kulik turned to Sergei. "We can't go to Marusia's empty-handed. We really ought to stop off somewhere and buy a gift of some kind—maybe some flowers."

"My very thought exactly!"

They hurried along and turned down a narrow cobblestone alley where they knew the nearest flower stand stood just off Market Square. But when they got there, they found the flower stand gone. They walked to another, but it too had disappeared. They decided to search for a shop of some sort, to buy perhaps a small trinket or some sweets. But to their dismay everything was boarded up.

They went on without a word. Only the snapping of branches of the few bare trees broke the silence. The clouds had drifted to the west and there was a blue-white glimmer from the new-fallen snow. Amid a myriad of stars, the moon threw long black shadows over the street. Pinsk was a ghost town tonight.

At the corner of Luninetska Street, they stopped before a gloomy little building with low, smudged windows. Over the sagging oak door was a sign: People's Tavern. They went inside and bought a bottle of vodka.

"We're going to have to keep this from my aunt." Sergei stuffed the bottle into his inside coat pocket. "If she catches wind of it, all hell will break loose."

At the Bohdanovich house, as before, they entered through the side door leading into the kitchen. The house was still; there appeared to be no one home. When they crossed the threshold they were almost startled to find Valentyn stretched out on a low divan, with his hands beneath his head, staring up at the ceiling. Logs crackled in the stove and the faint reflection of the flames flickered on his face. Puffing on his pipe, he couldn't have looked more contented, as if he didn't have a care in the world.

"Happy New Year, Uncle!" Sergei called out to him.

Taken by surprise, Valentyn rolled over onto his side. "Oh! Who's that? Oh! Welcome, welcome! What a pleasant surprise! Come in, you couldn't have found a better time. Happy New Year!

As you can see the house is quiet for a change. My old lady went out on an errand with Marusia. They said they'd come back by ten o'clock. Please, have a seat." Seeing the bottle of vodka, his eyes lit up and he winked. "I see you haven't forgotten your old uncle. To 1940! Let's drink like true bachelors!"

Hobbling to the buffet cabinet, Valentyn opened a bottom drawer and brought out a corkscrew and three glasses. He went to the pantry and returned with half a kilo of backfat, cucumbers, and a loaf of rye bread. Setting the food on the table, he filled up the glasses and made a toast: "To 1940! To health and fortune! To the future!" Then, smacking his lips and scrunching up his face, "One thing about our new liberators, they sure know how to make a good vodka, one that puts a hole right through the stomach."

When they started on their second round, Valentyn somewhat tipsy, propped himself on his elbow, and said, "My old lady should be back any minute now. She's going to make a scene, I just know it. Brace yourselves for the worst, gentlemen. If only she would take a swig herself now and then—but the matter is hopeless, she won't touch the stuff."

The clock over the cabinet ticked steadily away. It was now nine forty-five. Valentyn could feel the vodka going to his head. He turned curiously to Kulik. "Ivan, uh, didn't you say that's what your name was? My Marusia was rather impressed by you the other night. She'd never met a *moujik* who was so knowledgeable and able to express himself with such ease and precision. Why, it might as well have been Russian you were speaking, she said after you left. Yes, you made quite an impression on her. And for Marusia to say something like that is very exceptional, she's quite critical, she has a mind of her own."

He got up and tottering across the floor, almost falling over, he opened the door a crack and peeked outside. He was looking for his wife. Since she was nowhere in sight, he turned his attention back to Kulik. Giving him a wink, he said, "Who knows, young man, maybe you'll find yourself my son-in-law one of these days. You're a teacher you say, hmm . . . not bad, things could be worse."

No sooner had he spoken these words, when he shook his head, as if he were having second thoughts. "No, no. Pardon my saying so, but it would never work out. My Marusia could never stand to live with a *moujik*. She couldn't bear it. Hmm . . . but then on the other hand . . . maybe if you started being more receptive to Russian ways, maybe then she'd come around."

He fell silent for several minutes, tugging at his beard. Then he frowned, as a new thought occurred to him. "Good God! What if she were to go off and marry one of our new liberators!" He poured himself another drink, and swallowed it in one gulp. In a matter of minutes he forgot everything and went off in another direction, speaking loudly and with great insight.

"To live with women is a very difficult thing. You two are young, you don't know what awaits you. Marusia is still more or less manageable, but it's only a matter of time before she becomes like her mother. Efrosinia nags me from morning till night. First it's my beard and why don't I shave it off, then it's I sleep too long. Lately, as you've already heard, it's why don't I fix the sofa? I would just like to take an axe to it and smash it to pieces. The springs are so old and rusted there's nothing left to fix. My Efrosinia just can't seem to understand that. And now it's Lonia, and to make matters worse, Marusia has jumped in to help her. 'Go to Lvov,' they tell me. 'Go and bring Lonia home.' I would be happy to go, but it's not that simple. If I go to the train station and say, 'Please, I'd like to buy a ticket to Lvov,' the ticketmaster will tell me, 'One way is one hundred rubles, return is two hundred.' I realize it's not a phenomenal sum, but how am I supposed to cough it up? Money doesn't grow on trees."

Burying his head in his hands, he fell silent for the longest time. A new overwhelming sensation overcame him, one that he could no longer control. His voice quavered and broke. "Lonia, Lonia, my dear son, what I wouldn't do for you, if only I could. My son—my pride and joy, an engineering student, the top of his class. Tall, handsome, intelligent and—consumptive. That's the tragedy that has befallen my family—my father, my mother, two brothers, one sister. I managed to survive somehow and you see how it goes—it's been passed down to my children. It's a blessing Marusia is healthy."

Kulik felt genuine sympathy for Valentyn, whose face reflected such pain and suffering. He wanted to give him some hope and solace. Impulsively, he offered, "What if Sergei and I were to lend you the money? You could buy yourself a ticket and go to Lvov as soon as tomorrow."

Sergei jumped in. "What a good idea! I've got a hundred rubles in my pocket. I can give it to you right here and now."

"And I've got a hundred and fifty." Kulik reached for his pocketbook. "I've got another fifty in my room."

"Uncle, that'll be enough for Lonia to return home with you. And don't worry about repaying us, it can wait."

Valentyn accepted the money gratefully and after counting it twice, stuffed it in his jacket pocket, and said, "It might be a while before I can pay you back. I have to earn it first. And my hands aren't what they used to be. But don't worry, I was never in debt to anyone before, at least not for very long."

Kulik raised his glass, "To Lonia!"

"To Lonia! To our future engineer!" added Sergei.

The three men clinked glasses and the more they drank the merrier they became. Valentyn kissed the side of his glass and filled it up again. "It's now ten o'clock and, oh, I do think the drink has gone completely to my head. You two are young, you have better resistance. Come on, drink up!"

"No, thank you. I've had enough," Kulik said, in good humor. "Actually, we still plan to do some dancing before the night is over."

"Ah, but of course, I should have realized." Valentyn sank back into his seat. "How stupid of me. You didn't come to call on me. No, you came here to call on Marusia. What would two red-blooded young men want with an old man like me anyway, and on New Year's Eve? I certainly have no objection to Marusia going to the dance with the two of you." He leaned toward Kulik. "Pity you're so stubborn. You and Marusia would make quite the pair."

He refilled his glass, the drink loosening his tongue. "When I was young I loved to dance. The *quadrille* and the *venherochka* were all the rage back then. The music would play and the floor would go wild. If I may say so myself, I was quite the dancer. You'd have to lift your feet high off the ground and spin your partner in mid-air. It was such great fun. When I lived in the village I knew all the drinking songs. Sometimes the neighbors would get together and dance while I sang: 'So very high in the sky the eagles fly . . .'"

As Valentyn began on the second verse, Kulik and Sergei, pouring more drinks, joined in. The three of them sat on the sofa, filling the room with laughter and song. It was precisely at this moment that Efrosinia walked in.

"What on earth is going on here?" She could hardly believe her eyes. "You're drunk, all of you! Marusia, quick, pass me that broom over there." Taking hold of the handle, she rushed at the men.

"Auntie," Sergei said, "calm yourself, please. It's New Year's Eve, after all."

She glared at him. "Are you the one who brought liquor into my house?"

"Mother!" Marusia cried. "Don't start up. Not now."

Valentyn stumbled to his feet. He put his hand in his pocket, pulled out the money and waved it in front of his wife's nose.

"Efrosinia," he began, "I have very good news. The boys and I were celebrating—not the New Year, but the return of our Lonia. Yes, it's true. After tomorrow I'm leaving for Lvov. Here's the money for the ticket. The boys lent it to me. Now everything will turn out fine. I'll bring Lonia back and you'll be able to sleep nights again."

Efrosinia froze, speechless. Could it really be true that at last she would see her son again? Lonia would be home and in just a few days! Holding her shaking hands against her breast, she fell to her knees and wept and laughed at the same time.

Marusia looked closely at Kulik. "Are you drunk? You didn't strike me as the drinking type. Is it true, did you lend Father the money?"

"Yes, Marusia, with Sergei."

"That was very generous of you." She eyed her cousin with suspicion "Seryoza, why did you two come here tonight? Was it you who suggested this visit?"

"Yes, it was. Marusia, it's New Year's Eve, after all. In fact, it's almost eleven. Why don't you come with us to the dance? We'll have a grand time."

Valentyn went up to his daughter and whispered encouragingly in her ear. "Don't be so difficult, dear. Go ahead and have yourself some fun. Ivan Demianovich here seems like a decent fellow, a teacher, a historian, not to mention—good marriage material."

"Father!" Then to Kulik, apologetically, "Please don't pay any attention to him. He's had too much to drink. His mind always becomes jumbled when he's . . ." Then she caught herself. "Wait a minute, why am I apologizing to you? You're the one who got him drunk in the first place!"

"I'm not drunk, my little pigeon," her father called out. "I'm just happy. Go and welcome in the New Year. Dance the night away."

Rudely, without a further word, the girl rushed across the kitchen and disappeared into the living room. The two friends looked at each other, disappointed. Marusia had left them; they were convinced that she had retired for the night. But to their surprise, after barely fifteen minutes, she reappeared, her hair piled high, wearing a pearl-white evening dress pinched at the waist and low-heeled pumps. The young men were delighted. How beautiful she looked! Kulik had never seen anyone like her. How classic her features were and how soft and silky her complexion. Her beautiful body radiated warmth and tenderness and she looked lovelier than anyone could ever imagine. Kulik could not take his eyes off her. He lost his head completely.

CHAPTER 10

Everywhere one looked, couples were rapidly twirling each other about. The temperature was high and the air thick with cigarette smoke and the smell of cheap perfume. When the trumpets started to blare, the noise became ten times louder and the floor fell into a frenzy.

Kulik was beginning to get into the spirit of things and found himself tapping his foot to the beat of the music. Somewhere deep in the crowd he spotted Marusia with Sergei, dancing to a Tchaikovsky waltz. She was certainly the most striking girl there. He regretted having insisted that Sergei have the first dance with her and he waited impatiently for it to end. He tried to cheer himself up by reminding himself that he never really cared much for Tchaikovsky anyway, especially when the passages became melancholy and alternated with folk music. But Tchaikovsky aside, Kulik would have given anything to be on that floor with Marusia.

There was no slowing down. The dance floor was even more packed than before. Crowds of men and women thronged the doorway, smoking and drinking cold spiked punch, talking and laughing. Kulik was strangely attracted by the hubbub; he even forgot for a moment where he was. He felt a great desire to hear what people were saying, perhaps even to join in a conversation or two, but every time he caught a word, another drowned it out almost instantly. He moved on. A man came spinning his way, rather short, balding, his arms around a woman half a head taller than he. Kulik recognized him at once: it was Yeliseyenko, Chief of Education.

When the band began a slower tune, a voice called out happily from behind Kulik. It was Marusia. "Ivan Demianovich! We were looking all over for you." Then curiously, "Who are you looking at over there?"

Kulik shrugged, "Oh, just Yeliseyenko, the Chief of Education." Taking her hands in his, he asked, "May I have the next dance?"

On the stage, the musicians were thundering out "Rebecca," a popular love song about a Polish Jew in love with a beautiful woman. Although the song was very well received, it seemed out of place and not in keeping with the political mood of the day. It was just a matter of time before it, along with countless other songs, would be banned by the government, deemed petit bourgeois. But tonight no one seemed to care about that.

The drummer, a long-legged youth not much over twenty, whacked at his drums repeatedly, speeding up the tempo, slowing it down, then speeding it up even faster than before. When the saxophones suddenly erupted, the dancers, drunk and dizzy, became deafened by the musical explosion.

In the middle of all of this were Kulik and Marusia. Her eyes were shining; she looked radiant. At every step they took together, Kulik felt thrilled at how slight her form was and how delicate her features. When he took her hand in his and pressed it gently, she made no objection. He felt the warmth of her body next to his, and he knew that he had fallen in love with her. Pulling her toward him, he kissed her softly on her pale cheek. But to his dismay, she gasped and shrieked. Pushing him away, she said, "What was that for? Isn't it enough that I dance with you?"

Kulik's heart leaped. He couldn't believe her words. How mean-spirited, how utterly cruel she was. Why was he allowing this flighty, hypocritical small-town girl to toy with his emotions like this, to trample all over him? It pained him that she should take offence at a perfectly sincere and spontaneous gesture on his part. He felt mortified, ripped into a million pieces.

They danced on in awkward silence. Kulik hesitated to look at her. He thought sadly, "How tragic. So beautiful, so delicate, like a flower of the marsh, and yet so distant, so foreign." A chill passed through him; she suddenly felt cold and lifeless, like a porcelain doll.

When the music finally stopped, as he was walking with Marusia across the floor, Kulik was more than relieved to come across Sergei, who was leaning against the wall with a drink of spiked cranberry lemonade. They had just joined him, when, from the doorway, a voice shot out in a squeaky falsetto. It belonged to a slight man with epicene features. "Marusia Valentynovna! Over here!"

"Why, if it isn't Nikolai Nikitich!" Marusia waved at him excitedly. "How good it is to see you!" Then to her companions, and taking Nikolai by the hand, "May I introduce Nikolai Nikitich, the exceptional and renowned Pinsk poet. I'm sure you've heard of him."

Nikolai Nikitich looked around briefly and shook his head. "No, no, *nyet nyet*, Marusia Valentynovna. Haven't you heard? I've changed my name to Nikolai Kopitkin." Then nudging her in the arm almost playfully and winking, "A little Russian flavor's never been known to hurt a man, if you know what I mean."

He ignored Kulik and Sergei, addressing Marusia, "Haven't I seen these two fellows someplace before? Oh, yes, now I remember. I saw them at the teachers' conference." Pursing his lips, he looked Kulik over. "Why, if it isn't Ivan Kulik. Aren't you the one who gave that ghastly speech in Ukrainian? I must say, you certainly know how to stir things up. You had the participants virtually at each other's throats. This is what I think of you and your Ukrainian schools. Piffle!" Then back to Marusia again, "Certainly you didn't come here with these two fellows?"

Before Marusia had a chance to respond, Kulik, feeling tremendously insulted, spoke up, intending to put the poet in his place. "Nikolai Nikitich, have you ever gone to the zoo?"

Nikolai had not expected such a peculiar question. He crinkled his nose and cleared his throat. "Er, unfortunately, no."

"Well, in Prague I saw a beautiful chimpanzee whose imitation of humans was remarkable. The Czechs named him Potapka, which means imitator. If I might add, there's a striking resemblance."

No one had ever dared talk to Nikolai like that. He shot back haughtily, "In Prague, you say? I didn't think *moujiks* ventured that far."

"Oh, stop!" Marusia could barely contain herself. Looking profoundly embarrassed, she took Nikolai's arm, and hurriedly changed the subject. "Tell me, Nikolai, are you still writing?"

"Yes, naturally! How can I not write! Poetry is my muse, my elixir."

Marusia went on. "You have such a wonderful style. Do you remember last summer when you read to me from one of your books?"

"Yes, indeed, from *The Forgotten Book Of Verse*, if I'm not mistaken. I also read to you some of my reviews, which, if I may say so myself, were extremely favorable."

"Allow me to recite to you from my most recent collection. As you'll notice, my poems are no longer frivolous. They are now fearless and full of hope, and in them I give answers and an insight into what is going on around us:

> Hunger, cold and want
> Months, even years of struggle
> Listen for the Revolution . . ."

As he began the next line, Sergei cut him off. "Hey, Nikolai, why don't you try something like this:

> Hunger, cold and want
> I plop on my bed
> And snore and snore and snore some more . . ."

"Seryoza!" Marusia stamped her foot. "How can you be so rude?" Then apologetically to Nikolai, "Forgive Seryoza. As you can see he's had too much to drink."

At the sound of the word *Seryoza*, Nikolai froze on the spot and his eyes widened. He was shocked that Marusia had addressed Sergei in the diminutive, *Seryoza*, suggesting to him the two were more than the casual acquaintants he had assumed them to be. It was plain and simple: Marusia Valentynovna was associating with *moujiks!* "Excuse me, Marusia Valentynovna," he said quickly, hoping that no one had noticed that he was with these people, "I must be off. Give my regards to your father and mother. And how's Lonia? Is he still in Lvov? Well, goodbye."

The band began the rhumba. Kulik found himself mouthing the lyrics in Polish. Again he was alone. Sergei had gone off somewhere with Marusia. Kulik focused on trying to find a partner. He looked along the wall, around the podium, by the entranceway, but all the women seemed to be taken. His eyes strayed across the floor. Yeliseyenko caught his attention again. He was still dancing with the same woman. Kulik could now see her more clearly. She was very pretty, with big black eyes and a long, slender neck. There was something unusual about her and curiously familiar. Where had he seen her before? He watched her move across the floor. She was an excellent dancer, light on her feet, whirling and twirling gracefully, in a soft velvet dress that clung to her shapely body. It was almost as if she was oblivious to her partner and was dancing alone.

When finally the music stopped, Kulik, almost involuntarily, found himself drifting toward her. Who was this girl? As he moved closer, Yeliseyenko noticed him, and frowned. "You! I remember you from the conference. What do you want? Do you intend to ask this young lady to dance?"

Kulik hesitated a moment, then, ignoring Yeliseyenko, said to the girl, "Would you do me the honor?"

She smiled, nodded to Yeliseyenko, gave Kulik her arm and walked with him to the middle of the floor. She was as tall as Kulik, and when they danced, their eyes met. Where had he seen this unusual, lovely creature before, with eyes as black as the night? Suddenly he was seized by a wave of excitement. It was she, he realized, the girl from St. Barbara's Church! She drew back, startled. "Why are you staring at me like that?"

"Well, because . . . because, well, it's all quite odd. You're not from around here, are you?"

"What if I'm not?"

"You're not a teacher either."

"No." She looked steadily at him. "Do you always interrogate your dancing partners like this?"

"I'm terribly sorry. It was impolite of me. What's your name?"

"Zena. And yours?"

Kulik was surprised she did not give her patronymic, and even more surprised that she spoke in Ukrainian. "My name is Ivan, Ivan Kulik . . . You look familiar to me. I've seen you someplace before."

She was amused. "Is that what you say to all the girls?"

A Strauss waltz began. The floor filled with dancers, young and full of energy. Everyone was intoxicated, carried away by the significance of the night. They were not only celebrating the coming of the New Year, but the coming of a new era. History was in the making.

When at last the music slowed, Zena became surprisingly chatty, even affable, going on about the band, the music, the dancers, but when she mentioned the colorful decorations and the pictures of Stalin on the walls, their eyes locked. It seemed to Kulik that something odd had passed between them, as if they both harbored the same dark secret. He longed to ask questions, to speak, to exchange confidences, but did not dare. She looked away from him and seemed to become distant. Why, Kulik asked himself, had this young woman gone into the offices of the *Oblispolkom*? Could she possibly be a Soviet spy or an agent of some sort? He said casually, "On our way here we passed the *Oblispolkom*. Surely you know where that is? It used to be Father Mendiuk's house. One day party officials came and booted him out into the streets. Now he's no more than a beggar."

Zena broke free of his embrace and said quickly, "It was very nice to meet you, Ivan Kulik. Thank you for the dance. I'd better be off and find Yeliseyenko before he thinks I've abandoned him. Good-bye."

Before Kulik could say another word, she was gone. Why, he asked himself, had he gone and opened his big mouth? Why had he tried to corner her and in such an obvious way? Now he was left alone. He decided to return to the bar for another drink. As he was about to place his order, Dounia Avdeevna emerged from the crowd.

"Yoo hoo! Comrade Ivan!" she called. "So, we meet again . . . You're all alone? My, my! . . . First a blonde, then a brunette. Quite the Casanova. But how sad, now you're all alone, you poor dear thing." She lowered her voice. "May I give you a word of advice? Never trust beautiful women. You're better off looking for one with stamina and character, not unlike myself."

Kulik smiled. "What's become of your sailor?"

"Sailors! They're a reckless bunch. I'm interested now in the more stable professions like engineering, medicine, teaching . . ." She brushed up against him, "Yes, teachers in particular are very dependable."

Kulik stumbled back against the wall. He wanted to get out of there. Dounia Avdeevna, offended, threw herself back into the crowd.

Sergei came by, looking irritated. "Marusia just up and left. I don't know what came over her, but something obviously set her off. I offered to walk her home, but she wouldn't have it. She's so unpredictable and headstrong. What'll we do now?"

They were in no mood to participate in the festivities. Outside, the snow was now coming down heavily, so heavily that almost everything became invisible to them—the lamp posts, the buildings, the parked trucks. It was colder than ever. Kulik pulled his cap down over his ears and Sergei fumbled in his pockets for his gloves. They could hear the distant sound of cheers and applause. "Five, four, three, two, one! Happy New Year!"

They walked on, welcoming the New Year in silence. Nineteen-forty had begun.

CHAPTER II

For almost an entire week, chaos reigned in the Bohdanovich household. It began when Efrosinia snatched the money given by Kulik and Sergei from her husband's pocket and placed it under lock and key in the pantry. She had already decided what she was going to do with it: she was not only going to purchase the train ticket for him, but she was even going to take him to the station and place him in his seat.

All the while Valentyn was at a complete loss. He loved his son dearly and wanted to see him come home as much as his wife did, but he felt the demands being made upon him were far too great. True, initially he had agreed to go to Lvov, but was it really such a good idea? After all, he was old, nearing seventy, and he had no business traveling on trains, especially in these troubled times. He could have a heart attack or get mugged or something worse. And what about his arthritis? He racked his brain to try and find a way out, but there didn't appear to be one. And if he were to simply refuse to go, Efrosinia would go after him with her wooden spoon, something she did all too often. As much as he hated to admit it, everything was working against him.

In the midst of all this confusion, Marusia fell ill. When she returned from the New Year's Eve dance slightly after midnight, she collapsed on her bed with a throbbing headache. At dawn she woke with a temperature and by mid-afternoon it was higher. Efrosinia and Valentyn dropped all preparations for the trip to Lvov and turned their attention to their daughter. Although Valentyn was deeply worried about her, he was privately relieved that he could postpone his trip to Lvov, at least until she recovered.

Early one evening Efrosinia appeared at her daughter's bedside with a towel draped over her arm, holding a basin filled with cold water. The room was quiet; strips of light seeping in through the slats in the closed shutters cast faint shadows on the wall. A cold draft from beneath the floorboards chilled the air. With her eyes half open, her hair strewn over her pillow, Marusia lay buried under her eiderdown, unaware of her mother's presence. Stretching her arms languidly over her head, she took a deep breath, sighed, and rolled over onto her side.

Efrosinia laid a compress on her daughter's forehead and looked reprovingly at her. "Well, Marusia, you went to the dance and now look what's happened to you. You're white as a ghost." Then, angrily, "They took you there but they couldn't bother to bring you back. *Moujiks!* Just let them try and set foot in my house again!"

"Mother, keep your voice down, please." The girl massaged her temples with the tips of her fingers to alleviate the pain in her head.

"Don't you 'mother' me. Of course I'm your mother, I'm not your stepmother. If those two come anywhere near this house again, I'll chase them off like a pair of dogs. And that one, what's his name, Kulik? To think he even managed to win the old man over!"

At that moment Valentyn came into the room. Stroking his beard, he whispered in his wife's ear, "Let her rest. How do you expect her to recover if you never leave her alone?" He took the towel and basin from her hands, and setting them on the night table, pulled her out of the room.

Downstairs, in the hallway, he fidgeted, feeling compelled to approach her about something. Efrosinia watched him intently, guessing his intention. And just as she had expected, at last he came out with it.

"Efrosinia, let's be sensible about all this. Somehow it just doesn't seem right. It's about my trip to Lvov. How am I supposed to travel back home with Lonia on a crowded train? He might need medical attention. He'll be extremely uncomfortable and his condition might even get worse. And what if there are no seats available? Furthermore, the doctors might even refuse to discharge him from the hospital."

Folding her arms over her chest, Efrosinia narrowed her eyes and tapped her foot. She allowed him to go on.

"Uh, as I was saying, what I'm suggesting is that Lonia get better first, and then let him come home when he's fit to travel. Yes, that would make the most sense. I can certainly go tomorrow, but that might not be the best idea, uh, for Lonia, that is. And besides, Lonia is almost an engineer, it's just a matter of months before he gets his diploma . . ."

At that point, Efrosinia lost her patience and flew at him. "I see where you're going with this, old man. Talking in circles, as always. You have the money to buy your ticket and still you drag your feet! Marusia develops a slight fever and out of nowhere you feel obligated to nurse her back to health." Clutching his arm, she became more exasperated. "I'm going to get you on that train if it's the last thing I do. And shave off that ridiculous beard of yours and make yourself presentable! You can't be looking like that in Lvov!"

It was not long before a full-blown fight erupted. The shouting and screaming became so heated that the house seemed to shake. Marusia, unable to endure it any longer, got out of bed, stumbled to the top of the staircase and shouted for her mother. Efrosinia hurried out of the room to tend to her daughter.

Left alone, Valentyn went into the kitchen. He was more than grateful for this moment of respite. Spreading himself out on the divan, he put his feet up and fell into a doze. Barely ten minutes had passed when he was awakened by a strange grumbling noise. It was rather loud and raspy and was coming from somewhere in his body, beneath his chest. Before long he realized it was his stomach. It occurred to him that he had not eaten anything all day. Efrosinia had not only not prepared lunch for him but she hadn't made supper either, and now it appeared he was expected to go to bed without any food. Efrosinia had even neglected to light the stove, something she did dutifully every evening.

Valentyn grew more and more gloomy. The New Year, without question, was getting off to a bad start. He realized things were going badly for him. Perhaps he should give in to her demands, just get on that train and go to Lvov—at least then he would be left in peace. He pondered a moment. No, her expectations were unreasonable; she was simply unable to grasp the complexity of the situation. The more he thought about it, the more he felt a wrong was being done him. And he knew at that moment that he had to build himself up and stand up to her. But she wouldn't put up with it and in the end he would lose. No matter how he looked at it there was only one road for him to take, and that was the road to Lvov. Getting up, limping out into the hallway, he resolved to get it over with, to finally give in to her. He called out hoarsely, "Have it your way, old woman. Give me the money and first thing tomorrow I'll go to the station and buy myself a ticket."

At the sound of these words, Efrosinia flew down the stairs. "Did I hear you correctly? Did you say you want the money?"

"How else do you expect me to buy the ticket?"

Efrosinia shook her head. "No, no, no. I won't give you the money, not in a million years. Do you think for one minute I trust you? No! I'll go with you tomorrow and I'll buy the ticket for you. The train leaves at eleven in the morning. I've already made up three parcels for you to take with you. Now go get some sleep. You've got a long day ahead of you tomorrow."

Valentyn's stomach growled and he felt weak in the knees and exhausted. "You expect me to go to bed on an empty stomach? Oh, Efrosinia, your heart is made of stone. When I'm dead and buried, think of how you treated me."

"When you're dead and buried what difference will it make to you?"

It was not long before they started up again. Insults flew back and forth, doors banged, there were threats and shouts.

Marusia listened anxiously to her parents. But this time she was not so much disturbed by their arguing as she was by the manner in which they chose to do it. She couldn't help but hear what was being said, and she cringed at every word. It was the worst possible scene she could have imagined: they were going at each other in Ukrainian! Why couldn't they do it in Russian? And why did they have to use such dreadful Ukrainian phrases as "May you get cholera and die!" or "You old scarecrow in a pea field!" Pulling the covers over her head, she felt overwhelmingly distressed and embarrassed. She envied her friends whose parents were able to maintain well-balanced arguments in Russian without using even the slightest Ukrainian word. Why couldn't her parents do the same? She vowed to herself that when she married, all her arguments with her husband would be in Russian and Russian only.

From downstairs there came more expletives, more wailing, knocking, then a heavy thud, as if something went smashing against the wall. When at last the front door slammed, Marusia knew it was her father storming out of the house.

Silence reigned. She closed her eyes, and tried to nod off. Bits and pieces of thoughts floated across her mind; she began to reflect on the New Year's Eve dance. Why had she run off so suddenly? And who was that tall dark-haired girl dancing with Kulik? Where did she come from? Could she, Marusia, possibly be jealous of her? No! No! Marusia shuddered. "He's just a *moujik*. How could I have feelings for a *moujik*? True, he's managed to obtain an education and manners of sorts, but that language of his. Good Lord!"

Trying to redirect her thoughts, taking a sip of water from a glass her mother had put on her night table, she heard a vigorous knock on her door. To her surprise Kulik appeared on the threshold.

"What on earth are you doing here?"

"Good evening, Marusia. I've only come for a minute. You're quite pale, if I may say so."

"I'm sick, can't you see?" She could not help coughing. She seemed annoyed that he was there. "Why else would I be lying here? Count yourself lucky Mother's asleep. What do you want?"

"Sergei told me you weren't well and I thought I would visit you. I hope you're feeling better." He handed her a small box of chocolates.

She flushed and drew several long, deep breaths. Then she became even more insulting. "I don't need any consolations from you. And talk to me properly, not like a *moujik*. I can't bear to listen to you."

Kulik. pretended not to notice. He continued amiably, "What happened to you? Did you catch cold? The weather—"

She cut him off. "Did you come here to make idle chit-chat? Aren't you supposed to be attending some silly teachers' conference somewhere?"

Kulik stepped back, deeply affronted. He hadn't expected this. Forcing a smile, he resolved to leave before he lashed back at her, saying something he might regret. After he bade a quick farewell and turned toward the door, he was startled to find Efrosinia blocking his way. How did the old woman manage to creep in so quietly, like a cat? And how long had she been standing there listening?

"So, it's you!" She came at him almost instantly, her eyes fixed on him. "I see you chose to pay us another visit. Do you see what that dance of yours did to my daughter! She's been fighting a fever all week. As if I didn't have enough problems already."

"Mother," the girl groaned, "please, I have a headache."

Glancing briefly at her daughter, turning back to Kulik, Efrosinia's face worked with anger. "Why did you come back to this house? Do you have some kind of designs on my daughter? Some suitor you'd make! Hah! Letting a girl go home alone in the dead of night! That's a *moujik* for you!" Then a warning. "If I were you I'd leave while I still had the chance."

"Mother!" Marusia repeated, sitting up. "Please, just this once." Patting the side of her bed, she said, "Mother, come and sit down here beside me. Let's talk about Lonia instead."

"Lonia? What about Lonia?"

"Let's think about this rationally. It's about Father. He's not going to go to Lvov, and you know it. I've been thinking it over and maybe it's not such a good idea after all. It's such a long trip, and at his age. The train ride alone is bad enough, not to mention all the riffraff on board, especially these days."

Efrosinia listened with strained attention. She was finding herself inclined to agree, at least to a certain extent. Maybe it was too much to expect of him. The train ride was rather long and the cars, it's true, were now almost always filled with all sorts of bandits and thieves. Maybe it was best for him to just stay home. But these thoughts lasted only a moment. Stamping her foot, she exclaimed adamantly, "No! The old man is going! True, it may be a rough road, but in the end I don't think it will do him any serious damage. He's set to go tomorrow morning and that's that!"

"Mother!" Marusia raised her voice. "If Father does go, the situation will only get worse. He's already so weak and frail he can barely make his way around the house. How do you expect him to make it halfway across the country?"

Marusia suddenly fell into violent, hysterical weeping. Her voice trembling, she fixed her eyes in desperation on Kulik. "Ivan, you've got to help us, please. Do something! How can we get Lonia home? Oh, my poor, dear brother!"

Efrosinia too burst into tears. Grabbing Kulik's arm, she cried, "Maybe you'll go for my son?"

Kulik couldn't believe what he had just heard. This could only lead to some unimaginable bad end for him.

"Please, help my son!" Efrosinia squeezed his arm harder. "Bring Lonia home to me. I know you'll do it, in my heart I just know it. And if you won't do it for me, then do it for Marusia. I'll pray for you. Oh, thank you, son, thank you." She took hold of his hands and kissed them repeatedly.

Kulik looked at the two women. They were so pale and worn and wore such looks of infinite suffering, that his heart broke and he was afraid for them, but even more afraid for himself. If only he could get away from there and fast, before he agreed to do something he might regret. But suddenly he blurted out, "All right, I'll do it. I'll go tomorrow. I'll do it not for your daughter but for you, Efrosinia. I understand the tremendous grief you must feel."

He said goodnight and quickly left the house. A gust of cold wind swept in from the north and numbed his face. He could feel a deathly chill pass over his body. He walked in a sort of daze, unaware that his coat was unbuttoned and that he had left his hat and gloves in the Bohdanovich house.

It was only when he came to the first crossroads that he fully grasped the magnitude of the danger in which he had put himself. A wave of terror gripped his heart. Why had he agreed to go to Lvov? Was he out of his mind? Did he have some sort of death wish? Clearly he had not been in control of his faculties tonight. If he were to go, his absence from the conference would certainly spark suspicion. The NKVD would be notified immediately and get on his trail. His lodgings would be ransacked, his past would be dug up, his family sought out and investigated. It would be just a matter of time before he was snatched up in the dark of night and thrown into some deep, dark hole.

He became infuriated with himself for playing a kind of Russian roulette with his life. What were the Bohdanoviches to him anyway? Why, he had just met them a few days ago. He wanted to block out everything that had just happened, to go back on his word, but he had made a conscious decision and he had to bear the consequences. Rain or shine, tomorrow morning he would be on that train to Lvov. He tried to think how to handle this, to think of a plan to deal with the authorities. He could file for a leave of absence with the People's Commissariat of Education and say his father was ill or maybe that a close relative had passed away. That sounded reasonable enough. For a moment he felt confident that it would work, but his confidence did not last long. What if the authorities refused to issue him a pass? Or worse yet, what if they agreed to issue him a pass, then went on to verify his story? What if they found out what he was really doing? Why had he lied? What was he trying to hide? Was Lonia a nationalist? Were the Bohdanoviches involved in some kind of subversive activity? A simple request could lead to God knew what.

Home at last, he made his way up the stairs to his garret. Without lighting a lamp, he changed into his pajamas and sank into an armchair by the window. For the longest time he sat lost in thought, staring into the dark. A special form of misery began to take hold of him: suddenly he saw Marusia's pale face with her eyes red with weeping. She looked frightened, like a little girl, a child even, and she was shaking. Could she possibly appreciate and understand the danger he was putting himself in? That he was suffering for her benefit? Then at least his sacrifice would not be for nothing. But this feeling lasted only a moment. Was it possible she could be thinking of him or could she think only of her brother? Did she even feel grateful to him? Would she think of him when he was gone? He stumbled to bed, and wrapping himself in his blankets, shivering, tried to blot out everything that had happened. He tossed and turned all night.

Early the next morning, as he had promised, Kulik appeared at the Bohdanovich house. He had barely stepped over the threshold when he was met by the entire family, who, it turned out, had been sitting in the living room waiting for him since sunrise. Warm gratitude shone in their eyes and they were laughing and chatting. Efrosinia stroked her husband's arm almost affectionately, and Marusia, who had now recovered completely, sat quietly smiling on the sofa. Never had Kulik seen the family so calm or behaving so kindly to one another, never had he seen them all in such a good mood. Glancing briefly at Marusia's glowing face, suddenly he felt an unpleasant sensation in the pit of his stomach, an unpleasant sensation that grew stronger.

Is this how much his going to Lvov meant to them? Didn't they think of his pain? He was about to fling himself over the edge, to sacrifice his life for their son, and they couldn't bring themselves to show the slightest concern for his safety. Grudging their happiness, full of resentment, he thought, How wonderful to see them so cheery, and at my expense! Will they even give me a second thought when I get thrown into the dungeons of the Zovty Prison?" He was furious with himself for being such a fool. Why had he so readily agreed to put his life on the line? Suddenly he hated the Bohdanoviches; he felt nothing but loathing and contempt for them. They were selfish, crude, and petty, and he cursed the day he had set foot in their house.

But Marusia was excitedly waving a piece of paper in front of his nose. "Ivan! Ivan! Something wonderful has happened! Take this and read it!"

It was a letter from Lonia. Kulik read it aloud.

My dear beloved family,

Put your minds to rest, please. As I write this letter I am in the hospital, but not to worry as I am well on my way to recovery. In about a week's time I will be leaving Lvov with a fellow student who is passing through Pinsk on his way to Baranovichy. Don't send me any parcels because by the time they arrive, I will be with all of you in Pinsk.

With all my love,
Lonia.

Kulik stood dumbfounded, and then breathed a deep sigh of relief. With one stroke of the pen all his problems were solved. He was a free man again. What great news! Lonia was coming home, and on his own! Not only did the Bohdanoviches no longer need him, but he had gotten off the hook completely and so easily.

Looking into their faces, he saw them in a completely new light. They had not only become kinder and more understanding of one another but also more loving. They were not selfish and inconsiderate as he had believed, but quite the opposite. He felt guilty. How could he have doubted their sincerity? How could he have been so wrong about them?

Efrosinia stepped up to him, and squeezing his left arm, whispered her heartfelt thanks. He could feel himself reddening with embarrassment. If they knew what had been going through his mind just a moment ago, how much he had regretted becoming a part of their lives! And now he was being made into a hero, a savior. And for what? For a mere promise that never got fulfilled. After a moment he said, "This is wonderful news. I'm so pleased everything worked out."

Wishing them a good day, feeling completely invigorated, he made his way down the snow-covered sidewalk. The first lecture of the day would begin in about half an hour and he didn't want to be late. As he pulled his cap over his ears, he couldn't stop thinking of Lonia's letter. What struck him most about it was that it was written in Ukrainian, not in Russian, and his family hadn't even noticed, and if they had, they wouldn't have cared.

CHAPTER 12

T he next morning Kulik appeared at the Holzman Theater early, and taking a seat in the back row, watched the auditorium fill with teachers: men, women, young and old, some speaking Belorussian, some Ukrainian, but most speaking Russian. They all sat with satchels at their feet and writing pads on their laps, ready to take notes. When a tall, weedy man in his mid-forties with a turned-up moustache and greased hair was called to the stage, the buzzing of voices stopped. The man spoke loudly and arrogantly in a thick Russian dialect.

"Good morning, comrades. Welcome to the first teachers' conference of Western Belorussia. I am proud to say that the Pinsk region is to become a part of the new Belorussian Soviet Socialist Republic. Finally we are rid of the bloodsucking, bourgeois Polish imperialists and are united under the solid protection of mighty Mother Russia. Through our education system we will build a strong empire to serve all Soviet peoples."

Flipping through a pile of papers on a stand before him, he cleared his throat and went on. "We will start off this lecture with a brief introduction to the Belorussian language, and then we will concentrate on the Great October Revolution."

Kulik scribbled something on a piece of paper. His hand felt stiff and he found it difficult to keep pace with the lecturer's words. The theater was hot and stuffy. His neighbor to the right, a dark-haired, shabbily dressed young man, shifted uncomfortably, and then moved to the edge of his seat, squinting and craning his neck.

At first, Kulik assumed the man was so taken by what the lecturer was saying that he did not want to miss a single word, but it became evident he was having trouble understanding the Russian dialect.

Kulik returned his attention to his notes. After jotting down several lines, he felt a rather sharp nudge on his left shoulder. Assuming someone had accidentally knocked into him, he turned and was startled to find a government officer standing there, staring at him. The officer signaled sternly with his head, and Kulik got up and followed him out into the corridor. The officer prodded him toward the entranceway. As he heard the tapping of his own shoes against the gray concrete floor, Kulik was seized by dread. What was going on? Why was he being summoned, and by whom?

He immediately thought the worst. Black clouds were rapidly moving in. He was well aware that innocent people, particularly the Ukrainian intelligentsia, were being arrested *en masse*, executed or exiled to the northern stretches of Siberia: scientists, writers, artists, educators, all were being branded "bourgeois nationalists," "conspirators against the Soviet government," "elements dangerous to society" and so forth, and eliminated. Was it his turn now? Was he about to be dragged to his doom? He tried to tell himself not to jump to conclusions.

After a few minutes they came to the *Oblispolkom*, and went up two flights of narrow wooden stairs, to a large, dingy office with hardwood floors, a high ceiling, and small grimy boxlike windows. Behind an oak desk sat Yeliseyenko, Commissar of Education. He thumbed through a pile of documents, and after pulling out several sheets of typed pages, leaned forward and filled a heavy fountain pen from a small bottle of blue ink. After taking a sip of water from a glass on his desk, he finally looked directly at Kulik.

Kulik braced himself. Undoubtedly, the commissar had something on him, something serious, or he would not have summoned him here to his office. He had to try and find a way to protect himself, and fast. But how could he, when he didn't know how he would be attacked? He was about to be accused of some unknown horror.

Yeliseyenko rose from his seat, and with his hands behind his back, and his head bent, paced between his desk and the window. He seemed to be trying to decide what to hit him with first. He looked up from under his brows and said authoritatively, "I understand you are the headmaster of School Number Seven in Hlaby."

"Yes, that's correct." Kulik's heart thudded in his ears.

"Please, have a seat." Yeliseyenko glanced down at his notes, then looked up again. "Well, hmm . . . this is all rather interesting. Yes, yes, I remember you from the New Year's Eve dance. And now the question remains, what are we to do with you?" His eyes bore into Kulik, who felt as if he were being hit by a series of grenades. "The Pinsk region, and this includes Hlaby, has been affixed to the Belorussian Soviet Socialist Republic in which Belorussian and only Belorussian is to be taught. Why are you promoting Ukrainian in your school? Are you aware of the complications you are creating for yourself? It's becoming evident to me that you are a Ukrainian nationalist, perhaps even a saboteur of some sort. This matter can easily lead to very serious consequences."

So that was it. They already had a file on him! Striving to appear calm, Kulik drew a deep breath. He had to play their game; one small slip and it could be all over. He had to say something and fast, something to neutralize this accuser. But when he opened his mouth to speak, he was shocked by what came out—he didn't know where the words came from. "I understand why I'm here," he mumbled. "I know what you want from me." He was horrified. What a careless thing for him to have said! He had just implicated himself, admitted his own guilt!

Yeliseyenko grinned triumphantly and nodded, as if he had already convicted him. "So, you know what we want from you. In other words, you agree your behavior has been questionable. Everything is clear, yes, as though it were written on the back of my hand. You've decided to give instruction in your school in Ukrainian, that we are well aware of. But who authorized you to make this decision? We are a part of the Belorussian Republic and it is Belorussian, along with Russian, of course, that will be taught in the schools. Moscow has made its decision and its decision cannot, under any circumstance, be contradicted."

He went on. "And why are you biting your lip? And now you're shrugging your shoulders. Are you confused about something? Surely someone as clever as yourself could not have forgotten about the meeting last spring when the National People's Deputy Committee sectioned off the republics?"

When Kulik did not respond immediately, Yeliseyenko repeated, more harshly, "Have you forgotten?"

"No, I have not." Trying to collect himself, staring directly at Yeliseyenko, Kulik searched for a suitable reply. "I am proud not only of our Soviet regime but also to be a member of the greatest nation on earth." Then quite unexpectedly and to his dismay, he found himself going off in a different direction, one that he had promised himself to avoid at all costs: he became bold, even defiant—in short, a danger to himself. The words rushed out of his mouth before he could stop them. "I am confident, when the regime becomes better acquainted with the Pinsk region, it will undoubtedly reconsider its stand and attach the area to Ukraine where it belongs."

Yeliseyenko turned deep crimson and there was a dark, cold look in his eyes. He was furious. How dare Kulik, a mere civil servant, question the decision of the all-powerful regime! He was about to go on the attack, maybe even start up a psychological game, when he stopped, suddenly feeling unsure. He had to deal cleverly with the adversary before him; the onus was on him not to let the party down, even for an instant. He could not afford to be outsmarted and made to look like a fool. He was a distinguished Soviet representative now and had responsibilities to fulfill; he had to be strong and in control at all times. The Party had, after all, entrusted him with this new and very significant position, and it was his duty to watch out for and report any signs of treason. Jotting something on a piece of paper, pretending to make notes, he glanced now and then at Kulik from the corner of his eye to see if he could detect some discomfort or even panic. But Kulik's face remained blank.

Yeliseyenko began to recite standard Soviet phrases and slogans. Here he was in control. He shouted, "We live in the most democratic country in the world. The Soviet government is supreme. It ensures freedom and democracy to all the people of its republics. The Party is committed to preserving all national languages and promises to give special attention to schools, the sciences, and fine arts. All republics now stand firmly united under the sound protection of their older Russian blood brothers."

As Yeliseyenko talked on, he slipped into fluent Ukrainian; from his accent it was evident he was from somewhere in the Kiev area. Kulik was astonished. Yeliseyenko bit his lower lip, red with rage and embarrassment. He had just given himself away. He had been confident that his performance as a true Muscovite was perfect. But now he was exposed, stripped of his dignity. And, to make matters worse, he had betrayed his beloved Party. He had revealed a crack in the Soviet system. He felt like a traitor.

This made Kulik even more anxious about his own immediate future. He didn't believe a fellow countryman, out to prove himself to the Kremlin, would for one minute demonstrate compassion toward one of his own—quite the contrary, he would be more inclined to nail him to the ground. Kulik's lips became parched; he felt as though he were being prodded by a pistol to go out into a courtyard somewhere, where a single, final bullet awaited him. He strained every faculty to stay on top of things. Pretending not to have noticed Yeliseyenko's blunder, he shouted with a passion that amazed even himself, "Comrade Yeliseyenko, I am an honest and faithful citizen of our new and great Soviet Empire. I am proud to be a member of the most powerful mass movement in history, and I will fight alongside my blood brothers to the very end."

"Well, well!" Yeliseyenko clapped his hands, delighted. "It's good to hear you express such encouraging views. I commend you for them." Then, frowning, "Only I don't commend you for your teaching habits. When you return to your school, you are no longer to teach in Ukrainian. Is that understood? You are not to use Ukrainian under any circumstance. I am well aware you have no knowledge of the Belorussian language, but don't worry, that's not a problem. We're a nation of Soviet peoples and all Soviet peoples must speak Russian, first and foremost. In short, you will be teaching the children of Hlaby in Russian, which I understand you speak fluently."

Kulik sank back in his seat, and nodded. So that was their plan. Languages of the republics were to be encouraged, but only on a superficial level; Russian was to be extended in all spheres of social life. Talk of preserving ethnicity was a sham.

Yeliseyenko went on. "Allow me to speak candidly, Comrade Ivan. I know you're a historian with a degree from the university in Vilno—a fact, I might add, which is not to your credit. To put it simply, you have an education from a bourgeois institution where you were taught not only by non-socialist professors but also by pretentious, self-serving priests. You were educated in a hostile and unproductive environment. Take my advice and study the five volumes of Soviet history. Become a master of Marxist methodology and learn how to approach the phenomenon of scientific socialism; come to understand thoroughly the history of struggles between the ruling and exploited classes. Give added attention to the Communist Manifesto, and learn how the capitalist classes of all nations will be overthrown and eliminated by a worldwide working-class revolution."

Yeliseyenko, to Kulik's surprise, sounded almost friendly. "Should you succeed in re-educating yourself, I may in the near future be able to recommend you for promotion to some higher institution like a *gymnasium* here in Pinsk or a university in some other city. Do you understand what I'm getting at? Now I suggest you knock on that door." He pointed to the left, to a narrow gray door that appeared to lead to a closet or storage room. Kulik had not noticed it. "My secretary will prepare the specified books for you. Good day to you, comrade."

Kulik got up and made his way across the room. He felt a tremendous weight lifted from his shoulders. For today at least he could consider himself out of jeopardy. Nothing concrete had been compiled against him. He had to remind himself that it might be just a matter of time before they went after him again.

He knocked on the door, and opened it. Before he could enter, a woman rose from behind her desk and walked toward him. She wore a dark blue suit with cuffs, a white cotton blouse and black flat-heeled shoes laced up the front. She was tall and pretty and wore her hair pulled back from her face into a bun. It was Zena. Without so much as a nod, she walked over to Yeliseyenko's desk and handed him a folder with papers in it. The two put their heads together and exchanged several words. Then Zena turned toward her office door, and in a soft but official tone, asked Kulik to follow her.

Her office was small and dim; light from a narrow window seemed to stop at the pane. Her desk, with an Olympia typewriter and two black gooseneck lamps, was half the size of Yeliseyenko's, and its piles of papers were neat and looked well-organized. A grained pine bookcase occupied one wall and on another was a clock next to a framed photograph of Stalin.

Slipping a blank sheet of paper into her typewriter, Zena rapidly hit the keys. Ten minutes passed, then another ten. Somewhat irritated, Kulik said carefully, "Excuse me, but am I to be here much longer? I have lectures to attend."

Zena did not answer. She made notes in a logbook, then typed a few more pages. Another ten minutes went by, and at last, without looking up, she said in Russian, without a trace of an accent, "The order for your school is complete. Exercise books, Russian dictionaries, pens, textbooks, slates . . ." As she leafed through the list, she raised her brows. "A magnifying glass, a telescope . . . hmm . . . strange. Are you a naturalist of some sort?"

"No, not really. Actually, history is my weakness. Greek mythology, to be exact." Kulik was amused by her interest, which seemed to be candid and genuine. Their eyes met and she smiled. She was not the cold, oblivious government worker of just a few minutes ago. Who was this girl? What was going on in her mind? She turned away, and began to immerse herself in her papers. She avoided looking at him. Kulik felt impelled to try to get some kind of response from her. He started to talk about Greek mythology.

"Are you familiar with Greek mythology? Yes? Do you remember when Zeus, god of the sky and ruler of the Olympian gods, fell in love with the beautiful Europa, daughter of Agenor the Phoenician king of Tyre? While she gathered flowers by the seashore, he appeared before her in the guise of an exquisite white bull, and enticed her to climb onto his back. Then he sped away with her across the ocean to Crete . . ."

Before he could finish, Zena burst into a fit of laughter. "Oh, you really are funny, Comrade Ivan. And you're such a cynic! I also understand you're a bit of a hermit? According to my files here, you teach in some godforsaken place miles from nowhere."

"I'm headmaster of the grammar school in Hlaby, that's correct, but being a hermit—that couldn't be further from the truth." He was grateful that she had become more friendly and talkative. "Before I go, there's one more thing. Comrade Yeliseyenko said you would prepare the five volumes of Soviet history for me."

She got up from her desk, reached for the top shelf of the bookcase, and brought down several books bound in cheap cloth. Kulik made one last attempt to amuse her. He said jokingly, "Once I plough through these pages, I will most definitely embark on the road to truth. I might find myself not such a hopeless socialist after all."

Zena gave him a stern look. Her eyes quickly moved to the door and she signaled with her head, as if to warn him that Yeliseyenko might be listening on the other side.

In that instant Kulik saw that Zena was not the loyal, unquestioning government worker she pretended to be. He believed that they understood each other.

But barely a second later, Zena said mechanically, "The cost for the books will be twenty-five rubles."

Kulik rummaged in his pocket and paid the money, which he felt was exorbitant, thanked her and left the building.

An almost balmy wind was blowing in from the south, the sky was clouded over, and for the first time in a long time the falling

snow melted as it hit the ground. The warm front brought with it
a hint of spring. Kulik tried to collect his thoughts. He didn't know
whether to celebrate his freedom or to agonize over what was to
come. The day that had just passed was beyond his understanding: up until almost the last minute, he had not expected it to end
the way it did. He had not expected to be set free and he certainly
never expected to find someone like Zena in the offices at the People's Commissariat of Education. And suddenly he felt happy, so
astonishingly happy, that it almost frightened him.

CHAPTER 13

Kulik climbed the staircase to his attic, sat on the edge of his bed and asked himself question after question: Why had he been summoned to appear before Yeliseyenko? Had he displayed disloyal tendencies somehow? Was this a test of his endurance? A battle of nerves? A joke of some sort? And what was this talk about familiarizing himself with Marxist ideology? Was he being perceived as a possible threat, an adversary, an enemy to Communism? Maybe something dark and frightful was going to happen.

But before long he felt a surge of optimism. Wasn't he still a free man after all, free to go whichever way he chose? This freedom was worth valuing. His future even looked hopeful. Hadn't he just proven himself innocent before Yeliseyenko? Wasn't that why he had been released? When he had first been summoned, he was almost certain it meant his end, but things turned out differently: a stone was hurled at him and he was struck by a pebble. He began to think that maybe the new regime was not as brutal as he had believed it to be. Perhaps he had overreacted, perhaps he had not taken a true view of the situation.

But when he kept thinking about his meeting with Yeliseyenko, his reservations resurfaced and it became clear to him that he had indeed gone through an ordeal. He became upset again. He couldn't make sense of anything that had just happened. He was apparently on the verge of being convicted of some form of anti-Soviet activity, but what was this activity? He could be found guilty of thinking differently, or even thinking at all. When the time came for his arrest, there would be no trial and no judge, no notice to family and friends; he would be cast into some deep, dark hole, and left to die. He felt trapped by the utter absurdity of the situation he was in. He was falling deeper and deeper into a psychological abyss.

He tried to calm himself, to put things into some kind of perspective, but there was no logic anywhere and the real world as it was known, no longer existed. It was like a dream. Banging his fist against the side of his leg, and with his head exploding, he shouted:

"Damn these thoughts, damn them all!"

And there was Zena: her large, black eyes, her pale complexion, her full mouth. Suddenly she seemed to him to be a greater enigma than ever. Could she be trusted or could she not be trusted? He asked himself that question over and over.

Darkness had descended and his room became pitch black. Rising from his bed, he felt an overwhelming need for some distraction. Instead of switching on the lamp on his night stand, he threw on his cap and overcoat and hurried out. The air was cold and damp. He labored through the snow to get to the front gate, but he was happy to see that the sidewalk had been cleared in either direction.

He set out for Market Square. A round moon hung over the rooftops like a large silver disc in the black sky. Adjusting the scarf around his neck and pulling his cap down over his ears, Kulik walked up Zaliznitsa Street, and then down side streets. When he crossed a small laneway, which turned at an angle, he stopped suddenly. The Zovty Prison, the newly established NKVD headquarters, loomed before him like a great fortress, tall, impenetrable and forbidding. The walls were high and made of thick yellow brick, and small, barred windows looked down onto a bare yard enclosed by a wrought iron fence with barbed wire strung along the top. Although the building was dark, Kulik imagined he could hear noises coming from within: the clicking boot heels of the NKVD making their way up and down the corridors, the thud of heavy doors, plaintive cries from the dungeons. He looked for a light to appear in one of the openings, to see movement of some sort, but everything remained black and silent. And suddenly he had a strange feeling that he was not alone, that he was being watched from one of the upper levels. Not daring to stay any longer, he took to his heels and fled down the street.

At Beresky Street, he turned left, and came to the outskirts of town. He walked without any idea of where he was going. He began to think about Marusia. How strangely cold and indifferent she was. He could not understand her contempt for all that was not Russian. Ukrainians were despicable to her—she despised their faces, their mannerisms, their clothing. And yet she was one of them. Whenever she forgot herself, which was not very often, and spoke in her native tongue, her language was flawless, but when she talked in Russian, her sentences became strained and choppy and sometimes even incomprehensible. The stress of her words fell on the wrong places, her endings were frequently incorrect, and she constantly mispronounced words or misquoted phrases. Really, she was a rather pathetic, misguided provincial, who simply had to be in a constant struggle with herself.

At the end of a long, narrow street, Kulik came upon a wide-open space dotted with evergreens and shrubs. There was no sign of life anywhere and under the bright full moon the snow lay like a vast untouched carpet of silver-blue. Turning down a barely discernible pathway flanked on either side by a growth of young cedar, he walked past a large sign that read "Park of Culture and Rest." Putting his hands in his pockets, he walked further into the park, to the Pina River. The broad, deep waterway was now one long block of solid ice glistening under the starry sky like a sheet of glass. Tall, soundless forests along the river's edge cast long, shadows; everything in the park was in a hard winter sleep.

Setting out along the dark shore, Kulik felt a kind of peace and tranquility that could not be found anywhere else, especially not on the streets of Pinsk. The frozen waterway, the shore, the soft hills, were a dark silver-gray, blending into blackness. As he was passing the snow-covered bushes, he stumbled over something jutting out of the snow. It was a burlap sack. He picked it up and opened it: it held a large loaf of bread, a coil of kolbasa, and some cheese. Had a woman—a wife, a mother, a daughter—hidden this sack in the bushes for a loved one on the run? Now these tragic stories were probably a part of everyday life.

Then from the river came a soft, barely audible rustling sound. He turned his head, and saw something moving slowly behind a wall of reeds. He hurried toward it and jumped in front of a man well into his sixties, whose thin face was gray and colorless, almost translucent, and whose eyes watered from the cold.

The two men stood frozen in their tracks, staring at each other. Then the man, looking wildly and fearfully at him, flung himself around in an effort to flee. But he lost his balance and fell headfirst into the snow. Kulik rushed to help him up, and said reassuringly, "Please, don't be afraid. I'm not going to rob you, I'm not a thief. I'm merely out for a walk."

"In this bitter cold? How long have you been following me? Are you an informer?"

Kulik said to him, "I understand. In these troubled times everyone is a threat in one way or another. No one can be trusted."

The man's eyes wandered. Adjusting a ragged blanket over his shoulders and pulling an old scarf tighter around his neck, he glanced at the bushes and asked warily, "Have you looked inside the sack?"

"Are you being pursued?"

"We are all being pursued," was the answer. "Even the pursuer is being pursued. We are all traveling the road to Hell." He picked up the sack and pulled out the kolbasa coil and the bread and stuffed them inside his coat. Patting himself on the chest, he smiled vaguely. "A few minutes of warmth and the food will thaw out completely." Then he said abruptly, "You seem different from other people. If I may ask, who are you?"

Kulik told him his name, that he was a teacher in a nearby village, and that he was in Pinsk for a teacher's conference where he was being ordered to stop teaching the children in Ukrainian and teach them in Belorussian instead. He explained that the Pinsk Marshes were being annexed to Belorussia, even though most of the people were Ukrainian. "My lessons will prove interesting, to say the least," he said dryly, "since I don't speak a word of Belorussian and neither do the children."

The man raised his brows. "Do you speak Russian?"

When Kulik nodded, the old man's face lit up. "I'm happy to hear that. Your knowledge of Russian might help you find a way to get through the system yet."

"Do you live here in Pinsk?"

"I'm a drifter," the man said bitterly. "A homeless beggar. I had a wife, a daughter, grandchildren, but now everything is gone. I'm being hunted from one hole to another. In warm weather I make a bed for myself on the ground under a tree in a park or in the woods, and now that it's winter I look for any warm spot. I find food in trash bins, the dump, wherever I can. I have to keep moving from town to town, one step ahead of the police. I live in fear that tomorrow will be my last. I'm on the run, but there's nowhere to go, there's no hope, not for me, not for anyone. I would like to go to the West, but I don't know how to get there."

Kulik said carefully, "Do you know if your family is still alive?"

The man shrugged. "I heard that they were sent to Siberia, but others said they were gunned down in the fall of '39. Someone told me that they relocated somewhere to the Caspian outside of Grozny . . ."

He fell silent for a moment. "And the sack?" Kulik asked.

He said that he had stolen the food when people were distracted by a dispute. Then he said, "Sometimes people give me things." He looked around nervously. "I hope I can trust you," he said. He turned to go, but he had something else that he felt compelled to say. He pointed in the direction of the Pina.

"There beyond the bridge, do you see the steam rising above the treetops? It's from steam shovels. They're busy working to broaden and deepen the Bugsy-Dnieprovsky Canal. And do you know why they're in such a hurry to finish it? When spring comes and the ice melts into the Dnieper, through the canal, passage to the West will be opened up. The canal will give access to the Bug and along the Bug you'll be able to get to the Visla and so on all the way to the Baltic.

"And then the worst will come for us. The forests will be mowed down, and they'll take rye from the north, wheat from Volynya—all these goods will be loaded onto ships and sent east, straight to Moscow. Every grain of wheat will be squeezed out of the fields and every cow milked dry to try to fill government quotas. Everything will float downriver: meat, butter, oil, rye, lumber, wheat. . . . And our people? They'll go on working the fields but they won't prosper. They'll starve."

Kulik felt sick. The wind, and the river, the trees—everything felt dead around him.

"It's time for me to be on my way now, young man. May our paths cross again. First thing in the morning I'll be heading out. With a bit of luck I might even find myself in the West. Goodbye and may God bless!"

Kulik, alone, stood shivering. Then he began to hurry along the snow-covered lane, back toward the park gates, into the city. All night the man's miserable life gave him nightmares. The next day the conference was coming to a close, and he would be leaving Pinsk after a two weeks' stay and returning to the village. He was now almost eager to embrace the monotony of village life. Anything was better than Pinsk.

Sitting in the Holzman Theater waiting for the lecture to begin, he couldn't get the old man out of his mind. He prayed to God for the safety of that wretched victim, and for his own safety.

CHAPTER 14

K ulik sat near Paraska in the kitchen while she filled up
the stove and the logs snapped and crackled loudly. Fire-
light quivered on the opposite wall and before long the
entire school was warmed up. Outside a blizzard raged, probably
the worst of the season. The wind howled furiously, the windows
rattled, and huge flakes of snow slammed up against the frosted
panes. It was the end of January and the Christmas season had
just ended. There had been very little celebration this year; in fact,
Christmas Day had come and gone like any other. There had been
no friendly gatherings or meals in village homes, and no festivity
in the streets. No holly wreaths on the doors, no decorated Christmas trees in the front yards, no Nativity puppet shows in the village square, and no evening carollers. All religious celebration had
been branded bourgeois, subversive and illegal. The church bells
never rang because the village church had been gutted and boarded
up, and there was talk it would soon be turned into lodgings for
local officials and visiting NKVD men. News had spread from villages like Morozovich and Lopatina that churches had been set on
fire and burnt to the ground.

Paraska filled a pot with water and set it on top of the stove to
boil. She said to Kulik sullenly, "This is one Christmas I'll never
forget. On Christmas Eve my older boys got together with friends
to sing carols in the streets. When they just barely entered the
square, Cornelius chased them off with a stick. He hollered at
them, 'Another word out of any of you, and I'll call in the NKVD!
Siberia's just waiting for the likes of you! Hoodlums!'"

She sat on a small footstool, and stared vacantly into space. "What's this world coming to? Yesterday a bunch of peasants were picked up and shoved into a sealed truck. We heard they were headed for Arkhangelsk, far, far away in the north, on the White Sea. The sun hardly rises over the horizon there in the wintertime and it's always cold. They say the people have to work sixteen-hour days, and all they have to eat are gruel and rotten fish. This is our future. And what crimes did we commit?"

Kulik did not speak. The names Arkhangelsk, Kolima, Vorbuta, said to be the sites of slave labor camps, filled him with indescribable despair.

Paraska threw another log on the fire. She stared at the pot of water that was just starting to boil, her eyes filled with tears. With difficulty, she said, "My poor Philip is dying. Our house is poor and full of sickness. Philip's head throbs and he coughs all night. Cornelius and Leyzarov, those sons-of-bitches, still won't give him a pass to travel to Pinsk to see a doctor. They keep saying he's just being lazy and trying to get out of hauling logs for the new canal. I've pleaded and pleaded with them, but it's no good. My poor husband is suffering a slow, agonizing death, and they don't care . . ."

She wept bitterly. Then all at once, her expression changed and her eyes were on fire. She shouted in a voice that was not her own, "Murderers! Nothing but murderers, all of them!"

Kulik couldn't think of anything to say that would make her feel better. "How goes it with your cow Rohula?"

"Rohula had a calf late in the fall. But it's nothing to celebrate. I see you haven't heard. The Village Soviet has ordered that every cow in our region must produce a quota of ten liters of milk a day, and those liters are to be handed over to the regime. Ten liters of milk a day! How in God's name can Rohula come up with ten liters a day? Our forage is no good and all our cows are mangy, nothing but skin and bones. What does that leave our children? The villagers have begged Kokoshin for at least a cupful, but he just shakes his head and laughs, he blames the shortage of milk on poor farm management. He says that in Russia a cow produces up to fifteen

liters a day, and with no problem! He says that we're hostile and
anti-Soviet; he says that under the Poles, we were happy to give up
all our milk to the Polish masters. He keeps saying that all Ukrainians have bourgeois tendencies, that they're dangerous to any
socialist society. And all this for a cup of milk!"

Kulik looked gravely into her face. "And what happens to the
milk you get from Rohula?"

"They let me keep one liter, but that one liter is assigned to
the calf. My children are left with nothing." Then hesitating a
moment, brushing her hair away from her face, "The Poles were
ruthless, but they never squeezed the last drop of milk out of our
cows, and we were always able to find something for our children. Now there's nothing. Every day we're forced to drag our
milk to the Clubhouse, where they put it on wagons and take it to
Pinsk and from Pinsk, straight to Moscow. They've already begun
to take rye out of our storage sheds, meat from our root cellars;
they're even confiscating hemp from the old women. Grandfather
Cemen, may he rest in peace, was right. This is the beginning of
the end."

After Paraska left, Kulik continued to sit by the stove. After a
while the kitchen door was pushed open and Sergei came in. In
the dim light, he did not appear to be himself. His shoulders were
hunched, and he moved with effort. At the teachers' conference in
Pinsk, Kulik had noticed something strange about him, especially
toward the end. He had become withdrawn and uncommunica-
tive, and had settled himself in a chair in the back, against the far
wall. Something seemed wrong.

Kulik stiffened in shock when Sergei stepped into the light.
There were bruises on his cheeks and around his eyes. His left
ear was swollen; the lobe was caked with blood. It was obvious
someone had given him a terrible beating. Feeling utterly helpless,
Kulik tried to get him to sit him down on a chair by the stove and
take some hot tea. Sergei resisted.

"Let me stay on my feet a little longer. If I could just start walking and walking . . . If only I could run . . . just run."

Looking as if he were about to collapse, he made an obvious effort to pull himself together, and flicking his eyes about the room, asked, "What's become of Paraska? Has she gone? Yes? Good, we're alone. Are all your doors locked? Lock them now. Promise me you won't say a word to anyone. Even if they pump air into your stomach or shove their fists down your throat—promise me."

"Sergei, what happened to you?"

"Things are bad, very bad."

Kulik waited.

"Do you remember when I didn't show up for the lectures on Tuesday? Do you remember I left and never came back? Did you notice that the officials were not interested in my whereabouts? That's because they knew where I was. They knew everything. Everything."

"Sergei, what are you saying? Where were you?" Kulik was afraid to hear the answer. Then it came:

"I was at NKVD headquarters, in the Zovty Prison. Lieutenant Sobakin summoned me to his bureau. I was there exactly four hours. And believe me, the meeting wasn't pleasant. You can see what they did with me. . . ."

Kulik's head spun. "This is how it starts," he mumbled, hardly aware of what he was saying. "This is just the beginning. This is just the beginning."

Sergei went on. "The spider has already started to weave its web, and it's only a matter of time before I get trapped in it. When I first came into Sobakin's office that Tuesday, he was friendly, very friendly. He said, 'It's very pleasant to see you.' He patted me on the back, even offered me a cigarette, although he didn't offer to shake hands. Then his eyes started to glisten and I knew instantly it was all leading up to something very serious. And sure enough it was. He sat at his desk and wrote down my name, then the names of my parents, my family. After that, he smiled and started asking a lot of questions. What was my political orientation? What did I do before the war? Where did I study? Who paid for my education? Did I ever belong to any organizations? Did I belong to the Ukrainian Nationalist movement? Did I serve in the Polish army? What do I think of Cornelius, the Village Chairman? How do I feel about Buhai and Chikaniuk? Do I have something to say about Hrisko Suchok. And then . . ."

He lowered himself into the chair Kulik offered him.

"And then . . . What did I know about you, Kulik? Did I know where you're from? Did I know that you came from a bourgeois background? That you were the son of a servant who worked in a Polish rectory? Was I aware that you maligned Soviet policies? And that when you were a student, you were an active member of some Ukrainian nationalist movement that planned terrorist activities against Party members and the government? I tried to explain to him that I didn't know anything about all that, but he just sneered and said, 'Don't toy with me. I know you and Ivan Kulik are good friends.' Later he warned me, 'Just remember one thing: it's your duty as a Soviet citizen to disclose all information on conspirators.'

"When I tried to defend you, he turned red in the face and banged the table with his fist. He glared at me and said, 'Didn't you hear Kulik's speech at the conference?' I acted as if I didn't know what he meant. When I called him 'Comrade Sobakin,' he got up and came toward me. He said, 'Comrade? I'm no comrade of yours!'

"And how right he was. I was certainly no comrade of his, how could I have been? He had a .22 caliber pistol in a holster and I stood before him defenseless. He could have done anything to me that he wanted: he could have shoved his fist in my face, bashed in my head, broken my neck. He had the authority to wipe me off the face of the earth and not give it a second thought. And what could I do? Nothing, except spit in his face."

Sergei closed his eyes. He said quietly and seriously, "Sobakin knows you've been encouraging Ukrainian in the school; he accused me of supporting you. He made up charges against me: I distribute bourgeois nationalistic propaganda brochures at night; I belong to the Organization of Ukrainian Nationalists, and I've helped its regional leader, a man by the name of Litovsky, go into hiding; I vilify Stalin publicly and I'm involved in a movement to bring him down. The list went on, and I wondered how I could be guilty of all that. He wanted to force me to admit to everything and sign a confession.

"At first I tried to tell myself that it was all a big mistake and the new regime couldn't possibly behave like that. But I know this is their usual method of operation. The NKVD dreams up fake counterrevolutionary activities and then grabs victims everywhere and anywhere and gets them to answer for these 'activities'. I've heard that wherever they find a man, the crime is not far off. A lot of people end up signing confessions just from the hopelessness of it all. I made up my mind I wasn't going to break.

"In any case, Sobakin had three pages on me on his desk. He handed me a pen and said, 'Now you just sit there and write out your confession. Be honest. We know everything.' Then he left the room. He was gone maybe half an hour and when he came back he had a completely different attitude. He seemed friendly. He offered me another cigarette, and he said, 'Forgive me for losing my temper. We've got so much bourgeois riffraff around here, it's hard sometimes not to lose control. But I can see you're different from the others. You're bright, alert, you're precisely what our new Soviet system needs. I want us to be friends.' Then he looked sideways at me and said that if I agreed, it would be to my 'advantage.'

"He stood staring at me for a long time before he went on, saying that if we were going to be friends, we would have to trust each other. And that required teamwork. If I was treated unjustly, he would come to my aid without the slightest hesitation. He would be my supporter and true friend. 'If you happen to need money, advice, anything at all, just come to me.' Then his eyes narrowed. 'But, of course, friendship must be proven and more importantly, you have to prove your allegiance to the new regime. If you play your cards right, you may very well find yourself on the royal road to advancement.'

"I expected a proposition like this, but still I was thrown off guard. I said, 'I see, comrade.' The word *comrade* didn't bother him any more. 'Are you asking me to be an informer?'

"'An informer?' Sobakin burst out laughing. 'Any idiot can be an informer. No, no, what I want from you is your loyalty, I want you to be a government official. And mark my words, there's a big difference between informer and government official.'

"I asked him what was involved in being a government official.

"He said it's 'a most honorable post. You'll have the highest level of power in your village. You'll be its eyes and ears, its very heart. It'll be your responsibility to protect our great socialist motherland. You'll continue being a teacher, at least on the surface, but in reality you'll be working hand-in-hand with the NKVD, weeding out enemies of the state. You'll be performing an especially important task for the Party and the government.'

"He lowered his voice and leaned toward me. 'Now about Kulik. Of course, you'll continue your friendship with him, but it's most important that I be given accurate accounts of your encounters with him. As you've probably guessed, he's under suspicion. There are serious allegations against him. In Vilno he worked with the Polish secret police to quash the Communist Party, and during one of their attacks, four dedicated comrades lost their lives.'"

Kulik couldn't believe what he was hearing. "Sergei, do you believe any of this?"

"Of course not. I don't believe a word of it. And even if it was true, it would make me happy to know there would be four bastards fewer on the face of the earth. Of course, I pretended to be shocked, outraged, and luckily he bought into it. He was convinced he had found his man.

"He waved some papers in front of my nose and told me to read them carefully, and sign on the bottom when I was done. He said he believed we would work well together. There was a list of people who were under suspicion: acquaintances, friends, family members. I read everything: I was to be named 'government official' for Hlaby and surrounding area effective immediately, and if I performed well, I would be handsomely rewarded for my services. I was even given a quota to fill. It was all in black and white. I had to think fast. Finally I blurted out, 'I'm afraid I can't sign it, comrade. I'm not good at this sort of thing. I'll give myself away in an instant. If you like, I can be an aid or assistant to you of some kind, but a government official, I could never swing it. I'm not aggressive enough and I don't have much experience in dealing with people. Every grandmother in the village would see right through me in a minute.'

"Sobakin just stared at me with no expression while I was talking. Then he got up from behind his desk and left the room, shutting the door behind him. He was gone for several minutes, and when he came back again, he was much different, he seemed impatient. He lit a cigarette and said that all that was fine for now, but only for now. He said, 'I strongly advise you to give this matter careful consideration.' He said he would call me back there soon, and he was sure we'd be able to come to some sort of agreement. And one more thing—what just happened here, he said, 'well, it didn't really happen, if you know what I mean. Not a word, not to your family, not to your friends, not to a soul. If you tell anyone, I'll find out, and you know what will happen when I do.'

"He led me to the door, and when he opened it, the guards came in. They grabbed me by the arms and took me to the basement, where they roughed me up in a closed-off room. Then they dragged me down a narrow hallway and threw me into a dingy corner near the stairwell. They left me there for it seemed like forever, and then a door opened across from me and they came out practically carrying a man, half-dressed, with his hands tied behind his back. His face looked swollen; he couldn't walk, obviously. It was a horrible sight; they did it in front of me on purpose, to break me, to scare me. . . ."

Sergei's eyes filled with tears.

"I had to tell you about this; you had to know you're in great danger. I can't even begin to imagine what Sobakin would do if he found out we met here tonight. Be careful, Ivan, they're out to get you."

Kulik tried to sound optimistic. "There's no need for alarm, my friend, not yet. They don't have anything on us, at least nothing concrete. They're trying to corner us—they're getting closer, that's true, but there's still some time left."

But Sergei sat staring vacantly at the wall. Then he pulled himself up and opened the door a crack to peer outside. There was nothing there. Fumbling into his overcoat, he said quietly, "Well, it appears it's safe enough for me to go home now. Good night. And be careful."

Kulik went into his office and sat down at his desk, closed his eyes and buried his head in his hands. The NKVD was obviously trying to pin something on him They couldn't find anything, so they were inventing idiotic stories about his past. Then he tried to convince himself that since the NKVD had nothing on him, in the end he would be found innocent and be left alone. But then there came the inevitable question: why was the NKVD coming up with something, anything, no matter how outrageous? Why was he being targeted like this?

He had to admit the utter hopelessness of his situation. The wheels of Soviet justice had been set in motion; it was just a matter of time before he would be run down. He would be tortured physically and psychologically until he cooperated somehow and showed repentance. But repentance for what? Sabotage? Treason against the Soviet government? Propaganda? Agitation? He racked his brain for some logical explanation of all that was happening; he could hardly believe any of it could be true.

But the more he thought about it, the more frightened he became. The room was bathed in moonlight; long shadows fell across the walls and ceiling. The floor creaked. Suddenly Kulik felt he was not alone, that someone was in the room with him, watching. He was certain of it: he was being watched not only now but at all hours of the day—at night, during school hours, even in the early morning. But by whom? A neighbor, a pupil, a parent, Paraska, maybe even Sergei. But Sergei a spy? His entire being rebelled against the idea. "No, not Sergei. Never!" He must be slowly losing his grip. There was no logic left anywhere; the real world did not exist any more.

Informers were everywhere: everyone was spying on someone; no one was above suspicion. Maybe Sergei was spying on him after all, by pretending not to be spying on him, and if so, someone had to be spying on Sergei. This confusion and hysteria were occurring even in the most backward villages. The sane were becoming insane, the insane, sane. Everything was in a jumble.

Suddenly Kulik thought about Paraska. If anyone was spying on him, it would be Paraska. His heart leapt and he caught his breath. Yes, of course, why hadn't he thought of it before? Certainly she was spying on him and passing information to Kokoshin or Leyzarov. It all made perfect sense now! She never set limits on the things she said in front of him; she readily and openly attacked the state. And the way she went on about her cow Rohula. Wasn't she trying to get him to reveal something? Feverishly, he racked his brain trying to remember if he had said anything incriminating to her. No, he hadn't. He breathed easier for a minute, but before long he became tense again. What about Sergei? Was he an informer or not? The question was tearing Kulik apart. For a brief moment, he actually started to hope that Sergei *was* an informer—at least as an informer he stood a chance of surviving. His own life was coming to an end, he could feel it with all his heart, but for Sergei at least there would still be hope. He became determined that his good friend would not suffer the same ugly fate that awaited him, no matter what the cost.

Still in his clothes, Kulik sank into bed completely exhausted. Tired as he was, he couldn't sleep. The room was cold and drafty; he lay shivering, staring into the darkness. The constant ticking of the clock on his nightstand grated on his nerves. The night was still, almost too still, and all at once he thought he heard something, a kind of shuffling noise outside in the hallway, then footsteps. He was certain someone was about to knock on his door and within seconds it would fly open: it was the NKVD coming to get him. They would drag him out of bed, throw him into the back seat of some big black car and whisk him off to an unmarked prison somewhere. With no trial and no judge, like thousands upon hundreds of thousands of others, he would perish, unknown to family and friends.

His head pounding, Kulik got up and paced the room. He was still shivering. and suddenly he became convinced Paraska was there in the room with him, that she was hiding behind the chest of drawers, laughing at him, watching his every move, preparing notes to take to the secret police. He saw one of his pupils emerge, pointing his finger at him and shouting at the top of his voice, "Provocateur! Saboteur! Nationalist! Arrest him!" Excruciating pains shot across his chest. He could no longer separate illusion from reality.

He fell back into bed and pulled the covers up around him. Drenched in sweat, he tried desperately to shake himself free of his hallucinations. Finally, toward dawn, he fell into a fitful sleep.

CHAPTER 15

Around ten o'clock the next morning Kulik was sitting in his office when Cornelius entered, followed by a man and a woman. The man was tall, with graying hair and sharp features, and the woman, thin almost to the point of emaciation, was not much over twenty.

Cornelius handed Kulik several official documents, and announced, "Allow me to present our new teachers. They have just arrived from Pinsk."

Kulik scanned the papers. They all had appropriate stamps and seals and officially introduced the new teachers: the man, Liavon Maximovich Ivashkevich and the woman, Haya Fifkina Sruleyevna. The two stood side by side, erect, waiting patiently. They did not speak.

Kulik took them on a tour of the school grounds. He told them that classes started at eight in the morning and ended at one o'clock Monday through Saturday; the children were to arrive at school with completed assignments; singing classes were conducted in the afternoon right before recess; and lunch was eaten at their desks at twelve-fifteen. He showed them the classrooms, first grade to eighth, the school supply room, the staff room, and the storage closet. When the tour was finished, he asked them if they had found suitable lodgings. They had, and he told them he would see them first thing in the morning.

Kulik watched them leave the building. For some reason he felt uncomfortable. There was something about the woman he found unsettling, though he couldn't quite pin it down. Ivashkevich seemed like a decent, straightforward sort and even well-educated, but Haya Fifkina was young, almost too young, and he wondered how much teaching experience she had had, if any at all. She worried him.

And sure enough, on the following day the moment she stepped into the grade two classroom there was trouble. The children decided almost instantly that they didn't like her. They laughed and jeered at her and called her a scarecrow; she responded by calling them a bunch of backward *moujiks*, deaf and dumb, who would never amount to anything. She spoke a broken, barely coherent Russian, and this sent the children roaring, especially when she added stress to her 'r's' in an attempt to roll them in the Muscovite fashion. This set her off and she went storming down the aisles in a fit of rage, shouting, "Antagonists! Underlings!"

One afternoon she stood before the blackboard holding a history book, intending to give a lesson on the October Revolution. She called out to the class, *"R-R-R-R-Rebiatushky!"* The children began to laugh at her immediately.

Ohrimko Suchok, sitting by the door, watched her closely. Rubbing his hands and glancing around, he appeared to be up to something. When Haya turned her back to write a sentence on the blackboard, he took a slingshot and a small stone out of his pocket, aimed the stone directly at her and struck her on the side of the head. Haya screamed, and rubbing her head, faced the class, determined to find out who had done it. When no one came forward, she threatened to go to the headmaster at once. But the children only roared and clapped, pinned to their seats. She stormed into the hall and made straight for Kulik's office. Banging his door open, she cried loudly, "Hooligans! Delinquents!"

Kulik leapt to his feet. He was dismayed to find her so distressed. "Calm down, please. Collect yourself and tell me what happened."

"Hooligans! Delinquents!" she repeated. "Those children are unruly and antagonistic. They belong in a zoo!"

"Please, try and settle down." He tried to calm her by offering her a seat.

"They don't listen to a word I say. They're defiant and rude. And that Ohrimko Suchok is nothing more than a thug!"

Seeing how truly upset she was, Kulik tried to comfort her. "Don't get discouraged. I know it's difficult for you right now, but once the children get to know you, they'll settle down. I'll have a talk with Ohrimko right away. I'm sure things aren't as bad as they seem. May I make a suggestion? Perhaps if you conducted your lessons in Belorussian, at least in part, things might become a bit easier. Though they don't know either Belorussian or Russian, the children are more familiar with Belorussian, because it's closer to Ukrainian. Russian, I'm afraid, is completely foreign to them."

Haya's face suddenly changed; she seemed stunned and confused by what he had just said. She sounded quarrelsome. "Teach them in Belorussian? That's out of the question." Before long she started hurling Soviet standards at him.

"In our great Soviet Empire no one differentiates between Russian and Belorussian. To us it's all one and the same. In my hometown of Slutsk, for example, Belorussian is not taught in the schools anymore, only Russian, and we embrace it as our own. I suggest you stop maligning Russian policy and concentrate on educating your pupils in true Communist fashion. The Soviets have given us the ultimate brand of socialism, and as a result we're able to enjoy a free and happy life. We have our great leader, Joseph Vissarionovich Stalin, the most wonderful and compassionate man alive, to thank for all of this."

When Kulik showed no sign of agreeing with her, she left without looking back, and slammed the door behind her.

The next morning to everyone's surprise, Haya appeared in class looking refreshed and energetic, even with a twinkle in her eye. She seemed to have forgotten everything that had happened yesterday, and her looks had improved. Her unruly hair was neatly pulled back into a bun and her thin lips had a pinkish hue. There was even a touch of red in her cheeks. She showed every sign of wanting to set things straight. Smiling at the children, making a sincere effort to appeal to their better nature, she started the day with a lesson on the Russian language.

"Children! Children!" She clapped her hands. "Listen closely: *Cyenia*. *Cye* and *nia* make *Cyenia*. Now repeat after me, *Cye-nia*."

But the children barely had a chance to open their mouths, when Ohrimko threw up his hand. He shouted out before being called upon, "Excuse me, Comrade Sruleyevna, but what does *Cyenia* mean?"

Haya, irritated, looked at him. "It's the name of a *malchik*, of course."

"And what's a *malchik*?"

"Oh, you stupid little boy. Just pay attention and not another word out of you! Now sit down."

When she turned her back to the class and began to write on the board, Ohrimko, to the amusement of his classmates, stuck out his tongue and shot a paper airplane across the room.

Without question, Haya's biggest problem was little Ohrimko. He was a troublemaker, he was ignorant of the school rules and had no desire to behave himself. He not only quarreled with his classmates, but he beat them, often until they bled. He couldn't leave even the girls in peace, and enjoyed pulling their braids and kicking them from behind. In the schoolyard he was feared more than Lucifer himself. Just a few days earlier, he had jumped on Philip Mak, a boy two years older than he, brought him to the ground, and punched him in the face until he was black and blue. The children worried about whom he might attack next.

One day when the bell rang and the children were let out from their classes, Ohrimko thought of another scheme involving Haya Fifkina. He really wanted to get her this time. Hiding behind the schoolyard fence, peering from between the palings, he waited for her to come out. He was holding a snowball, which he had packed so firmly it was as hard as a block of ice. When Haya at last opened the door and walked into the yard, the boy raised his arm over his head, and as hard as he could, hurled the snowball straight at her, hitting her in the back. Haya shrieked, and losing her balance, fell into the snow. Ohrimko laughed and cheered. He sang out loud, "Haya rode on a goose high in the sky, until she came upon the Sabbath day, oy vey, oy vey, oy vey."

Scrambling to her feet, red with rage, she ran after him. "You again!" she cried. "You little brat! Wait till I get my hands on you. What you need is a good thrashing." She almost grabbed his collar, but like a bolt of lightning, the boy took to his heels and raced down the street.

When Haya appeared in school the following morning, prepared to discipline Ohrimko in the harshest way she could think of, to her dismay, she was met by complete chaos: the children were running around laughing and screaming; a few boys were wrestling on the floor kicking over desks and chairs; paper airplanes were flying across the room; and in the far corner several little girls were making a great fuss over something, jumping up and down, giggling and pointing to the floor. Haya had never seen such disorder. No one seemed to notice her standing in the doorway.

"Order!" she cried out. "Order in the classroom! Everyone sit down. Immediately!"

At the sound of her voice, the children fell silent and quickly scrambled to their seats. Haya looked for Ohrimko. He sat at his desk, bent slightly forward, wiping his nose with the cuff of his shirtsleeve. His chest heaved with suppressed laughter. It was instantly clear to her who had instigated this latest episode.

"What's been going on here?" she demanded. Then with a look of absolute horror, she cried, "Who did this?" She pointed between her feet, where there were chalk marks everywhere. "Who's responsible?"

Beneath the desks, all the way from the blackboard to the door, the entire floor was covered in chalked crosses.

"You little insubordinates, all of you! This is inexcusable!"

She swung around and made for her desk, hopping over the crosses as if she were afraid to step on one. Wide-eyed, their mouths agape, the children watched in silent amazement. They had just witnessed a spectacle. What they had suspected all along was true—Haya Fifkina was living proof of their suspicion: Jews were afraid of crosses, and if they touched one, let alone stepped on one, they would be cursed.

Haya lashed out at them. "Anarchists! Provocateurs! Ignoramuses! Don't you know crosses are symbols of subversion, a fabrication of our oppressors? We don't put up with that kind of nonsense anymore, we stand liberated, and all thanks to our Russian blood brothers."

Clutching her head, she murmured under her breath, "Oy vey, where have I ended up? In some dismal, backward hole, with no hope and no future, just a band of counter-revolutionaries!" She wagged her finger threateningly at the children. "The education inspector is coming from Pinsk any day now and I intend to tell him everything. Every one of you will get a flogging with my special birch rod! Understand?"

She turned to Ohrimko. "Come here, young man."

The boy slid from his seat, and watching her closely, edged his way slowly toward her desk.

"Wipe off those crosses! Right now!"

"I didn't do it."

"Liar!"

"That's the truth."

"I'm telling you, wipe off the crosses!"

When Ohrimko shook his head, Haya Fifkina lost control of herself, and lunging forward, grabbed his ear. She tried to drag him to the ground.

"Wipe off those crosses! Wipe them off, I tell you, now!"

Ohrimko, kicking and punching, tried to break free, but Haya kept him down with a firm grip. After a moment, managing to free his right leg, he kicked as hard as he could, striking her several times, once in the belly, twice in the head. Screaming, she let go of him. The boy raced to the blackboard, grabbed a wooden ruler from the ledge and started striking her with it. She covered her face with her hands, trying to protect herself from the repeated blows. The struggle continued for several minutes, until somehow Haya managed to knock Ohrimko across the floor. Breathless, she ran down the corridor and into Kulik's office.

"Anti-Semitism! Anti-Semitism!" she cried. "This school is riddled with anti-Semitism. I almost got killed! I refuse to take it anymore. I didn't fight for the emancipation of the proletariat and train to become a teacher so I could be run down by a band of fascists!"

Kulik was astonished. "Calm down, Haya, calm down. Please sit down. Now, tell me, what fascists are you talking about?"

"Those little monsters I've been assigned to teach. Fascists, all of them! And that Ohrimko Suchok is the worst of the bunch. I demand his expulsion immediately!"

She was in great distress and shaking. Her flat chest heaved with emotion, while tears rolled down her cheeks. Kulik tried to find something to say to calm her down, but he stopped short, afraid anything he said would only set her off even more.

She was thin, very thin, like a twig, and she seemed so helpless standing there trembling, almost tottering. He wondered how she had come to be here in Hlaby, so many miles from nowhere. She was not a teacher by any means, but a child, a mere child, who ought to have stayed home with her mother. With sympathy growing in him, he said at last, "I agree, it's a very trying situation, but you must not forget that it's a difficult time for the children as well. There's been a complete overhaul, not only in the school system, but in everyday life. It'll take time for them to adjust. All I can suggest is that you try and make them like you."

"Try and make them like me?" Her eyes bulged. "They'll never like me. They're hostile and aggressive. In fact, the entire atmosphere here is unbearable." Then looking at him coldly, "And you! You're talking to me pretending to be my friend, but you can't fool me, not for one minute. I know you're the one responsible for creating adverse sentiments here. It's because of you the children are the way they are."

She had barely uttered these words, when the door was thrown open and Ivashkevich came into the office. Having heard Haya's accu-

sations from the hallway, he immediately rose to Kulik's defense.
"You're being too hard on our headmaster, Haya Sruleyevna. After
all, the Soviet schools are only just beginning to be developed here,
and to ensure a smooth transition, we all have to work together.
The headmaster only just recently landed the post here himself.
You can't hold him accountable for your unfortunate incident."

"I can't hold him accountable?" Haya shot back. "You mean to
say I can be murdered by one of my pupils tomorrow and the little
monster will go free because our good headmaster here cannot
yet be held accountable? What kind of place is this?" She pulled
a handkerchief from her pocket and blew her nose. "I don't have
any peace anywhere, I'm terrorized wherever I go. In the classroom I'm harassed nonstop; out in the street I get sticks and snowballs hurled at me from all sides. And all because I'm Haya Fifkina
Sruleyevna, a Jew. Under Soviet law we Jews now have the same
rights as all citizens of the Soviet Union. Everyone is equal. The
activities going on in this village are subversive and illegal and it's
my obligation to bring them to the attention of the authorities."
She stormed out into the corridor, shouting, "You haven't heard
the last of this! I'm not through with you yet, not by a long shot!"

Silence fell over the room. Ivashkevich stood against the wall
awkwardly, not knowing what to say or do. Kulik sat at his desk,
trying to appear calm. After several minutes, the two men glanced
at each other. Finally, clearing his throat, Kulik said, as if nothing
unusual had just happened, "Comrade Ivashkevich, please have a
seat. How are things going with the third graders?"

"I have nothing to complain about, really. But on the other hand,
I don't have anything to boast about, either. The children don't
understand me and I only understand about every tenth word of
theirs. In all honesty, when I was assigned to this school I really
thought I'd be amongst fellow Belorussians, but that's not the case
at all.

"I think our new regime has made a serious mistake in not connecting this region to Ukraine. I don't think our new leaders are
quite the humanitarians they claim to be."

Kulik was completely rattled by Ivashkevich's remarks. He looked suspiciously at him; something was not quite right. The atmosphere became strained. Kulik hesitated, asking himself question after question. Why did Ivashkevich so brazenly and unabashedly take it upon himself to openly challenge the new regime? Certainly it was not because he was reckless, or incapable of seeing how dangerous such talk was. Was he testing him? Trying to provoke him in some way? Did he expect his defenses to be down, especially after the scene with Haya Fifkina? Something was wrong. He began to suspect that Ivashkevich had a secret plan of some kind. And then his worst fear turned to reality: Ivashkevich was an informer! This fellow teacher with whom he had exchanged friendly words, even the occasional anecdote, this man who showed only his good nature, was in fact a trickster, a government agent sent to spy on him. Kulik had a horrible feeling of helplessness; his heart pounded. He knew he had to do or say something to throw Ivashkevich off track. He said firmly and with conviction, "The Soviet regime has made no mistake, Comrade Ivashkevich, I assure you. Our good liberators always have in mind what's best for the people of our great nation."

"You really think so?" Ivashkevich smiled uneasily. He could not hide the fact that he was very much discouraged by Kulik's response.

"Absolutely." Kulik reached across his desk. "Take a look at this microscope." He carefully picked up the instrument and handed it to Ivashkevich. "It's quite magnificent. Our school has never seen anything like it before. The Soviets, by providing something of this caliber, show that they truly care about quality education for the masses, from the factory worker to the peasant."

As Kulik spoke, he felt Ivashkevich's eyes on him, weighing his every word, as if looking for a break in his voice or hesitation of some kind. Ivashkevich was waiting for him to make a slip or to do or say something incriminating so he could take it to the authorities. Kulik watched Ivashkevich watching him, and he wondered if Ivashkevich doubted him as much as he doubted Ivashkevich.

When finally the expression on Ivashkevich's face seemed to suggest he was giving up on his little game, Kulik, at least for a moment, was able to let down his guard.

Ivashkevich had lost the first round, and as if realizing this, in an attempt to mask his intentions, began to mouth propaganda. "You are correct, Comrade Kulik. We must forever be grateful to Joseph Vissarionovich Stalin for our liberation and for the good fortune he has bestowed upon us. Just to see an instrument like this microscope or the fish tank in the sixth grade is enough to convince anyone that the new regime is truly generous and wonderful."

After finishing this speech, Ivashkevich adjusted his shirt collar, abruptly excused himself and hurried out the door. As he disappeared down the corridor, Kulik couldn't help but wonder, who had truly come out on top, he or Ivashkevich?

The bell rang. Recess was over and classes were resuming. Kulik, still at his desk, took a deep breath. The dark clouds hanging over him were forever descending, and before long they would consume him completely. Although he had gotten off easy today, he knew that with each day there would be new and more formidable hurdles to leap. He was upset and very tired. The future looked grim, if there even was a future, and the past had been blown into little pieces. Tomorrow would no longer be a day like any other, but the beginning of a new and more terrible challenge.

Kulik's thoughts were in a tangle. He tried to read through some papers. But no matter how hard he tried to concentrate on his work, he couldn't get Ivashkevich out of his mind. The truth of the matter was, Ivashkevich was a government agent, an informer, with one purpose—to get him, Kulik, on even the flimsiest of suspicions. Yes, he understood it all now; he was being pursued, and by someone in the school, and now more than ever he had to watch his every step.

To further complicate things, the unfortunate incident with Haya Fifkina grew bigger and bigger. News of trouble at the school spread like wildfire and it was not long before every house rang with the scandal. Small groups of women gathered to gossip in their yards, men argued in the streets, and officials in the Clubhouse called emergency meetings. Everyone was shocked to learn that Ivan Kulik, the new village headmaster, was an anti-Semite. And it didn't stop there: he was not only stirring up the children, but also promoting anti-Semitic sentiments everywhere in the region. When these very serious allegations reached his ears, Cornelius took it upon himself to confront Kulik.

"What's been going on here?" he demanded. "Word has it you're pumping the children up with anti-Semitism. It's a good thing Haya Fifkina caught wind of your actions before they got out of hand. She's already reported you to the Pinsk authorities."

"What are you talking about?" Kulik asked.

"Don't fool with me. I'm the Village Chairman and I know everything that's going on around here. You set the children against Haya Fifkina for the simple reason that she's a Jew. And that sort of behavior is subversive and punishable by law. Our free and liberty-loving regime has sent Haya Fifkina here to teach the children, not to be maligned by them."

"What are you insinuating?" Kulik stood up. "Your accusations are absolutely unfounded, not to mention ridiculous. Haya Fifkina was welcomed here just like any other new teacher. And as far as the children are concerned, I know they've gotten out of hand, and first thing tomorrow disciplinary measures will be taken. But to imply that in some way I riled them up is absolutely preposterous."

Cornelius kept up his attack. "You're asking for trouble, Comrade Kulik. Take my advice and run the school like a devoted servant of the state. Teach the children the true spirit of revolution. And teach them to like Jews. Make them understand ours is the most democratic country in the world where everyone is equal and Jews are just as equal as anyone else."

Cornelius had much more to say; he was determined to get Kulik to see things in the proper light. "We're all one and the same, and I'll prove it to you. Take, for example, the merchants of Pinsk. Just last week, weren't they all rounded up and interrogated, then imprisoned equally? The Poles, the Ukrainians, the Jews—no one group got discriminated against. Hah! So there you have it, we *are* all equal!"

Kulik listened to Cornelius's idiotic rant with increasing exasperation. He wanted to grab him by the scruff of the neck and hurl him out the door. His patience was wearing thin.

Cornelius went on. "You, comrade, are a product of a bourgeois society and you're tampering with the minds of our young children, teaching them perversity and anarchy. You must prepare your lessons in such a way that the Party and our glorious leader Joseph Vissarionovich Stalin are above all else revered and praised. The children, especially the younger ones, must know how their parents suffered under Polish oppression and how Olivinski, the Polish tyrant-landowner, enslaved and demeaned them. They must understand that the new Soviet government is their great liberator and they must forever show their gratitude. The new regime not only cares about educating the masses, but also about doing away with illiteracy in the most backward of villages. Who do you think brought this microscope and the fish tank to the school? Our new regime, of course. They spent two thousand rubles on these items because they care. Allow me to say it again: subversion must be quashed at all levels to ensure our new system runs smoothly and productively. I, as a Soviet citizen, will do my utmost to make sure this happens."

As this continued, Kulik completely lost track of what Cornelius was saying. He saw Cornelius' thick, cracked lips moving soundlessly under his moustache. But the words *fish tank* and *two thousand rubles* caught his attention. He was curious to learn why the new regime had so generously parted with such a substantial sum of money. He said, "You mean to say the new school instruments were purchased by the government and sent here to our school?"

"Yes, that's right." Cornelius opened his eyes wide and blinked. "Our government is committed to providing the best education for all children of the Soviet Union, whether they live in urban centers or in backward, isolated villages. We're all treated equally.

The instruments were brought from Pinsk by car, and I myself unloaded the boxes and helped carry them into the school. The villagers were thrilled to see their children with such modern tools."

Talking louder and louder and faster and faster and becoming more impassioned, as the words flew out of his mouth, it was not long before he let the truth slip.

"Yes, it was a great job to raise that money and everyone participated. The people worked hard to enable the new regime to buy the instruments for the school. It was our regime's idea, and if not for our regime, we would have nothing. A meager amount was requested from every household, and naturally the people complied. And why did they comply? Because the people *are* the government—it's all one and the same. The government is run by the people, the money is collected from the people, given out by the people, for the people."

Kulik listened with mounting anger and contempt. He now understood everything. He said bitterly and sarcastically, "So it is *we the people*, or rather, *we* the government, who, according to you are one and the same, who are giving us our fish tanks whether they have the money or not? People like Paraska, for instance? Is she part of the government?"

Cornelius' small black eyes flickered, filled with rage. He said sharply and disdainfully, "How dare you challenge the government. You are a subversive, and I can see by the light in your eye that you're not one of us." Then a warning, "The frozen wastelands of Arkhangelsk are not far off, in fact they're beckoning you as we speak. And in case you didn't know, the NKVD is already hot on your trail."

Kulik's heart thudded, "Why, that's ridiculous. I'm a simple, humble teacher and I have had no political affiliation whatsoever other than with the Communist Party."

Cornelius laughed ironically. "You don't fool me for one minute. Even Kokoshin and Leyzarov are on to you."

"Did they send you here? Is that why you're here?"

"No one sent me here. You think I'm stupid, don't you? I came here because I know what's going on. I'll have you know I have a good nose; I can smell a traitor when I see one. I didn't make my way up the Party ladder because I'm thick in the head; no, I made it because I get the job done. I can see where your sympathies lie as clearly as I can see the light of day. You claim to be of peasant stock, which may be true, but in spirit you're a bourgeois. We know about your past. In Vilno you obtained a bourgeois education and associated with subversives. And subversives are the great enemies of Communism and must be dealt with immediately. We live in the most democratic country in the world, where the masses rule. The workers have finally overthrown the ruling classes, and we must fight to preserve this wonderful new life of ours, no matter what the cost."

Kulik lost all self-control, and flew at Cornelius. "You're nothing more than a buffoon! I've heard enough. Get out of here before I throw you out!"

Cornelius's face lit up with a sardonic smile. "Hah! I see I've touched a nerve. The aloof and self-important headmaster has lost his temper. Just like a balloon he went 'pop!'" Then with a snarl, "We'll get you, you wait and see. Already you're being watched. It won't take long now. And a word of advice, if you ever dare utter another word against Jews, it'll be off to NKVD headquarters with you!"

"Get out of here! Now!" Kulik almost choked with rage. Lunging forward, with all his strength he grabbed Cornelius by the collar, and punched him in the face, knocking him down.

"Help! Murder! Help!" Cornelius cried. He managed to scramble to his feet and make a run for the door. But he was no match for the stronger and younger Kulik, who quickly tripped him up, dragged him across the floor, and hurled him out the front door into the yard. As he landed in the snow, Cornelius cursed and howled at the top of his lungs, "Damn you, bourgeois! Your head will roll for this!"

Kulik slammed the door and bolted it shut.

CHAPTER 16

To everyone's surprise, pinned to the wall outside the grade one classroom was a long sheet of paper with an elaborate, detailed cartoon drawn by a steady and capable hand. It was a caricature of a young boy with tousled hair and an upturned nose, who clutched a ruler in his left hand, aiming it like a spear at a woman. The boy wore a fierce, nasty expression and bore a strong resemblance to Ohrimko Suchok. The woman, skinny with frizzy hair, looking very much like Haya Fifkina, was scrambling through a window trying to escape from him. Several children were penciled in at the bottom, crouched on all fours, peering fearfully from under their benches. Under the drawing was written:

It is not a ruler but a spear
Haya Fifkina, beware!

At recess, almost all the children gathered around the drawing, laughing and talking at the top of their voices. A few older boys elbowed their way to the front to get a better look, while several girls stood on tiptoe, shouting and pointing excitedly. One little girl in a blue frock and gray knitted stockings, standing near the drawing, twirling her braids, took it upon herself and for the benefit of all to read the words aloud, "It's not a ruler, but a spear . . ." As she read, the children fell into an uproar. Enjoying the attention, just as she was about to start on the next line, suddenly Ohrimko appeared and charged toward her. He was red in the face and fuming with rage.

"Why don't you just shut up!" he shouted at her. "You're just a dumb old girl. It's not funny!" Raising his arms, with all the force he could muster, he pushed her to the ground and kicked her in the head. When her nose started to bleed, horrified at the sight of blood, she picked herself up, and made for the door as fast as her little feet could carry her, down the corridor, straight to the headmaster's office. Standing in the doorway, panting and gasping, wiping her tears with the cuffs of her blouse, she smeared blood all over her face.

Kulik saw her and leapt up in horror. "Good God," he cried, "what on earth happened to you?" Before she could answer, he pulled her into the kitchen, filled the basin with warm water, and washed her hands and face. Later he applied poultices to her cuts. "Who's responsible for this?"

The girl cried out, "Ohrimko Suchok!"

Kulik was shaken. Ohrimko Suchok was an incorrigible boy, hopeless; he was at a loss with what to do with him. He wanted to call the boy to his office at once, but he wasn't sure how to handle him. Ohrimko had just been disciplined for attacking Haya Fifkina, and with no noticeable results. Finally, Kulik decided to wait until the end of the day, until classes ended, to allow himself time to think of a plan. He considered suspending him and sending him home, keeping him after school, giving him a good thrashing. . . . When the bell rang, he had come up with the perfect solution, one that had just popped into his head. It was rather unconventional, but he was confident it would have a positive effect. He sat at his desk, patiently waiting for Ohrimko to knock on the door.

"Come in, young man." Kulik rose to his feet. His tone was calm and composed and there was even a smile on his face, which he didn't attempt to hide.

The boy stared. He didn't know what to make of this. He expected the headmaster to be enraged, fuming, but he certainly did not expect him to be smiling. He anticipated the worst and was very frightened. Any moment now, any second, he would get a flogging a thousand times worse than he had ever had before. Drawing a deep breath and standing without moving a muscle, he closed his eyes tight and waited for the onslaught to begin. But there came no sound of a switch, no pain to his palms, no heavy breathing of the headmaster over his head. There was only silence. Slowly opening his eyes, to his surprise he saw the headmaster sitting quietly at his desk with his hands folded, still with that same strange smile on his face. Ohrimko watched him closely, convinced he would spring on him at any moment.

Kulik motioned to him. "Come here, young man." That his tone continued to be soft, even kindly, further confounded the boy.

Creeping timidly toward the desk, Ohrimko wanted only one thing: for the punishment to be over and done with. He suspected the headmaster was up to something and whatever plan he had for him he was certain would be brutal.

Kulik watched the boy but didn't speak. He was thinking. As he was about to say something, before any words came out, to his great surprise, the boy burst into tears; his entire body trembled. He couldn't stop crying.

"Ohrimko, what's wrong?" Kulik was amazed to see the school bully in such a state of distress. He had expected defiance and anger from him, but not tears.

The boy continued to whimper. "It's my legs. They're sore. My father beat me last night, he beat me with a nettle switch and now I can barely move." Rolling up his pants, he showed Kulik the cuts and bruises on his legs.

Kulik was deeply disturbed by what he saw. Even though Ohrimko was the biggest bully in the school and made life miserable for everyone, there was a kind of helpless sadness in his eye that had to arouse sympathy. For the first time he saw the boy not as a little monster out to create pain and misery for others, but as a lost, confused, lonely child trying to get attention.

The boy stood hesitating, rooted to the spot. The thought of getting another beating all but paralyzed him. Suddenly he saw the headmaster rise to his feet and come toward him. Any second now and everything would be over. He would grab him, strike him, finish him off right then and there. But instead Kulik took hold of his left ear. Pain shot through the boy and he let out a cry. He was guilty and now he was about to pay. He had beaten up a defenseless little girl and he deserved what was coming to him, and probably more. He waited for the flogging to begin. But instead of a flogging something completely unexpected happened. The headmaster made a very peculiar sound and his mouth twisted with disgust:

"Ugh! Ohrimko, this is completely unacceptable. We simply cannot allow this sort of thing to go on. Your ears are filthy!"

The boy stood dumbstruck. He turned red with shame and embarrassment. It was true he did not take kindly to soap and water and very rarely washed his face, let alone his ears. But why was the headmaster making a point of it now? Wasn't he there to be punished? When the headmaster opened the top drawer of his desk, Ohrimko was sure he was going to take out a switch or something equally unforgiving. But instead he brought out a small parcel wrapped in newspaper and tied with brown string.

"Here, Ohrimko," he said, "this is for you. I bought it in Pinsk. Something tells me that at heart you 're a good boy."

For the longest time Ohrimko stood looking dazed, his eyes round with wonder. Edging toward the desk carefully, he leaned forward and grabbed the parcel. Peering inside, to his great astonishment he found half a dozen candies in thin paper wrappers, everyone a different color. He could hardly believe his eyes. No one had ever given him such a treat before, and straight from a candy store in Pinsk!

The headmaster urged him on. "Go ahead and take one."

Ohrimko hesitated a moment and then popped an orange candy into his mouth, all the while keeping an eye on the headmaster. He was certain something big and painful was about to happen to him, and soon. No one received candy for punishment; that just did not happen. The headmaster was merely toying with him before moving in for the kill.

And sure enough, barely a minute had passed when, pacing the room, the headmaster all at once turned on him with a scowl. His tone was stern and abrupt.

"Ohrimko, do you enjoy being a bully? Do you enjoy teasing others and cracking their knuckles? Do you? Why don't you answer me? Very well then, I'll answer for you. I believe you do not. That's why I want to discuss something with you today. I want to give you a job—a very important job. I realize everyone says you're a troublemaker, but I disagree, I feel deep down you're capable of better things, much better. And I'm willing to give you a chance. But first I must have your full cooperation. What I propose to do is make you chief of your class. Your job will be to make sure none of your classmates get out of hand, and if they do, you must report to me immediately. I want you to take this assignment very seriously. Do you think you can handle it?"

The boy's mouth dropped open. He had expected a lot of things, a thrashing, expulsion, but class chief? Drawing a long, deep breath, he scrambled to respond. Things couldn't have turned out better. Of course he would be class chief, and of course he would make a good one, probably the best. Why, he already had a considerable following among both boys and girls, and to keep them all in line would not only be easy, but great fun. Hah, if someone dared not to listen to him, he'd show them! And suddenly he began to think of himself as rather important. There was no one who even came close to rivaling his qualities in strength and leadership. He thought, The headmaster sees I'm strong and I have the power to make everyone afraid of me. I already have the class under my thumb, so I'm the natural choice for class chief.

"Well, Ohrimko." The headmaster looked at him from under his brows. "What will it be?"

"Yes, I can do it," he shouted.

Kulik smiled slightly at the boy, pleased his plan was starting to take effect. "I knew you would agree to my proposition, young man. Keep in mind, being chief is no easy matter. You must set a good example to the rest of the class at all times. You must be the paramount influence. For example, you can't get into any more fights, or beat up girls, or cause trouble for the teacher. It's important for you to listen and show respect to Haya Sruleyevna. You are not to threaten her in any way. Don't hang your head, young man, we all learn from our mistakes. And one last thing: you are behind in your lessons. You must work hard to catch up to the rest of the children. Why, little Tolik already knows the entire alphabet, and by heart. If you apply yourself you can overtake him easily. Chief of the class must surpass everyone in all respects."

Ohrimko screwed up his mouth and gulped hard. The headmaster's plan was beginning to take on a sour note—it was definitely more than he had bargained for. True, he looked forward to keeping his classmates in line, but the part about doing his homework didn't appeal to him one bit. On even his better days, he didn't enjoy listening to what was going on around him in class, and he had no desire to work through his arithmetic or spelling drills. Suddenly, being class chief didn't look as appealing as it had a moment ago.

When the recess bell rang, the headmaster called all the second graders together and made his announcement: Ohrimko Suchok was to become class chief. Shocked and shaken, the boys and girls banded together to raise their objections. Desperately they pleaded with the headmaster to reconsider. They argued it was completely unfair to grant Ohrimko the upper hand; it would only give him license to terrorize them, without being held accountable by anyone but himself.

When this news reached Haya Fifkina, she couldn't believe her ears. She was completely beside herself with anger. After having launched a formal complaint to the People's Commissariat against Ohrimko Suchok and before even receiving a response from them, she was furious to learn that the headmaster had gone and appointed him class chief. Ohrimko was a belligerent child, her worst pupil, and if anything, deserved a good thrashing, certainly not a pat on the back. She was convinced this was all some kind of plot to drive her out of the school for good. She vowed to take this additional information to the authorities in Pinsk, in the hope that it would strengthen her case against Kulik.

The very next day, entering her classroom, prepared for disaster, Haya Fifkina was completely taken aback to see that the children were not shoving and lunging at one another or yelling in rough, teasing voices—they were lined up behind their desks, their hands folded before them, shouting in unison, "Good morning, Citizen Haya Fifkina!" Haya stared at them suspiciously, then walked over to Ohrimko and looked him straight in the eye. Obviously this impish little brat, who for some reason was pretending to be a model pupil, was responsible for this. He definitely had something up his sleeve. She turned to look at the blackboard. It had not only been scrubbed clean but even polished. On the ledge lay a neatly folded damp cloth and next to it a row of chalk. She didn't know what to make of any of this.

"Well, well, children." She put her hands on her hips. "What a delightful surprise. Thank you. Now please, take your seats." Feeling immensely pleased, she reached for an exercise book on the far side of her desk, ready to begin the first lesson of the day. Looking up briefly to ensure that order still reigned, she found Ohrimko on the edge of his seat, eagerly waving his hand. He looked confused.

"Yes, Ohrimko?"

"Citizen Sruleyevna, I would like to ask you a question, um . . . er . . ."

"Come on, come out with it, boy. Don't drag your tongue. What is it?"

"Well, about your lessons. Why can't you teach us in Ukrainian? We don't understand anything you say. If you taught us in our own language, then things would be easier for us all."

"Oh, *rebiatushky, rebiatushky*," Haya waved her hand. "If only I knew how to speak Ukrainian, if only. But not to worry, soon you will come to understand Russian and speak it as though it's your mother tongue. Then I guarantee everything will flow as smoothly as butter. Today we'll start our lesson by reviewing the alphabet. Everyone together now: A, B . . ."

Following Haya's voice, the children strove to do their best. Even Ohrimko mouthed letters he had never before pronounced. When Haya assigned a short spelling exercise, the children applied themselves diligently; some even came up with correct answers.

These improved conditions should have created a better environment in the school as a whole and formed a stronger relationship between teacher and headmaster, but events took a different turn. Haya became more mistrustful of Kulik, was hostile and aloof toward him, and managed to convince herself that with the NKVD on his trail, he was desperate, and had turned the children into exemplary pupils to protect himself. She had heard of these sorts of tricks, tricks used typically by counterrevolutionaries. But what worried her most was that if Kulik succeeded in painting himself in a better light, her life would again become a living hell. Things would go back to the way they were, if not worse. The children would start harassing her in the classroom and on the street again, fights would break out, Ohrimko would become defiant once more, and of course Kulik would go back to spreading anti-Semitism.

But as the days passed, the children's performance actually improved. The biggest change came in Ohrimko. He was not only on his best behavior most of the time, but proved a more-than-capable student. He worked doggedly through his additions and subtractions, and was even able to write the letters of the alphabet all the way to the letter 't'. And to add to this, he didn't neglect his chief duties; he took them very seriously. One day when Anastasia stuck out her tongue at him and scribbled something on the wall beside her desk, Ohrimko interrupted the class and escorted her to the headmaster's office. And when Tolik and Fedko got into a brawl at recess, Ohrimko was there to break it up; he grabbed them both by the scruff of the neck and hurled them in opposite directions. Ohrimko was determined to do the best job he could. He was now at the top of his class.

Kulik was thrilled with the boy's progress. He believed that the more a child misbehaved, the greater his cry for help and approval. Scolding, punishment or rejection served only to more firmly entrench this negative self-image. A child, especially a child like Ohrimko, riddled with defenses like aggression, anger and violence, must have his self-worth and self-esteem built up in a constructive way. By appointing him class chief and demonstrating he was worthy of this position, Kulik felt he had turned the boy around. It was no secret that he had a soft spot for him, something Ohrimko was well aware of and took pride in.

Early one morning, as dawn filtered through the school windows, Kulik sat behind his desk, pen in hand, buried in paperwork. Unable to sleep, he had been up since four that morning, flipping through textbooks, writing reports, and reviewing assignments. With the stove refilled with firewood, the warmth beginning to penetrate the room, he started to grow drowsy. His eyelids became heavy, and in no time he nodded off. When he woke, he glanced at his watch and saw it was only seven forty-five; he had been asleep for no more than a few minutes. The sun was rising on the horizon and soon the school bell would ring.

As Kulik delved back into his work, he heard noises outside. There was an abrupt screech, followed by the low humming of a motor car. Peering out his window, he was disturbed by what he saw: a big black car parked in front of the school gates. The doors were closed, and the windows were tinted green. It was not an ordinary auto, but an NKVD car; the people called it the "Black Crow." Black Crows could be seen everywhere these days driving through towns and villages. Kulik had seen many slinking up and down the streets of Pinsk—Sovietskaya, Karalyna, in and around Market Square, at first only in the dark of night, then eventually in broad daylight. They never seemed to rest, stopping only briefly in the rear of NKVD headquarters to dump off their load of victims before returning for more.

Was the Black Crow coming to get him? Openly, in daylight? He backed away from the window and waited. He heard the car doors open and slam shut, and the sound of voices, then footsteps coming closer and closer. They were already in the school, walking down the corridor, gradually and evenly, coming to get him.

And suddenly there it came, the dreaded knock on the door. On the threshold stood three men: Yeliseyenko, Iofe Nicel Leyzarov and Simon Stepanovich Sobakin.

Sobakin stood in the middle, with Iofe Nicel on his left and Yeliseyenko to his right. Without moving, dressed in heavy gray overcoats and knee-high leather boots, they cast quick glances around the room. There was a constrained silence that seemed to last forever. Finally Kulik blurted, "Welcome to the school, comrades."

Sobakin pushed his way into the room. "Good morning, Comrade Kulik." He spoke brusquely; the visor of his cap was pulled down over his forehead and shaded his eyes. "We've come on official state business. We're conducting an investigation of the school and would like to see your documents, pass books, and your teaching certificate."

Kulik pulled a folder from the bottom drawer of his filing cabinet and handed it to Sobakin, who examined every page carefully, deliberated briefly, and passed them on to Leyzarov.

"Hm . . ." Leyzarov muttered, scratching his head. "Yes, everything appears to be in order." He scanned the last page, and to Kulik's great alarm, quickly folded the documents in half and slipped them into his satchel.

"Now, Comrade Kulik," Sobakin again, "we'd like you to accompany us on an inspection of your school. We trust you're running it in true Soviet fashion and that everything is in accordance with Soviet law." Turning, he stepped out into the corridor, paused, and set out to the right, with Leyzarov and Yeliseyenko close behind. Kulik trailed by a few steps.

In the corridor, they stopped to examine the bulletin board. They seemed pleased with it. At the top of the board, in the center, was a large picture of Stalin, and directly below it an article on a recent demonstration in Red Square. On the left was a list of about twenty honored *kolkhoz* workers from the region.

The men moved on to the grade two classroom. Haya Fifkina stood before the blackboard, giving instruction in arithmetic. Today, in a navy skirt and a freshly ironed white cotton blouse, with her hair twisted back in a loose braid, she looked particularly presentable. Using thick, bold strokes she carefully and slowly wrote 12+9=? Holding a ruler in her left hand and tapping her right with it, she called out:

"Who knows the answer? Georgi?"

No answer.

"Tolik?"

From somewhere a thin little voice: "Twenty-one."

"Very good, Tolik." Turning back to the board, Haya proceeded to write 14+11=? "Who knows the answer? Ohrimko?"

Ohrimko winced and fidgeted in his seat. He stared down at his hands with great intensity and started counting with his fingers. Finally he looked up and said, "Twenty-five."

"Good. Very good."

It was when Haya was writing another equation on the board, that she noticed the three government officials standing in the doorway. Their unexpected appearance completely frazzled her, and she gasped and jumped back, knocking against her desk. She had no idea how long they had been watching her, and being caught unawares made her not only nervous but incapable of thinking straight. She went off into a frantic giggle. Not having the slightest idea of what to say, grasping at anything, she lost all self-control, pointed to the back of the class and shouted:

"That's him! That's the culprit I wrote you about! That's Ohrimko Suchok!"

The children watched her with confused delight, chattering loudly and poking each other. Laughter broke out. One little boy fell off his seat and started to cry, while another sent a slate flying across the room. The class was now in complete uproar.

"Comrade Haya!" Sobakin, stamped his foot in a show of outrage. "Please, collect yourself and get on with your lesson." Then turning sternly to the pupils, "Quiet! Quiet in the class!"

Taking long, deep breaths, the more Haya tried to calm herself, the more shaken up she became. The children had now gone completely wild and there was no way to calm them.

"Children! Children!" She clapped her hands, trying desperately to restore order. "We are now going to review the alphabet. Repeat after me, A B . . ." Trembling and gasping, suddenly she broke off. Tears gushed down her cheeks, and she wanted only to escape from the room. Then to her great relief, the bell rang. It was recess. She was saved. The children quickly gathered their belongings, formed a line against the wall, and exited the room.

Leyzarov turned to Haya seriously.

"Comrade Haya, I would like to talk to you. We're here today because we have a deposition from you. In it you accuse the headmaster of subversive activity and anti-Semitism. You claim he promotes these sentiments in both the school and throughout the village. Is that not correct?"

"Yes," she squeaked out.

"Do you have proof of your charges?"

"Yes."

She started to revive. Her voice became stronger, more self-assured. "Yes, I do, as a matter of fact. The children harass me on the street and in the school. They call me beanpole and hurl snowballs at me. Several weeks ago they drew crosses across the classroom floor with chalk to scare me and mock me. They wanted to see if I, a Jewess, would dare touch one with my foot."

Then breaking down, she began to cry. "The feelings of anti-Semitism are deep-rooted here, no doubt about it, and Comrade Kulik does nothing to smooth them out. On the contrary, the children are not only being encouraged to hate Jews, but they're being taught acts of subversion."

"Tell me, Haya," Sobakin said sharply, "these children who harass you, are they from your class or from the higher grades too? Now let me see. What about this Ohrimko Suchok? I believe he's a second grader?"

"Yes, and he's the worst of them all. I wrote to you about him. He's cunning and deceitful and doesn't obey any rules. He's like a wild animal. He sits right over there!"

Sobakin smiled condescendingly. "Your charges are certainly reasons for concern, but it appears to me the real problem lies not in the children, but in your inability to control them. You're the teacher and therefore you and not the headmaster are responsible for your pupils. From what I see of the situation, you haven't established any kind of rapport with the children. To put it simply, you've failed to earn their respect."

Haya's eyes bulged and she shot back hotly, "If I'm responsible for my class, then why did our good headmaster Kulik interfere with my instruction and appoint Ohrimko Suchok class chief? How is it, I ask, that the most unruly pupil in the entire school suddenly attains the most honorable and entrusted position? What have you to say about that?"

Kulik had been standing near the door. Haya had just launched a most dangerous assault against him and he knew he had to move quickly to defend himself. He hastily stepped before the officials.

"Allow me to straighten this matter out, comrades. In the first place, I'm not a subversive of any kind or an anti-Semite, for that matter. The very notion is absurd and repulsive to me. As you can see for yourselves, everything in the school is run and has been run in strict conformity with Soviet policy. Haya Sruleyevna is at odds with me for making the worst pupil in the entire school chief of his class. Perhaps I acted in haste, I admit, but since the boy responded to no measure of discipline, I decided to run a sort of experiment—one of positive reinforcement, so to speak, one that would encourage him to attain a higher level of importance and self-esteem. And if I may say so myself, it's been a great success." Then turning to Haya, looking directly at her, "Tell me, honestly, Comrade Haya, after the incident with the crosses, did Ohrimko's behavior worsen or improve? Why, wasn't it just yesterday that you came into my office with only good things to say about him?"

Haya turned white and stammered. "I . . . uh . . . I . . ."

Yeliseyenko tapped his foot impatiently. "Well? We're waiting for an answer. What have you got to say to this?"

Glancing helplessly and frantically about the room, looking pleadingly at the officials, she broke down completely. "Oh, it's true, the problem is not Ohrimko, at least not any more. The real truth is it's horrible here and I hate it. Please, comrades, I beg you, get me out of here, transfer me to another school, one closer to Moscow. I can't bear it anymore. Ohrimko did improve, in fact he's even become a good student and a good influence on the others, but still, it's not enough. I implore you, send me to a Russian school. I feel so cooped up here. No one, including the villagers, understands a word I say and I don't understand them."

Yeliseyenko patted her gently on the shoulder. "All right, Haya, we'll take your concerns into account when we investigate this matter further. But you must collect yourself, please. You'll be hearing from us shortly." Then he looked briefly at his watch, and signaled to his colleagues. "Now we must be off to the next class."

The men hastily made their way down the corridor to the grade three classroom, where Ivashkevich was bent over his desk, leafing through a pile of papers.

"Comrade Ivashkevich?" Yeliseyenko poked his head through the door. "Excuse the interruption. We're running an investigation of the school today and would appreciate a few minutes of your time. May we?"

Looking up, somewhat startled, Ivashkevich took off his spectacles and shoved his papers aside. "By all means, come in, please."

Yeliseyenko wasted no time in getting down to business. "We'd like to ask you a few questions regarding the school. How long have you been teaching here?"

"About two months."

"And how do you feel about the school? In other words, in your opinion is it being run efficiently and effectively?"

Ivashkevich hesitated. "Things aren't bad. However . . . how shall I put it . . . uh . . ."

Sobakin snapped, "Out with it, we don't have all day."

"Well," Ivashkevich said, "to put it simply, I find teaching here rather difficult. The people in Hlaby are not Belorussian as I was led to believe. The children can't speak a word of it and I have to start from scratch—quite literally from the alphabet. It's created a big headache for me. From what I understood, when the regime assigned me here, I would be among fellow Belorussians, but this is not the case at all. Everyone here speaks Ukrainian."

Visibly agitated, Yeliseyenko pretended to ignore what he had just heard. He started up again, this time about Kulik. "And what about the headmaster? Do you find him competent and reliable?"

"Oh, yes, quite, and I might add, the charges of subversion and anti-Semitism building up against him are complete nonsense. Not only is Comrade Kulik a good headmaster but he's an upstanding citizen. Why Haya Fifkina has built a case against him, I don't know. In my opinion, she's created a mountain out of a molehill. Allow me to speak candidly—our headmaster did a wonderful job in turning that young Ohrimko around. We were all convinced he was hopeless, but Comrade Kulik proved us all wrong and I applaud his efforts. Kulik is setting a fine example for the children and is encouraging them not only to work hard but to take their schooling seriously."

Yeliseyenko glowered. He said abruptly, "Yes, in any case, I'm sure before long we'll get to the bottom of this whole mess." Then after taking a slip of paper from his coat pocket and reading it, he cleared his throat and brought up another matter. "Hrisko Suchok and Cornelius Kovzalo—I would like to speak to these two men right away. I believe they live here in Hlaby. Would you be so kind as to bring them to the office immediately?"

Eagerly, Ivashkevich rose from his seat, and grabbing his overcoat from the closet, set off for the village. Barely ten minutes passed before he returned with the two men. The first to come through the door was Cornelius, followed by Hrisko Suchok.

Yeliseyenko called out, "Grigory Osipovich Suchok."

"Uh, that's me, comrade," Suchok pulled off his big sheepskin hat, and crumpling it between his hands, bowed obsequiously.

"Ohrimko is your son, is that correct?"

Suchok flushed a deep crimson. This was the very question he wanted to avoid, and at all costs. He started apologetically, "Yes, he's mine. He's a troublemaker, no doubt, and I'm the first to admit it. But I'll have you know, I've already taken serious steps to set him straight. I thrashed him until he was black and blue all over and couldn't walk for a week."

Yeliseyenko seemed unimpressed. "Yes, well, yes." Then looking him in the eye, "Tell me, did the headmaster ever call you to the school regarding your son's behavior? And if so, did he discuss with you the incidents involving Haya Fifkina?"

"Yes, as a matter of fact he did." Suchok loosened the top button of his overcoat. He felt extremely nervous standing before such important government officials. "Exactly one month ago, on a Thursday I believe it was, I came to see the headmaster regarding my boy. I begged him to teach him a lesson once and for all—to stretch him out on a bench and give him a good whipping or to strap his knuckles until they cracked. But he refused. He said he came to our village to teach the children and not to beat them. Uh, if you don't mind my saying so, I think our headmaster is too soft-hearted. I think he lacks a certain toughness, which I believe is necessary for this job. As you can very well see for yourself, even though I'm a simple man, I was forced to take matters into my own hands. And now, thanks to my firm stand, my Ohrimko's finally learned his lesson."

Yeliseyenko looked sternly at Suchok. "About your son's assaults on Comrade Haya. I find this sort of behavior extremely alarming and it sets a dangerous precedent. I'm suggesting it was you who riled him up at home, and that it was you and not the headmaster who encouraged him to be anti-Semitic. A boy of seven has to get his ideas from somewhere. It's obvious to me Ohrimko got them from you."

Suchok's eyes popped and he let out a little yelp. "God help me if I should be guilty of such a thing! I want you to know I'm a good, hard-working Soviet citizen and could not even bring myself to think such thoughts, let alone utter them. I have to tell you, my wife and I have good friends among Jews as we do among our own people. And let me say, there's good and bad in both. Allow me to explain. Just last summer in the Pinsk marketplace Isaac Zimmerman tried to swindle me out of a bag of beans—he's a worthless crook who tips his scales. And then another time I stopped to visit Bobli Abramovich. When I brought my eggs to her stall, she not only gave me a good and fair price, but she even offered me tea and cakes. A fine woman and a sweet soul, may God bless her and her family."

Yeliseyenko shook his head indignantly. He had heard enough. He quickly changed his line of questioning. "What did you do during Polish occupation?"

Suchok tried to be sensible. "I had a small tract of land. Two-tenths were arable, eight-tenths swamp. My old lady and I worked hard day and night to keep our family fed."

Suchok looked worried. He couldn't stop thinking about his son. Disaster was about to strike, he was sure of it, and he wanted to be prepared. With not much confidence in himself, wringing his hands, he sputtered, "About my boy, I give you my solemn word you'll have no more trouble from him. He'll be like an angel. Please, just give him another chance. And if he should dare step out of line again, I'll beat him so hard his eyes will jump out of their sockets."

Yeliseyenko at last lost his temper. He ended abruptly, "That'll be all for now, Suchok. But remember, we're not finished with you yet. You'll be hearing from us soon. You may go." He swung around to Cornelius. "Comrade Cornelius. You are the Village Chairman, I understand?"

"Yes, that's right." Cornelius gave a slight bow. Unlike Suchok, he felt completely at ease and was extremely honored and happy to be in such fine company. He boasted, "I am the one who is responsible for the village and I report directly to the higher authorities in Pinsk on a monthly basis. I want you to know, I keep my eyes wide open and can spot counterrevolutionary activity in a split second. And I have the school under my watch too. The headmaster, how shall I put it, is a bit of an, uh, nonconformist . . . And when I learned he provoked the schoolchildren and set them against Haya Fifkina, I couldn't keep myself from getting involved. Why, just the other day I came to the school to have it out with him, to teach him a thing or two. I told him the children must not only be taught tolerance but that they must be given lessons on the Soviet constitution." Then leaning forward, as if speaking in confidence, "Allow me to tell you something about Comrade Kulik. He may be headmaster of our school, but he has no understanding of law and order. I said to him, 'You've got to teach the children to like Jews. Things are getting more and more out of hand around here. There's disruption in the classrooms and unrest in the village.'"

Pausing to scratch his head, thinking of where to go from there, in the end he dropped his train of thought and went on at length about himself. "I'm a simple man, from a simple family, and I have no education from a university, like Comrade Kulik. But I'm a loyal Soviet citizen. As you probably know, I fought hand and foot against the Polish imperialist army and they even threw me in jail for my Communist beliefs. And I endured terrible injustices, until, of course, our Soviet brothers liberated us. As you can see, I've made my way up from nothing to Village Chairman. Therefore, I speak candidly when I say I think the headmaster is . . ."

Yeliseyenko cut him off. "Enough! Your sentences are without beginning or end and you make no sense." Then somewhat more calmly, "Now let's go back to the beginning, let's go back to the day you came to the school to confront Comrade Kulik. What happened exactly?"

"Well, things were not too pleasant. Kulik grabbed me by the scruff of the neck and threw me out the door. On the porch he kicked me with the tip of his boot so hard I was bruised for the longest time after. I can't even begin to explain how painful it was to sit."

Yeliseyenko shook his head. "Cornelius, you're an idiot from beginning to end. I don't blame the headmaster for kicking you out, and I can't say I wouldn't have done the same. You should know your place by now and shouldn't stick your nose where it doesn't belong. Tend to matters in the village and leave the operations of the school to the headmaster. Understand? We're finished with you now, you may go."

Silently, in a huff, Cornelius made for the door. Out in the yard, he ran, stumbling. Things had turned out badly for him; he brooded over it all the way home. His very vital comments and observations had not even been taken into consideration, and his impressions of the headmaster had been ignored completely. How could this be? After all, wasn't he the Village Chairman, an important figure in the region, appointed by the Party? Why had the officials treated him so disrespectfully? No matter how hard he tried, he couldn't understand it.

All the while Kulik stood in the middle of the room with his hands behind his back. He was considerably on edge. The room felt hot, and his temples throbbed. After witnessing the circus with Haya Fifkina and Ivashkevich, and later with Suchok and Cornelius, he didn't know what to make of it all—it seemed so ridiculous, like some big joke. Now it was his turn. He braced himself for the final round.

Sobakin was the first to speak. He said severely, "Well, Comrade Kulik, what are we to do with you? Hmm? We know all that's going on, in fact we've been watching you for some time. No, you can't hide anything from us. But because we live in a democratic society, the most democratic in the world, we've agreed to hear you out. I'm sure once you explain yourself, everything will be cleared up."

Lighting a cigarette, he smiled slyly and went on. "I understand you used brutal force to throw the Village Chairman out of the school. Your unorthodox method of excusing him is not, and I repeat, *not* in line with Soviet policy. To make a public display of a Soviet representative is no light matter. It's equivalent to making a mockery of the government itself."

Kulik's voice barely obeyed him. "In the first place, when I threw Cornelius out of the school, I felt I was not throwing out a government representative but a rude and ignorant person who was wasting my time. I had a stack of papers to mark, not to mention a list of school matters to tend to."

Sobakin gave him a piercing look. "Cornelius is an idiot, that has already been established, but the truth of the matter is he came to you regarding a very serious problem—one of anti-Semitism. And quite plainly you refrained from hearing him out. Now as a result a scandal has erupted, and a scandal in the school, especially one of this magnitude, does not redound to your credit. And furthermore, where Ohrimko is concerned, it appears some strict disciplinary action needs to be taken, something you've neglected to do. From where I stand, it's plain to see you've demonstrated nothing but hostility toward the new system. I understand you've even been sabotaging the Clubhouse meetings."

Kulik felt as if he had been stabbed in the back by a thousand knives. The game had taken on a more dangerous spin, more dangerous than he could have brought himself to imagine. Evidence was being compiled against him, evidence built on lies and pretenses, and these lies and pretenses were enough to send him to his doom. He had to watch his every move and to prepare himself for whatever came his way.

Looking at Sobakin, suddenly he was overcome by feelings of hatred and revulsion such as he had never felt before. He wanted to rip apart the man's flesh, to strangle him, to shout: "How many deep, dark secrets are buried behind that heavily decorated uniform of yours, Simon Stepanovich? How many innocent men, women and children did you murder today? How many mass graves did you fill? You're nothing more than a beast, there is no humanity in you."

His heart beating rapidly, Kulik tried to calm himself. He said to Sobakin soberly and carefully, "Your accusations are all without foundation. It's true Ohrimko Suchok created trouble for Haya, but to deem him, or even me for that matter, an anti-Semite because of this is simplistic and premature. The boy has been impossible, I agree, not only toward Haya, but also toward his fellow classmates and many of the villagers. He repeatedly hurled rocks and snowballs at passersby, and on more than one occasion people came to the school to complain about him. And about anti-Semitism, I might add, in Hlaby there is no such thing because the villagers for the most part don't really know what a Semite is or what it means. In fact, prior to Haya Fifkina's arrival, there were no Jews in the village. This is an out-of-the-way place where people for the most part are simple-minded and accustomed only to their own kind; visitors rarely pass through. I'm working hard to try to reeducate the children and to help them adjust not only to our new social order but also to the Belorussian language. I have dedicated myself to helping create the best Soviet state I possibly can. And I trust, of course, I will have your full support in this."

Sobakin had long since stopped listening to Kulik. Staring directly ahead of him, he seemed as if he had already come to his own conclusions. He said with a supercilious air, "It's clear to me we've been led on a wild goose chase. Obviously Haya is new at her job and prone to hysteria. The way I see it, the problems in the school are standard ones, and with proper attention in time they will work themselves out." Then directly to Kulik, in a show of friendliness, "Vanya—I hope you don't mind me calling you by your diminutive—you're still a young man and have a lot to learn. Despite all your shortcomings, all in all, you did the right thing with Ohrimko and I commend you for your efforts. A fine job indeed."

Swinging around, he called out to his colleagues, "Well, gentlemen, it looks like we've been here long enough. Shall we be on our way?"

In a great clatter, the men found their way out of the school and across the yard to the big black car that stood waiting for them by the gates. Kulik heard the motor start up and he watched the car push off along the snow-covered road in the direction of Pinsk. His nerves were shattered. Everything that had happened was real and frightening, and yet nothing was as it seemed. He felt as if he had been tossed from one hand to another, kicked and punched, roughed up. The government officials had played their usual games and applied standard intimidation tactics, but somehow he had been able to withstand them all. They had tried to break him, to confound him, to frighten him, and they had failed. But how long before they came after him again? And in the next round he might not be so lucky.

————

Early the next morning before classes started, Kulik summoned the Suchoks to his office with the intention of somehow resolving, at least in part, the situation concerning their son. He expected the family to knock on his door sometime around seven, but to his great surprise, the door banged open and Ohrimko came flying across the room. His face was red and bruised and he was crying and whimpering. His father came after him waving his fists, followed by his wife.

"Get on your hands and knees and kiss the headmaster's feet!" Suchok grabbed hold of his son's collar and kicked him from behind. "Beg him for mercy! This will be the end of your disobedience once and for all. You've been a troublemaker long enough!"

Tears streamed down the boy's cheeks as he threw himself on the headmaster, grabbing at his ankles. He whimpered louder; his words were barely audible.

Kulik looked on with shock and outrage. "Stop this exhibition at once!" he yelled. Seizing Ohrimko's arm and pulling him up, he sat him on a chair next to his desk and handed him a handkerchief. He tried to calm him down. "Hush, quiet! I don't want to hear any more of those noises from you." Then glancing sharply at Ohrimko's father, "I intend to put an end to this entire matter right now, but calmly and rationally, and in a civilized manner."

Suchok's face, as bullish as his son's, crimsoned. "I'm trying to straighten my boy out once and for all. He's always up to no good. Why did you call us here this morning? What did he do now? If there's one thing he responds to, it's a good thrashing. Maybe if you did the same he'd be better behaved in school."

Kulik gave Suchok an icy glare. "I don't want to see this sort of display in my office again. Brutality only gives rise to more brutality, and it solves nothing. Ohrimko has done nothing wrong, that's not why I called you to my office today. Now, please, have a seat."

Turning back to Ohrimko with a reassuring smile, he walked over to the filing cabinet, pulled open the top drawer and took out a large cardboard box. He handed it to the boy. "Here, son, this is for you."

The boy sat frozen, his eyes fixed on the box, not knowing what to do with it. He thought maybe his punishment was inside—a rod or a leather strap. He was trembling all over.

When the headmaster lifted the lid, Ohrimko's eyes lit up in astonishment and disbelief. Inside there were all kinds of things he had never seen before. It was all too good to be true, he couldn't believe his eyes! First he pulled out a bright red box engine with six driving wheels, then a car, then another and another, then a handful of rails, some curved, some straight, all with small teeth at the ends.

"See these teeth at the end of the rails?" Kulik said. "When you attach them to each other, you can form a track. You can make it any shape you like. Don't be shy. Come and help me."

The headmaster and Ohrimko worked together quietly to assemble the parts, and before long a track in the shape of an ellipse filled the entire desk. Kulik placed the locomotive on the rails and then he and Ohrimko hooked up the five additional cars. From the box Kulik brought out four small batteries, tucked them into an opening on the side of the locomotive, and pressed a button. Almost instantly the engine took off, pulling all five cars behind it. The boy watched in excited fascination. Never had he seen anything so remarkable— a toy moving by itself, not pushed by anyone. He watched the train go round and round for the longest time, hypnotized by it.

Kulik was delighted by the boy's reaction. He thought to himself, An impoverished child far from civilized society—with this small toy, the whole world has opened up for him.

Kulik turned to Ohrimko's father. "Do you have a big enough table at home for this train?"

"Oh, yes, yes." Suchok fawned, squinting and bowing. He was completely thrown off guard by what had just happened and wondered how it was that his son came to be so handsomely rewarded, and for being a troublemaker! It didn't make any sense to him. Nonetheless, he was overwhelmed by the headmaster's generosity, and felt deeply honored at the special attention accorded his son. "The table's very big and strong. Yes, yes, very big. I built it myself just last spring from some oak planks."

"Wonderful." Kulik was delighted. Then turning to the boy, "Son, this train is for you because you've earned it. Your behavior in school this last week has been outstanding and your schoolwork has improved even beyond my expectation. If you have trouble putting it together once you get home, I'll gladly come by and help you. Now go on, run along."

At that moment Ohrimko's mother, who until now had sat quietly, suddenly clasped her hands. She shouted, "Good Lord! For something like this to happen to our family!" Then shaking her head, "No, no, we absolutely cannot accept such a fine gift. A toy like this is not for the likes of poor, ignorant *moujiks* like us. No, Ohrimko cannot accept it."

Ignoring his mother, Ohrimko quickly and eagerly took apart the train set and put the pieces carefully back into the box. He put it under his arm, thanked the headmaster, bade him a good morning and scooted out the door. His mother and father followed close behind.

Kulik watched the family cross the yard. Ohrimko's father was looking proudly at his son and telling him, "It's truly a wonderful gift, son. You're very lucky. Work hard in school and maybe one day you'll learn how a real train works. Maybe one day you'll even become an engineer. You just might be the first in the Suchok family to make something of himself."

Kulik believed that the problems with Ohrimko had been solved. But he knew that the issue at play was not what it appeared to be on the surface. It was not about an unruly child, but about a system of provocation, manipulation, and intimidation. It would break whomever it chose, and by whatever means. He was just thankful that this day had started as well as it had.

CHAPTER 17

Rather unexpectedly, an NKVD man moved into the small wooden house next to the Bohdanovich home. He was of average build and height, in his mid-forties, with thick graying sideburns. He left his house every morning at precisely the same time, carrying a bulging satchel, and hurried down the road toward the city center.

Marusia watched him from her living room window. His presence made her suspicious and resentful. Peaceful Luninetska Street, rarely disturbed by the sound of a motor car or even a horse-drawn cart, now for the first time had a stranger in its midst, and not just an ordinary stranger, but an NKVD man at that. Even Marusia's parents noticed his comings and goings. Efrosinia went to the trouble of learning his name: Simon Stepanovich Sobakin.

One morning as Simon Stepanovich came out of his house and walked down the narrow walkway to the street, he glanced over a low hedge at the Bohdanovich house, only a few meters away. The movement of a curtain caught his attention. Someone was watching him, spying on him. He crossed over into his neighbor's yard, peered in the window and became completely enthralled. He saw a girl there, very pretty, not much over twenty, her face fresh and full of life, framed by a pile of lovely brown hair. The two gazed at each other for a few seconds. Then, extremely embarrassed, the girl fled. Sobakin pressed his face against the glass and tapped on the window several times, trying to get her to come back. He was smiling, delighted by this unexpected encounter, and with someone so lovely, so charming!

Marusia was mortified, angry with herself for having spied on him in the first place. To make matters worse, she was certain it would be only a matter of time before he appeared at her door and introduced himself to her. And sure enough, the following Sunday, shortly before noon, he came to call. But he did not come alone; he arrived in the company of a man, younger than he by a good fifteen years, and not a stranger to the Bohdanovich household.

Old Valentyn was the first to greet the visitors. "Why, Nikolai Kopitkin!" He extended his hand joyfully. "The esteemed Pinsk poet. What a pleasant surprise! Come in, come in! You haven't forgotten us after all!"

Nikolai shook hands with the old man, and bowed. "Good day to you, citizen. How's the family? In good health, I'm sure. In any case, I've come by today with a friend who also happens to be a neighbor of yours. May I introduce Lieutenant Simon Stepanovich Sobakin."

"Ah, our new neighbor, of course!" Valentyn turned to the lieutenant. "I've heard so much about you. Finally we meet. It's an honor to have a government dignitary in my humble abode. Truly an honor."

"Please, no need for ceremony." Sobakin, distracted, said impatiently. "Just treat me as you would anyone else."

Valentyn offered the men refreshment, and the three sat and chatted for several minutes about the weather. Hearing their voices, Efrosinia hurried in from the kitchen, wiping her hands on her apron. When she saw Sobakin, she was stunned and baffled. How did a prominent NKVD man, a lieutenant at that, come to be in her living room? And why was he laughing and drinking, with, of all people, her husband? A man of such high standing never casually and openly socialized with his neighbors like that. Narrowing her eyes suspiciously, she wondered why he was here. Was he looking for something or maybe someone? Was he on a mission of some sort? She studied his features closely: his high rounded cheekbones, his slanted blue eyes . . . She thought she detected a vague craftiness in his expression. Sobakin looked at her as if he had read her thoughts. "So, *Mamasha*, you think you recognize me, is that it? Have you seen me some place before?"

Efrosinia answered slowly, "You look familiar to me. Yes, I'm sure I've seen you before, but I can't quite recall where. Maybe at the marketplace or the town hall. Your eyes are small, and they have a strange shine to them, a shine, if I may say so, that's almost diabolical."

"Diabolical!" Sobakin slapped his knee and burst into a fit of laughter. He was finding the lady of the house most amusing. "Efrosinia Sofronovna, don't you think you are being a little hard on your new neighbor?"

As she was about to reply, Valentyn, knowing all too well the looseness of his wife's tongue, was quick to cut her off. "Comrade Lieutenant, please excuse my wife. She has a habit of speaking before thinking. Don't pay any attention to her."

Having said this, he prepared himself for a scene, a scene like no other. He had challenged her openly, and before such a formidable guest. His wife was short-tempered and outspoken and with a blink of an eye could bring disaster upon the whole household. Second after second passed, but for some reason she did not utter a word. Watching her nervously, he became totally confounded when she sank into an armchair with her hands on her lap, almost as if she had resigned herself. She did not appear angry; but calm and composed. Valentyn remained on his guard. Something was definitely brewing in that old head of hers, not unlike the calm before the storm. Then without giving her husband a second glance, Efrosinia turned to Sobakin and said, quietly and seriously, "Tell me, comrade, what good is a father who's so lazy he can't even bring himself to travel to Lvov to bring home his ailing son?"

Finally there it was, she had come out with it. Valentyn grumbled at her, "I knew you'd be up to your old tricks, I should have known. Now you're even bringing our guests into it!" Then apologetically to Sobakin, "As you can see, my wife's not responsible. . . ."

"Not responsible! Hah!" Efrosinia shot back. "Is that what you call it? Why, you old goat! You're nothing more than a parasite!

Our son's in Lvov somewhere, maybe even dying, and instead of going after him, you just stretch yourself out on that godforsaken sofa and nod off. You don't care what happens to him, you don't care about anything."

Growing more and more wound-up, not realizing what she was doing, she fell to mimicking her husband, something she did often when she was at the end of her rope. Exaggerating her gestures, pulling at her chin, she looked and sounded remarkably like him: "'Leave it be, precious, it's all in God's hands, precious. We cannot change what was meant to be.'"

Then looking to her guests for encouragement and support: "I ask you, gentlemen, should I give up on my Lonia simply because he's in 'God's hands'? And am I to wait for 'God' to put him on the train and to bring him home from Lvov? And am I also to believe that that stupid sofa that has been screeching for well over a year is in 'God's hands' too? Will 'God' take a hammer to it? Have you ever heard anything so ridiculous? The truth of the matter is I have a lazy, useless husband whose greatest challenge of the day is getting up in the morning."

Sobakin, in an effort to appear polite, said, "Uh, yes, I agree, the situation regarding your son appears most unfortunate. May I ask, have you had any contact with him?"

Efrosinia's mouth dropped open. She was struck dumb by Sobakin's interest in her son, who was a total stranger to him. She suddenly saw in him the answer to all her prayers. Why hadn't she thought of it from the start? He was an official, a man of distinction, who had connections in all the right places. If anyone could bring her Lonia home, it was Sobakin. Her eyes welling with tears, she looked at him as her savior and said hastily, "We receive a letter about once a week. But it's always the same: 'Dear Family, I'm feeling much better and the moment I feel well enough I shall come home'; or 'Dear Loved Ones, bear with me a little longer'; or 'My Dear *Mamasha*, I will be home in a few weeks.' Every letter we receive is the same, full of hope and promise, but Lonia has yet to show his face. Here, read the letters for yourself." From a drawer in a small table by the sofa, she brought out a wooden box holding a pile of envelopes tied with string.

Sobakin reluctantly took them from her. The old woman's complaining had already more than tested his nerves, and he was rapidly losing what little patience he had left. The truth of the matter was, her Lonia was of no concern to him, he couldn't care less if he was alive or dead. He had come there only to meet the girl. After quickly scanning the room, he started to read the first letter with feigned interest.

"My dear ones, please don't worry about me, I'm still in the hospital, but any day I expect to be released. A month ago I hemorrhaged and things looked rather grim, but happily my lungs are on the mend and I am almost as good as new. See you soon. Yours, Lonia."

Sobakin opened other letters and read them aloud. In one, Lonia wrote that he had moved into an apartment on Lichakivsky Street and was even attending classes daily at the university, preparing for exams; in another, Lonia was completely healthy, but not yet able to return home because he was still under observation by doctors at the clinic; in yet another, Lonia was fully recuperated and would be visiting Pinsk very soon.

When Sobakin had finished the last letter, he was in a terrible mood. The girl had not showed up. Fuming, practically throwing the letters on the table, he was ready to leave. He had wasted enough time. As he got up and excused himself, Efrosinia was quick to grab him by the arm. Had she not been in such a state of distress, she would have noticed the anger and resentment in his face. Her voice trembled. "What do you think, Lieutenant? I know the letters are from Lonia, but my daughter Marusia disagrees. She believes they are all forgeries."

"Marusia?" At the sound of the girl's name, Sobakin paused. She could make an appearance at any moment. And probably he could win her over by simply pretending to take an interest in her brother, by asking about his studies, his health, or why she thought his letters were forgeries. Yes, that would work. A few minutes passed, but still no sign of the girl. His blood boiled. Where was she? Why hadn't she come? What if he had missed her? What if she had left to go into town to run errands or visit with friends? He felt his face grow hot with exasperation. He wanted no more of this bothersome family and their trifling problems. Damn them! Forcing a smile, he indulged the old woman one last time.

"If you don't mind, *Mamasha*, permit me to copy your son's address. I understand your profound grief. It's really unfortunate. However, from his letters it appears that your son is fine and even enjoying his time in Lvov. But then on the other hand, if your daughter believes the letters are forgeries, well, of course, that's another matter. If she's here, perhaps I could talk it over with her." He added, "I'll personally look into this matter. Within a week I promise you will have your Lonia home with you."

The old woman was overwhelmed by the NKVD man's generosity. "Will you really bring my Lonia home? Bless you. Bless you. I will never forget your kindness." Taking his hands in hers and squeezing them tightly, she whispered with quavering emotion, "Now I understand what being a true Russian means."

The warmth of Efrosinia's grip filled Sobakin with loathing and disgust; almost instantly he pulled away. Moving toward the door, he signaled for Nikolai to follow. He was not about to waste a second more of his valuable time. Obviously the girl was not in the house. Storming out of the room, not watching where he was going, he almost collided with someone standing in the hallway by the staircase. She was very pretty, with lips the color of raspberries and there was a penetrating scent of lilac around her. Sobakin stood thunderstruck. It was Marusia! His heart gave a thud. The girl tried to pass, but he blocked her way.

Valentyn, seeing his daughter, hastened to beckon her into the living room. "Marusia, you've come in the nick of time." Then to Sobakin, "Allow me to introduce my daughter, Maria Valentynovna."

Sobakin, more than delighted, extended his hand. "Simon Stepanovich. I'm pleased to meet you."

With flushed cheeks, she said quickly, "Is it true? I overheard what you said. Will you really bring my brother home?" She didn't try to hide the fact that she had been eavesdropping.

"Yes, I will, Maria Valentynovna." Sobakin liked what he saw: tall, slender, very pretty, a full bosom. "Before the week's end." He was seized by a rush of excitement.

Marusia dropped her eyes. She felt confused and disoriented. Sobakin had a penetrating and hungry look in his eyes, as if he were devouring her with them. His powerful presence was everywhere in the room. After a long and terrible moment, to her great relief she caught sight of Nikolai standing by the window. She cried, "Why, Nikolai Nikitich! Good to see you. Just the other day I picked up the *Polissian Pravda* and read one of your poems. Very curious; in fact, rather surprising."

Nikolai coughed and said hotly, "Maria Valentynovna, I believe I already made it clear to you on a previous occasion—I no longer go by the name Nikitich. I now use my pseudonym, Kopitkin. A poet of rapidly growing renown such as myself ought not to have a *moujik* name like Nikitich, but rather a strong, solid Russian one. Hence, the name Kopitkin."

"Excuse me." Marusia was embarrassed. "Nikolai Kopitkin, yes, of course, I'm sorry, it must have slipped my mind. As I was saying, I read your poem and was most impressed by it. Your political message was very striking, even uplifting. Quite a change from your usual style, I must say."

"Yes, that's correct, Maria Valentynovna." Nikolai was now more than willing to discuss his craft. He combed his hair back with his palms. "My preoccupation with flowers and nature is over—too bourgeois, too trivial. I now write about the times, about revolution and the inevitability of socialism. I look reality in the face, so to speak."

Sobakin, who had been following the conversation with marked interest, let out a loud, abrupt laugh. He found Nikolai Kopitkin's writing a waste of time in general, and inessential to the common cause. True, Nikolai was trying to better himself by Russifying his name, and was even perhaps succeeding on the surface, but still, at heart he was a *moujik*, and all the name-changing in the world would never fix that. Slapping Nikolai on the back, he decided to have a little fun with him.

"Nikolai, have you ever written about frogs? They're here in your primordial mudlands by the thousands. Surely their mere number ought to have brought you inspiration. And not to worry, if your poem doesn't work out, our new Soviet Union has plenty of good editors. They could iron things out for you in a flash. Hah, hah, hah!"

Nikolai's mouth twitched with irritation and he could feel the tips of his ears burning. Sobakin had gone too far with his insults and he resolved to put a stop to it. He said haughtily, "First and foremost I am a poet, and, I might add, not just an ordinary poet, but a Soviet poet. I write for the betterment of socialism and society. If our regime requires that I relate some kind of allegorical message involving birds, or even frogs for that matter, then, of course, I will put my pen to work. Poetry is the nation's guide and conscience. It depicts the basis of revolution."

Sobakin, still laughing, punched Nikolai playfully on the arm. "What an old card you are! If only we had more of your kind around. We'd take the world by storm!"

Nikolai Kopitkin seethed with anger and resentment. In an attempt to save face before the Bohdanoviches, he decided to laugh off this humiliation, to treat it like some big joke. But looking at Efrosinia, then at Valentyn, then at the girl, he was dismayed to find them shifting awkwardly, straining to contain their embarrassment. He thought they were probably thinking to themselves, Poor Nikolai Kopitkin has just been mowed to the ground, and so mercilessly or Poor Nikolai Kopitkin, the renowned Pinsk poet, is so misunderstood.

Marusia felt that Sobakin had demonstrated a cold cruelty she would not have wished upon her worst enemy. She felt sympathy for Nikolai, even to the point of defending him in some way, but then she recalled the way he had acted at the New Year's Eve

dance. During their brief encounter, Marusia had addressed her
cousin Sergei in the familiar, Seryoza, thereby demonstrating that
she was directly and closely associated with him, a *moujik*. On top
of that, Nikolai had arrogantly and rudely snubbed her and walked
away, leaving her standing there. There was absolutely no reason
for her to show any sympathy for him now. Instead she decided
that Nikolai Kopitkin was a self-serving, irresolute louse who got
what he deserved.

And as for Simon Stepanovich, he seemed to derive pleasure
from his own cruelty. There was something unpleasant and
revolting about his face, and the airs he assumed made her wince.
Quickly she concluded that he would make a dangerous liaison
and she should stay as far away from him as possible. She felt afraid
of him. But at the same time something was pulling her toward
him, something she didn't understand. She felt oddly restless, finding it difficult to repress an emotion building inside her. Could she
possibly be feeling physically drawn to this crude and offensive
NKVD man, old enough to be her father, and who reported daily
to the Zovty Prison? The thought made her shudder.

However, she found herself no longer thinking of him as an
agent of the Kremlin carrying out unthinkable deeds, but simply
as an official, respected, a dignitary. She tried to untangle her feelings toward him, but the more she tried, the more confused she
became. His harshness and brutality were becoming attractive to
her; even his uniform was arousing in her a passion she was finding difficult to understand. Could it be she was ready to embrace
the devil himself?

Valentyn, picking up his glass, called out, "Another round for
our guests! Marusia, pour more drinks."

Marusia quickly filled up the glasses, including her own, and sat
down in an armchair opposite the NKVD man, who settled on the
sofa next to Nikolai Kopitkin. Her cheeks were flushed. The drink
had gone rapidly to her head. Sobakin kept staring at her. She was
slender, pleasing to look at, so innocent and spontaneous, and her
movements so supple. She was everything he had heard about

provincial girls from distant republics, and he wanted her all to himself. And though her face was fresh and youthful, and her flesh almost like silk, there was something very grown-up about her. With each passing moment he became more and more enthralled by her beauty. Everything about her fired him up. And the more Marusia sipped her drink, the more exuberant she became.

Giddily, perhaps even unconsciously, she became flirtatious, unexpectedly displaying a new sensuality. She smiled, laughed and tossed her head. Sobakin grew wild with excitement. He fixed his attention on her swelling breasts. The power of her own femininity intoxicated her. And hers was a femininity like no other, capable of capturing the heart even of a cold and hardened NKVD man. She found the prospect thrilling.

The guests stayed late into the night, and at last some time around midnight they bade their farewells. After locking up the house, Valentyn and Efrosinia retired, but Marusia lingered in the living room, trying to sort out all that had happened. She couldn't get Sobakin's face out of her mind. It was round and puggish, pockmarked, in many ways unattractive, even ugly. His slanted eyes were stony and lecherous. His loud voice, his big, rough hands, just the mere thought of him made her shudder. He had an animal presence and she felt as if she were being slowly consumed by him, eaten alive.

Nevertheless, there was something intriguing and captivating about Sobakin; an unknown force seemed to be drawing her toward him. He was a Russian officer, influential, a man of consequence. Never in her wildest imagination had she ever dreamt she would meet a man like that. She was flattered by the attention he paid her. He was not only an important government agent, but a man of honor, a man of his word. After all, he had promised to bring Lonia home, and she truly believed he would do just that. With this comforting thought in mind, she went to bed, and fell into a sound sleep.

The next day, some time in the early afternoon, there was a knock on the front door. Marusia, racing out from the kitchen where she was helping her mother prepare lunch, opened the door to a small blond boy, not more than ten years old. He shoved a largish paper-wrapped parcel at her, and took off down the street. There was a card affixed to the parcel: *For the charming and effervescent Marusia, with best regards, Simon Stepanovich.* She ripped off the wrapping and gasped in disbelief. It was a shiny black coat, softer than anything she had ever seen—it was a Persian lamb! She had never seen anything so beautiful. She had always dreamed of owning such an exquisite coat, but it was always just that, a dream. And now as if by a miracle she owned one. She saw herself as the luckiest girl in the world.

With great care she took the coat out of the box, and half closing her eyes, brushed it tenderly across her face, delighting in its velvety softness. Then something cold and stiff scratched against her cheek. Sewed just below the collar was a label in large italic letters: *Kranza.* A chill ran down her spine. Yuri Kranza had been a well-known Pinsk furrier. Just last Christmas he and his family had disappeared; his shop was now empty and boarded up. It was rumored that they had been shipped off to a camp somewhere in Siberia. The coat slipped out of her hands and fell to the floor. She hated the coat now, and she hated Simon Stepanovich even more. Her thoughts went in circles, and kept returning to the label: *Kranza.* She kicked the coat away from her; she wanted to destroy it, to rip it to pieces.

But after a few minutes, her mood changed. She knelt to pick up the coat and softly, with the tips of her fingers, began to stroke the back, the sleeves, and the lapels. What was the point of worrying about the Kranza family now; after all, they were gone, and nothing would bring them back. And anyway, there was no concrete evidence about what happened to them, it was all just rumor and speculation.

Thus with a clear conscience, she laid the coat carefully out on the sofa: it was double-breasted, bell-shaped, with cuffed sleeves, undoubtedly the latest fashion in Western Europe. It was so soft and lovely, too lovely to throw on the floor. And it was her coat, given to her as a gift, a coat that distinguished and sophisticated women even in Moscow would have hungered for. As its owner, she felt very privileged and important. She ripped off the label, and hurled it into the fireplace, where it sizzled a moment, and turned to ash.

In the kitchen, she stood before the full-length mirror by the door and admired herself. "How gorgeous I look, how absolutely gorgeous!" It certainly flattered her: it made her lips redder and fuller, her eyes greener, deeper, and it made her skin lighter, almost as white as snow. She couldn't get enough of herself.

"Mother! Father!" she shouted at the top of her voice. "Come look at me. Something wonderful has happened! You won't believe your eyes."

Valentyn and Efrosinia met their daughter in the doorway. They tried to speak, but words failed them.

"Isn't it wonderful?" Marusia went on. "Don't I look beautiful? Yes, it's from him, from Simon Stepanovich. The coat is absolutely amazing, I'll be the envy of the entire city." Burying her head deep inside the coat collar, closing her eyes and taking a long, deep breath, she felt as if this might be just a dream. But it wasn't a dream, the coat was real, very real, and it was hers. She cried, "It cost a total of three hundred *zlotys*, and now it's mine, all mine. Imagine!"

Efrosinia, dressed in her usual black loose-fitting housedress, clasped her hands against her chest. "Three hundred *zlotys*! That's a small fortune. It's definitely nothing to sneeze at." This was all too good to be true. Such an expensive coat, three hundred *zlotys*, and just for her Marusia. Beside herself with joy, her voice quavered and broke with emotion. "That Simon Stepanovich, he's a Russian in the true sense of the word: generous, kind-hearted, always striving for the betterment of others." At that moment, she was struck by the immense possibilities this very unusual gesture could open up, not only to Marusia but to the entire family. Quickly she took her daughter's hand in hers.

"Now, Marusia, let's be sensible about this. Simon Stepanovich is a high-ranking Russian officer and he's well-connected, not to mention he's taken a rather strong liking to you. Having someone like him in our lives will certainly put us at an advantage."

But the words were barely out of her mouth, when she had second thoughts and wanted to take them back. She gazed at her daughter anxiously. The truth of the matter was that Simon Stepanovich was not a man in the normal sense but an NKVD man, and NKVD men were the political police, they tortured innocent people in the dungeons of the Zovty Prison, and murdered them. Efrosinia wanted to tell her daughter to stay as far away as possible from Simon Stepanovich; she wanted to tell her to return the coat immediately and not to see him again, but she held her tongue. She was undergoing an intense inner struggle. When at last she did speak, she was horrified by the sound of her own words—it was almost as if it wasn't her voice at all, but someone else's, and the voice, incredibly, was praising Simon Stepanovich.

"It's true, Simon Stepanovich's eyes are on the small side, and rather piercing, but when one looks beyond that, one can see he's a caring and thoughtful individual; obviously his heart is in the right place. He's offered to bring Lonia home, hasn't he? Who would have expected such compassion from a man like him?" Then with a forced smile, trying to sound convincing, even to herself, "As you know, there are many nasty things being said about the NKVD as a whole, but believe me, they're all only rumors. NKVD men are people too. They feel and think just as we do, and they also have their compassionate and vulnerable side."

Avoiding her daughter's eyes, she went on, "Don't agonize over your feelings, child. I know you're confused. I want you to know it's perfectly natural to have a physical attraction for a man, even if he happens to be an NKVD man. The worst thing to do is to fight your feelings. Before the war when the Poles were in power, many of our girls fell in love with men in the Polish secret police, and married them. The only difference now is the secret police happen to be Russian. Falling in love with a Russian is no different from falling in love with a Pole. It's really quite natural."

Her eye fell on her husband sitting by the window, shaking his head. She snapped at him, "What's your problem, old man? What are you grumbling about over there? Are you disagreeing with me? Do you want to ruin everything for us?"

Valentyn scratched his head and shrugged. "I don't like it. That coat I mean, I don't know . . . No good will come of it. It's certainly expensive, but . . ."

He fell silent, trying to think what to say next. When he started up again, he was bolder and more resolute. "Marusia will pay for it in the end. Our daughter is beautiful and with her beauty she'll pay. I would return the coat immediately. 'Thank you very much, Simon Stepanovich,' I would say, 'but I cannot accept such a fine gift.' He's going to charm her, woo her, but in the end she'll be the one to pay. Mark my words, he'll bring her nothing but grief. And when he's done with her he'll cast her aside and in a flash, he'll be gone. Try and find him then! If you want my opinion, Kulik would be a far better suitor: he's well-educated, he holds a good position as school headmaster, and after all, he's one of our own."

"Kulik!" Efrosinia repeated. "What nonsense! I've never heard anything so silly. A village teacher, with a small salary, and no future? Hah! Do you really want your daughter to while away her years in some dark, godforsaken hole surrounded by filthy, illiterate *moujiks*? She's headed for bigger and better things than that. If she plays her cards right, Simon Stepanovich is her ticket to happiness and prosperity. He has an enviable position with the regime, he's a well-respected officer, and he'll go far in the Party. True, he's a Russian, and maybe a bit on the mature side, but we can get used to that. And he's promised to bring Lonia home. All he has to do is make a phone call, ask a few questions, and Lonia will be as good as home."

Efrosinia walked over to look at several photographs hanging over the cabinet. She took down one of the larger ones, and sat on a chair beside the sofa. The photograph was of Lonia as a boy of nine or ten, smiling and holding a ball. Her eyes filled with tears.

"My baby, my poor baby, good lord! I can't believe it, my baby's coming home at last!"

———

Two days passed uneventfully. Efrosinia busied herself preparing for Lonia's arrival, with Marusia's help. Valentyn for the most part lay on the sofa dozing or reading the newspaper. On the third day, the same blond boy appeared at the door with a parcel. It was from Simon Stepanovich, and this time it held a skirt and a small bottle of French perfume. There was no label on the skirt: it had been snipped off. But its quality and style showed clearly that it could have come from only one shop: *Kranza's.* Marusia turned pale and thought about the Kranza family again. They were certainly gone, and their shop was shut. She closed her eyes, and tried to organize her thoughts. The skirt was so attractive and stylish, made of the thinnest, finest wool, and the perfume had come all the way from France. What harm could there be in her keeping them? It certainly wouldn't hurt anybody, and it certainly wouldn't bring the Kranzas back. This was simply a gift from a generous admirer. The skirt would look stunning with her white cotton blouse, or maybe with the red angora sweater her mother had made for her on her last birthday.

The extravagant generosity of Simon Stepanovich was overwhelming. The attention he was giving her was like nothing she had ever experienced. It made her feel wonderful: feminine and beautiful. Excitedly, she hurried down the hallway to tell her parents, but something held her back. Talking to them about Simon Stepanovich would only start more arguments, something she wanted to avoid. Their quarrels always gave her a headache, and she didn't want anything to spoil her good mood. She took the gifts upstairs to her bedroom, and hid them in the back of her closet.

A week went by and to Marusia's surprise Simon Stepanovich did not pay a visit. She wondered what had become of him. A couple of times she even got up early to look for him through the living room window. But he was nowhere to be seen. Where had he gone? Was he hiding someplace? What was he up to? She began to feel uneasy.

And then, to her great surprise, another thought popped into her mind—maybe he was with another woman. She was shaken by jealousy, a new feeling for her. Had he lost interest in her already? For a moment she believed that he really had found someone else.

But then she was struck by another thought, a frightful, shocking thought. "What if he's not with another woman, what if he's in the Zovty Prison?" She couldn't erase this violent image from her mind and it stayed with her for days.

Finally, on the following Sunday, around seven in the evening, Simon Stepanovich appeared at the Bohdanovich house. Without bothering to knock, he walked into the kitchen and to the table where Efrosinia was peeling potatoes. He was in full NKVD uniform, and he was holding a pair of black leather gloves. He looked worn and ill, as if he hadn't slept for days. Efrosinia looked up at him, startled. "Is that you, Lieutenant Sobakin?" She got up, drying her hands on a dishtowel. "Why, comrade, you look like the living dead!"

"I must admit, *Mamasha*, I'm totally exhausted. I've been swamped with work these past few days."

Efrosinia looked at him closely. There was something particularly disconcerting about him tonight and she never hesitated to say what was on her mind. "Your face is stone gray and your eyes are all bloodshot. What have you been doing? What kind of work can possibly make a man look the way you do?"

Simon Stepanovich frowned and before he knew it, he snapped, "What business is it of yours?" Then he looked away. He had to try and restrain himself, at least until he got what he had come for. Marusia was nowhere in sight.

Giving Efrosinia a broad, exaggerated smile, he said, "Yes, *Mamasha*, the reason I came by tonight was to discuss your son. I found out a few things about him. He's quite an exceptional young man. He has not only caught up with the studies he missed while he was in the infirmary, but he's at the top of his class. He'll be an engineer before you know it. You should be very proud of him. But unfortunately, I'm sad to say, he won't be back this week as I promised. My official who visited him on Lichakivsky Street was quick to advise him not to interrupt his studies because it could greatly affect his graduation. But happily, this doesn't include the spring break. *Mamasha*, Lonia will be home when the snow melts."

Sobakin slipped his hand into his pocket, brought out a sealed envelope, and handed it to Efrosinia, who ripped it open and burst into tears. Before her very eyes was a photograph of her son taken only recently. "Oh, my dear Lonia," she cried, kissing the picture over and over. "You're alive! You're alive!" Then, frightened, "But how thin you are and your face is so drawn and hollow, it has no life. You look like no more than a skeleton." For a moment she stood mournful and dejected, as though she had just received news of his death. But Lonia was not dead, he was alive and she had a photograph to prove it. Lonia was alive!

In an outpouring of gratitude, grabbing hold of Sobakin's hand and pressing it to her cheek, she exclaimed, "Oh, Lieutenant, thank you! Thank you!" She shook with excitement. Lonia was alive and that was all that mattered to her now. It was already late January and in just a few short months her son would be home. "I can't believe it's true. Oh, Lonia, my son!"

Sobakin watched the old woman with mounting disgust. Her thin graying hair, her skinny arms, and her faded black frock, which she seemed to wear all the time, made him wince. She was loathsome to him. This whole nonsense of her missing Lonia was becoming tiresome and burdensome and he had no desire to continue with the charade. But still, for the next little while at least, he had to find a way of humoring her, of getting on her good side. His eyes wandering, he said, "Yes, *Mamasha*, from what my official tells me your Lonia is as eager to see you as you him. You have everything to be thankful for."

Efrosinia, taking in his every word, threw up her arms as if set free from a terrible burden. Tears of joy streamed down her cheeks and her heart raced. Rushing to the doorway, she shouted, "Marusia! Come quickly, I have wonderful news!"

A few seconds later, Marusia appeared in the doorway, out of breath. "Mother, what on earth is going on?" Stopping short upon seeing Simon Stepanovich, she murmured, "Company? Oh, I didn't realize we had company." Blushing, quickly smoothing her skirt, she looked awkwardly at him and smiled. Efrosinia ran to give her daughter a hug.

"Oh, Marusia, we have such good news! It's about Lonia. Look, he even sent us a photograph. He's well and he's coming home in April. Lieutenant Sobakin, bless his heart, is the bearer of good news tonight."

The mention of her brother's name threw the girl into a whirl of emotion. She couldn't believe her ears. "Did you say Lonia's coming home? Mother, why, that's wonderful news. The best news ever!" Swallowing her tears, unable to contain her happiness, her cheeks turned a deep red and she looked on fire. She was about to thank Simon Stepanovich, but something made her stop. Thanking him was not as simple as it seemed. In her heart she felt an unexpected thrill. Never before had she seen such a powerful man. His thick, big hands, his graying sideburns, his broad chest, all this became attractive to her in a full-blooded way. His face and bull neck burned hot and there was a savage determination in his eye that hadn't been there a moment before.

Sobakin was unable to take his eyes off her. His blood tingled. He stood fierce and silent, watching her intently. Finally he said, "Marusia Valentynovna, would you do me the honor of accompany-ing me to the cinema tonight? I understand there's a wonderful film playing at eight o'clock."

Efrosinia was quick to answer for her daughter. "Don't you think it's a little late, Lieutenant? It's unexpected."

Sobakin tried not to show his impatience. "Nonsense. The night is young and I hear the film is superb. Well, Marusia Valentynovna, what do you say, shall we make a night of it?"

The girl moved away, feeling uncomfortable and embarrassed. "Perhaps mother is right. Maybe another time."

"Why another time? If we leave right now, we'll make it on time. What's wrong with tonight?"

"Well, I don't know. I'm really not prepared to go out . . ."

"What's to prepare for?" Sobakin almost snapped. He was coming to his wit's end. The two women were wasting his time, and it made him furious to see how ungrateful and mistrustful they could be, even after he had gone to such lengths to promise to bring their Lonia home. Trying to remain calm, he said, "My good ladies, I'm simply one good neighbor inviting another out for an enjoyable evening. *Mamasha*, I guarantee you your daughter will be well taken care of. You have absolutely nothing to worry about. She'll be in good hands, you have my word."

In the end, although somewhat reluctantly, Marusia and her mother agreed that it would be perfectly acceptable for Marusia to go to the cinema with Simon Stepanovich.

The girl started timidly toward the doorway, and, looking briefly at Sobakin, said, "Please excuse me a moment while I freshen up." After a short time she returned with her hair pinned up, wearing a brown double-breasted coat belted at the waist and with a knitted shawl over her shoulders.

Simon Stepanovich glanced at her with disapproval. Shaking his head, he said, "No, Marusia Valentynovna, I want you to wear the coat I gave you. Go put it on, please." She hesitated, but left the room, and returned a moment later wearing the Persian lamb.

Sobakin's eyes glittered and blood rushed to his neck. "You look absolutely stunning!"

He took her by the arm, said good night to Efrosinia, and led Marusia down the back staircase on their way toward the city center. The snow-covered street was dark and empty, illuminated by the lighted windows of the houses they passed. They walked in silence; the only sound was the crunching of snow beneath their feet. When a cold blast of wind came from the north, the girl lifted her coat collar to keep warm. Just before they reached the first crossroads, they saw a big black car parked on the side of the road. The motor was running and the chauffeur, dressed in NKVD uniform, stood leaning with his back against the driver's door, smoking a cigarette. When he saw them approaching, he threw down his cigarette and opened the back door.

Simon Stepanovich had made no mention of a car. Marusia hesitated. When she felt his hand at her back, pushing her into the back seat, her heart skipped a beat. She said quickly, "Why don't we walk, I'd much rather walk. It's no more than fifteen minutes into the city."

Sobakin let out a hearty laugh. "You silly girl. Why walk when we have the luxury of a car?"

She settled by the window behind the chauffeur and Simon Stepanovich nestled in beside her. Her pulse beat fast; she was feeling restless and on edge. To her dismay, she noticed that the car had picked up speed and was heading not in the direction of the cinema, but rather, eastward, toward the railway station. Unconsciously squeezing her hands together, she cried out in distress, "Where are you taking me? Why are we traveling in the opposite direction?"

Simon Stepanovich smiled. He brought out a bottle of whiskey from under his seat and took a drink. Then he leaned toward the girl, and stroking her under the chin with his forefinger, whispered quietly, "Why all these questions, my lovely? And why don't you trust me? You really ought to calm down." He took another drink. "First I thought we would go the Zalizny Café for a bite to eat, and then later head over to the cinema. There's no harm in that, is there?"

The girl retreated into her corner. More than anything she was afraid of losing her self-control. Glancing at him, she was horrified to notice how revolting he looked in the dim light. Her heart beat violently. The trap had been set and she could feel herself falling headlong into it.

Finally the car stopped, not in front of the Zalizny Café, as Simon Stepanovich had promised, but before a large dilapidated wooden building with a sign over the main doors: Railway Hotel. Sobakin got out of the car, and after talking with the chauffeur, leaned inside and grabbed her by the arm. Pulling her toward the hotel, he pushed her through the door, into the middle of a spacious foyer, dimly lit by two shale-oil lamps. The walls were covered with a faded yellow wallpaper, and the floor was sooty and damp. The girl was absolutely petrified of Sobakin and of what he might do to her. She wanted to run out the door as fast as her legs could carry her, but she found herself unable to move and stood numbly, in a kind of daze.

Sobakin went up to a small desk against the wall, and called for the concierge. A plump, unkempt, middle-aged woman appeared and nodded to Sobakin to follow her. They climbed a creaky wooden staircase to a darkened corridor lined with doors. The woman pulled a key from her pocket, threw the first door open, and disappeared down the stairs.

The room was small, dingy and poorly lit; two tiny windows with sheer curtains overlooked the street. A dank and musty odor rose from the floorboards; on the roughly plastered walls were patches of mildew. There was a bed at the far end piled with tattered linen and beside it a small table with two rickety chairs. In the center on an old writing desk covered by a clean cloth, was a tray with bread, sausages, fruit compote, boiled eggs—and a bottle of vodka. Marusia felt that the walls were closing in on her; she was completely at Sobakin's mercy. Stealing a glance at him, she was horrified to see how huge he was. With his clenched fist he could easily knock her down, even knock her unconscious. Not able to move a muscle, deathly pale, she could feel only a kind of sick dread.

"Well, Marusia." Sobakin picked up the bottle from the table. "Shall we have a drink?"

"I don't want a drink."

"You don't want a drink? You stupid girl." He burst out laughing. "You think I intend to bite you or something? Now, I'm warning you, don't give me a hard time. Come here beside me."

She backed up against the wall. "Stay away from me, Simon Stepanovich. You're despicable. You're a monster and a drunk." Sobakin threw off his overcoat and hurled it across the room. He sat on the edge of the bed, took off his shirt and kicked off his boots. "Very well," he said, "if you won't join me, I'll drink by myself."

In no time he had gulped down three glassesful, and started in on the sausages. Smacking his lips and belching, he poured himself another drink. Marusia, fixed to the spot, knew that he was going to make his move.

"Marusia, come over here." He patted the bed with his hand. When she didn't respond, he said more loudly and forcibly, "Come and keep me company. Be a good girl, you don't want to make me angry, do you?"

Marusia remained unmoving.

Sobakin looked her up and down. "I said come here. Now! You peasant girls are all alike; you pretend to be so fresh and coy, but you're all just a bunch of whores. Come here and show me a good time." He waited a moment, then rose angrily from the bed and staggered toward her, grabbing hold of her arm. "You little bitch."

Marusia saw herself being dragged to her doom right then and there. An awful wail broke from her throat. For a brief moment, she thought she was going to faint, but then an uncontrollable fever seized her. She became violent, her eyes on fire. Ripping her arm out of his grip, she screamed at the top of her voice, "Get away, get away from me!"

Simon Stepanovich was surprised and pleased by her sudden burst of energy. "My, my, the peasant girl has spunk! I like that. It adds to the excitement." Then crushing her in a horrible embrace, he thrust his lips against hers. She struggled to break free, but Sobakin tightened his grip and pressed her closer to him. He whispered in her ear, "How did an ordinary *moujik* girl like you ever manage to become so beautiful? You're just what my Russian blood needs." Throwing her on the bed, he slipped his hands under her skirt and grabbed at her thighs. She kicked and screamed, but was smothered by his weight. Her battle was being lost. Sobakin raged on. Tugging at her wildly, he ripped her blouse, and pressed his mouth against her neck and her breasts. She was saturated with the smell of drink, and felt as though she had died and gone to Hell.

When Sobakin fumbled to unbutton his trousers, suddenly, with an astonishing show of strength, the girl jerked her small frame forward and started to kick him. Her eyes gleamed; she looked like a woman possessed. At that very moment she thought of something and cried, "You think you've won. You think you've won, but you've really lost. Hah! Hah! Hah!"

"What? Just shut up." Sobakin ignored her.

"Did you look at me? Did you take a close look at me? Didn't you notice I have bags under my eyes and my forehead is broken out? You're worse than a bull. Even a bull knows when to leave the cow alone. Don't you know about a woman's monthly cycle? Hah! A fine time you've chosen, Simon Stepanovich!" She laughed hysterically.

The NKVD man, confounded by her strange behavior, pulled back a moment. He muttered, "What? You mean you've got the woman's curse? You're menstruating?"

Raising his body, he staggered to the table, and grabbed the vodka bottle. Marusia jumped off the bed, picked up her coat, and rushed to the door. She could sense him coming after her—any minute now he would seize her by the neck and pound her to the ground, maybe even kill her. Clutching the doorknob, she heard him call after her, "Marusia! Marusia!" His voice sounded unusual, distant, even muffled. Turning her head, she was startled to see him slouched on the bed, his head hanging. He mumbled, "Well, Marusia, it's too bad, we could have had ourselves such a good evening. Maybe next time." He got up and, dragging himself to the window, called down to his driver, "Eros! Go fetch me another girl!"

Outside, the girl ran frantically in the direction of Luninetska Street. She was terrified that she was being followed, that Simon Stepanovich was on her heels, that he would catch up to her, rip off her clothes, and discover she had tricked him. Then he would beat her mercilessly and defile her. Paralyzed with fear, her head pounding, she ran through the deserted streets, every few seconds pausing to look over her shoulder. After about twenty minutes, breathless, she found herself safely on the doorsteps of her house. Slamming the front door open, she flew past her father in the hallway and stormed into the kitchen, where she found her mother stoking the wood stove.

"Mother, mother! Oh, mother it was awful!" She could not stop crying. Efrosinia stood dumbstruck. Marusia ripped the Persian lamb off her back, threw it to the ground, and stomped on it. "Damn bastards, all of them! Mother, he stank of drink and corpses. He was so repugnant."

"Settle down, my darling, shh, settle down. It's over. It's all over." Efrosinia took her daughter in her arms and gently patted her, while she asked in a low whisper, "Marusia, tell me, did anything happen? Did he . . ."

"No, mother no, no, no, nothing happened." Marusia was now even more hysterical. "Nothing! Nothing!"

Efrosinia pulled a handkerchief from her pocket and wiped her daughter's cheeks. "My poor, poor child. What are we going to do now? There's nowhere for us to turn. We should really go to the police, but how can we go to the police when Sobakin is the police? What are we going to do?" She wept, feeling her daughter's pain, as if it were she herself who had just gone through the ordeal. She stroked Marusia's hair and rocked her in her arms. "I took care of you when you were sick, I sang you lullabies to get you to sleep at night, I marveled at your first steps. And now a filthy bastard appears and like a wild cat attacks a harmless lamb. May his teeth rot and fall out in Hell. Damned NKVD man! Lucifer!"

In their tight embrace mother and daughter did not notice Valentyn standing in the doorway. Shaking his head and tugging at his beard, he sang out to them, "Didn't I tell you? Didn't I say all along that Kulik would have been a better match?"

CHAPTER 18

It was no longer a secret that Iofe Nicel Leyzarov was having an affair with Dounia Avdeevna. In the beginning it was all quite hush-hush because Leyzarov went out of his way to exercise extreme caution: every other night, late, after everyone was asleep, he set out for Dounia's house in the village of Moro-zovich and returned to his quarters in Hlaby by early dawn. For the longest time this arrangement went on undetected. Then one day everything changed. For some reason Dounia insisted that Leyzarov either spend the entire night with her and return home some time after breakfast, or visit her directly at lunchtime and return to Hlaby before nightfall.

This new schedule did not affect Leyzarov too much, since Dou-nia was more than capable of satisfying his sexual needs as easily in broad daylight as in the dead of night. But what did bother him was being seen by the villagers. Almost instantly, to his great dis-may, gossip broke out and spread like wildfire, and before he knew it all eyes were on him. He heard people whispering behind his back, and at the Clubhouse meetings the snickering never stopped. On a number of occasions he overheard villagers chuckling and murmuring, "That Dounia sure knows how to reel them in," "She has them begging for more," and "There's certainly enough of her to go around. Hah! Hah! Hah!"

What bothered Leyzarov most about this gossip was not so much that he had been found out, but rather that it seemed to sug-gest Dounia was involved with more than one man. And it was not long before he began to suspect that there was indeed more to the picture than met the eye and that he just might be the brunt of an even larger rumor. As the days passed, he felt as if his presence in Dounia's life was beginning to play a smaller role and even that she was growing indifferent to his needs. Gradually he became convinced that Dounia Avdeevna had taken up with another man. It troubled him deeply to think he no longer held exclusive rights to his love nest and that after six long months he was about to be cast off like an old shoe. He waited for the moment to come, for that proverbial slap in the face, but happily, and to his surprise, nothing happened—at least not for a while.

As the days passed, Leyzarov basked blissfully in the warmth of Dounia Avdeevna's bedroom. With all his fears of unfaithfulness quashed, he felt infinitely grateful for the attention she was bestowing on him. In fact, in his heart he began to feel the birth of a new sensation—could love be taking the place of infatuation? His urge to be with Dounia was uncontrollable. Separation now seemed inconceivable to him; if anything, he felt their special bond strengthening. This woman, Dounia, had been his lover for almost half a year, and he began to feel their affair could go on for another six months, maybe even forever.

At the same time, it seemed incredible that he should have fallen in love with her. She was not a beauty by any means, and often when he looked at her, he couldn't quite figure out what it was about her that kept him coming back: she was fat, her face was lumpy and crude, and her long stringy hair looked like a dirty old floor mop. There was no gentleness or softness in her gestures, and her vulgar laugh repelled him. She was the loudest and most grotesque woman he had ever known.

But despite all that, there was something exceptional about her. She was passionate, cruel and sensual, always bursting with new appetites and adventures. The blood in her veins boiled and when she shivered it was with a kind of drunken excitement. She was skilled in the art of lovemaking, always throwing herself frantically and shamelessly into the pleasures of the flesh. Her caresses were brutal, wild, and she did not hesitate to succumb to the dictates of her body. Leyzarov had never known a woman like this, so ready to lose herself again and again. He felt a deep lust inside him and yearned after her day and night, like a famished animal.

Interestingly enough, it was not only the force of lust that bound Leyzarov to Dounia but also the force of the palate—she was as good a cook as she was a lover. Dounia Avdeevna worked wonders in the kitchen, concocting the tastiest omelets, the most succulent cabbage rolls, and her boiled beef was mouth-watering. In her cellar she stored an assortment of cured foods like pickles and sausages and she always had a generous supply of potatoes, beets and carrots. And if that wasn't enough, with her many connections in the Pinsk marketplace, she always made sure that her pantry was stocked with Iofe's favorite foods, one of which was pickled herring. Iofe really lived the good life and believed that indeed everything was better and happier under Stalin's Constitution.

One night at Dounia's, Leyzarov happened to overstay his visit, and instead of setting out at his usual time just before nightfall, he prepared to take his leave at a few minutes past midnight. Dounia was cross, and pushed him impatiently toward the door.

"Off with you! It's later than I thought."

"Why are you so eager to be rid of me, my dumpling? We were having ourselves such a good time." Then, laughing, "If I didn't know any better, I'd think you were seeing another man."

"Oh, my long-nosed soldier," she shouted after him, "how ugly you are after all. The dark scares you, is that it? If the Devil catches you by the seat of your pants, how will you defend yourself? Just remember, praying is subversive. All it will do is land you in Siberia!"

"Not to worry, my little dumpling," he called back, already in the yard, "I have no need for prayers. With my pistol I'll stop the Devil dead in his tracks."

Whistling happily, in good spirits, Leyzarov walked briskly from the edge of Morozovich onto the main road that led back to Hlaby, guided by the moon and stars. When a blast of frigid air swept across his face, he turned down the earflaps of his sheepskin hat. Invigorated by the brightened sky, he quickened his pace and listened to the crunching sound of his footsteps. He delighted in the frosty stillness.

He couldn't be a more contented man—not only did he have a good position with the Party as Representative from the District Committee of the Pinsk Region, but he also had a little something on the side. No, indeed, life was not passing him by. True, at times he found his Party duties tiresome, especially when expropriating land from peasants or confiscating their provisions, and the long hours of Party meetings were becoming increasingly boring, but at least there was one place he had totally and exclusively for himself—his little love nest. It was there that he was able to concentrate on his own needs and forget about the common good.

"Yes," he said aloud as he walked along the frozen marsh, "I'm a lucky man. Dounia, you're the woman for me . . . It's true you were not blessed with the beauty and softness that might inspire a painter or a poet, and your love of food has pushed you out in all directions, but you're mine, all mine."

Suddenly he noticed a solitary bush on the right side of the road. It thrust out of the snow like a huge wicker basket, cold, dark, and unmoving. Dried leaves dusted with frost dangled from its limbs, and a sprinkling of pink petals looking very much like roses clung to its lower branches.

"How odd," he thought, stooping to examine it. "Exposed to the harshest of elements and still it clings to life. The leaves look almost green and the petals look so fresh and alive. Why hadn't I noticed it before?"

Beyond the bush, there was nothing but a vast, empty, silent plain. Leyzarov knew the trail between Morozovich and Hlaby like the back of his hand, and even in the dark of night he was able to tell where he was along the path. Looking to the right he remembered that exactly at this point about a quarter kilometer from the road was a clump of alder shrubs that continued southward all the way to the Stryy River. So why had this peculiar bush never caught his attention before? A scattering of snow fell, and the moon, climbing up between the trees, slipped behind the clouds. When the moon re-emerged he turned back to the bush. As he bent to examine a limb on its left side, longer than the others by about a foot, he heard a strange, cackling sound. When the lower branches began to rustle, he edged his way forward, trying to get a better look. Several seconds passed. Then as if out of nowhere a largish object soared swiftly upward, and landed with a heavy thud directly at his feet. Completely bewildered and rather frightened, Leyzarov jumped back. A sharp, shrill cry pierced the silence. Leyzarov stiffened like a board. Something horrible was staring up at him; it had eyes that were penetrating and shiny, like live coals

"Caw! Caw! Caw!" Then again, "Caw! Caw! Caw!"

Gradually the thing came into full view: it was smaller than he first thought, soft and roundish, with a pointed head, sporting a crest of brush-like feathers. After a moment an enormous spread of plumage appeared, displaying iridescent greens and golds with rich vibrant peacock-blue markings.

"Well, I'll be damned." Leyzarov scratched his head. "If it isn't the peacock from the Olivinski manor. What's it doing here in the middle of nowhere scaring me half out of my wits?" Then sneering, "Cold, are you? Well, come here; let me put you out of your misery."

When he reached to grab it by the neck, the bird sprang upward instantly, and flying into the air, released an earsplitting yelp. Leyzarov put his hands to his ears to muffle the noise. When finally the bird settled a little further away, Leyzarov once again lunged forward and tried to snatch it, this time by the tail, and almost grabbed hold of its feathers. The peacock flung itself around, screaming louder and more wildly than before. Leyzarov was thrown completely off balance and fell into the snow, where he lay for a minute or two. When finally he regained himself and sat up, he was astonished to find the peacock staring at him, flapping its wings, as if it was taunting him.

"Why, you useless peafowl!" he exploded. "I'll get you once and for all!"

Rising to his feet, he reached for his holster, pulled out his revolver, aimed and fired it. The peacock, frightened by the noise, scrambled behind the bush to safety. Several seconds of silence followed. Leyzarov listened, and not hearing a sound, aimed and fired again, this time randomly into the bush, hoping to somehow bring the bird down. When the silence continued, he became convinced he had finally finished it off. Then as if out of nowhere a strange, deafening, almost pain-filled wail erupted, followed by a series of shorter, fainter ones.

Leyzarov muttered hotly, "That damned bird is still alive!"

Panting heavily, thrashing through the snow, it was not long before he caught sight of the animal in the open field. It was dragging its right leg behind it, slightly opening and closing its fan as if in distress. A bullet had landed in its right upper thigh and it looked as if it was about to collapse.

"I've got you now," laughed Leyzarov victoriously. "Come here and let me finish you off."

But the bird, flapping its wings frantically, somehow managed to move further from Leyzarov, who chased after it, firing shot after shot. He shouted at the top of his voice, "You stupid bird! I'll get you if it's the last thing I do!"

It dragged itself farther and farther on its healthy leg. Leyzarov took aim and fired his last shot. A long wail erupted from somewhere in the darkness, and then came silence. The bird dropped to the ground, dead. Iofe hastened to examine his kill, and when he saw the animal lying limp and motionless on a smooth crust of ice, he shouted loudly, "I got you, you bourgeois bastard! I won!"

As he bent to pluck a feather out of its wing for a memento, suddenly he heard a cracking sound beneath his feet. He was horrified to find he was standing not on solid ground but in the middle of a pond, and the ice beneath him was starting to give way. He could feel his body slowly slipping into the ice-cold water. His muscles cramped and he went completely numb. Cursing the bird for having lured him there, he was certain his life was about to end, either by drowning or by freezing, whichever came first. His blood pulsated in his temples and his head whirled. Kicking the water, frantically trying to stay afloat, he began to realize that his boot heels were touching bottom and that the water actually reached only to his waist. He turned ever so carefully, and, with the tips of his fingers, searched for ice thick enough to support his weight. But the cold was becoming more and more painful, and he was starting to experience a tremendous loss of strength. When finally he found a chunk thick enough, he placed his palms flat upon the surface, and with all his strength pushed himself upward and pulled himself out of the water.

With his clothes already stiffening, somehow he managed to stumble back onto his trail. Without thinking, he took to his heels and fled, not toward Hlaby, but back toward Morozovich, to Dounia Avdeevna's. He ran so fast he thought his heart would explode. Another ten minutes and he would be at Dounia's door, comfortable under a thick, warm eiderdown, being nursed back to health, spoon-fed hot teas with liquor and maybe later a little chicken soup. He had to keep moving, to keep his blood circulating. Never had he taken part in such a race, a race for life, and he was doing his best. The frozen wasteland was rapidly closing in on him.

Then all at once things got worse. A cold blast of wind blew in from the north and thick flakes of snow began to fall heavily. "Trouble," Leyzarov murmured as he forced his way into the driving snow. Chills rushed through him, his teeth chattered, and he could no longer feel his hands or feet. The cold cut through him like a knife. His well-trodden path was quickly becoming snow-filled, and with each step he had to fight deep wind-driven heaps of ice and snow. He no longer knew whether he was going in the right direction. The bitter cold was beginning to affect his mind. He prayed feverishly for the lights of Morozovich. Desperately, hopelessly, he called out Dounia's name over and over, but his voice bounced off the plains and became lost in the emptiness.

Terrified and desperate, Leyzarov began to weep. He didn't want to die. He became convinced that his frozen corpse would be found in the morning, perhaps by some local peasants, or even by his comrades. His life, which had been a very full and rewarding one, not only as a prominent Party representative but as a lover was over, and all because of a stupid bird. Dropping to his knees, his strength gone, he began to imagine what it would be like for Dounia when she came to identify his body. Her bitter tears, her misery, her suffering. Poor Dounia!

As he sank deeper into the snow, he caught a whiff of smoke. The smell intensified and a waft of warm air swept across his face. Raising his head and straining his eyes, he could see a faint stream of smoke billowing out of a chimney close by. He was on the outskirts of Morozovich! What great luck! Stumbling to his feet, he tottered toward the outlying houses. Dounia's was the third on the left; he recognized the cleared walkway leading to her front porch. He had never been so happy to lay eyes on her small wood-framed house, old and decaying as it was, with its sagging roof and lopsided shutters. Crawling up the front stairs, his face coated with crystals of frost, he banged on the front door, waiting anxiously for it to open, for Dounia to appear, to take him into her big, fat embrace, to warm his body in hers. But to his great horror when the door finally did open, it was not Dounia standing there, but Kokoshin, and in his night clothes!

Collapsing on the threshold, Leyzarov was carried inside, stripped of his clothes, and placed in Dounia's great walnut bed. Half-conscious, shuddering, he fell into a fearful broken dream, barely aware of what was going on around him: there were vague shuffling noises beside his bed, the splashing of water, the sound of voices, first a man's, then a woman's. The warmth of the room penetrated him. Struggling to bring himself to consciousness, through drooping lids he saw enormous shadows on the gray walls, and heard a whispered conversation. It was not long before he fell into a deep sleep.

Leyzarov slept for two days and two nights; he slept like the dead. When he finally woke it was to excruciating pains in his entire body. His hands and legs were a purplish blue, and he could hardly move his toes. There was a throbbing in his head and his cheeks burned. Rolling onto his side, he looked around in utter confusion. After a moment everything started to come back to him and he realized where he was and that he had gone through a terrible ordeal. He made an effort to call Dounia's name, but felt too weak and tired. Burrowing into the pillow, he closed his eyes and dozed off again. He was grateful to be alive.

When finally he woke again, his first thought was of Dounia. The peacefulness of her room, the pale light creeping in through the window, the faint odor of garlic from the kitchen, everything around him made him feel calm and contented. His eyes strayed across the room. An old painted chair piled with towels and linen stood by the door and next to it was a cheap oak bureau cluttered with various odds and ends. Several items were strewn across the floor—undergarments, stockings, shoes. The room was small, almost bare, not the kind of room one would think of as a lover's retreat. But it was special to Leyzarov, dear to his heart. He was a lucky man to have a woman like Dounia Avdeevna. Closing his eyes he pictured her big, soft, body pouring out over his, her bosom on his chest, her half-open mouth releasing crude chuckles. The mere thought of her made him quiver. Without question, he was coming back to normal.

He opened his mouth to call her, when like a flash his horrible ordeal came back to him and he began to relive it bit by bit. But it was not the ordeal on the pond that really upset him; it was the ordeal that followed, the ordeal on the doorstep of Dounia's house. Suddenly he remembered vividly: it had not been Dounia who had greeted him at the door that terrible night. It had been a man! With rage boiling up inside him, his heart pounding violently, he screamed out one word:

"Kokoshin!"

Everything was clear to him now. Dounia was unfaithful, and he had caught her red-handed. His pride was wounded; he felt crushed and humiliated. He was horribly jealous of Kokoshin; the mere thought of being replaced by him was almost unbearable.

Kokoshin's red nose, his scraggly beard, his quavering, arrogant voice, all rushed at him like cold water.

"The joke's on me," he muttered miserably. "I've been replaced like a dog." He was angry, not so much with Dounia, but with himself for not having seen it coming.

While he was trying to climb out of bed, Dounia walked through the door. She was carrying a tray of food and a small bottle of greenish ointment.

"And where do you think you're going?" she exclaimed good-naturedly. "I thought I'd bring you something to eat. I see you're already feeling better."

Setting the tray on the nightstand, she frowned at him. "That was quite some adventure you put yourself through the other night. In your fever you kept shouting and shooting at something, and cursing. What was all that about? Well, never mind." Then fussing with his bed covers, "Let me roll up your sleeves, I'll put some ointment on your blisters."

As Dounia rubbed his arms and legs, he watched her in bitter anguish. His vanity had been hurt; he had been played for a fool. The words at last broke from his mouth, "Dounia, you've betrayed me. How long has this affair with Kokoshin been going on?"

"Oh, Iofushka," Dounia looked at him peevishly. "I really can't stand to hear you whimper like this. You ought to calm yourself. And don't be such a poor sport. I'm not made of glass, I don't break easily. I'm a woman of many needs, and the truth of the matter is, I've become bored with you. I like change in my life and excitement. You don't own me."

Leyzarov gasped in shock. With his whole heart he hoped it was all just some big joke. He was so intent on being reconciled with her that he was willing to forgive and forget everything she had just said. After all they had been through together, how could she just brush him off like that, and without the slightest sign of remorse? For a brief moment he hated her. He hated her obesity, the roundness of her shoulders, and her unhealthy color. She was common and crude and repulsive to him. His heart was in pain.

Dounia remained indifferent; she felt she had done nothing wrong. Leyzarov no longer interested her and she wanted to be rid of him, it was as simple as that. She felt obliged to tell him to go away, that he ought not to pester her any more, and just as she was about to do that, she was struck with an idea. She decided to make him an offer.

"Iofushka," she whispered, "I've been thinking. I have a proposition for you and it's quite a generous one, one that I thought up all by myself just now. It's like this: you can remain my lover as long as you agree to share me with Kokoshin. It's up to you."

Leyzarov could not believe his ears. He was willing to give way to some extent, but there was a limit to what was and was not acceptable to him. Red with anger and confusion, he remained speechless for the longest time.

Dounia looked impatiently at him. "Is that a no? Well, Iofushka, then it looks like it's goodbye." She shrugged, a look of disappointment passed across her face and vanished as quickly as it appeared. "I must admit, it was fun while it lasted. Come here and give me one last kiss."

Grabbing hold of his head, almost crushing his jaw, she thrust her thick red lips upon his. Leyzarov felt a pang, then long spasms shot through his body. Soon all feelings of resentment disappeared and he began to experience pleasurable sensations. He wanted to have Dounia the way he had always had Dounia, with her fierce embraces, her brutality, her abuses. Out of breath, his deep-seated lust for her intensifying, in a split second he decided to surrender himself to her demands. Sharing her might not be such a bad idea after all—it was not as if he was being cut off completely. Dounia was a substantial woman with more than enough to go around. And Kokoshin wasn't that bad, a good sort really, a bit obnoxious at times, but it was not as if their paths would ever have to cross. Then remembering the endless supply of bread and sausages Kokoshin regularly confiscated from local villagers, he smacked his lips and smiled to himself. Yes, this arrangement might work out better than he thought. And before he knew it he had accepted the new arrangement enthusiastically.

Dounia was delighted by Leyzarov's turnabout. Twirling his hair with the tips of her fingers, she whispered softly and joyfully in his ear, "Ah, there, Iofushka, I knew you'd come around."

Thus the threesome—Dounia, Leyzarov, and Kokoshin—comfortably and unabashedly settled into their new lifestyle. They reveled in their shamelessness, not caring what anyone thought or said, engaging in thrilling round-the-clock orgies. When Leyzarov arrived at the front door, Kokoshin left by the back. Kokoshin would bring cheeses, breads, and kielbasa; Leyzarov, whisky. Things could not have worked out better and the two men even started to like each other. If they happened to meet along the way, they greeted each other with a sort of camaraderie, exchanging playful, knowing glances. Soon their visits with Dounia began to coincide, and passionately devoted to her as they were, with the aid of liquor, they soon discovered a new kind of ecstasy. The threesome now spent their days and nights together in wild scenes of sex and scandal.

The shocking story of the *ménage a trois* spread quickly: two representatives of the national Party and a Morozovich schoolteacher engaging in lewd, licentious, sexual escapades. There was talk of dancing, drinking, and all-night carousing. Legends were created about Dounia—the unappeasable seductress, a Siren, who lured men into her boudoir and bound them in salacious misbehavior. Her sexual appetite was said to be so great and insatiable that she was capable of accommodating the entire Red Army.

In Hlaby the teachers of School Number Seven, including Headmaster Kulik, were well aware of the goings-on in the shabby little cottage on the edge of Morozovich. Although this debauched trio did not set a good example for the people of the region, especially for the young, they did provide a much-needed distraction from the pressures of everyday life. Leyzarov and Kokoshin had begun to neglect their duties. From early February there had been a dramatic decrease in the number of Clubhouse meetings, and in the few that were called, the two men were absent more often than not. Almost all political duties had come to a standstill: wages were no longer confiscated, men were not rounded up and sent to work on the Bugsy-Dnieprovsky Canal, and land was no longer expropriated. Even Cornelius, the Village Chairman, who normally busied himself in and around the Clubhouse with various tasks, felt as if he were on holiday.

Everyone was grateful to Dounia Avdeevna for having taken the two Party men off their hands. It was because of her that the entire region was experiencing a sort of mid-winter thaw. The men wallowing in drunkenness and adultery at all hours gave the villagers a break from their misery. They couldn't have been more pleased.

But Dounia was beginning to feel restless and unfulfilled. Leyzarov and Kokoshin were no longer meeting her needs, and she started to look for a change, a new kind of thrill. And it didn't take long for her to find it; in fact, it was a place she had had her eye on for the longest time—the Hlaby school. The prospects there looked very good indeed, with three eligible men to choose from, all very different from one another: Sergei, Ivashkevich, and Kulik. But she decided that Sergei was much too young and inexperienced, and that Ivashkevich, overweight, middle-aged and balding, was possibly even impotent. That left Kulik as her next target. Not wasting any time, one night when the clock struck eleven, she threw her cloak over her shoulders, wrapped her head in a long knitted shawl, and made for Hlaby. When she reached the school, she went around the back to Kulik's living quarters, and, happy to find the door unlocked, went inside. Kulik, who was at his desk working on some papers, looked up in astonishment.

"Good evening, citizen!" Dounia called out in a sing-song voice, looking somewhat flustered. "Forgive me for coming here so late, but I'm at a total loss. I don't know what I'm going to do. I'm not prepared for my morning class and I desperately need your help. It's about a lesson in mathematics. The fourth graders need to be taught fractions. I'm here because I didn't know where else to turn."

Kulik gazed at her, incredulous. "Fractions? You came here in the middle of the night because of *fractions*? Well, fractions are not such a big mystery, but unfortunately it's late and I'm ready to turn in for the night. Why don't you come back in the morning? I can review the lessons with you before classes start." Rising from behind his desk, eager to be rid of her, he tried to push her out the door.

"Oh, what a wonder you are." Dounia lavished a seductive smile on him, "Are you trying to get rid of me already? Why, I just got here." She winked at him. "Does it make you nervous being alone with a woman in the middle of the night? I won't attack you, I promise." She took off her cloak, plopped herself into an armchair and threw back her arms. Kulik waited for what would come next. At last she confessed, "The truth is I'm so miserable. I just had to get away from those two bulls back at my place. I've grown so tired of them. They don't excite me any more." Then, flushing, "I need someone who will bring a new kind of sensation into my life, a new kind of passion, if you know what I mean."

Kulik saw her point at once; he knew where she wanted to take him. But he said, "You mustn't talk of Comrades Leyzarov and Kokoshin like that. They're upstanding members of our national Party. You could find yourself . . ."

Dounia looked Kulik over, and burst into a fit of laughter. "I must say you're a strange one. You're what, twenty-five, thirty? Here you are, a grown man, talking to a hot-blooded woman with desire on her breath and what do you do? You behave like a babe in arms with the taste of your mother's milk still on your tongue." Then sardonically, "Tell me, Ivan, how do you manage to stay so chaste, so virtuous?"

Kulik was now terribly exasperated. Dounia's penetrating scent was permeating everything in the room. He had never found any woman so repulsive. "Wasn't it mathematics you came here for?"

"Oh, Vanyoushka, Vanyoushka." Her voice dipped up and down. "You're a greenhorn, such a greenhorn." Becoming more and more animated, laughing, slowly she spread out her big, fat thighs. She went on with alarming familiarity, "That's what I find so intriguing about you. I'm here to make you an offer, a rather delicious one, I might add, one that you won't be able to refuse."

Kulik was at the door, fumbling for the knob. He could feel the cool wafts of air seeping through the cracks. Dounia had got out of the chair and was coming at him now with her arms wide open. He said loudly, "Dounia, this is not a good idea. I'm the school headmaster and I have responsibilities. If the villagers caught wind of any kind of indiscretion on my part I'd be ruined. No, no, you must leave immediately."

Dounia withdrew several paces. Rejection did not sit well with her; she took great offense at what he had just said. She was determined to get back at him. With her hands on her hips she said maliciously, "Oh, I see how it goes. You're saving yourself for that green-eyed girl, Marusia. Poor Vanya. Poor, stupid, little Vanya. You pine after her night and day, you put her up on a pedestal, and while you do all this what does she go and do? She goes out till all hours of the night with Sobakin. Where to? To smoke-filled taverns and dingy hotel rooms. Yes, your pretty little princess has fallen from grace. Her parents dreamed of a big church wedding, flowers, bridesmaids, guests from the entire region, but as it turns out your little innocent prefers the taste of vodka. It's no secret Sobakin's got lucky with her. Now you know—she's just as bad as the rest of us."

Dounia fell silent a moment, and when she spoke again her voice was completely changed. "Ivan, what I am about to say to you is for your own good. Don't trust women, especially pretty ones like Marusia. They'll always prove unfaithful. Just throw an expensive coat over their shoulders or place jewels on their fingers and within minutes they'll turn into whores."

Kulik was stunned. "Marusia . . . you say . . . with Sobakin . . . ?" She was such a strong and independent girl with pride, dignity and character, not to mention intelligence. She would never allow herself to be victimized like that. Kulik refused to believe it. It had to be a vicious lie. Dounia was a disgusting conniver who enjoyed upsetting people. He wanted to grab her by her stringy hair and hurl her out the door, and was moving toward her when to his great horror, he read it all in her face: her small squinting eyes, the faint wrinkles on her forehead, her twisted, mocking grin, everything about her demonstrated a kind of smugness. It was possible that this detestable and repulsive woman before him was telling the truth. He felt a horrible chill.

Throwing herself back down in the armchair, flinging one leg over the other, Dounia straightened her skirt and smoothed her hair. She said with sparkling eyes, "Oh, Ivan, how nice and cozy it is in here. I could use a drink about now. I'm terribly thirsty. How about it? We could drink to our new-found friendship. Well, what are you waiting for?" Then reprovingly, "And don't look so glum. That green-eyed hussy isn't worth your time. You'll be over her before you know it. Besides, she's not the only girl around. If you haven't noticed, I'm ready to throw myself at you."

Dounia's fat, flabby body, her plump arms, her vast chest repelled him beyond measure. He had to find a way to get rid of her. He considered just telling her to get out, but in the end he did not dare. Then to his own surprise a plan came to him, a plan that was brilliant and fool-proof.

"You say you want a drink?" he asked. "Then a drink it is."

Grabbing his coat and hat he hurried out the door. "I don't have drink in my quarters but I know where to get some. Make yourself at home. I'll be back in about twenty minutes."

"Now you're talking!" Dounia called after him. "And remember, I like it hard and strong. Make sure it's at least eighty proof!" Then beaming, very pleased, "I see you know how to entertain a woman after all!"

As the clock on Kulik's desk ticked away, barely twenty minutes had gone by when he reappeared in the doorway; not with a bottle in his hand, but with Kokoshin at his side.

"Oh, my little dumpling," Kokoshin rushed at her with open arms. "So this is where you've been hiding. Leyzarov and I were wondering what had become of you. Comrade Kulik said you came here with questions about arithmetic, but I know you better than that. You came here looking for a change, for something a little younger perhaps? But as you can see, tonight is not the night. Come back home with me. There's plenty to drink there."

When Dounia and Kokoshin finally left, Kulik slammed the door shut and shot the bolt. Taking a deep breath, he reminded himself over and over again to make sure that in future all doors were locked the minute school was dismissed. A reenactment of tonight's events was something he wanted to avoid at all costs.

CHAPTER 19

Luck, it seemed, was on Dounia Avdeevna's side. It all started with the regional pre-election campaign. Leyzarov and Kokoshin, thinking about Dounia's late-night rendez-vous with the headmaster of School Number Seven, began to fear that she was about to drop them for him. Clearly she already had designs on him, and so whimsical and unpredictable were her mood swings of late, it might be just a matter of time before she would be gone from their lives forever. They couldn't bear the thought of losing her, she was all that mattered to them: Dounia knew what love should be, and they needed to possess her and to be possessed by her exclusively.

Putting their heads together, they came up with a solution: they would nominate her for candidate for Deputy of the Village Soviet of B.S.S.R. and would make her the only candidate, ensuring her victory in the spring. They were confident that such a demanding and prominent position would leave her little time for anything else, especially for involvement with the handsome young headmaster.

Of course Dounia was thrilled by this nomination, and as the two men had hoped, she could think of nothing else. The prospect of representing the masses of her region enthralled her, and consumed her day and night. Feeling a great sense of pride and honor, she began to devote all her energy to preparing herself for this very important post. News of her nomination spread quickly, and before long everyone came to understand that Dounia Avdeevna was going to be their next Deputy. Not only was she the *prime* candidate, she was the *only* candidate. Every day, standing on wooden crates in the village square, she gave impassioned speeches, and in the evening she walked from house to house, knocking on doors, swearing allegiance to the most wonderful party on Earth, the Communist Party.

The pre-election campaign went into full swing, and at the end of March, a general meeting was called, which all inhabitants of the region were asked to attend. Young and old alike flocked to Hlaby and crowded the small Clubhouse, eager to witness the unfolding of the democratic process. Villagers had been informed that they, the people, formed the foundation of the greatest working-class revolution in history, and as a result, were now eligible voters, and come spring, would be electing a Deputy of the Village Soviet of B.S.S.R. Gone was the authoritarian Polish government where discrimination reigned; the wealthy Polish landowners had been obliterated by great Mother Russia and the land given back to the people, and these very same people, the proletariat, now had a voice in government. Today they were being called upon to hear the nominee for Deputy of the Village Soviet, and hearing her would enable them to cast their ballots competently and decisively.

Up front, on an elevated platform behind a long rectangular table, sat the two Party representatives, Kokoshin and Leyzarov. They were dressed appropriately in drab high-collared army jackets and trousers tucked into black leather boots, but their faces were puffy and they appeared rather unsteady. Their breath smelled of drink.

Leyzarov was the first to speak. "Comrades, let the meeting begin! It's wonderful to see such a fine turnout today. You have come from far and wide, from Lopatinsia, Morozovich, Kriveselo, and Hlaby. Today is the day for the pre-election when all of you, the peasants, the backbone of our great nation, will meet the candidate to best represent you in the Village Soviet of B.S.S.R. This is a wonderful time in Soviet history. The former bourgeois Polish occupiers and landowners elected to parliament their own people, while you were only spat upon. No vote by the working masses was allowed. Now, comrades, you have a voice—a voice that will ring not only throughout the nation but throughout the world. In the spring there will be elections, and whomever you choose to vote for, will, as representative of your region, take up the honorable position of Deputy of the Village Soviet of B.S.S.R. Today we have one outstanding candidate with us, one who is most deserving and, of course, a natural choice. Her name is Dounia Avdeevna Zemlankova."

Looking at Dounia, throwing her a warm and affectionate smile, Leyzarov's blood tingled and he felt a rush of emotion throughout his body. When his eyes locked with hers he saw her mouth quiver and her chest heave. This intimate exchange lasted only a second before Leyzarov once again officiously addressed the crowd.

"In a few minutes I will introduce Dounia Avdeevna to you, but first, you the people, must, in accordance with our democratic process, vote in a presidium. For those of you not familiar with the term, a presidium is a standing committee in the Communist organization that serves as the organ of a larger body. As you can see, behind me are four empty chairs, chairs that must be filled with the most upright citizens, ones who will best represent you today."

Leyzarov had barely finished when a voice erupted from a front-row seat. It belonged to Cornelius, the Village Chairman. He leapt to his feet, his beady black eyes flashing. "The voice of the common man is finally being heard. I take this opportunity to vote our wonderful new candidate for Deputy of the Village Soviet onto the presidium: Dounia Avdeevna Zemlankova!"

At the sound of her name, Kokoshin rushed in, clapping, much pleased, "Excellent choice! Excellent!" He patted Cornelius on the back. "I commend you for your fine decision, Comrade, you couldn't have selected anyone more deserving."

Cornelius smiled sheepishly. He had not only made a favorable impression on both Leyzarov and Kokoshin, but had steered the pre-election meeting in the right direction. He felt quite proud of himself. He resolved to say more, but just as he was about to open his mouth, Kokoshin zoomed in from behind and shoved him back in his seat.

The crowd watched closely.

In the meantime, Dounia had found her way onto the platform and taken one of the center seats. Today was a great day for her. Glancing at her two lovers, she couldn't have been happier or more contented. She was exceedingly grateful for what they had done for her and vowed that, once elected, she would be the best deputy possible. Tears welled in her eyes and her cheeks flushed a deep red. The two men were enthralled by the success of their plan. The crowd appeared to accept Dounia as their future Deputy and even seemed delighted to have her on the presidium. Yes, the meeting had got off to a good start indeed, and there seemed to be no reason why it shouldn't continue in much the same way. The men were confident that the remaining seats for the presidium would be filled with equally deserving citizens.

Leyzarov addressed the crowd. "Citizens, I want to congratulate you all, the meeting is moving along splendidly. It is now time to fill the remaining seats of the presidium, the most prestigious seats in the house. And I want you the people to decide who will—"

He was interrupted by laughter and jeers from the back of the hall. Then a lone voice called out: "Marko Tovkach! I vote for Marko Tovkach to sit on the presidium!"

Applause erupted, followed by more laughter. Before long a large, burly man with crooked legs and a scraggly beard, clutching a black skullcap, was pushed onto the platform. He stood gaping at the throng, scratching his head.

Leyzarov watched in horror as Tovkach took a seat on Dounia's right. "This must be some joke," he thought, trying to contain himself.

Tovkach was a notorious drunkard. Just the other day at dusk he had been found lying on the edge of Pashensky's field with an empty vodka bottle. Lucky for him he didn't freeze to death. And now this bleary-eyed lush was not only on the presidium but seated next to the future Deputy of the Village Soviet. This was an absolute outrage! Leyzarov was speechless.

In that instant someone else shouted, "My vote goes to Marsessa Kunsia!"

The crowd roared even more loudly. Leyzarov was totally beside himself. He turned to Kokoshin for help. The meeting, which had started out in such an organized and civilized manner, was being transformed into a sideshow. Leyzarov looked closely at the faces before him, suspecting sabotage. Rage boiled inside him; his face felt hot.

Marsessa scrambled up onto the platform and took a seat on Dounia's left. She was a particularly unkempt woman in her mid-forties with a pinkish blotchy face and graying hair. Her big eyes flashed wildly about the room and her mouth was twisted into a crazed grimace. It was no secret that Marsessa was unlike the other villagers; in fact, there was nothing normal about her. To put it simply, she was mad, she had gone mad years ago around the age of twenty. For some reason she was fond of funerals, and whenever a procession wound its way into the cemetery, she was not far behind, wailing and bawling at the top of her voice. She was also notorious for hurling obscenities at passersby and for singing songs, one in particular, her favorite, which she sang over and over: "The bulls are horny as hell. The cows are in heat. It's spring! It's spring!"

The villagers tolerated her. She was affectionately known throughout the region as the Madwoman of Hlaby.

Leyzarov tried to appear composed, but anger got the better of him. First a drunk and now a lunatic had found their way onto the platform, and in a matter of minutes had managed to transform the meeting into a circus. Things had got completely out of hand. Desperately he tried to think of ways to boot the two off the presidium, to replace them with suitable and deserving representatives, but then another voice ripped through the Clubhouse:

"My vote goes to Ostap Pavlovich Bubon!"

This time the laughter broke into a roar. Old Bubon, partly senile and half-blind, wasted no time in hobbling up to the front on his cane. He wore loose-fitting trousers patched at the knees and a shabby gray overcoat. His wife, who had been unfaithful to him with the local butcher, had died mysteriously years ago, and immediately after her death, and ever since, he called all women whores and Jezebels. Bubon had been suspected of killing her, but somehow he had slipped past the law.

Leyzarov stood on the platform ready to tear out his hair. He was now certain the meeting was being deliberately sabotaged. The most imbecilic, the most obnoxious people in the region—a madwoman, a drunk, and now a wife-killer—had just been granted the most distinguished seats. Things couldn't possibly get worse. Desperately, he appealed to the crowd, "Comrades! I'm sure some of you must have other candidates in mind. In the name of democracy, please give me their names." Swallowing hard, visibly rattled, tugging at his shirt collar to loosen it, he looked anxiously at the faces before him.

At that moment Kokoshin stepped in and tried to help restore order. He waved his arms. "Citizens! Citizens! I give you one last chance. Look around you, I'm sure there are people more worthy to represent you today than the three who presently grace our platform. Please, give us more names."

But the crowd remained unresponsive. Feeling that the situation was hopeless, he conceded. "Then it's agreed. The outcome is clear, the people have spoken." Reluctantly he jotted down the names of those on the presidium in his ledger book, and slipped the book into his pocket. Finally when things appeared to settle down, to everyone's surprise, another voice shot out from the crowd, "On behalf of the presidium, I vote honorary seats be granted to Stalin and his top advisers!"

The two Party men froze and their mouths dropped open in horror and disbelief. Things had gone from bad to worse; the meeting had now turned into a complete debacle.

Kokoshin leaned over and whispered to his partner, "This is nothing more than a travesty. They're planning to sit Stalin in line with a group of dimwits! We've got to do something."

Leyzarov agreed. "It's definitely a conspiracy. Someone's going to pay, and dearly!"

Before either could think of a response, several young men started dragging chairs onto the platform and placing them on either side of Tovkach and Bubon. One young man in blue-gray trousers, with tousled brown hair, took a framed picture of Stalin down from the wall and with great care set it on the seat of one of the chairs.

The crowd roared and heckled.

Tovkach, Marsessa and Bubon sat happily on the platform, enjoying the best seats in the house. Did they consider themselves dimwits? Certainly not. Tovkach always had enough to eat and drink, and he was too smart to complicate his life with a nagging wife. Ostap Bubon would have whacked his cane over anyone's head who called him a dimwit. He wasn't a dimwit; he was smart, because how else would he have landed a seat on the presidium— and next to Stalin!

Kokoshin tried to restore order.

"Attention, people! Attention! The time has now come for me to introduce to you our foremost candidate who will take up the honorable position of Deputy to the Village Soviet. The village Morozovich, in conformity with our existing order, elected a candidate for our electoral neighborhood, the very respected and cultured worker, Dounia Avdeevna Zemlankova. Now, allow me to say a few words about Dounia Avdeevna.

"She is the daughter of a proletarian family and her father, Avdeya Zemlankov, is a well-known, revered laborer. Most of you are aware that old Zemlankov, with his horse and cart, still today hauls furniture, barrels of tar, and beer in and around Pinsk. When the need arises, he also moves the city's garbage to the dump on Kostibyoushka Hill along the Pina. The proletarian origin of Dounia Avdeevna is indisputable. She is a dedicated worker who herself has labored as a bricklayer for the construction industry and later was a merchant in the Pinsk marketplace where she sold salt herring from her barrels. Now she has taken up the honorable position of schoolteacher in Morozovich, where she is beloved by the children and deeply devoted to her work. Her family is working-class and bears the torch of the revolution. They are the true citizens of our new civilization. A big round of applause for Dounia

Avdeevna Zemlankova, our future Deputy of the Village Soviet of
B.S.S.R.!"

Although the crowd applauded rapturously, the three undesirables on the platform did not seem to be paying any attention
to what was going on around them. Ostap, leaning on his cane,
could actually be heard snoring, and Tovkach stared at his hands
and played with his fingers. Marsessa was lost in her own world,
rocking her body back and forth, mumbling under her breath, constantly repeating herself.

While Kokoshin addressed the crowd, Marsessa's mumbling
grew louder and more pronounced, and before long she began
hurling insults at everyone around her. All eyes fell on her. Cornelius, who was sitting in the front row came forward and shouted,
"Will you just shut up, woman! You're disrupting the meeting. You
sound like a chicken with its head cut off." Then under his breath,
"Stupid hag."

Marsessa caught his last words, and went cross-eyed. Spring-
ing out of her chair, hissing like a snake, she went at him. "You of
all people have the nerve to call me a stupid hag! I'm no hag, and
I'm certainly not stupid. The people didn't choose you to sit up
here on the presidium, did they? Look who's stupid now? Horse
thief!" Then turning to look at the picture of Stalin, she smiled and
winked. "Hah! I told him off, didn't I, Joseph Vissarionovich?"

"Enough! Enough!" Leyzarov stamped his foot angrily. "Another
outbreak will not be tolerated. If you're not called upon, you have
no right to speak. These are the rules of the house. Now sit down,
both of you."

Cornelius, in defiance of Leyzarov's orders, swung around to
face the crowd. The audience of about two hundred seemed to
be expecting him to take the stand and say something important.
And he, Cornelius, Village Chairman, appointed by government
officials in Moscow, had a lot to say.

"Comrades!" he shouted, "I feel compelled to say a few words.
You must be very proud of yourselves. A meeting was called in the
dead of winter and you all took the time to be here today. It's obvi-

ous to me that you clearly understand the importance of solidarity and I commend you for that. In just a few short months, in the spring elections, we will officially vote in Dounia Avdeevna as our Deputy of the Village Soviet. She will go to Minsk and talk about our villages and make a good impression on the higher authorities there. Because of her, we will undoubtedly get special treatment. You see what having a smart and dedicated Deputy means! Our lives will become enriched and we will live out our days in happiness and contentment. Come spring, all that will be left for us to do will be to sing and dance and be merry.

"And the best news of all is that at the start of May our generous new regime will be assigning our region a *kolkhoz*. And a *kolkhoz*, for those of you who don't know, is a huge socialized agricultural unit operated by enormous harvesting combines, tractors, mechanical equipment and other machinery. It's most impressive. Industrialism is the birth of the working-class revolution. A new age indeed lies ahead for the common working man—no more horses and oxen on our vast tracts of land! We are re-establishing our agricultural system, where all workers will be equal, and all property will be held in common ownership. Yes, it's true, the former Olivinski estate is ours for the taking. The property, as you know, is immense—it has a barn, a pigpen, a chicken-coop, fields of wheat as far as the eye can see, even a duck pond—everything is there just waiting for us. A *kolhoz* is a remarkable place, it will not be owned solely by one oversized, greedy capitalist landlord; on the contrary, it will be operated and managed by you, the working masses, the backbone of our great new nation! History is being rewritten. Through collectivization you will see socialism at work, where everyone will be equal. A woman will be equal to a man and a man to a woman. It's even written in the Constitution."

At this point, everyone in the Clubhouse was startled by a loud banging noise. All eyes fell on Bubon, who was striking the floor with his cane.

"A woman equal to a man?" he shouted. "Never! Those damn bitches, nothing but Jezebels!" He yelled so loud the veins on his neck stood out. "They'll never be equal to a man. Never! They're all sluts, whores, every last one of them!"

Cornelius walked up to the old man and said contemptuously, "Don't interrupt me when I'm talking. Keep your stupid comments to yourself."

He was about to seize Bubon and pull him off the platform. But when the old man raised his cane and aimed it directly at his head, Cornelius backed off. He knew how strong Bubon was. Stepping aside, he turned his attention back to the audience.

"Now where did I leave off? Oh, yes, the *kolkhoz*. The *kolkhoz* is an extraordinary place and it has its own set of rules and regulations. At the beginning of May, we will release all our animals into the vast fields of the former Olivinski estate. The horses will be housed in the barn, the cows in the shed, the pigs in the pigpen, and the chickens in the chicken-coop. We'll feed the horses oats and hay, and say, 'Eat! Eat! There's plenty more'. The cows will get the best feed money can buy, and our buckets will overflow with milk. Experienced workers will come all the way from Moscow and show us how to shear our sheep, and we'll also have special milkmaids. If we work hard together, we'll all prosper." He raised his arms as if to embrace the crowd. "Glory to Stalin! Glory to the greatest friend of the people!"

Marsessa sprang out of her seat. "*Kolkhoz*, hah! To hell with your *kolkhoz*! Your mother won't live to see the day I give up my cow to your stinking *kolkhoz*! Never!" Then to the people, "Did you hear? Cornelius wants to seize our horses and our sheep. He wants us to give up everything. All his life he was a filthy, miserable, good-for-nothing, and now he wants everything for nothing."

"Not me, you stupid woman," Cornelius shot back at her, "it's the regime, the regime wants everything for nothing. Your brain is fried; you don't understand the first thing about socialism. Now shut up and sit down." He turned sternly and reproachfully to the crowd. "Shame on you for voting such a featherbrain onto the presidium!"

"Comrades! Comrades!" Kokoshin waved his hands. "We are now coming to the end of our meeting, but before I call it a day, I would like to ask Dounia Avdeevna, our new Deputy, to say a few final words."

Dounia rose from her seat and looked lovingly at the crowd. Her hands clasped in front of her, she cried out, "What joy! What absolute joy! We are witnessing history in the making. Labor has triumphed! My dear friend and colleague Comrade Kokoshin has called upon me to say a few words. Well, let's see, what can I talk to you about? About life? My life has been gray and uneventful like the lives of most proletarians. I was born in Pinsk to the family of Avdeya Zemlakov. My *papasha*, by hauling various wares in and around Pinsk and operating a junk cart, somehow managed to provide for us. And when I grew up my *papasha* sent me to school. Even though I'm a proletarian, my life has been enriched by education. Never underestimate the importance of education! And now I'm a teacher. If you're interested in my grandfather, allow me to say a few words.

"During the dark, gloomy, oppressive days of the Czar, my grandfather settled in Pinsk, where he worked as a tailor. And that's how the Zemlankov family came to be from Pinsk. I'm very honored that you, dear people, have granted me the honorable position of Deputy of B.S.S.R. Our regime, I want you to know, is very fair and generous and because of this, I love it very much, and I know the regime loves me too because I'm an honest and cultured laborer. Our regime doesn't like capitalist landowners and greedy, self-serving farmers, and I don't like them either. I say, death to all the *kulaks*!

"And in spring the elections will come and you will officially choose me as your deputy. I am grateful to all of you for this chance. I will go to the meetings and tell the authorities how nice and hardworking you all are. I will say to the regime: please build for the people of the Pinsk Marshes big factories, develop their farms, and expand their cities. And don't worry, people, I will also say to the authorities: burn their churches and chase their priests out of the seminaries. Destroy the last vestiges of oppression and set them free. Yes, I will say all this, and just for you."

Pausing a moment, she appeared to be searching for something or someone in the audience. Shaking her head, she said seriously, "You have a total of thirteen teachers in your region and not one of them is here with us today. How curious! How discouraging! But on the other hand, if they are truly preoccupied with school matters, then, naturally, I won't hold it against them. A teacher, dear people, is like an ant that pulls a weight greater than itself. Grammar, arithmetic, geography and so on, must all first be absorbed by the teacher and then deposited into the heads of the pupils. This mission is a very difficult one because your children, as we all know, are a bunch of morons. But not to worry, our teachers are smart and educated people. They are trained to chase ignorance from their little heads and replace it with the light of knowledge. That's why I'm not angry with our teachers for not being here today, because I myself am a teacher, and I know the great challenges that face them. You did the right thing when you chose me, a Morozovich schoolteacher, for Deputy. I will work hard and find the absolute best way to represent you. Hurrah for Stalin! Hurrah for our new regime!"

"Hurrah!" echoed the crowd. But they were growing restless.

Clapping his hands, Leyzarov quickly adjourned the meeting. The Clubhouse emptied in a matter of minutes.

Walking along the road, bundled in her tattered coat and headscarf, Marsessa Kunsia was making her way home. A group of young people passing by her, teasingly asked if she would sing them her "bull song."

Giving them a big smile, without a word, she spun around and cut across the frozen meadow. Far from the ears of the crowd, with the wind hitting against her back, she burst into song.

"The bulls are horny as hell. The cows are in heat. It's spring! It's spring!"

CHAPTER 20

K ulik reread the letter for the tenth time.

Dear Comrade Kulik,

We are enclosing our debt to you and we apologize for not contacting you any sooner. Because we started receiving letters from Lonia a few weeks after your visit, we didn't need your generous loan after all. Happily, Lonia writes he should be arriving in Pinsk sometime at the end of April. Thank you for your good will and we remain forever grateful.

Sincerely,
The Bohdanoviches.

Kulik's heart sank. The letter read like a standard piece of business correspondence; there was no invitation to visit, no interest in his affairs or his well-being. It was obvious Marusia had written the letter, yet for some reason she hadn't signed it. He despised her indifference, her matter-of-fact tone, and he became convinced she wanted to distance herself from him. "It's no secret Sobakin got lucky with her." Dounia's harsh, brutal words went through his head over and over again. How could Marusia have succumbed so easily? Obviously, the Bohdanoviches no longer had any use for him, Kulik, or for his money. Because their Lonia was finally coming home, Kulik's friendship no longer mattered to them. He was deeply hurt.

And to make matters worse, the isolation of village life was not helping his state of mind. In fact, it was causing him horrible spells of depression. More than anything he wanted to lose himself in the city, where he could walk into a crowd and remain anonymous. Since learning of Marusia's affair with Sobakin, he could find no peace. Jealousy and revulsion tore away at him, causing him bitter pain. "If only . . ." he murmured to himself hopefully, "If only she and I could have . . ." But before finishing this thought, he sighed in anguish. "Marusia has fallen prey to a wild beast. Sobakin has already sunk his sharp fangs into her tender flesh." These dismal thoughts rolled around in his head, mixed with other thoughts about the village, which seemed to him like a kettle of boiling water. It was one incident after another.

For a brief moment Kulik felt grateful that he had not attended the village meeting. He had not attracted attention to himself and, at least for the time being, he was free from scrutiny. But was he really free? Was anyone free anymore? Danger lurked in all corners and the Party henchmen saw and knew everything.

With these disturbing thoughts streaming through his mind, Kulik was startled by a knock on the door. He was surprised to find Boris Paspelov, the newly appointed school inspector, standing on the threshold. He was a young man in his thirties, his sandy-colored hair oiled and combed back smartly. A thick mustache concealed his upper lip and his left eye twitched slightly. He was dressed in a neatly pressed overcoat, carried a bulging leather satchel, and his black leather boots shone. He was clutching several documents.

"Good day to you, Comrade Kulik," he said, tipping his cap. "How are things in your school?" He cleared his throat. "Well, in any case, we'll see about that soon enough."

It was clear at once that he took his job very seriously. After scanning the room, he walked to the bookcase behind Kulik's desk and took down a volume from the top shelf. As he flipped through the pages, shaking his head, he made several unintelligible remarks and scribbled something in his notepad. Then he made his way to the filing cabinet, where, starting with the top drawer, he pulled out folder after folder, studying each one thoroughly. Almost half an hour went by before he turned his attention to Kulik's desk. He rummaged through the drawers, turning papers upside down, ripping open envelopes, and scattering pencils and paper clips across the floor. When finally his eyes rested on several boxes piled in a corner, he looked very serious. "Unacceptable," he stated. "This is completely unacceptable."

Without another sound, he went out into the corridor, and after briefly inspecting the bulletin board outside the office door, walked into every classroom, where he sat quietly in the back row, carefully observing the lessons and making copious notes. Classes had barely finished, when, rather huffily, he called all the teachers into the office for a meeting.

"Unsatisfactory!" he snapped at them. He turned to Ivashkevich. "Comrade Ivashkevich. You don't pronounce names correctly. Your diction is improper and reeks of provincialism. The children are all confused. For example, you say *Lyavon*, but you should really say *Lyev*. It's as simple as that! Haven't you heard of Lyev Nikolayevich Tolstoy? Well, he's *Lyev* Tolstoy and not *Lyavon* Tolstoy."

Ivashkevich shrugged. "Lyev Tolstoy is a Russian writer and naturally he has a Russian name. In Belorussian there are no *Lyevs*, only *Lyavons* and therefore *Lyev* Tolstoy becomes *Lyavon* Tolstoy. In England, for example, *Lyev* Tolstoy becomes *Leo* Tolstoy. In France, *Léo* Tolstoy. *Lyevs* are found only in Russia and nowhere else. And since the regime has made our school a Belorussian one, we'll continue to say *Lyavon* and not *Lyev*."

"A Belorussian school!" Paspelov stared at him haughtily. "You're not about to teach me what kind of school this is! First and foremost this is a Soviet school, and in Soviet schools there are no *Lyavons* only *Lyevs*. Understand?"

Visibly disturbed, Paspelov paced the room for a while with his arms folded, looking down at the floor, after which he turned his attention irritably to Sergei. "I listened to your geography lesson, and it was most unsettling, to say the least. You mispronounced all the place names. For example, Kiiv should be Kiev, Lviv, Lvov, even Polissia should be Polyessia. I am sorry to say, these are serious blunders and I am obliged to bring them to the attention of the People's Commissariat of Education once I return to Pinsk."

Having said this, clearly disturbed by the state of affairs in School Number Seven, he set his eyes on Kulik. "Your lesson in ancient history, comrade, was very troubling. Every historical reference you alluded to was a distortion of the worst kind. For example, under Sagron, the Assyrian Empire was not only the . . ."

"Uh, not Sagron," Kulik delicately corrected him, "but Sargon."

"That's what I said. Sargon! In any case, when teaching ancient history you should really focus on truly great rulers like, uh, like . . ."

"Sargon?" Kulik tried to be of help.

"Yes, like Sargon," repeated Paspelov, laying special emphasis on the letter 'r'. "However, by giving lessons on Sargon, you are not to ignore the integral part our great Mother Russia played in the development of ancient history."

"Excuse me, Comrade Inspector," Kulik said, even more carefully than before, "but Russia did not exist in ancient times."

Paspelov stood looking rather shaken. Collecting himself as best he could, forcing a smile, he strove to keep up appearances. "Yes, yes, it seems to me you are correct, after all. My memory fails me. It's been a long time since I studied history, let alone ancient history. Of course, of course, how could I have forgotten?"

Kulik and Sergei exchanged brief glances, deriving great pleasure at seeing Boris Paspelov make a complete ass of himself.

Shuffling uncomfortably for a moment or two, Paspelov stepped up to Kulik, and patting him on the back, said in a condescending tone, "I'll have you know, Comrade Director, you've made a good impression on me today. You seem, if I may speak bluntly, well-informed and intelligent. This is a pleasant change, I must say, from what I normally come up against." Then looking straight at him, "In any case, I'm confident that by the time I see you again you will have straightened up this whole mess regarding your ancient history classes."

He glanced at his watch, collected his things, and hastily made for the door, where he called out, "I'm running late. Till next time. I have yet to look in on Dounia Avdeevna. Good day to you."

In the road, Paspelov got behind the wheel of his black sedan and set off for Morozovich. Kulik watched him disappear into the distance. Feeling almost sorry for him, he muttered, "Prepare yourself, Boris Paspelov. Dounia Avdeevna is about to eat you alive."

Had Boris Paspelov known what awaited him in the Morozovich schoolhouse, he would have bypassed it by ten kilometers, at least. According to his calculations, Dounia Avdeevna still had a few more classes to teach before the end of the day and would be in the school for another two hours. That would give him enough time to carry out a full inspection of the classrooms and to conduct an interview with her afterward. As he pulled up before the front doors, which were slightly ajar, he was surprised to hear singing coming from somewhere inside. It was a deep, husky voice, almost masculine, and horribly out of tune. "I lost my virginity to the man I adore. I lost my virginity . . ."

Paspelov quickly got out of his car, and stepping into the school, looked up and down the hallway trying to determine where it was coming from. As the voice struggled to reach a high C, he realized it was coming from a room at the far end of the hall. He poked his head in the door.

"Oh!" a woman shrieked, startled by the intrusion. "You scared me half to death. I wasn't expecting anyone. Who are you and what do you want?"

"Good day. My name is Boris Paspelov and I am the new school inspector. I was sent by the People's Commissariat of Education in Pinsk and I am here on official state business." Then, curiously, "Was that you I heard singing?"

Dounia nodded and began to complain. "Ah, yes, it was me you heard singing. Singing, that's my only salvation. I'm going mad in this horrible dead place. It's not fit for human habitation. The people here are from the Dark Ages."

Paspelov looked at her disapprovingly, took out his notepad and jotted down a few lines. Raising his head, he said severely, "There are still two hours left of school. Where are the children?"

Dounia brushed back her hair from her face. "They went home about an hour ago."

"Did you dismiss them?"

"Yes, I couldn't bear it anymore, they were driving me crazy. They're just a bunch of spoiled, sniveling brats."

Paspelov tensed. He was becoming quite perturbed. For a teacher to take such liberties was unheard of. He stormed at her, "And who gave you permission to do that?"

Dounia threw back her head. She was growing increasingly impatient with his questions. "Hah! Now you want to read me the bill of rights!"

"If I have to, I will. As inspector, my job is to visit schools and verify that all students and teachers are working in compliance with the new order. From what I see here already, this school is full of irregularities."

"Full of irregularities? You've got a lot of nerve coming here and bothering me with irregularities! I don't have time for your nonsense. And your approach is most unfriendly and disrespectful." She added, "I suppose you haven't heard . . . I'm not just the mere teacher you think I am. I'll have you know, I've just become the leading candidate for Deputy of the Village Soviet. The people have voted me in. Yes, I'm to be the next deputy. As you must now understand, I've been kept very busy, and I haven't had time to waste on schoolwork. My head is brimming with ideas, night and day. Meetings, meetings, every day I must attend meetings— there's no end to them. And the speeches I have to prepare! And on top of all that, the peasants and workers have to be organized, the posters put up. As you can see, I'm a very busy woman."

A constrained silence followed and the tension in the room intensified. The truth of the matter was that Paspelov was completely stunned to hear of Dounia's candidacy for regional deputy; in fact, this was the first he had heard of it. The news literally left him speechless and made him wonder how such a crass and grossly underbred woman could be nominated to so responsible and dignified a position. This was a complete mystery to him. He didn't want to believe it, and chose not to believe it. He decided that she was making up a story.

He said firmly and with a great deal of authority, "I am the school inspector and I shall conduct my inspection of your school as I see fit. Now, if you'll excuse me."

Pushing her aside, he proceeded to rummage through her classrooms, fidgeting in desks, sifting through papers and examining closets. When after about an hour he returned, he looked indignant and disgusted.

"This school is in appalling condition. It's worse than a pigsty. There's scribbling on the walls and the floors are filthy. The benches are all scratched up and dusty, and the blackboards look like they've never been cleaned. All that's missing in this dump is a broken window."

Dounia caught him up at once. "Actually, one of the little monsters broke a window just last week and I had to send a peasant especially to Pinsk to get it fixed. Why, it cost me almost thirty rubles!"

Paspelov wrote several lines in his notebook, looked up at her briefly, and wrote some more. Then he asked to see her lesson preparations.

"Lesson preparations?" Dounia shrugged. "What do you want with lesson preparations? Do you think I'm so stupid that I have to record everything on paper?" After briefly examining her nails, rolling her eyes, she pointed to a small wooden table with a lopsided pile of papers on one side and a stack of copybooks on the other. "If you feel you must do something, go right ahead, get it out of your system. That's the work of the children over there. Take all the time you want."

Paspelov promptly made for the table. He thumbed through the papers, and leafed through the copybooks, all the while shaking his head, muttering under his breath. He could hear Dounia humming at the other end of the room, and saying, "Oh, grammar, arithmetic. Trying to teach these little delinquents is an absolute horror."

Waving a copybook in his hand, Paspelov came toward her. "This work is dreadful. This is not writing, it's scribbling! And there are hardly any teacher's corrections anywhere, and if there are, they're either too sloppy to make out or just plain wrong. How do you expect the children to learn anything?" He turned his attention to a pile of papers that appeared to be arithmetic homework. "Why, you don't even know your fractions! This is an outrage!"

"What do you mean?" Dounia was offended. "Of course I know my fractions. I'll prove it to you. Here, for example, is an apple. If I cut it in half, I get two halves. And if I cut the half in a half, I get a quarter. Simple!" She faced him with her hands on her hips. "Hah, and you say I don't know my fractions?"

"And how do you add a half and a third? How do you multiply an eighth by a quarter? And what's a common denominator?"

"Common denominator? Hmm . . ." Dounia scratched her head and thought a while. Finally she shrugged. "Quite honestly, it slips my mind for the moment. But it's no big deal, these little monsters could do very well without these common denominators of yours. Besides what do they need to know them for anyway? Look at me, I'm doing just fine and I'm even a teacher, not to mention the soon-to-be Deputy of the Village Soviet."

She looked at him with contempt. "Your attitude is terribly hostile and imperialistic, Comrade Inspector. You're putting on airs as if you're well-read, but you don't fool me, you're a fake. I wouldn't be surprised if you never went past grade five. Do you always attack women as if you were a general?"

Paspelov was completely unprepared for her degree of insolence. "Do you realize whom you are speaking to? This, Dounia Avdeevna, could cost you your job! I am the school inspector and I was sent here by the People's Commissariat of Education."

Dounia rushed back at him. "School inspector, hah! You're nothing more than a flea! You were born a flea and you'll die a flea!"

"How dare you!" Paspelov could not believe his ears. "You're an illiterate and vulgar creature, you have no place in a school, let alone becoming a candidate for Deputy of the Village Soviet. I will be certain to brief Yeliseyenko, the school superintendent, on the mess here. Then we'll see who the flea is!"

At this fiery moment, to Boris's great surprise, as if out of nowhere, two government officers entered the room. They were both in official army uniforms and their chests and lapels were heavily decorated. Revolvers dangled from their holsters. The taller of the two, Paspelov noticed, was carrying what appeared to be a bottle wrapped in brown paper.

"Dounia!" Kokoshin rushed to her, and looked into her face with concern. "What's going on in here? We heard all the racket from outside. Is everything all right? Have you been waiting for us long?" Then catching sight of the inspector standing against the wall, he raised his brows suspiciously. "Who's that?"

"His name's Boris Paspelov. And he's been harassing me all afternoon. It's a good thing you came when you did. He was just about to hit me."

At that moment Paspelov felt rather dizzy. It was precisely then that he realized whom he was dealing with and how dangerous the situation was that he had created for himself—it hit him like a ton of bricks. He had battled with the wrong person; it was now obvious Dounia Avdeevna had friends in high places, and these friends, with just a wave of her hand were capable of bringing him down. Wiping his forehead, swallowing hard, he gathered his belongings quickly and made for the door. In a faint voice, he bade farewell and hastened to his car.

Dounia shouted after him sarcastically, "Good day to you too, Comrade Paspelov. Who's the flea now? Hah! Hah! Hah!"

The sun was setting, and a harsh and bitter wind coming in from the north piled the snow in large heaps against the schoolyard fence. It was so cold outside one could hardly breathe. With his hands trembling upon the steering wheel, the snow-covered countryside rushed past Paspelov, who felt he was having a bad dream. He knew it was the beginning of the end for him. His ascent up the Party ladder had stopped before it had gotten started, thanks to Dounia Avdeevna, future Deputy of the Village Soviet of B.S.S.R.

CHAPTER 21

One day Ohrimko Suchok's grandmother appeared in Hlaby and took him to her house in a faraway settlement somewhere beyond Kolodny, in the heart of a deep forest. She brought him there to make him a winter coat from wool she had spun herself. Although Ohrimko's grandmother was planning to bring him home in just a few days, Kulik already found himself missing the boy. He had an empty feeling, and he thought how glad he would be to see the boy come breezing through the door of the school, his big bright eyes shining and a broad smile on his face.

But thoughts of the boy became intertwined with other thoughts, grave and serious, and he began to feel uneasy. He could not understand or put into words what was troubling him. He missed Ohrimko, and felt as if the boy's absence would trigger something horrible and disastrous.

When Ohrimko had been gone for two days, Paraska came out of her small wooden house some time before noon, and crossed the road to the school. The day was cold and blustery. It was late March, but it felt more like the middle of January. Dressed in a ragged overcoat two sizes too large for her, and with a crudely spun shawl wrapped around her head, she suddenly stopped in the road and strained her ears to listen. There was a peculiar sound coming from the near distance—it was the rumbling of a motor car, coming closer and closer, toward her. What she saw made her heart thud. It was a car, but not just an ordinary car. It was an enclosed black police car.

"It's the NKVD!" she screamed. Scared out of her wits, she ran headlong into the school. "Director! Director! They're coming! They're coming! Lord have mercy on us!"

Kulik, jumping up from behind his desk, hurried to the window. Peering outside, he whispered in a voice that was not his own, "It's the Black Crow."

"Oh, my God! Oh, my God!" Paraska clutched her chest. "Just when I thought things couldn't get any worse! My Philip's slipping in and out of consciousness. He's at death's door. My life's a living hell and there's no end in sight. What misfortune! What misfortune! And now of all things, the Black Crow!"

With each passing second the rumbling grew louder. At last the car swerved to the right and came to a screeching halt by the schoolyard fence. The front and back doors flew open and out came six NKVD men, all in long gray army coats with rifles strapped over their shoulders. One of them Kulik recognized immediately: Simon Stepanovich Sobakin. As he watched the men, he was convinced they had come for him. Why else would they have stopped at the school?

The NKVD men grouped together a moment, then hurriedly broke up into two groups: the first, under the command of a sergeant-major, started for the village, while the other, led by Sobakin, did not turn into the school as Kulik had expected, but made for Paraska's house. When she saw that, Paraska's face filled with dread and she shook like a leaf. A fearfully unnatural cry ripped from her throat, and half-hysterical, she threw herself outside, crying out the names of her children: "Lida! Maria! . . . God, no! Don't harm my children!" Lifting her overcoat up to her knees, running through the deep snow, somehow she managed to catch up to the men just as they were about to open the door of her house. Weeping violently, she tried to push her way in front of them. "What do you want from us? We're law-abiding citizens. We've done nothing wrong. My children! Please don't harm my children!"

"Out of our way!" A heavy hand landed on her shoulder and pushed her aside. The alarm on her face intensified when she recognized the man standing over her. It was Sobakin.

"Why do you look so shaken up, my dear?" He gave her a mock-ing grin. "No need to be scared. Nothing is going to happen to you. Now come on, grab hold of yourself. Besides, we're forever grateful to you. Remember on our last visit when you gave us that fine feast? That was most kind and generous of you."

Clearing his throat, he spat between his feet, and motioned to his men to follow him inside.

Paraska's children, seeing the strangers enter the house, were frightened and tried to hide. Three-year-old Danilo crawled under the table and screamed for his mother.

Sobakin walked across the room without saying a word. Slip-ping his hand into his leather shoulder bag, he brought out a piece of paper and read harshly, *"Philip Semionovich Braskov!* Does he live here?"

At the sound of her husband's name, Paraska's agony was inde-scribable. Looking frantically from one NKVD man to another, she said, "Philip, that's my husband. He's over there on the sofa. As you can see he's very sick. I don't expect him to make it to the morning." Then with tears gushing from her eyes, her voice breaking, "Please, don't harm him, I beg you. He didn't do any-thing wrong."

Sobakin stepped up to the dying man and poked him in the ribs with the butt end of his rifle. He said roughly, "Come on, get up, Philip Semionovich. Why haven't you been reporting to work at the Bugsy-Dnieprovsky Canal? Our records show you're deliber-ately trying to thwart its construction."

"Lieutenant Sobakin," pleaded Paraska, "he's not conscious any-more. He doesn't know what's going on around him."

A sneering voice shot out from across the room, "Not to worry, Paraska. Your Philip will be fine. We've prescribed the perfect remedy for him and you should be grateful to us. We're sending him off to a health resort. I hear there are several really good ones in Siberia. Hah! Hah! Hah!"

With a wave of his arm, Sobakin ordered the two officers to remove Philip from the sofa. One grabbed hold of his legs, while the other slipped his hands under his shoulders. The dying man stirred slightly and let out a low moan. The movement was too much for him. Blood oozed from the corners of his mouth and his eyes rolled from side to side. Six-year-old Svetlana, who had been crouching behind a chest of drawers jumped out, and with a look of terror on her face, clutched at her father's arm. "Papa! Papa! Wake up!"

Paraska rushed to her daughter's side, and scooping her up in her arms, kissed her face repeatedly. She cried, "He's dead! Dear God, your father's dead!"

Sobakin came forward, and touched his heels. He said matter-of-factly, "He's cold, stone cold."

The officers dragged the dead man across the floor, and threw him outside into the snow. Sobakin called after him, laughing, "Well, Philip Semionovich, you've gone and outsmarted us. You son-of-a-bitch."

Finished with Paraska's house, the NKVD men, accompanied this time by Iofe Nicel Leyzarov, jumped into their black car and headed for the other side of the village, to the home of Hrisko Suchok. As they entered the gates of his yard, Hrisko, who had been splitting wood by the side of his shed, dropped his axe, and took several steps back. His heart beat wildly; he knew that something dreadful was about to happen to him. His only choice was to try to run. He turned and headed to the threshing barn. He frantically jumped over a low wattle fence, and rushed toward a grove of alders, hoping to lose himself in the thicket. The men ran after him, and, before he knew it, Suchok was surrounded. A single bullet ripped through the air and struck him in the nape of the neck. He fell to the ground dead. A red stain seeped into the snow. Sobakin stepped up to the corpse and kicking it onto its back, shouted to his comrades, "We just got ourselves another son-of-a-bitch!"

In the meantime Iofe and one of the officers stormed into Hrisko's house, where they found his wife hiding behind the stove. She was frozen with fright, scarcely able to stand, looking like a cow about to be taken to slaughter. The officer pulled her out by the hair, and dragged her, screaming, into the Black Crow. Over and over she cried out the name of her son.

Inside the Black Crow it was dark. Sobbing and praying, it was not long before she realized she was not alone. Someone else was there, mumbling and whimpering. It was a woman in great distress, and she sounded very much like Marsessa Kunsia, who, disoriented as she was, had grasped the horror of her situation. Seeking the warmth of each other's bodies, the women huddled together and wept.

A shroud of doom had fallen over Hlaby. The village was silent, but tense and restless. Paraska, pale and emaciated, moved like a zombie, and was no longer of any use to herself or to anyone around her.

For the next several days the villagers busied themselves washing the bodies of the dead, preparing them for eternity. Two pine boxes were quickly constructed and the dead men were laid inside. Twelve stocky young peasants with round pink faces, lifted them up on their shoulders, and slowly walked to the cemetery. The villagers trailed behind, chanting softly and weeping. Some carried long sticks with icons framed in colorfully embroidered cloths, while others clutched at crosses hidden inside their coat pockets. Once in the cemetery, standing over the freshly dug graves, one elderly villager took it upon himself to speak. He began in a low, doleful voice:

"Such is the funeral of Hrisko Suchok and Philip Braskov, the first in our village to be buried without a priest. May God bless them. . . . Our Father, who art . . ."

As the coffins were lowered into the ground, the sun appeared from behind a mass of clouds. It shone brilliantly and joyfully, and there was an unexpected warmth in its glow. A gentle breeze swept across the faces of the mourners. The hard winter was finally retreating. Spring was in the air.

CHAPTER 22

The great heaps of snow piled up on either side of the roads and on the walkways began to recede, and water dripped from the rooftops to gather in large pools. Trees and bushes had been freed of their winter covering; the ice on the Stryy River was melting along the shoreline. The village was slowly and surely showing signs of life.

With the promise of warmer weather came spring fever, and Kulik was feeling every bit of it. The long winter months had made him weary and crestfallen; he longed to get away, if only for a day. Although the horrific scenes from just a few days ago had severely dampened his spirit, something new seemed to be taking place within his young heart. Change was in the air and he was ready to embrace it with full force.

Pinsk! How long was it since he had been to Pinsk? The unknown awaited him there: all he could expect was the unexpected, since he was sure that the city had changed so radically in the past several months that it would seem like another place entirely. The puzzling and short-tempered Yeliseyenko of the People's Commissariat of Education, was there, the enigmatic, attractive Zena, the repulsive Sobakin and, of course, the beautiful green-eyed Marusia. At the thought of Marusia his heart dropped. Had she really given herself to Sobakin, as Dounia Avdeevna had so relentlessly maintained, or did he still stand a chance with her? Perhaps love was still in the air. The prospect of seeing her again filled him with inexpressible joy, but it soon faded. No one, including Marusia, could be trusted.

Putting these negative thoughts aside, Kulik placed Ivashkevich in charge of the school, and hitching a wagon ride with a local peasant, made for Pinsk. There were several school matters for him to settle there; for example, more pencils were needed, the calligraphy workbooks had been used up, there was no more ink, and several slates needed to be replaced. He also intended to ask Yeliseyenko why a new teacher had not yet been assigned to replace Haya Fifkina.

In Pinsk, the wagon lumbered slowly through a winding residential street, then looped round a corner and entered Market Square. On the east side of the square stood the Roman Catholic Church, and on the north side was a wall of small dim shops with signs over the doors, but with their windows boarded up, barred, or covered with faded newspapers and various proclamations. There were no bakeries, the fabric shops had disappeared, the fish stores, the fruit markets . . . The soul of the town was gone, it was hardly a place to visit, let alone to live. Even the passersby seemed drab and dull. Although Kulik was grateful to be out of the village if only for a day, he yearned to be some place else entirely, another city, another part of the world.

Kulik thanked the driver for the lift and slipped him a few rubles. A handful of peasant carts had already collected, not in the middle of the square as they had used to do every Tuesday and Friday, but along the sides, against the church wall. He was disheartened to see how dead the place was, especially on a Friday morning. It used to be so vibrant, so full of life! The fruit and vegetable stalls, the sound of cattle, the endless barrels of pickles and salt herring—all gone, along with the troops of little children laughing and chasing each other through the square, and the townspeople haggling with peasants over prices.

As Kulik was crossing the square, a broad-shouldered peasant with a face shaped like a potato, hurried toward him, and flashed open his oversized coat to expose huge pockets sewn into the lining from scraps of fabric. Each pocket held various items: in one there were perhaps six eggs, in another a slab of salt pork, and in still another a chunk of stale black bread.

"How about some eggs today?" the man asked eagerly. "I'll give you a good price, they're fresh this morning."

Kulik politely declined and continued on his way. After a while another man came up behind him, rolling a small makeshift hand-cart on wheels.

"Good morning to you, sir," he called out, tipping his cap. "May I interest you in some finery today?" Turning his cart to face Kulik, he showed remnants of coarse fabric and various nondescript odds and ends, including some cheap jewelry. "Maybe you'd like to trade your watch for some fine linen?" The peddler pulled out several pieces of cloth and held them up. "A little something for the wife, perhaps?"

Kulik walked on. The morning was bright and cheerful and the air sweet with the fragrance of spring. As he was about to turn down one of the side lanes, he heard a man and a woman arguing loudly about something.

"I'll give you five rubles," the man shouted.

"Five rubles! Hah!" the woman shot back. "That's not nearly enough."

"Well, then here's six!"

"Six? Not on your life! You can keep your six, I want ten!"

Kulik stopped. It was Valentyn, shaking his head and gesticulating at a middle-aged peasant woman.

"Ten rubles!" he yelled at her. "For what? A handful of half-rotten garlic?"

"Citizen Bohdanovich!" Kulik hastened toward the old man. "How goes it?"

Valentyn's eyes lit up. "Ivan! Ivan Kulik! Good to see you, young man! What brings you to our fair town?" Then, frowning, "I hope you're not looking to buy some garlic. This woman here wants ten rubles for three heads. It's nothing short of highway robbery!" He shrugged. "As you've probably noticed, there's not much to buy in the market these days. Everything is empty and locked up. Such are the times we live in now."

Delighted to find a familiar friendly face, Kulik invited the old man to have a drink with him. He knew a tavern nearby where

245

they could have a comfortable chat. But. when they stopped before the shabby two-story building, Kulik's smile faded. The place was padlocked. They looked at each other gloomily. Kulik was quick to make another suggestion. "There's a rather pleasant spot just a few minutes from here. When I came to Pinsk for the teachers' conference, I went there several times. I could use a bite to eat. What do you say?"

They walked to the stone building with its grimy façade. Kulik glanced through the paned windows and was relieved to see that the place was filled with people. They were huddled around long wooden tables covered with white tablecloths, talking, laughing, eating and drinking. The air was thick with tobacco smoke. The atmosphere seemed different from the way it had been when Kulik had visited it several weeks earlier. When they entered, a stocky woman in a uniform with epaulettes came up and blocked their way. She wanted to know whether they had trade union passes. Kulik was astonished by the request.

"Sorry." She shook her head. "This tavern is for trade union workers only. You'll have to take your business elsewhere."

They walked through dirty puddles of melted snow, past several ramshackle hotels and a string of dusky shops, all boarded up. Before long they tried another tavern, but there too they were required to show passes to prove they were workers from the railroad or shipbuilding yards.

Kulik thought, "A new hierarchy has been established, and in the world's first classless society!"

Old Valentyn, as if picking up on Kulik's thoughts, grumbled under his breath, "Before the war all you needed to go to a tavern was money. Why, you could practically drink together with a general!"

At last they were able to enter a small building called People's Tavern, where they ordered a bottle of wine and some black bread and sausages. The only other patrons were several men and a woman sitting in the far corner sharing a pot of beer, talking quietly. When the food and drinks arrived, Kulik asked, "Well, my good friend, tell me, how are things with Lonia? Has he come home yet?"

"Lonia, Lonia." Valentyn's face clouded and he sighed deeply. "It's a complete mystery to us. He writes often enough, but he still hasn't found his way home. My old lady is beside herself with worry. Even I'm starting to believe there's something wrong. And to make matters worse, Marusia insists his letters are forgeries."

Kulik was genuinely surprised by the news. "When I got your letter with my money, I assumed everything was going well and that Lonia was finally on his way home."

Valentyn finished his glass of wine, and quickly started on another. He became bitterly sarcastic.

"My two women have involved themselves with a knight in shining armor. And some knight in shining armor he's turned out to be! He's like a hawk after a hen; the hen flaps her wings and tries to get away, and the hawk swoops down and grabs her by the neck. One second and 'snap!' it's all over."

Kulik refilled the glasses. "Is it serious between Marusia and Sobakin? I understand they're quite the pair. I thought there would be a wedding by now, that you'd have yourself a Russian son-in-law."

"No, God forbid!" The old man's eyes flashed. "Sobakin will never get his hands on my daughter, not if I have anything to do with it. Besides, there can never be a wedding."

"How can you be so sure of that?"

"Because the son-of-a-bitch is married. He has a wife and children, two boys and a girl, in Moscow. Marusia found this out from a friend of hers." He drained his glass. "Sobakin's a swine. First he promised to bring Lonia home to us, but those were just empty words; he was trying to worm his way into Marusia's heart. He gave her expensive gifts, God knows where he got them—a bottle of French perfume, a fur coat, a skirt, and then . . . time for Marusia to pay him back. Lucky thing she got away from him unharmed, if you know what I mean, but just by the skin of her teeth. From the very start Sobakin had something terrible in mind for her."

He shook his head. "My Marusia should have known better. How long it took her before she got wise to him, and what a price she had to pay!"

A long silence followed. Valentyn rested his elbows on the table, and stared at his drink. "We haven't heard the last of Sobakin, not by a long shot. And on top of it, he rents rooms in the house next door to ours. Every night he returns from the Zovty Prison with blood on his hands. The tortures our people endure in there! Sobakin is the Devil personified." Then looking at Kulik, with regret, "I told Marusia over and over, from the very start, that you would have made a better suitor. But unfortunately every time I mentioned your name, she just rolled her eyes and laughed. I don't know what's wrong with that girl. She never listens to a thing I say."

Kulik winced. Trying to maintain his composure, he shrugged and said, "I'm really not interested in your daughter. She wanted a Muscovite and that's what she got. I'm sorry things didn't work out for her; though. Naturally, I wish her the best."

Eventually the conversation took on a lighter tone. Kulik went on about life in the village, while Valentyn complained about his wife. After about an hour, they shook hands and parted company.

It was now almost one o'clock. Kulik had only a few hours left to settle his school matters before catching his ride back to the village. He headed for the People's Commissariat of Education and was delighted to find Zena in Yeliseyenko's offices. She was seated at her desk, writing something with one hand and holding buttered bread in the other.

"*Bon appetit!*" Kulik called out cheerfully from the doorway.

She looked up smiling. "Why, if it isn't Ivan Kulik. Good to see you. Please, have a seat. Are you hungry? You're welcome to some of my bread."

"No, thank you. Actually, I've just come from a tavern."

Zena laughed. "I assumed that much. I can smell the drink on your breath from here. Why don't you have some tea, it'll take off the edge, at least before Yeliseyenko gets back. He left for a meeting about an hour ago, he should be back very soon."

248

Zena filled a cup with hot tea from a sealed thermos and handed it to Kulik. "Well, what's brought you to Pinsk?"

"Oh, nothing much, just a few simple school matters. We need some supplies—ink, slates, copybooks. And I'd like to talk to Yeliseyenko about a replacement for Haya Fifkina. Our school has been short-staffed for some time now."

Zena looked sharply at him. She said quietly, "Are you looking for trouble?"

Kulik was stunned by her question, and felt an uprush of alarm. He didn't understand what she meant by it. Why did she speak so directly to him? Why would she speak at all? Her words obviously had a hidden meaning. Was she up to something?. He felt that all at once he could see right through her; he could read it in her face. She wasn't just a secretary as he had thought, she was a government agent, trying to get him, rattle him, to hook him in some way.

But the more he thought these thoughts the more afraid of them he became, so afraid that in the end he chose not to believe them after all. This lovely young woman with the soft, dark eyes and the warm, engaging smile could not possibly be a spy for the Kremlin. But he remained on his guard and watched her carefully.

She put her elbows on her desk and ran her fingers through her hair. "Ivan, how you've changed since I last saw you. You've aged so. I can see your heart is heavy and you're filled with worry. You seem afraid."

Kulik did not respond. He had to believe that she really was an informer, out to get him. Although her voice was smooth and pleasant, there was definitely something menacing, even underhanded about it. And she seemed to be deriving a bitter enjoyment from deceiving him. He was on to her now, and he waited for her to start up one of her cat-and-mouse games. And sure enough, she didn't waste a second. Drawing her chair a little closer to him, she whispered softly, "Theatrics and secret negotiations. They're all around us. The stage is out there in the streets, and inside here are the planners and directors."

"Planners and directors?" echoed Kulik, looking around. "What do you mean?" He was greatly troubled by what she had just said and he could feel her moving in on him. A slip of the tongue and she could finish him off, just like that.

Then unexpectedly, her face changed. She looked helpless and miserable and her mouth twitched with nervous tension. He saw her once again as an ordinary, harmless girl who had simply come to People's Commissariat of Education to find work as a secretary. Was she really unveiling herself before him and risking everything? If only he could open up to her in the same way she was opening up to him. He wanted to believe in her, more than anything he craved sincerity, but sincerity, he very well knew, was a thing of the past. One wrong move and everything could be over. He understood how difficult it must be for her to reveal her feelings, to take such a chance, if that's what she was doing.

Suddenly he became convinced of her honesty, and in that split second he resolved to reveal himself too. As he opened his mouth to speak, to disclose his innermost thoughts, he stopped short. No! he could almost hear himself shouting, I will not fall into her trap, not at any price! He saw before him again, not the pretty young secretary with an office in the People's Commissariat of Education, but a formidable force to be reckoned with. Her show of courage, her vulnerability, were all too obvious—it was just a great act.

He had to recognize how attractive and young she really was, twenty-five at the outside. He was determined not to allow himself to be drawn in by her. An oppressive silence hung in the air. He studied the room. Although the walls were a dingy yellow and there were water stains on the ceiling, her office was clean and well-organized. He said at last, "I must say, you seem quite contented here. Your office is bright and comfortable, even inviting. You appear to have it all, a good salary, an enviable position in the government." Then, deliberately, to get a reaction from her, "It certainly doesn't seem to be the kind of place where hard-nosed inspectors are sent out to harass and intimidate poor, unsuspecting village teachers."

Zena shifted uneasily. "I take it you are referring to Inspector Paspelov? From what I understand, he's no longer in our employ. Apparently someone in your village cut his career short. Sobakin recommended him highly, and then the next thing I know he's been terminated. I hear he's been resettled somewhere in the interior."

Kulik felt a sense of overwhelming danger. He thought, So that's it! This tidy little office is more than just an office; it's much more like a workshop, where, as Zena just pointed out, planners and directors work together to make or break people.

There were faint lines under her eyes and her smile seemed forced and contrived. She was obviously disturbed by something. "Ivan, there are no listening devices here and I'm not two-faced. I want you to believe that. Oh, you don't know me, you don't know a thing about me, because if you did, you wouldn't . . ." At that point Kulik changed his mind again. This attractive young creature could not be an informer as he had suspected, she was direct and trustworthy. He decided to open his heart to her. She would never betray him, he was sure of that now.

"Zena," he said, "our lives are empty and our minds are dead. Only a few months have gone by and what a strain on the nerves it's been. You go out and don't know if you'll make it back home, you stay at home and don't know if late at night you'll be dragged out of bed with a rifle at your back. You're afraid to meet with friends and family, you're even afraid of the sound of a car coming. We've been robbed of good humor and our dreams are nightmares. Zena, your eyes are on fire, they're like magic. I've decided to take a chance. You're free to report me if that's what you want. I can't go on living in silence."

Zena said, without looking up, "You have nothing to be afraid of, Ivan. I'll never betray you. As the old saying goes, a healthy oak should not fear the storm."

Kulik smiled. "Your analogy is a thin one, Zena, and doesn't really offer me much consolation. True, a healthy oak may weather a storm, but how does it protect itself from an axe or a saw? And what if this axe or saw is handled by a lunatic or a buffoon? Then all the trees may fall, and they may fall senselessly and randomly, one after the other, including your oak. Everything and everyone has a breaking point. Even you, Zena."

She threw back her head and laughed. "Now you're talking nonsense. I think we've both said enough for one day."

She wrapped her bread in brown paper and put it in a drawer. Then she got up and walked to the window. The warm rays of a magnificent mid-afternoon sun touched her face. The air smelled sweet with the freshness of spring.

Kulik watched her tall, lean form throw an elongated shadow across the floor.

He thought, My God, she's beautiful! Why hadn't he seen it before? Her golden silky skin, her full raspberry mouth, her slightly aquiline nose—so young and tender. But her features showed strength and determination. This was no ordinary girl!

Zena walked back to her desk, frowning. She said, "You study me like a book. The slightest change in my expression makes you hesitate. You dissect me into the smallest of pieces, like a scientist, and you can't bring yourself to trust me. Why can't you accept me for who I am?"

Kulik did not know how to respond. This lovely dark-haired girl was a stranger to him. Who was she really? He said to her, "The first time I ever saw you . . . was over on Sovietskaya . . . you were going into St. Barbara's Church . . ."

Zena said ironically, " Thank you for being so honest. And do you think that I didn't know you saw me? Well, I saw you watching me, but did you see me watching you?" She lowered her voice. "I see you're not yet acquainted with the new order of things. You have a lot to learn. To keep one's physical and mental balance, one must exercise extreme caution at all times. The road ahead is very wet and slippery ."

Folding her hands on her desk and leaning slightly toward him, she whispered barely audibly, "Allow me to give you a word of advice. About your request for a replacement for Haya Fifkina— don't ask for one. The Party could very possibly send you a new teacher who is an informer. And are you sure there isn't an informer in your school as we speak? They're everywhere, they listen to everything, and they fill out reports. You must learn not only to avoid danger but also to identify it. It could be your doctor, a farmer, a fellow-teacher, even a pupil. It could be anyone."

Kulik listened with growing apprehension. He stood up and, gazing at the floor, his shoulders hunched, he muttered half to himself, "Something dark and ominous is moving in on me. I can feel it with all my heart . . . it's just a matter of time before . . ."

As he struggled to finish his sentence, Zena walked over to him and took his hands in hers. "Ivan, you mustn't lose control of your senses. I'll never push you off a high cliff, you've got to trust me. You must find the strength somehow to fight back. You'll find your way, I know you will. I can see it in your eyes, my heart tells me. Perhaps we'll see each other again somewhere soon."

Her eyes welling with tears, she embraced him and kissed his lips. "Yes, we'll definitely meet again and soon, but far away from this horrible place. And now you'd better go. Yeliseyenko is due back any minute. Stay away from him, stay away from the entire Commissariat."

Pushing him from her, she quickly opened the door and said goodbye. Kulik hurried down the corridor and into the street. The sun seemed unusually bright for this time of year, the end of March, and the last snow had nearly melted. Overcome with a feverish passion, all he could think of was taking Zena into his arms and showering her with kisses. He feared for her life more than for his own. How much longer would it be before she gave herself away? Would they arrest her before they took him? It was Zena who mattered most to him now.

Coming to an intersection and crossing Luninetska Street, Kulik didn't notice that he was on the road where Marusia lived. She was the farthest thing from his mind.

CHAPTER 23

Nowhere in the land was spring so vibrant and generous as it was in the villages of the Pinsk marshlands. In the forests the tender young leaves unfolded, the sky was a clear blue and birds twittered loudly. The fields burst with the smells of overturned damp earth and manure, and the unpaved roadways turned to thick layers of coffee-colored mud. The sun's warmth sank into the thatched rooftops of the scattered run-down cottages, seeping through their narrow windows and doorways. Spring had finally arrived, filled with hope and promise.

A flock of wild ducks returning from the south flew briskly over Hlaby. Somewhere to the east, over the Stryy River, came the cawing of foraging gulls, and emerging deep from the shadows of a stand of dark, dense firs, was a golden eagle, spreading its wings wide and soaring high into the sky. The damp and swampy forests roared and echoed with life.

In School Number Seven the morning bell had not yet rung. The children had already collected in the yard and were shouting and laughing, chasing each other, playing ball or hide-and-seek. When a flock of geese glided over the school grounds in a v-shaped formation, the boys took off their caps and threw them into the air, shouting, and the girls soon joined them, throwing up their kerchiefs.

Kulik, standing by the school door watching the children play, could not stop thinking about Ohrimko, still hidden away at his grandmother's cottage. His father and mother had been taken from him and he had been left orphaned, to hide in the depths of the forest like a common criminal. Every night Kulik prayed that the boy be kept safe. Officials of the new regime were watching and waiting for his return; they threatened the villagers, demanding to know where he was. But there was not a soul alive willing to reveal the wet and forested pathway that led to the house of Ohrimko's grandmother. For the time being at least, the boy was safe.

Very quietly, about once a week, dressed in dark clothes, with a large sack over his shoulder, Sergei stole out of the village and set out on the long trek to the little cottage in the bog. He carried small amounts of money, some clothes, food and various trinkets. Ohrimko, who anxiously awaited Sergei's visits, ran out to greet him, and asked him about his parents. Had they returned home yet? Did his mother miss him? Did his father finish building his wooden horse? Sergei tried to comfort the child by assuring him that his parents loved and missed him and would come for him as soon as they could. He would have given anything to free the boy and his grandmother from the misery that had descended upon them.

On his most recent visit Sergey resolved to be straight with the boy, to tell him the truth, but when he tried to speak, he could not utter a word. He simply took Ohrimko in his arms and giving him a big hug, whispered, "I'll be back in a few days."

Ohrimko was so young and innocent, and already his life had taken a senseless turn. His father had been murdered and his mother probably taken away to slave in a concentration camp in the far north. Ohrimko deserved to know the truth, and as painful as it would be, Sergei was determined to tell it to him on his next visit.

Up on a small hillock, just north of the village, was the cemetery, where there were two freshly dug graves marked with crude oak crosses. In one, covered with wreaths made from dandelions and mint sprigs, lay Hrisko Suchok. Chikaniuk, Suchok's neighbor, had looked through the chinks in his barn, and seen Sobakin gun Hrisko down, mercilessly and senselessly, as he ran in desperation toward the distant forest.

In the other freshly dug grave Philip lay, next to his father Cemen. Every morning at the crack of dawn Paraska arrived at the cemetery with a small bouquet of wildflowers that she had picked along the way. In her coarse cotton dress, her legs bare, she would lay the flowers on the grave, drop to her knees and utter the Lord's prayer. She was hardly recognizable, having grown even thinner and more pale these past few weeks. There was no solution in sight to her problems, and all she could do was weep into her handkerchief. Her sobs reverberated across the grounds, and died outside the entrance gates.

Spring was everywhere; the marshland throbbed with life. The villagers were quick to feel the season's benevolence—the warm, gentle breeze brushed softly against their faces, everything became fresh, alive, and beautiful. It seemed as if the hardships of the long winter months had finally come to an end and now all living things were able to breathe freely and easily again.

Zachary Buhai, with rolled-up trousers and shirtsleeves, spent his days sitting on a bench at the side of his house basking in the sun. Looking toward the river, he thought to himself, "Soon the Stryy will rise above its banks and flood the fields. Before the water pours into the village, I'll pull my fishnets out of the attic and set them along the fence. I'll be more than ready for those fish. Hah, watch me reel them in by the dozen!"

With each passing minute came more signs of spring. The warmed earth woke large congregations of frogs, and in the early evening, their croaking echoed across the countryside. From morning till night wild geese soared across the sky. No other creatures symbolized the coming of spring in the marsh like these flocks of migrating birds returning north.

But with spring came rain and lots of it, and it was not long before the raging waters of the Stryy River started to overflow their channels, moving unconstrained toward the low-lying fields. Small rivulets started to seep into village gardens, and soon dampened the earthen floors of the houses.

Buhai jumped with excitement, rushing to set up his nets. "Fish! Fish! I'll have more of them than I can eat. I'll pickle them, I'll smoke them . . . Hah, I remember my father talking about a flood that forced people to run for high ground. The river got more than ten times as much water as its bed could hold and everything was swept away. What a spectacle that must have been! This flood will be even bigger and better!"

A few kilometers east of Hlaby along the Stryy, close to Morozovich, a dyke constructed of compacted dirt and piled alder twigs started to leak in three places. As the water rose, it collapsed the dyke and washed out a wooden bridge over it. The bridge was a link between Pinsk and the settlements along the south shore, of which Hlaby was one. For the villagers on the south shore, the flood was a godsend: it meant that government officials, agitators and propagandists, all coming from Pinsk, no longer had access to their area and they would be left in peace, at least until the bridge was rebuilt, which could take weeks, even months.

Only to Iofe Nicel Leyzarov did the collapse of the bridge bring unhappiness and frustration. Since he was in Hlaby at the time, it meant that his pleasures and irrepressible passions were cut off. Because Morozovich was on the north shore, there was no way he could reach his love, Dounia Avdeevna. Kokoshin, on the other hand, happened to be in Morozovich during the collapse, and was now reaping the benefits. He was with Dounia; he possessed her totally and wholly. Undoubtedly the two were spending endless hours in her big, fluffy bed, rolling about, playing out scenes of sexual desire. Leyzarov seethed with anger and resentment.

Standing by the schoolyard fence, Kulik looked toward the Stryy. The narrow, fast-flowing river was roaring toward the Pinsk dyke, slamming repeatedly up against its dirt walls, already penetrating it in several places. The water swelled higher and higher and before long became a sea of foaming whitecaps: reeds were ripped from the banks, logs floated by, and small animals were swept away. Dark clouds collecting overhead promised more rain. It was just a matter of time before the village would be deluged with water.

Gazing over the marshland, Kulik, taking a deep breath, filled his lungs with the damp air with its smell of bog and waterfowl.

A breeze rose up from the low-lying fields and in the distance he could see nesting geese drowned in the flood of the blue-gray mist. As Kulik's thoughts drifted, there came a familiar voice from over the fence. It was Sergei. "Hello, my friend. Are you ready to check out the snares with me?" Sergei wore a cap with a black visor; an empty sack was flung over his left shoulder, "Maybe we'll get lucky today and find ourselves a duck or two. But we better hurry before the rain starts up again."

"I'm ready, but why do you carry only one oar?"

"What do you want another oar for? Besides, this is all I could find."

In a ditch close to a nearby shed, lay a broad wooden boat with peaked bow and stern. They lifted the boat onto their shoulders, carried it to the river and set it afloat. Kulik climbed in and settled on the crossboards, while Sergei, giving the boat a shove into deeper waters, jumped into the stern. The boat moved silently and easily, rippling the smooth, calm surface on either side. Kulik slipped his hand over the edge and watched the water curl up between his fingers.

The boat headed for a clump of thick bramble bushes. Sergei steered it through an opening between them. The branches on either side were closely entwined and the pale daylight struggled to pierce the tangled foliage. A gray-brown grebe with a dense, silky breast sang softly above them. Before long, the current started to run up against the sides of the boat. Sergei worked the oar harder, trying to fight the rushing water. The boat pitched and tossed on the waves. Paddling quickly, Sergei managed to set the boat on the river's course, where it traveled with little effort. They passed thick clumps of willows, then swiftly moved to a spread of covering of last year's grasses. In the distance wild ducks could be heard chattering and flapping their wings. As they moved farther downriver, the sound of ducks was closer.

"The snare I set is just beyond the riverbend." Sergei pointed to a stand of willows. "Maybe there's something waiting for us already."

And sure enough, in a covering of reeds and cattails lay a plump male duck, with pale wings, which at a distance flashed a silvery-blue. It lay dead, strung by its neck. Paddling the boat closer, looking at Kulik, Sergei said sarcastically, "Hah! I'm just as good at catching ducks as the NKVD are at catching people."

Quickly untying the snare, Sergei shoved the duck into his sack and put it in the helm of the boat. They traveled on toward a broad stretch of river, where another snare was hidden deep in a clump of bulrushes.

"It looks like we're ahead of the game," shouted Sergei. He opened his sack and stuffed another bird inside.

Pushing farther and farther downriver, they passed mighty walls of alders and willows that swayed gently in the breeze, creaking and singing their low, grave songs. The boughs of the trees were closely interwoven and the canopy of leaves was pierced here and there by slight shafts of daylight.

Sergei looked round uneasily, and said slowly, quietly, as if he were having trouble believing what he was about to say, "The heart of the marshland has no bounds. It's completely hidden from the NKVD, even though they see everything and they never sleep. This is the only place where one can really feel safe."

Kulik looked apprehensively at his friend and shook his head. "Maybe for the moment, but it'll take a lot more than the thicket of these marshes to save the life of a hunted man."

As Kulik spoke, he was struck with an idea. "Sergei, if only we could do something about this. Our people have got to organize and form a resistance movement of some kind, we've got to fight back."

Sergei leaned toward Kulik. He was unusually serious. "It's already happening. In Zeleny-Klin a resistance movement is forming. Young nationalists are setting traps for government infiltrators, and they're setting those traps just as I set them for these ducks. They're even getting guns. A week ago outside the village Koshirshchina, a secretary of the District Committee was shot dead. Of course the NKVD are wild with anger and they swear revenge. It's possible Iofe or Kokoshin are next on the hit list—especially Kokoshin."

"Kokoshin? Why him?"

"Because he heads the spy unit for our Village Soviet. And not only that, he makes lists of all the 'undesirables', the 'enemies of the people', and hands them over to the higher authorities in Pinsk. He authorizes all the arrests. He's directly under Sobakin's jurisdiction and he takes his orders from him."

"How did you find this out?"

"He pulled me aside one evening, grabbed me by the collar, and reminded me that Sobakin has not forgotten about me, and that one day soon I would be recalled to Pinsk. He said that certain charges, quite serious charges, were being compiled against me."

A spasm shot through Kulik and his voice trembled. "What are you going to do?"

"Run. Hide. But where? They'll find me wherever I go. It's just a matter of time . . ."

Sergei hid his head in his hands. Kulik did not utter a word.

They continued to float downriver. On the left bank a great blue heron came to feed on frogs and fishes, and near the river's edge in the bulrushes and cattails, nests of deep-water ducks had gone afloat. It was not hard to imagine something dreadful lurking in the marsh, behind the dark, dense foliage, watching them.

Sergei looked about him. His face was grave. "It seems so quiet and serene here, as if no one can do us any harm. It's almost the perfect place to calm strained nerves. But the serenity is deceptive, it's even insidious. There are eyes all around, hidden, following our every move." Glancing at the tips of the bulrushes, where he could see patches of sky, he whispered, "And Buhai—he's an informer. Kovzalo, too. About Chikaniuk, I'm not sure. Kokoshin meets with them all on a regular basis. About Ivashkevich I'm not so sure either."

"Ivashkevich?" Kulik echoed the name, barely audibly. This could confirm his worst suspicions.

"Yes. Let me tell you a few things about Ivashkevich, and then you tell me what you think. When you were in Pinsk the other day, I invited him over for a drink, to check him out, so to speak.

Well, he got quite drunk and started in on Ukrainians. 'You were oppressed by the Poles,' he said to me, 'and now the Russians are sinking their teeth into your skins. But you're like weeds in the *chernozem*, when you're pulled out of the earth your roots spread and you take over the fields again. No one can kill your spirit.'

"Then he said, 'In Hlaby you have a school Belorussian in form and Russian in content, and the children don't know either language. They're expected to know Belorussian, but they have to take their lessons in Russian. And the only language they know is Ukrainian. It's just a big mess. The regime should be better informed about who really lives here in these marshes, that's what I think.' He said that maybe he'd go to Moscow himself and set things straight.

"When he got up, he lost his balance and fell. I dragged him upstairs to my bed, and within minutes he was out like a light. It's a good thing he didn't take his drunken babble out on the street; he would have been arrested in no time. It seems to me he was bona fide, but I'm not sure—an informer or not an informer? I can't tell. If he really is an informer, Kokoshin will get little benefit from him because, as you can see, drink has a way of loosening his tongue, and if he's not an informer, then, well, we'll just have to wait and see."

They made their way through the almost impenetrable thicket, amid the buzzing of insects and the soft swish of grasses. They breathed in the scent of moistened trees and swaying sedges, and watched long-legged birds wade in shallow water and poke their long beaks into the water to catch fish. They heard the sound of the wind and with a quavering in their hearts felt the earth rumble beneath them.

CHAPTER 24

Pinsk was drowned in sunlight, and the broad, ramose chestnut tree, lighted by magnificent cream-colored flowers, towered high above the roof of the trim and tidy Bohdanovich house. Marusia, looking through the open window of her living room, was happy to feel the warmth of spring on her face. Watching flocks of geese soaring high above the treetops and small red squirrels scrambling from tree limb to tree limb, she thought suddenly of Sobakin. His heavy face, with dark pouches under his eyes, haunted her night and day. And to add to her nightmares, he lived in the house next door. Although a wooden fence separated their two properties, from his upstairs window he had a full view of her garden. Marusia felt as if his eyes were always on her.

Her only consolation was in knowing that almost always, into the late hours of the night, he worked in the Zovty Prison. What exactly he did there she didn't know, or rather, she didn't want to know, but the one thing she knew for certain was that each time he passed her house he stared hard at her windows. There was no doubt in her mind that she aroused him and he wanted her at any cost. More than anything she regretted having gotten involved with him in the first place. Now she was paying the price. She knew that if their paths crossed again, she would not be so lucky as she had been when he took her to the Railway Hotel. His great drunken body would descend upon hers and crush it. The girl had seen him only once since that awful day. As she sat reading on her front porch, he had come up behind her, and tried to explain away his behavior.

"I acted like a drunken boor," he said. "I was a pig. That'll never happen again, I assure you. I even said to my chauffeur Pyelushkin, 'With the most beautiful flower in all of Pinsk, I acted like a barbarian. Hit me, Pyelushkin, come on, punch me.' But he refused. 'I won't punch you, Lieutenant,' he told me, 'my hand is heavy and I'll only knock you out, and where will that get me?' Marusia, I beg you, please, forgive me. It was the drink."

Sobakin's breathing was heavy and agitated. Dropping her book, she had rushed past him into the house before he could stop her, and slammed and locked the door. Remembering every lurid detail of his assault on her at the hotel, Marusia realized how far she had gone down a slippery slope. How could she ever have become involved with this monster, she asked herself again and again. Could it possibly be that she had actually been attracted to him in some way, or had she been tempted by his high-ranking position in the Party? Whatever the answer, her life was now one of misery and regret. Every time she saw a chauffeur-driven black government car drive by, the mere thought of Sobakin sitting in the back seat filled her with repugnance and despair. She had always loved taking long, leisurely walks along the avenues of Pinsk, looking into shop windows or meeting with friends, but now that luxury did not exist for her; she was no longer free to do as she pleased. Everything had changed. She was afraid to go outside her house, even into the garden, for fear she might meet him. Occasionally she would slip out for a walk at night, with a friend or her parents.

One evening, having seen Sobakin leave for the Zovty Prison and assuming he would be there the entire night, she mustered up the courage to go for a walk on her own, something she hadn't done for several weeks. Unfortunately, what she didn't realize was that for some reason he had returned to his quarters almost half an hour after leaving, and now sat at his desk buried in paperwork. Precisely at the moment that Marusia came out her front door, Sobakin raised his head and glanced out the window. What he saw was thrilling to him. Marusia was starting for the street, heading toward the city center, and alone! He couldn't believe his good fortune.

Quickly putting on his boots and overcoat and throwing water on his face, he ran out the door. Walking swiftly along the sidewalk, he managed to catch up to her at the crossroads. Without being seen, he came up from behind and forcefully grabbed her arm. Marusia cried out and made a fruitless effort to break free. Clutching her in a fierce embrace, he began to drag her toward an alleyway, away from the city center. "Let me go, you drunkard!" she screamed at him, struggling. "Where are you taking me?"

Sobakin smiled. "To the Park of Culture and Recreation. We can take a stroll along the river. I know how you like to take your walks. And we'll have all the privacy we need. The park has pretty well emptied by now. Don't look so upset, I won't hurt you. What's wrong, don't you like me any more?"

Sobakin pushed her through the park gates, down several pathways to the river. An ominous swirling of the current could be heard, and with dusk falling, the water near the banks looked black and bottomless. He shoved her toward a bench facing a clump of reeds at the water's edge and pushed her down.

"Marusia," he breathed and grunted savagely, "you drive me out of my mind."

The girl sat stiff and motionless, made sick by the stale smell of his body. She shuddered as she felt his big hands crawl up her back, around her shoulders, onto her breasts. He pulled her to him and held her in a crushing embrace. As he forced her down on her back and climbed on top of her, she felt that her entire body was about to be destroyed. Gasping and writhing, trying to get away, she twisted herself forward, and bending her left arm, with all her strength somehow managed to jab her elbow into his jaw. Sobakin stifled a cry. Blood gushed from his mouth, and moaning, he loosened his grip and took a handkerchief out of his pocket to tend to his wound. Marusia broke free to make a run for the pathway, but he reached out and grabbed her by the neck.

"I'm going to finish you off right now," he yelled, and dragged her toward a clump of bushes.

Marusia kicked and screamed; her face was on fire. She shouted, "Rape me! Kill me! You disgust me. You have black circles under your eyes because you don't sleep at night. Murderer! Monster!" Growing more and more enflamed, gasping for breath, she lifted her leg and swung her knee as hard as she could into his groin. He howled from pain. She took to her heels and ran as fast as she could out of the park gates. She raced down the darkened streets for ten or fifteen minutes, to her house, where she burst in and went directly to her room.

This violent episode played on Marusia's mind over and over and at night she struggled with nightmares. She did not mention it to her parents, who noticed a change in her, but asked no questions. Her mother was distressed to see her daughter so miserable and watched her closely, suspecting the worst. Marusia became a virtual recluse. For the longest time she stayed in the house and didn't venture even into the garden. She busied herself sweeping, dusting, washing. But Sobakin's face was always there. The appalling scenes were re-enacted in her mind again and again, and chills rushed up her spine at the thought of his cold fingers upon her flesh. She had no appetite. There was nowhere for her to turn for help, not to her family, not to her friends, and not to the authorities. The thought of Sobakin coming to track her down paralyzed her with fear; she was convinced that in the end he would get her, one way or the other.

It was some time before she dared even to open her bedroom window to let in the cool night air. After almost four weeks she felt her body slowly reviving. Her panic attacks, which had recurred daily, were fading away. She began to enjoy spending her evenings with her parents in the living room, chatting and listening to the radio. With each passing day she grew stronger. She made up her mind not to be beaten by Sobakin.

One evening she had become so thoroughly weary of being a prisoner in her own home that she resolved to go out. Although she had built up considerable confidence, she dared not make a move until she was absolutely certain Sobakin had left for the night. Standing behind the curtains of her living room window, she watched for him to come out of his house. And sure enough around seven in the evening, he hastened down the walkway, undoubtedly on his way to the Zovty Prison. He was wearing his usual loose-fitting white shirt belted at the waist and trousers tucked into high black leather boots. A Nagant pistol protruded from his holster and in his left hand he carried an overstuffed attaché case. The girl watched him stop suddenly, look around, then set his eyes on her house. She jumped back and froze. Sobakin stood there staring at the living room window for a moment or two, then hurried through the gateway and into the street.

Marusia felt intensely relieved as she saw him disappear into the distance. He was gone and would not return until morning. At least for tonight she was free to enjoy and explore the city streets again. Throwing a light shawl over her shoulders, she told her mother and father she was going for a walk, and started for the city center. In her flower-printed cotton dress and low-heeled pumps, her shoulder-length hair blown by the wind, Marusia attracted the notice of passersby. Her brilliant smile lit up her face. Men could not take their eyes off her—she was so shapely, so pretty, so young.

As a pale moon showed itself on the western horizon, Marusia reached the crossroads. Suddenly a stout and buxom woman in her mid-fifties appeared from a row of small run-down cottages. She was poorly dressed with a tattered scarf over her head and bast sandals on her feet. It was Lukeria Philipovna, Sobakin's landlady. Her husband was the former postmaster. She looked Marusia over, and said contemptuously, "I watched you come out of your house. Are you out searching for Lieutenant Sobakin? You can't get enough of him, is that it? Before the affair goes any further, maybe you should consider writing his wife in Moscow. You shameless whore!"

Marusia was bewildered and upset. Her neighbor had never acted like this toward her before. Lukeria went on, working herself up, her face red. "And what do you think he does into the late hours of the night in the Zovty Prison? Take a walk over there right now and listen to the screams coming from the basement.

And you don't even care about what they did to your own cousin. Your cousin Sergei—"

Marusia fled, trembling, her pulse beating wildly. She wanted to get as far away from Lukeria Philipovna as she possibly could. As she paused by a lamp post to catch her breath, she was relieved to see her good friend Nadia walking out of a nearby lane. The two girls had graduated together from the gymnasium and had talked about moving to Minsk and studying at the university there. Marusia greeted her friend happily and went to kiss her on both cheeks as was the custom, but Nadia drew back, murmuring nervously and hurriedly, "Uh, I'm in a great rush today, Maria Valentynovna. I can't talk. Good-bye!" She made off quickly without looking back.

Marusia was so shaken she was scarcely able to move. Her best friend had just shunned her; everything in her life had come crashing down. She was overcome with a bitter loneliness such as she had never felt before. Her head bent, she drifted slowly along the sidewalk until she came to a row of small shops. She stopped before Radion Smushka's grocery store and peered through the window. Smushka had always had the best selection of rolls and breads and the tempting smell of pickles and smoked sausages always wafted from his doors. But now the shop, like all the others along this stretch, was dark and empty. Smushka had only one daughter, who, Marusia remembered, had been married off during the winter to some minor government official. Shortly after their wedding, the two were arrested one night by the secret police. No one knew whether they were alive or dead. As Marusia stood before the window, she was startled to see a man come out of the shop door. It was Radion Smushka. Looking at her with deep hatred, he spat between his feet, and disappeared into his shop, slamming the door behind him.

Marusia burst into tears. She felt shattered and powerless and in her heart there was indescribable pain. It seemed to her that she was being punished and that this punishment was pressing down upon her and suffocating her. And about Sergei?

Drawing a deep breath, Marusia walked on. The air was warm, but she felt strangely cold and could not get the damp smell of the closed shops out of her nostrils. Before she knew it she came to Market Square, which was filled with people under a sea of red flags. As she edged past a group of *Komsomol* members shouting to each other in Russian, suddenly a familiar figure emerged from the crowd and started toward her. It was her godmother, Olga Nikolayevna. The girl hadn't seen her for quite some time and she was delighted to encounter a smiling face.

"Ach, Marusia." The godmother gave the girl a hearty embrace. "Let me have a good look at you. I can't believe it, is it really you? How grown up you are! How beautiful! I'm so terribly glad to see you." She squeezed the girl's arm painfully hard, her eyes welling with tears. "Marusia, you've got to help me, I beg you. My sister and her family have just been arrested. Please, Marusia, you've got to do something, I know you have influence. Maybe if you gave *him* a good word, if you know who I mean, he'd listen to you. Please, Marusia, talk to him. I beg you, for the sake of the children."

Marusia was filled with dread. "What do you mean by *him*?"

"Why, your lover, of course. Sobakin. You're my last resort. Please, Marusia, please help me."

Marusia drew away from her. "My lover? He's not my lover. We went out only once, but now it's over. I was wrong about him, I made the biggest mistake of my life. Can't you understand that? Why can't anybody understand that? I despise him! He's nothing to me! Nothing!"

Olga Nikolayevna replied with cold triumphant hatred, "My, my, what a fancy lady you are now, why, one could easily mistake you for a Muscovite. And what have you really become? An NKVD man's whore." The woman wanted to say more, but for some reason held her tongue, turned and walked away, all the while muttering venomously under her breath.

Marusia shook; she was helpless against a flood of tears. Completely losing her head, she began to run away from the square. But she could not get away from the emptiness surrounding her.

She had made one bad mistake, which she regretted with all her heart, and now because of this, her entire existence was dissolving before her eyes, and she wondered in agony what was to become of her. The simple-hearted geniality of the townspeople was gone for good, and their once forgiving and gentle eyes now crushed her with loathing and contempt. Marusia wanted to bury herself in some deep, dark hole and forget about everything.

CHAPTER 25

A heavy black cloud had fallen over Marusia's house; she and her parents lived in gloomy solitude. No friends came to visit, neighbors no longer stopped to chat, and passersby pointed their fingers and whispered, "The girl who's taken up with Sobakin, the crudest and most brutal NKVD man in all of Pinsk, lives in that house. May she rot in Hell!"

Everyone avoided the Bohdanovich house like the plague.

Marusia no longer ventured into the city center or even took walks in her own neighborhood. She stayed in her own back yard, where for hours at a time she sat on a bench under an apple tree, reading or writing in her journal. At least there she found a haven.

One evening when the sun was setting, she decided to go out into the garden and catch a breath of air. She sat on a bench and noticed that along the low fence, there was a bed of geraniums that seemed to be drooping and pale. As she looked at them, wondering if she should fetch them some water, suddenly there came a loud, harsh voice from over the fence. It was Sobakin.

"Good evening," he called out, a strange and contorted smile upon his face. "What a wonderful night. Perfect to just sit and dream."

Revulsion and contempt surged through her. But for some reason she did not feel afraid. She continued to sit there, unmoving.

"What's wrong with you today, Marusia? Aren't you going to chase me off the way you always do?"

Before she could do or say anything, Sobakin stepped over the fence, and sat down beside her. He lit up a *makhorka* cigarette.

Marusia felt a spasm in her chest. There was only one thing on her mind and she could not contain herself. Even her parents had heard that people had seen Sergei dragging himself out of the prison. "What did you do to my cousin? Why did you beat him?"

Sobakin shrugged. "Cousin? What cousin?"

"Sergei Stepanovich Viter, the schoolteacher from Hlaby."

"Sergei Stepanovich? Oh, yes, yes, Sergei. I remember him now. Apparently he was called into the Zovty Prison and interrogated without my knowledge. Yes, that's how it happened. I must apologize on behalf of my creatures. They're probably the ones responsible. I had no idea."

"Creatures?" The girl raised her brows. "What creatures are you talking about?"

"Why, the riffraff of the secret police. They're all just a bunch of hooligans, low-lifes, if you know what I mean. They give the NKVD a bad name. Unfortunately, I can't control everything and be everywhere at once. Let me assure you it won't happen again. Soviet law prohibits beatings of any kind, especially by the police. What happened to your cousin had to be an isolated incident. In any case, I'll look into it." Then narrowing his eyes, "Did Sergei complain to you?"

The girl turned pale and bit her lip. "No, he didn't say a word. I happened . . . um—to hear from someone who saw him coming out of the prison."

There was a constrained silence. Finally Sobakin started up again. "As I was saying, Marusia, this is a terrible misfortune and it will not happen again. I give you my word of honor."

"Your word of *honor*?" shouted the girl. "And what do you do in the Zovty Prison, Lieutenant? Let me tell you what you do. You arrest innocent people, you throw them into the dungeon, you beat them and torture them, you even kill them!"

"Marusia, Marusia." Sobakin laughed a little. "You're working yourself up into a fit. In fact, you're becoming hysterical. Calm down. I assure you, the Soviet government is doing all it can to establish peace and stability. Naturally, a few people get arrested now and

then, but this is completely normal. Our government is merely looking out for the best interests of its citizens. I'm sure you'll agree,
there isn't a nation on earth that doesn't take measures to deal with
its criminals."

"Criminals!" Marusia shouted at him. She felt she might kill
him. "What crimes did my cousin Sergei ever commit? Is the
daughter of Radion Smushka a criminal? And what about her husband? Where are they now? What's become of them? And what
about my godmother's family—are they criminals too? Even their
six-year-old daughter? What are the charges against them? Tell
me! Tell me!"

Sobakin began to show signs of annoyance. He said through
clenched teeth, "The innocent we set free."

But Marusia would not stop. "Why don't you just tell me the
truth? You're a liar! A murderer and a liar!"

Sobakin looked at her coldly. "You're a very stupid girl, Marusia Valentynovna. If you keep on like this, you'll find yourself in
a pot of boiling water. You don't understand the first thing about
Communism. Allow me to explain it. Actually, it's very simple:
if a farmer wants a good crop, he has to sow only the best seed,
but first he must separate it from the chaff. Joseph Vissarionovich
Stalin, the greatest architect of socialism, is this country's 'farmer',
so to speak—like the farmer, he wants to produce only the best.
It's with his help and only with his help that we'll build the perfect
society. Generations to come will thank us for our work . . . "

"You freed us from Polish oppression, that's true. But now the
shops have disappeared and the markets are empty. . . Why is that?
What are you doing?"

Sobakin said sharply, "Marusia, you're young and naïve and
you're walking a very fine line. I suggest you acquaint yourself
with the proletariat movement, so you can understand how it
works." He took a long, deep drag on his *makhorka*. "In the meantime I would watch my tongue if I were you. A word of advice:
before you start criticizing something, you should really have a
better understanding of what it is you're criticizing. Believe me,

in time when the people get accustomed to the new order, they'll learn to appreciate everything that's being done."

"And what about my brother? You promised to bring my brother from Lvov. Where is he?"

Sobakin smiled and lit another cigarette. His voice became softer and more friendly. "I've been trying to help your brother for quite some time. As a matter of fact, he's one of my top priorities. If only you knew what I've gone through on his behalf: I've conferred with my contacts in Lvov, I've made innumerable phone calls, I've even written letters." He moved a little closer, and whispered to her, "Marusia, I have some surprising news. Brace yourself. Your brother is going to get married."

"Married?" echoed the girl, astonished. She turned toward Sobakin, and stared at him. Was he telling the truth? She thought that if she could only see his eyes, they would tell her everything. But the sun was setting over the houses and it was growing dark.

Sobakin went on more soberly. "Unfortunately, it appears there's a problem with your brother's engagement. His fiancée, whose name is Oriska, is the daughter of a Ukrainian nationalist—in other words, a counterrevolutionary. Lonia has gone a bit too far by getting involved with this girl. From my end, I'm doing all that I possibly can to help him out of this mess."

"Lonia, mixed in with counterrevolutionaries? I can't believe it!" Marusia caught her breath, and burst out loudly, "Why are you doing this? Why are you making things up? You're just stringing me along! For what purpose?"

Sobakin grimaced. "Maybe it's better that you don't believe me. After all, it's not a pleasant thing to face up to. But soon you'll see that I'm being truthful. Your brother is planning to come home for the summer holidays, and then he'll tell you everything himself."

Sobakin sounded so self-assured and so in control that Marusia became uncertain. What if there was a chance he was telling the truth? What if Lonia really was coming home? She was so desperate to see her brother again that she was willing to believe anything. Drawing a deep breath, she put all her suspicions aside, and stealing a glance at him, made herself believe that he was telling her the truth.

But a second later, everything changed again. He was sliding closer to her, slipping his arm around her back, breathing heavily. When she caught a whiff of drink on his breath, she pushed at him, crying, "Get away from me and stay away from me! You make me sick! You're a drunk and a liar! I hate you. And why don't you ever clean your teeth?"

As he continued to grope her, Efrosinia came running out of the house, shouting, waving a broom. "Get away from my daughter right now or I'll bash your head in!"

Sobakin, taken aback, jumped to his feet. *"Mamasha."* He spread his arms in self-defense. "Marusia and I were simply having ourselves a little chat. You shouldn't get so excited. It's not good for your blood pressure." Straightening his shirt collar, looking very perturbed, he flung himself around and hurried back to his yard.

Marusia burst into tears. "Oh, Mother, he touched me. I feel horrible, just horrible."

"Calm down, dear child, calm down." Efrosinia took her daughter in her arms and hugged her until her body stopped shaking. When Marusia finally regained herself, they went back into the house. In a corner of the living room, dim lamplight cast long, muted shadows over the walls, and from the window the pale moonlight struggled through the half-closed curtains.

Valentyn lay on the sofa in his pajamas, dozing. When he heard the women enter, he slipped his arm under his head and without looking up, gave a prolonged yawn. He crooned as if to himself, "Ah, here is my daughter, at last, my devoted daughter. And what has she gone and done? She's rolled to the very edge. I could hear Sobakin and her cooing from outside the window, like a pair of doves." Stressing every syllable, he went on as though she wasn't there. "My daughter's head has been turned by a lieutenant from the secret police. She's completely lost her senses. And now we've got nothing but trouble."

He stroked his beard, and looked directly at Marusia. "Didn't I tell you Ivan Kulik would have been a better match? Didn't I tell you? Ivan's a decent, intelligent young man, and one of our own. Why couldn't you just listen to me?"

Marusia shot back hotly, "Don't talk to me about Kulik, Father. I told you a million times, I have no interest in him. Why don't you just leave me alone once and for all? Why must you always attack me?"

Valentyn smiled ironically. "Don't you have a few things confused, daughter? It's Sobakin who's always attacking you, not I. From what I see, he can't seem to keep his hands off you."

Efrosinia quickly jumped in. "Stop it, old man! Stop it right now! Leave Marusia alone. You're only making her more miserable than she already is. And what good will it do? She's learned her lesson all too well and now she has to find a way to deal with the consequences. We all do."

She grabbed her daughter's hands, and pressed them tightly to her breast. She whispered, "Is there any news of Lonia? Did Sobakin say anything to you?"

"Oh, Mother! He's a liar; he's been lying all along. Every word of his is nothing but a lie! He says that Lonia is getting married, but you can't believe a thing he says."

Efrosinia turned white. She buried her head in her hands and wept quietly, her small, thin frame shaking. "Lonia, Lonia, my poor baby, what has become of you? Are you healthy or are you ill? Are you alive or are you dead?"

She rocked back and forth, growing increasingly restless. Then she looked at her husband and it was clear something was beginning to set her off. "Did you hear, old man? Did you hear what your daughter just said? Were you even listening? Lonia is still in Lvov and he's not coming home after all. Well, what have you got to say about that? And better yet, what do you plan to do about it?"

Valentyn scrambled to his feet, and as fast as his old legs could carry him, made for the kitchen door, calling out, "Don't start on me again, old woman. I know exactly what you're aiming for. Your nagging is going to be the death of me yet."

Efrosinia caught his arm. "You're not going to get away from me so easily this time, and you know perfectly well what I mean. You'll go to get Lonia if it's the last thing you do. First thing tomorrow you'll go to the train station and buy yourself a ticket to Lvov. Then you'll get on that train and bring Lonia home. If you don't, I swear, I'll set the house on fire, I'll hang myself, but I'll murder you first."

Efrosinia's excitement grew increasingly intense. She went on for several minutes more; suddenly her voice faltered and broke. She sank into an armchair opposite the sofa, and sat unmoving, her face buried in her hands. Finally she turned gloomily to her daughter. "Oh, Marusia, what's happening to our family? Will we ever see Lonia again? My little boy, what's become of you? My poor little boy."

She shook her head and said to Marusia in bewilderment, "And you, what am I to do with you? Come here, let me take a good look at you. My, my, how you've grown. You're not a child anymore, you've become a beautiful young woman, too beautiful for your own good. If I were even half as beautiful as you when I was young, do you think I would have ended up with your father? Not in a million years! Look at him, he's become glued to that broken-down sofa of his. And that stupid beard he's decided to grow—it makes him look like an old goat! My word, if things had been different, I would have found myself a handsome government official or maybe even an officer in the army. But in my day officers and officials were different, they were honorable and respectable, not like today. Today, oh, God, they're nothing more than vultures, raping and stealing wherever they go. Bandits, all of them!"

Listening to her mother go on, the color drained from Marusia's face as if something had just occurred to her. Her single thought was of her cousin, Sergei. She cried out: "Oh, no! Sergei! Good Lord, what did I do? What did I do? I made a mess of things. Mother, I accused Sobakin of beating Sergei in prison, and I accused him straight to his face! Now he'll finish Sergei off for sure. I had to go and open my big mouth. When will it all end? When will it all end? May God help Sergei!"

Efrosinia rose; her cheeks were sunken and she looked like a dead woman. She murmured in a monotone, "Marusia, do you think it's possible our Lonia might really be getting married?"

"No, Mother, no! Sobakin's lying. How can you even think that? Lonia would have written to us. Sobakin's just looking for another way to get to me. But it'll never work. I'll never submit to him. Never! Never!"

Efrosinia said quietly and dreamily, "Lonia is getting married, I can feel it in my heart. Soon we'll have ourselves a wedding."

Marusia was taken aback and rather frightened. Efrosinia went on, "I know Lonia is getting married because last night I had a dream. In my dream there was a church, much bigger than our cathedral, and in the belfry a bell rang, at first it tolled, then it rang out joyously. Then there was procession of young women dressed in long white gowns, they were carrying baskets of flower petals and throwing them everywhere along the path. They were followed by a young woman with long golden hair dressed like a bride with a wreath on her head. Next to the woman a young man was walking all in black, even his shirt and gloves were black. But his face didn't look like a groom's face. It was pale yellow and he looked wasted and miserable and his eyes were red and sunken. He looked old. It was Lonia! He and his bride followed the procession into the church and the doors banged shut behind them and the bells stopped ringing. The dream was so real, it was almost as if it wasn't a dream at all. Then every-thing became clouded . . ." Her voice broke.

Marusia ran to her mother and flung her arms around her. She had never seen her like this. "Mother, get hold of yourself, please," she cried. "Calm down, shhh . . . calm down. It was just a dream, a stupid dream! Stop crying. Everything will turn out all right, you'll see. Lonia will be home before you know it."

She tore away from her mother and ran upstairs to her room, slamming the door behind her. Falling onto her bed and burying her head in her pillow, she wept bitterly. The sound of her ago-nized sobs traveled into the hallway, down the stairs, and filled the entire house.

CHAPTER 26

Everything appeared to go well on this beautiful sunny June day. To begin with, early that morning, Sobakin, in his full NKVD uniform, carrying his overstuffed satchel, unexpectedly and hurriedly left for the Zovty Prison. In the Bohdanovich household, things had settled down considerably. Marusia woke around nine, made breakfast and went about her usual household chores. No one dared mention Sergei, and even Lonia's name was not whispered. It was almost as if the normal flow of life had been restored, at least on the surface.

Just before the clock struck noon there came a knock on the front door. It was the postman with a telegram addressed to Marusia. She ran to tell her mother the good news. "Mother, Mother, it's from the *Oblispolkom* about my application for a teaching position. I'm being called in for an appointment today at two."

Efrosinia, knitting a shawl, put her needles down "Have you given this enough thought? Is this what you really want? To become a teacher?"

"Mother, it's about time I did something with my life. Besides, we can certainly use the money. And with all these things happening around us, we still have to go on. And Father's not . . ."

"Father!" Efrosinia cut her off. "Don't start with your father again. Just look at him. As usual, he's snoring away. Such a hypochondriac! You see how he got out of it again? You see? Didn't I tell you he'd find a way? Mark my words, he'll never make it to Lvov, he'll never go for Lonia. He's full of excuses, nothing but excuses. Now he claims he can't buy a train ticket because in order to buy

278

a ticket he needs a special pass from the NKVD, but before he can get this pass, he says, he must apply to NKVD headquarters, and it could take weeks for them to process it."

Turning on her husband who was stretched out on the sofa, "Get up, old man, I've just about reached my limit with you! Get up before I do something I might regret!" She was about to grab him by the arm, but clutching her head, she burst into tears. "Lonia, my poor Lonia, what a high price you have to pay for having such a father."

"Oh, Mother!" Marusia stamped her foot. "Enough already! You've got to stop tormenting yourself like this. You're driving us all crazy, and it's not doing anyone any good."

She took her mother's arm, sat her down in an armchair and gave her a glass of water. Then she massaged her shoulders and back until she calmed down. When Efrosinia began to sink into drowsiness, Marusia slipped a pillow behind her mother's head, lifted her legs onto a footstool and covered her with a blanket. Then she took her letter and rushed out to go to the *Oblispolkom*. It was almost two o'clock.

She felt today was the day she would achieve something. Having a job would be a way not only to help her parents financially, but also to escape the pressures in her life; namely, to get away from Simon Stepanovich. She felt confident about her prospects of getting work, because not only was she well-educated, but she spoke Russian, and fluently at that. She tried to clear everything from her mind that might affect her optimism.

The *Oblispolkom* was an imposing stone building covering a big chunk of the block, five stories high and surrounded by a narrow, empty courtyard. The large, rectangular windows on the lower level were protected by iron bars. There was a continual flow of people through the front gates; pigeons roosted under the eaves above the main entrance. Marusia was intimidated and even a little frightened by this impressive and important place. On the second floor, she stopped before a massive brown wooden door marked People's Commissariat of Education. She knocked, turned the oversized brass knob, and entered timidly.

Yeliseyenko, Superintendent of the National Division of Education, sat at his desk, jotting something in a notebook. His flaxen hair was oiled and combed back from his pale, puffy face. He wore horn-rimmed glasses. Marusia silently tiptoed to put her envelope on the corner of his desk and sat down in a chair opposite him. Yeliseyenko looked up unsmiling. "Well, Maria Valentynovna. We've looked over your application with great interest. So, you want to be a teacher? And you specified you wanted to teach in a village. Hmm . . . interesting. Well, your credentials certainly qualify you." He took a folder from his desk drawer and scanning the papers, asked, "How is your Belorussian?"

Astonished, Marusia laughed nervously. "Uh . . . I don't really know Belorussian. But I know Russian. I can certainly teach in Russian."

"Teach in Russian?" Yeliseyenko shook his head. "Regrettably, we have no openings for Russian teachers at the moment, especially in the villages. We do, however, need Belorussian teachers, for as you well know, we are now part of the Belorussian Soviet Socialist Republic. Of course, should you decide to apply to an urban institution, there might be an opening there somewhere." Then looking questioningly at her, "If I may ask, where did you learn Russian?"

She shifted in her seat and said apologetically, "Unfortunately, I didn't learn Russian in school because when I went to school our land was occupied by the Poles, so naturally all my schooling was conducted in Polish. I picked it up here and there, wherever I could."

Yeliseyenko smiled. He found her attempt at Russian most humorous. "Yes," he said, "Russian is the language now most commonly used, and your attachment to it is commendable. I realize you're eager to make a favorable impression, and, I might add, your ingenuousness is certainly appreciated. However, the truth of the matter is your speech is flawed. For example, your diction is off and your inflections are improper." As Yeliseyenko continued, he lapsed, perhaps unconsciously, into Ukrainian, and without a trace of an accent.

Marusia was dumbfounded: the Superintendent of Education, a man of position, was speaking to her in, of all languages, Ukrainian, just like a *moujik*! How could this be? She was shocked to learn he was not a Russian as she had assumed, but a Ukrainian like herself. She couldn't understand why a man who had managed to climb so high up the Party ladder would deliberately undermine himself like that. Was the Ukrainian so deeply ingrained in him that no matter how hard he tried, he just couldn't quash it? Or maybe he wasn't undermining himself at all, maybe he just wanted to make fun of her, to reduce her to the mere provincial she really was. She became increasingly uneasy. She had worked so hard and for so many hours to perfect her Russian, to sound authentic, and now it was all for nothing. But she refused to believe she had given herself away so easily. Confused and embarrassed, she spoke up. "Excuse me, comrade, I'm at a loss here. It seems strange that you just spoke to me in Ukrainian, which, from what I understand, is a Russian dialect. I was led to believe Russian was the official language now, to be used in all facets of life. Have I been mistaken?"

Yeliseyenko got up and, running his fingers through his hair, walked across the room to the window. Marusia was surprised to see how short he was, perhaps a head shorter than herself. He opened the window wide– the air was fresh and clean and the clatter of horses filled the room. After a few minutes, he turned and began what appeared to be a carefully crafted propaganda speech, in Russian.

"Well, Marusia, you don't seem to understand the aim of the Soviet Union. First of all, Ukraine is a recognized republic and therefore, naturally, has its own language and culture, which must be maintained and preserved. Ukrainian is not a dialect of Russian as you seem to think, but a separate language. We also have other great nations in our midst such as Azerbaizan, Georgia, Chechnya, and so on. And all these nations have their unique cultures and languages that must first and foremost be protected. I might add, they have all, including Ukraine and Belorussia, happily and voluntarily joined together to form the USSR, the greatest democratic nation on earth. And of course, being a member of this great union bestows the highest of honors."

He flipped through some files and handed her a folder. "If you have any hopes of working here, you must read this list of reference books. It's compulsory reading for anyone seeking a teaching position. I have to add that before any decision is made you will be examined thoroughly on these texts."

Marusia scanned the titles and quickly noted that all the required reading material was in Russian. If Belorussian was the official language as Yeliseyenko had just pointed out, why were the books in Russian only? This was cause for further confusion and she tried her best to make sense of it. Although she would have been the first to admit that she did not know much about the new regime, the one thing she did know was that in order to get anywhere she would have to learn about it and ultimately to contribute to it, to accept it with blind devotion. She was prepared to do that. But reading through all this material could take days, even weeks, and time was something she didn't have. "Excuse me, comrade," she said. "Allow me to be direct. About a teaching position . . . I am most eager to find work . . . You must understand, my father is old and feeble, and my mother is not well. We need to live somehow . . . I thought you might find me a job right away, maybe in a village somewhere. . . ."

"A village? Hmm . . ." Yeliseyenko thought for a moment. Then he shrugged and shook his head. "Unfortunately, as I've already mentioned, without knowledge of Belorussian your prospects don't look very . . ."

Just then a phone rang behind a closed door. The faint sound of a woman's voice could be heard, then the opening and closing of drawers, and before long Yeliseyenko's secretary, wearing a plain navy dress with white cuffs, and a string of fake pearls, came into the office. She put a stack of files on the corner of his desk, and whispered something in his ear.

Yeliseyenko rose, looking distracted, and said quickly, "If you'll excuse me, something unexpected has just come up. I'll be back in about fifteen minutes." Grabbing a folder from his drawer, he hurried to the doorway, where just before he left, he called out to them, "Zena Maximovna, meet Maria Valentynovna. Maria Valentynovna is applying for a teaching position, in a village school, it appears. Please go ahead, ladies, get acquainted with each other."

Zena turned to Marusia and extended her hand. Her voice was low and pleasant. "Good to meet you. We haven't actually met, but I know your name is Maria Bohdanovich. I saw you at the teachers' New Year's Eve dance. You were there with Ivan Kulik and your cousin, Sergei, I believe."

Although Zena welcomed Marusia affably, she was surprised to see her in the offices of the People's Commissariat of Education. Like so many others in the city, she had heard about Marusia and Sobakin. She wondered how such a lovely girl could have gotten involved with someone like him. Sobakin was a known and feared NKVD man, with a face like a pumpkin, and he was married. "So you want to teach in a village? Do you like village life?"

"I don't really know." Marusia shifted uneasily. "I've always lived in Pinsk, but I thought I might like to try something different. Life in the country would certainly be slower and much more peaceful than in the city. This appeals to me. Sometimes it's good to get a fresh start in life."

Zena immediately concluded that what Marusia really wanted was to escape Sobakin. She wanted to warn her, to say, "Don't make matters worse by going to a village somewhere. At least in the city there are places to hide: you can slip behind a building, call on friends, lose yourself in a crowd. But in the village you'd be like a sitting duck. Good God, think it over!" But she said, "A teaching post might be difficult to find, but Yeliseyenko has been promising me an assistant for some time now. If you'd consider office work, I'll talk to him. Of course, I understand you have your mind set on teaching, but in the meantime . . ."

Color rushed to Marusia's face. She had not expected anything like this. She was so thrilled she hardly knew what to say. "A job? Here? In the *Oblispolkom*? Why, that would be wonderful! Yes, yes, I'll take it if the position is available."

Suddenly the prospect of working in the city became more appealing to her than working in a village; it was almost as though she had read Zena's thoughts. Indeed the city would be much better for her. Zena smiled. "I'll see what I can do. If Yeliseyenko gives his approval, we'll be contacting you. You should be hearing from us in a day or two. Goodbye for now."

Marusia went down the stairs and into the courtyard in a dream. The possibility of working in the *Oblispolkom* overwhelmed her. A job there would transform everything. She couldn't wait to tell her mother that she might soon be earning her living.

The next few days were spent in painful suspense. Marusia tried to keep busy with housework, and even took up needlework. When at last she turned her attention to the books assigned by Yeliseyenko, she managed to settle down. On the third day she opened the door to a messenger who handed her an envelope. She ripped it open and could not believe her eyes. Tomorrow at noon she was to come to the *Oblispolkom* offices, to the Department of Education and start her new job. Completely overwhelmed, she let out a cry of joy.

At precisely twelve o'clock the next day, Marusia mounted the stairs of the *Oblispolkom*. Quickly checking her dress and smoothing her hair, she entered Yeliseyenko's office. He was sitting at his desk, head bent, flipping through some books. His shirtsleeves were rolled up to the elbow and he wore a huge ring with a blue stone on his left hand. He didn't seem to realize that she was standing there, and stepping closer to his desk, she wanted to say something, but couldn't think of anything. Yeliseyenko looked up and seemed startled to find her standing over him. Glancing at his watch, he said, "Twelve noon on the dot. Excellent. Excellent." He got up. "Please, come with me."

He ushered her into an adjoining room and returned to his office. She was surprised to see how small this room was, only slightly larger than her kitchen pantry. It had dark oak flooring, a relatively high ceiling and dismal gray-green walls. The room was stuffy, but a long, narrow window looking down onto a busy street helped to brighten it. There was a cheap pine desk, which obviously belonged to Zena, who was not there, and a peeling veneered table stacked with papers. On the wall hung a large picture of Stalin.

After a moment, Zena appeared in the doorway carrying several heavy cloth-bound binders. Looking somewhat distracted, she greeted Marusia, and asked her to have a seat; she would be with her shortly. She sat at her desk and slipped a sheet of paper into the typewriter. Her fingers raced across the keys.

Marusia hadn't a clue about how to type, and she began to feel inadequate. Watching Zena, she remembered when she had first seen her. It was at the teachers' dance. A blue dress came to mind, carefully waved shoulder-length hair, a chunky gold necklace. Yes, and she had danced with Kulik, they had held each other in a rather familiar way and moved easily across the floor. She remembered how she, Marusia, had suddenly fled the dance. Had that been a girlish whim? An act of jealousy on her part? She couldn't possibly have been jealous about Kulik.

"Well, I'm done at last," Zena said cheerfully, getting up from her desk. "I hope I haven't kept you waiting too long. Congratulations on your new position." She reached up to pull a ledger from a high shelf. "This is where we keep our records. It must be filled out every day. It's self-explanatory really. In any case, if you have any problems, don't hesitate to ask."

At first the two women exchanged only brief comments, but after only a few days they became more communicative with each other. Marusia chattered in her broken Russian, much to Zena's secret amusement.

"Are you from the Pinsk area?" she asked Marusia one day.

Marusia was startled by the question. Because she spoke Russian, she had assumed Zena would have thought her to be from some other place, possibly even from the Russian interior. Feeling offended at first, she decided that Zena meant no harm by it. "Yes," she said, "I was born in Pinsk. I've lived here all my life. And you? What about you? Where are you from?"

"I'm from Kishenky, on the eastern shores of the Dniepre. It's a lovely town, it's famous for its rolling flax fields. I miss it terribly."

Marusia adjusted easily to the office routine, and proved herself capable. By the end of the second week the two women had formed a friendship and had even come to address each other in the familiar. They began to exchange confidences.

"What do you look for in a man?" Zena asked one afternoon.

"I haven't really worked it out yet."

"Don't tell me you've never been in love?"

"No, as a matter of fact, I haven't. If the right man were to come along, then I suppose I might fall in love. But in general, I don't trust men. They're too aggressive, too domineering, too chauvinistic."

Zena was convinced the girl was hiding secrets from her. She looked much younger than her twenty years, but there was a fierce determination about her that seemed to reflect a more mature knowledge. Zena couldn't help but admire the bold front Marusia presented; at the same time she found it puzzling that such a clever and beautiful girl could have gotten involved with Sobakin. Her hostility toward men clearly reflected her inner turmoil.

Marusia turned to Zena. "What about you? Have you ever been in love?"

"Well," Zena smiled mysteriously. "Put it this way. I've come across many men and most are not unlike cats on the prowl. First they sniff and howl, then they get ready to pounce."

"They get ready to pounce, all right. And believe me, there's nothing pleasant in that."

"But if you find the right one, nothing could be more wonderful."

"The right one! Hah! The right one most likely will be the one who'll swoop down on you and catch you unawares. And he won't stop at anything until he has his way. He'll make you scream in pain."

"What a strange one you are!" Zena looked at her in surprise. "How can you be so cynical? Surely you don't believe all men are like that?" Without thinking, she asked, "Is that what *he's* done to you? Has *he* made you like this?"

Marusia drew back and turned pale. "What do you mean?"

Sobakin's name was on the tip of Zena's tongue; she wanted to say it, to confront her, but she didn't dare. To cover up, she blurted out Kulik's name instead.

"Kulik?" Marusia laughed. "What a thought! Ivan Kulik! Why, he wouldn't know what to do with a woman if he had one right in front of him. He's so utterly boring, so uncultivated, and he talks like the lowest of peasants. All he seems to do is lecture—about language, about education, about this, about that. He goes on and on, and he doesn't know when to stop. I realize he's educated, I believe he has a degree in history or philosophy or something, but there's something peculiar about him. I think he lives in the dark with one foot stuck in the mud."

"What is it exactly that you don't like about him?" Zena was surprised at her vehemence.

"Everything. His language is crude and vulgar, and he almost never speaks Russian. I can't bear the sound of his voice, or the way he walks, or the way he throws his head back. He's absurdly awkward, not to mention stubborn. The world is changing around him and he refuses to change with it. He's recessive, unenlightened. He's such a, a—a *moujik!*"

Zena found these remarks extremely annoying. Kulik might deserve a lot of criticism, but ridicule was not one of them. Surely Marusia could not really believe what she was saying. Zena, not wanting to start an argument, said, almost dreamily, "I happen to think Kulik is quite charming. As a matter of fact, I could see having a son by him. And I would want that son to be just like him."

Marusia stared at her. "A son? By him? Why? So, like his father he could dig a hole in the ground, crawl into it headfirst, and stay in the dark forever? What joy would there be in a son like that?" The words spewed from her mouth like water from a fountain. Feeling that she might have said too much, she bit her lip. She had the urge to tell Zena she didn't believe her own words, not all of them anyway, and that they had just somehow come out. More than anything she wanted to take back all the nasty things she had just said.

Feeling strangely uncomfortable, she struggled to find the right thing to say. Something seemed to be giving way inside of her. She looked helplessly at Zena, and for a brief moment the two women exchanged sympathetic glances.

CHAPTER 27

On the outskirts of Hlaby, the vast fields of rye had shot out their tender green stalks and were now gradually forming small ears of grain. A tawny black-headed horse trotted between the fields, pulling an old farmer's cart with high sides. Kulik sat in the front on a seat made of straw and next to him, handling the reins, was Chikaniuk. The two men were on their way to Pinsk, Chikaniuk to the marketplace to tend to some minor business matters and Kulik, to the Gosbank, the State Bank, to obtain teachers' wages for four neighboring schools, including his own. In his satchel Kulik had a list of all the teachers' names and the earnings owed them for the past month, which came to a total of three thousand rubles. First he would have to visit the *Oblispolkom* and get his papers verified, then wait in the long line at the Gosbank. He knew even before setting out that his mission could not possibly be accomplished in one day. The line at the Gosbank would undoubtedly be very long, much longer even than the line at the food cooperative.

As the cart rolled and bumped along, Chikaniuk remarked, "The rye over by Krive Selo has been completely drowned out by rain this year." He pointed toward a cluster of modest wooden houses with tin roofs, surrounded by towering willows. "Well-to-do farmers live in Krive Selo. Why, one could call them more landowners than farmers. Take Yuri Karral, for instance. He owns a fine big house, with over fifty acres of fertile fields, not to mention thick green forests and pasture lands. As you can imagine, life has been good to him. And now with all his wealth he's more miserable than anyone. I wouldn't want to be in his shoes for all the money in the world."

"How so?"

Chikaniuk gave him an ironic glance. "Do you think the Soviet Regime is about to come around and shake his hand and congratulate him for his accomplishments? Of course not! He's been branded a bourgeois, a *kulak*. In other words, an enemy of the people. His days are numbered."

The men fell silent. The sun had just come up over the horizon; Kulik could feel its warmth on his back. The rumbling of the cart made him drowsy and his lids grew heavy. Chikaniuk started up again at some length.

"You're an educated man, Director, so tell me, what do you think, is there a God or isn't there? I realize I don't have much schooling, but I'm not stupid either. I don't understand it. Leyzarov says that there is no God, that God is just a fabrication. But during the days of the Czar, lawyers and judges believed in God, and when a witness appeared in court, for example, he had to swear on the Bible. Things are so unclear now, I don't know what to think. Under the Poles, we had priests and churches and we went to mass every Sunday, but now everything has been turned inside out. Does God exist or not? I think maybe Leyzarov's right, that maybe God doesn't exist, because if He did, He'd show His face from behind the clouds once in a while. What do you think?"

Kulik forced a smile. "So many deep thoughts for so early in the morning." He hoped that this chatterbox would be quiet.

But Chikaniuk went on. "I have so many unanswered questions. My head is just brimming. Take life, for example. It's so short, and I would really like to know what it's like when we die. Do we just stop existing or are we reincarnated? And then there's Hrisko Suchok . . ." His voice dropped to an uneasy whisper. "I saw Hrisko Suchok murdered. That bullet, why, it took the last breath right out of him; he let out a little yelp, spread his arms out wide, then he fell down. It was all over, just like that. One minute he was there and then he was gone."

"I understand you saw it all happen."

"Yes, I saw the whole thing. Hrisko was like a rabbit . . . the rabbit flees and the hunter . . . bang! and it's over. Hrisko didn't break any laws, he didn't commit a crime. He got killed for nothing. And even if he did break the law, he shouldn't have been gunned down the way he was. Every civilized system has its laws and the accused is always innocent until proven guilty. But there's no such laws here; there's no law, where a man gets run down like an animal."

"I heard that the NKVD man who shot him was only trying to scare him—he aimed above his head, but it was an accident that somehow the bullet hit the back of his neck instead."

Chikaniuk's lips twitched. "That's not the way it happened. And it wasn't just any NKVD man that shot Hrisko, it was Sobakin. I saw him standing at the corner of Hrisko's house. I saw him aim and pull the trigger. One shot was all it took. Hrisko dropped to the ground, dead. And there wasn't any investigation, nobody questioned the witnesses afterward, there weren't any murder charges. And Sobakin just goes on as if nothing's happened—preaching about this happy, new life of ours under the Soviet sun."

The more Chikaniuk talked, the more tense Kulik felt. Why was Chikaniuk saying all this; why was he being so reckless and open about everything? Kulik began to suspect that he might be an informer. But then he noticed that Chikaniuk was nervous and uncomfortable. And when he began to stammer, Kulik felt sure he was being straight with him.

"I . . . I . . . I . . . shouldn't have said the things I just said, somehow they just came pouring out of my mouth. Please, Director, I beg you, don't take my words to the authorities because if you do, I'm as good as dead."

"To the authorities?" Kulik turned to look Chikaniuk in the eye. "Don't worry about me. Kokoshin hasn't approached me about becoming an informer and I hope it stays that way."

Chikaniuk gave a sigh of relief. "That's a good thing you're on to Kokoshin. He listens in on people. He stands by the door of every house and pricks up his ears like a dog. He's made Buhai into an informer and told him to spy on Kovzalo. And he's told Kovzalo to spy on Buhai. It's like being caught in a spider's web. Everyone is spying on everyone else. We hear Paraska's been told to spy on you."

"Paraska?" Kulik's heart thumped. "To spy on me?"

"Yes, but not to worry, so far nothing's come of it. Paraska doesn't have it in her, she's too simple-hearted, if you know what I mean. 'To keep an eye on the director?' she would say. ' Tell me what it is exactly I have to look for.' I heard Kokoshin wanted to recruit me too, but it hasn't happened yet."

As the cart rumbled forward, they came to the small village of Plishny, and onto a narrow dirt road that led to a bridge over the Strumien River.

"They're preparing the *kolkhoz*." Chikaniuk pointed to the left. "Just yesterday Leyzarov inspected all the buildings on the old Olivinski estate. He said the land was so big it could easily take care of a hundred heads of cattle, and he said there's also more than enough room for horses, geese and pigs. It seems that now everything is for the *kolkhoz*. There's already a waiting list to get in: Buhai, Kovzalo and a couple of fellows from other villages have signed up. It's just a matter of time before it swings into full gear. I hear the garden there is enormous and the orchard is filled with fruit trees. Leyzarov says there's more than enough of everything for everyone; we're going to build a paradise."

Chikaniuk said that recently, while Leyzarov was giving a speech to some peasants, out of nowhere a raven swooped down from the sky toward Leyzarov and almost struck him in the head. The bird circled the crowd several times, cawing, and finally perched on a tree branch. "Some say that the raven is bad luck, that it means war."

Kulik looked at Chikaniuk and said quietly, "I don't think it's come that far just yet."

"You don't think there will be war? Then why are the Bolsheviks preparing dugouts by the Bug River ? Why are trucks traveling there nonstop full of lumber? And why did they widen and deepen the Bugsy-Dnieprovsky canal? The answer is simple: to transport ammunition to the Front. I know this for a fact. I served in the army myself and I know what things are for. If the Russians are making dugouts, it means the Germans are getting ready to advance, and if the Germans advance there will be war. I tell you, war is in the air."

After crossing the Strumien River for at least half a kilometer, the two men continued along a bumpy dirt road, past several settlements and farmsteads. At last they came to another bridge, this time made of concrete, which led directly to the outskirts of Pinsk. There were rows of small whitewashed cottages on both sides of the bridge, most in a state of disrepair, with sagging porches and warped shutters; pots of drooping flowers stood on the windowsills. Groups of children played by the roadside, laughing and talking.

Kulik watched them as the cart passed. What about these children? Did they have a future or would it blow up in their faces? He closed his eyes and thought about his own childhood when he played in his grandmother's yard or with his friends along the banks of the Stryy. Life then seemed so easy, so uncomplicated. Now everything was so incredibly confusing. All at once Kulik looked urgently at Chikanuik.

"What if the authorities find out about our conversation today?"

Chikaniuk flinched. "They won't."

"How can you be so sure? When they take you to headquarters, when they rough you up, kick your teeth out, break your arms, then everything will come out."

"I'll never talk, and especially when it comes to you, Director. But if worse came to worse, I'd only have the best things to say. I'd say you're an upstanding citizen and that you have nothing but the greatest respect for the new regime."

Kulik continued to go at him. "But what if they won't believe you? And no matter how much you plead and cry, they still won't believe you. They'll beat you and they'll keep beating you until you break. Haven't you heard the old saying, 'Moscow does not believe in tears'?"

"Even if they torture me, I still won't talk. And besides, you've got nothing to worry about, you've said nothing against the regime, nothing to implicate yourself. As a matter of fact, I'm the one who's said too much."

Kulik began to feel afraid, not so much of Chikaniuk but of himself. He was afraid of every word he might utter and of every gesture he might make. Everything and anything could be used against him. Knowing how easy it could be to make that fatal slip, he resolved to play it safe from then on. He started carefully to pay homage to the new government:

"Yes, well, in any case, this is our new regime now and we must learn to live with it and appreciate it. Glory be to our new leaders."

Chikaniuk looked at Kulik askance and scowled. He said disdainfully, "Yes, we must learn to live with it, even if it has no written law. We must learn to live with it in the same way we would live with typhoid or cholera or cancer." He sighed. "There's no way out."

Finally the cart reached Market Square, and Kulik, jumping down, pulled his small traveling bag from behind the seat. He thanked Chikaniuk for the ride and crossed the square, to Neberezna Street.

It felt good to mingle with the bustling crowds, to walk past blocks of buildings and busy roadways. But when he came to the middle of a crossroads, trying to decide which way to go, he was gripped by a rush of alarm. He couldn't get Chikaniuk out of his mind. Even though he was sure Chikaniuk was being straight with him, the man still posed a measurable threat. If the authorities grabbed him and took him to the Zovty Prison for interrogation, he would undoubtedly break after the first round, and that would spell the end for Kulik.

There was no freedom anywhere anymore, and one wrong move could cost you your life. Even silence could bring disaster. Kulik knew that the only way he could protect himself completely would be to go immediately to Sobakin and report everything Chikaniuk had said. But that was out of the question. He could never be an informer. Never. The mere idea of such betrayal made his blood run cold.

By the time Kulik arrived at the *Oblispolkom* and knocked on Yeliseyenko's door, it was already ten o'clock. As usual the superintendent sat behind his desk buried in paperwork. He looked troubled, as if he had too much on his mind. He said quickly and rather distractedly, "Comrade Ivan, what brings you to Pinsk?"

Kulik handed him the sheet of paper with the teachers' names. Yeliseyenko studied the list carefully. After several minutes, he mumbled something under his breath, picked up his pen, and signed the paper. "I suggest you go to the Gosbank immediately. There's probably a considerable queue already. But you just might be lucky and get your money today."

Kulik hesitated. "Uh . . . if I don't get the money today, what do you suggest I do?"

"Well, then, you'll have to stay until tomorrow and go to the bank first thing. That won't be a problem. I'll issue you a pass stating that you're here on official government business."

Kulik thanked Yeliseyenko and started for the door. When he heard someone come in from Zena's office, he turned and was surprised to see Marusia standing there, holding some papers. She flushed, and a couple of sheets slipped out of her hand and fell to the floor. Kulik hurried to scoop them up.

"Marusia?" he said. "Do you work here at the *Oblispolkom?*"

"Yes, indeed she does!" Yeliseyenko said. "I have an excellent worker on my hands. I don't know how I ever managed without her." Then to Kulik, "You'd better be on your way. I believe you've got a lot to do."

As Kulik turned to leave, Marusia gave him a faint smile, which he returned. Her profile was even more beautiful than he remembered, and today her hair was brushed neatly away from her face and piled on top of her head. Her expression was different; no longer cold and challenging. She actually seemed friendly.

"My God, how beautiful she is," he said aloud to himself, out on the street. "Her job has transformed her. She looks so different, so elegant, so mature. I almost didn't recognize her." He couldn't get her out of his mind.

After walking for about ten minutes, he came to the Gosbank. The queue was longer than he expected, extending over several blocks, and ending only steps away from Market Square. He took his place behind a corpulent woman in a worn dress with a flimsy scarf over her head. She hardly moved, but from time to time she emitted long, drawn-out sighs. The line advanced very slowly, it barely moved at all; the people stared ahead blankly, and did not talk to one another. They were mainly government workers: teachers, postmen, factory workers, firemen, laborers, district committee members and so on, all holding cheques or certificates of some sort. Hour after hour passed while the line inched forward. An endless chain had formed behind Kulik; it spilled onto Market Square and looped around the far end. The people behind him were as passive as those in front of him.

It was now three o'clock. Four hours had passed and Kulik guessed it would probably take that many more before he got his money. He kept thinking about Marusia, about how stunning she was, and how changed she seemed. "She was so different today, and so different toward me. What's come over her?"

A long time later a voice erupted from a megaphone near the bank doors. "Attention people! Attention! There's no more money left in the bank! Come back tomorrow!"

There was some grumbling, but for the most part the queue started to break up as silently as it had formed. Within minutes there was not a soul left in sight.

It was a quarter to five. Kulik, walking down Karalyna Street, remembered that the *Oblispolkom* closed at five, so Marusia should be getting ready to leave for the day. He knew that to get home, she had to go down Karalyna; he slackened his pace, looking over his shoulder to see if she was coming. And sure enough, there she was, crossing over to the other side, walking briskly, a small brown purse under her arm. He turned and started toward her.

"Ivan, is that you?"

"Yes, it's me," he answered, pleased to see her in a friendly mood.

"Did you get your money?"

"Unfortunately, no, I have to go back tomorrow."

She smiled. "So, you're still going to be here tomorrow? Zena and I were talking about you the other day. She thinks you're a rather decent fellow. I think she might even like you."

Kulik laughed, embarrassed. He felt a twinge of guilt: he couldn't deny that he had strong feelings for both women. At Luninetska Street, Marusia said cheerfully, "You must come to the house and say hello to my parents. Father will be delighted to see you. He's so terribly fond of you."

Opening the front door, she called out, "Father! I've brought a visitor with me. You'll be pleased."

As they entered the living room, Valentyn pulled himself up off the sofa, and came toward Kulik with open arms. "Young man, how nice that you've come for a visit! A pleasure, always a pleasure to see you. And you, Marusia, are you done with work already? Excellent. There's nothing I want more than to see the two of you together."

"Oh, Father, stop it," Marusia said crossly; a touch of pink came to her cheeks.

While Valentyn and his daughter exchanged words, Kulik walked to the window and pulled back the curtains. All at once a dreadful chill took hold of him. "What have I done?" he murmured. "What have I done? It was a mistake my coming here today. I'm putting my life on the line."

Marusia heard him. "Putting your life on the line? What on earth are you talking about? What's wrong?"

"It's Sobakin. He lives in the house next door. He's always watching."

Valentyn did not hesitate to jump in. "Yes, in the house next door. He's settled there, in rooms on the top floor. He's like a poisonous snake and he wants my daughter. He even got her to . . ."

"Father! Please! Stay out of it!"

Father and daughter went at each other again and Kulik regretted having stirred things up. He noticed the old man had shaved off his beard. Efrosinia had finally got her way. He tried to change the subject. "By the way, have you heard from Lonia?"

Valentyn shook his head grimly. "Lonia. Lonia. In his letters he promises to come home for the summer. So many letters arrive, one after the other, but no Lonia."

"Where's your wife?"

"Efrosinia's at the train station. She's there almost every day. She's convinced herself that Lonia is coming home, and when he does she'll be there to greet him with open arms, like when he was a little boy. Every day at five-forty-five the train arrives from Lvov, but never with our Lonia. Efrosinia just waits for the next train. But it's always the same, no Lonia. My wife's no longer able to perceive reality in the normal way and it frightens me. Yes, I believe she's losing her mind."

He lowered his voice and the words trembled on his lips. "Lonia won't come today, or tomorrow or the day after. He's not coming home at all. Ever."

"Father, stop talking like that! You're frightening me. Why don't you go and get Mother? It's late and she should have been back a long time ago. I hope she hasn't had any trouble. Go and bring her home, please."

Valentyn remained unmoving, staring at the floor. Finally he said, "I suppose you're right. I suppose I should go and get her. She probably nodded off on one of the benches."

As he took his hat and cane and made for the door, Kulik also got ready to leave, but Marusia was quick to take his arm. Looking a little piqued, she said, "Ivan, please don't go. Stay and wait for Mother. As a matter of fact, just the other day she was asking about you, and she even said that the two of you had some kind of business to settle. It's true, she never really liked you very much, but now somehow she's warmed up to you. Isn't that the truth, Father?"

"Yes, yes." Valentyn looked at her vaguely. "I suppose it's true if you say so, but to be honest, I don't know anything about it. Well, in any case, it's a good thing she's asked for you, because then I'll still get to see you when I come back."

Descending the porch stairs, Valentyn pulled his pipe out of his pocket and lit it. He looked up at the sky and muttered, "Oh Lord, please don't let her be in one of her moods."

CHAPTER 28

Marusia and Kulik sat in the living room in awkward silence for a moment. Then she moved closer to him, her arm touched his. Her face was a little flushed. She smiled and said with a tremor in her voice, "At last we find ourselves alone and without witnesses."

Looking uncertainly into her green eyes, his heart melted like hot wax. He knew she wanted something from him, and he wasn't sure he could help her. She broke into sobs. "Ivan, I need your help. Please, don't refuse me."

Kulik wanted to hold her in his arms and comfort her, but he said hesitantly, "I don't know that I can be of any use to you. What do you want me to do?"

She rushed out of the room, to return a few minutes later holding a small wooden box. Her voice breaking, she said, "Lonia, my brother Lonia . . . Oh, I don't know what to make of anything anymore. Here, take a look at these letters. The box is full of them. Each and every one of them is signed 'your loving brother'. But I don't believe he wrote them. Something's happened to him, something terrible, I can feel it with all my heart. Mother can't bring herself to accept the truth, she's made herself believe they're from him, but I know they're not. This isn't even his handwriting."

Kulik took the box from her and examined the letters. Some were written in pencil and hard to read, others were in bold blue ink. Most were two to three weeks old, with an address from a street in Lvov. Their style was the same—mechanical, detached, even strained. They didn't read like letters from a young man to his loving family.

Marusia looked fearfully at Kulik. "What's your impression of them?"

Looking through them again, he said at last, "Well, I'm not really sure. In most of the letters he says he's fine and he's spending most of his time studying. In this last one here, he promises to come home to Pinsk for the summer holidays. The second half of June is not that far off. Why don't you just wait and see what happens?"

The girl flew at him in a frenzy. "I asked for your *impression*, not your *interpretation!*"

Kulik put the letters back in the box. "In all honesty, Marusia, I don't know what to say about all this. The only thing that is clear to me is that someone has been tampering with these letters."

She shrank back. "Oh, my God! It was Sobakin! I should have known. The entire time he's been promising to bring Lonia home what he's really been doing is stringing me along. I know it now! He doesn't care if my brother lives or dies."

"What do you want me to do? Do you want me to go to Lvov?"

Marusia's face brightened and she clutched his arm. "Would you, please? I have no one else to turn to."

When he met her desperate gaze, he blurted out the first thing that came to his mind. "You know I'd like to help you, but you have to realize this is a very difficult matter. . . . Well, I suppose I could go . . . but I definitely couldn't go before the summer holidays because that would raise suspicion at the school. I wouldn't only lose my position—I'd most likely be arrested by the NKVD and thrown into . . ."

Suddenly his throat ran dry and he could not go on. What was he saying? He was embroiling himself in a situation where he could easily be picked up by the secret police and convicted on some trumped-up charge. And her relationship with Sobakin certainly wouldn't help his case. He decided at that moment that it would be best for him to leave the Bohdanovich house immediately, and not involve himself any further in their affairs.

With all these thoughts rushing at him at once, he looked up and met Marusia's eyes, welling with tears. He felt he had to make her feel better. He said thoughtfully, "There's one other possibility, but you must promise to keep it secret. Agreed? I have a friend who lives in Lvov. He's a colleague of mine from my university days. I'll write him today and ask him to make some inquiries. I'm sure he won't refuse."

Her face took on a look of almost stunning gratitude. She said softly, "You're a decent man, Ivan. I was so wrong about you. You're different from what I thought."

She had become completely transfigured by her love for her brother. "You're different, too," he said. "You've changed in so many ways. You're actually even friendly to me . . ." He broke off and then added, "Yet, at the same time you're still . . ."

"I'm still . . . what? Why don't you finish?"

"Well, you're still trying to be something you're not. Why do you deny who you really are, especially with everything going on around you? You can't block it from your mind forever. You're a strange one, Marusia, and I can't quite figure you out. In spite of all that's happening, you still insist on speaking Russian. And your Russian isn't as good as you think it is and it's filled with all kinds of Ukrainian intonations. The only one you're fooling is yourself."

Marusia was about to give him an angry answer, but controlled herself to keep the peace between them.

They fell silent, and as the sun set, the room darkened. Marusia got up to switch on a small lamp by the sofa. She looked at Kulik and said with great effort, "Ivan, I meant to ask you, have you seen Seryoza lately? How's he doing? Is he all right? He hasn't come around for the longest time."

Not knowing what to say, Kulik blurted, "He's fine. He was quite sick for a while, but now he's better."

"Sick?" Marusia looked incredulously at him. "What do you mean, sick? Seryoza's never been sick a day in his life. What was wrong with him?"

"I think he had the flu."

"The flu? Why are you lying to me? And I thought you were actually starting to be straight with me. I was even coming to trust you."

"What do you mean?"

"Oh, don't pretend with me. Seryoza was never sick with the flu, and you very well know it. No, he was taken to the Zovty Prison and beaten! I know that just as well as you. Some people told me. Why can't you trust me, why can't you be open with me?"

Getting up from the sofa, Kulik said calmly, "For our own sakes, Marusia, I think it's best we drop the subject right now. Things will only get too personal and we'll end up quarrelling and saying things we might regret. No? You really want me to go ahead? All right then, I'll tell you. I have to be very careful with what I say to you because your thoughts aren't always clear, you're impressionable and confused, and you close your eyes to the truth." Then he added, "You're very charming, and I believe you're struggling to find your way out, but I'm not sure you ever will. So I think you can understand why I can't trust you, at least not yet."

She listened to Kulik with close attention. Her small delicate features tightened. Was she truly as inane as he said she was? Was she actually preventing herself from thinking things through?

She settled herself on the sofa, and, patting the seat with her hand, said almost cheerfully, "Ivan, come here and sit next to me. That's better. Am I causing your blood to tingle? Oh, you, you . . ." she ran the tips of her fingers along the contours of his face. "What a forehead you have. You don't even have the slightest crease. Such a fine, strong chin and your features are so heavy and bold. And that gleam in your eye! So devious! What were you like as a child? You must have given your parents a hard time."

Kulik smiled. "I was a handful, I have to admit. I climbed the highest trees and destroyed crows' nests."

"Did you get into fights?"

"All the time. I fought everybody and anybody, big or small. There wasn't a day I didn't have a black eye or a bloody nose. The neighbors all agreed I would either grow up to be a criminal or a great man. But as you can see, I've become neither. I'm simply a Soviet civil servant of the lowest rank."

"Were you ever in love?"

"I don't know—love is so fleeting. And besides, love today has taken on a whole new meaning, it's become burdensome and painful. It's lost its appeal. Is there a point to falling in love, to getting married, when they can knock on your door at any time, even on your wedding day? . . . But let's not talk about depressing things. Better to think of something pleasant and enjoy the moment."

Marusia who had turned towards him, felt she had not had a good look at him before. His straight black hair was combed back neatly, his handsome face was clean-shaven. There was something definitely appealing about him, something she had not really noticed until now. Kulik could feel his pulse throb, and impulsively, he leaned toward her, put his arms around her and kissed her on the mouth. She responded.

Then suddenly she tensed and pushed him away. Her demeanor changed completely and she gasped. "What are you trying to do to me? You men are all alike, all of you! Leave me alone!"

No sooner had she pulled herself away, when there came a tapping on the window. It lasted only a few seconds. Rushing to the window, she pulled the curtains slightly apart, peered outside, and whispered nervously, "Ivan, I think there's someone out there."

The two stood in silence and listened. When they looked out again, they saw only the branch of an elderberry bush brushing up against the lower pane.

"I'll go outside and take a better look." Kulik started for the door, but Marusia grasped his arm.

"No, don't go. It was probably nothing."

It occurred to her that it was around this time that Sobakin left for the Zovty Prison. She quickly concluded that her worst nightmare had come true: it was Sobakin at the window! Looking frantically at Kulik, she could feel her heart begin to pound faster and faster. Taking his hand in hers and squeezing it tightly, looking deep into his eyes, she knew she could never forgive herself if anything were to happen to him.

CHAPTER 29

It was well past nine o'clock when outside the Bohdanovich house there were a series of ear-piercing screams, followed by shouts. Marusia instantly recognized the voices of her mother and father. Turning on the lights, she ran outside to find her parents stumbling about in the darkness.

"I'll catch that damn thief if it's the last thing I do," Efrosinia was yelling. "I'll break his legs in two, I swear!"

Seeing her daughter, she called out, "Marusia, did you hear anything from the house? There was someone prowling around out here, trying to get in through one of the windows. Oh, if only I got a better look at him." Then catching sight of Kulik by the door, "And you, what a fine product of a man you are! You should have gone outside right away, grabbed him by the collar, and called the police. The police would have known exactly what to do with the likes of him!"

Efrosinia rushed into the house to see if anything was missing. She held up her long black frock so she wouldn't trip on it. When everything appeared in order, she went into the living room and plopped herself down on the sofa. Brushing a few loose strands of gray hair from her face, she drew a deep breath. Then she fixed her gaze upon Kulik, standing by the doorway.

Kulik winced. He knew that he was not exactly her favorite person, and it was just a matter of time before she would start berating him. But for some reason she ignored him. Her face worked and from her mouth came a series of strange, broken sounds; she seemed to be trying to say her son's name. Weeping, she repeated these sounds several times.

A tremendous feeling of grief and sadness overcame Kulik. The old woman had such a huge burden to bear, as she sat there on the sofa alone and powerless, a mere bundle. But she started to recover herself. A smile came to her lips. And indeed, when she spoke, to Kulik's surprise she did so quite easily, even matter-of-factly. For some reason she began to recount the events of her day. She looked straight at him, and seemed to be addressing him directly, but she didn't seem to see him.

"I went to the train station today and waited for the train from Lvov. I expected Lonia to be on the five-thirty-five, but he wasn't. I waited three hours for the next train. Hundreds of people got off, carrying all kinds of bundles and parcels. They were all bumping into each other and squeezing through the gates. I searched for Lonia, but again he was nowhere to be seen. Then my old man showed up and tried to get me to go home. But I made up my mind to stay on and wait for the express train to arrive in an hour and a half because I was sure Lonia would be on board. Valentyn said he would stay and wait with me, but that was only because he didn't want a scene. Then the train came and there was no Lonia. I wanted to wait for the next one, coming in at dawn. I was ready to spend the night on one of the benches. Then my old man came up with a very good point. 'What if Lonia decides to come by truck? There are a lot of trucks on the road these days traveling back and forth carrying supplies. He might easily hitch a ride with one of them.' So I finally agreed to come home. But, as you can see, I didn't find my Lonia waiting for me here. No, all I found was a thief trying to break in through the living room window—and you."

When Efrosinia finished she stared before her as if she hadn't said anything at all. She seemed oblivious to everything around her. Then she turned to Kulik. "Well, young man, tell me, what's brought you to Pinsk?"

Kulik sat down on the sofa. He was about to answer, when suddenly from beneath him came an incredibly loud squeak. The squeak was so loud that even Valentyn, who had just sauntered into the room, gave a start.

Efrosinia turned on her husband. "Did you just hear that, old man? It was the sofa again! Are you ever going to fix it?" Then to Kulik, "Look at him, he doesn't care about anything. And he calls himself man of the house! Man of the house, hah! What do you think, young man, is he a man like all other men?" She shook her head. "If this is a man like all other men, then God help the species!"

Valentyn's face reddened with anger. "This time you've really outdone yourself, old woman."

"Outdone myself? Does the truth hurt? The only good thing you've done lately is shave off that ugly beard of yours. And how long did that take you? Three months!"

She stopped short. Her mouth quivered and she buried her head in her hands, shaking with sobs and muttering to herself, her lips barely moving. Clasping her hands, she cried, "Oh, Lonia, my poor Lonia." Then again she seemed to rally. Seizing Kulik's arm, she stared into his eyes. "What do you think, young man, did my Lonia really get married? Yes, he did! He got married, I know he did." In a sort of trance, she smiled strangely. "I was there, at the wedding, and it was the most beautiful one I have ever seen. The church bells rang for the whole town to hear. My Lonia looked very handsome, all dressed in black. And I saw his bride too. How lovely she is, so tall and strong and self-reliant."

Marusia rushed at her and shook her, "Mother, stop it! Stop it right now! What are you saying? You've got to pull yourself together. You're letting your imagination run away with you again." She whispered to Kulik, "Forgive Mother, she hasn't been herself lately. As you can see she's become so disoriented by everything. And she's been having such terrible mood swings. I'm so afraid something inside of her may be snapping."

She tried to get her mother to go up and lie down, but Efrosinia resisted her.

Kulik could see the old woman was being torn apart. He had never felt so sorry for anyone as he did for her. No sooner did he feel this way, when Efrosinia seemed to change again, and this time there was a gleam in her eye. Looking at Kulik, she said cheerfully, "Ivan, how nice of you to come and visit us. Come on, get up, take Marusia by the hand and let me take a good look at you. What a pair! Your hair is black as coal and my daughter's is soft like cotton batting. Go on, walk across the room. Let me take a good look."

"Oh, Mother, please!" The girl flushed. "Don't you know when to stop?"

But Efrosinia concentrated on Kulik, measuring him carefully. "Just look at him, Marusia. My, my, what a fine young man he is, *moujik* or no *moujik*. How is it that I didn't see this before? He has such a proud walk, like a true gentleman. So tall and robust, not to mention handsome and educated." She threw a contemptuous glance at her husband. "He's nothing like you, you old goat. You clawed me like an animal. And if you had been let loose in some fine home, you would have broken all the furniture. Take a good look at him, it's never too late to learn a thing or two."

Valentyn snarled, "Don't you think you've said enough for one night, old woman? Why don't you just go and lock yourself up in your room and give us some peace and quiet for a change."

"You want to get rid of me? Why? So you can entertain our young visitor and drink your vodka? Is that your plan? Well, I assure you, I'm far from finished."

From the window the almost-full moon threw pale streaks of light upon the four walls. A warm breeze rustled the curtains.

Efrosinia fixed her attention once more on Kulik. "Ivan, when I look at you I think of my Lonia. He's about your age, big and strong, and his hair is dark like yours, only his eyes are brown, not gray and deep-set." Then, with hope, "Maybe you could help me. You're young and full of energy. Maybe you could go to Lvov and find Lonia. You could bring him home to me. Will you? Yes? Bless you, son, bless you."

Encouraged, Efrosinia managed to calm down. She gave her arm to her daughter who drew her into another room.

Valentyn was more than happy to be rid of his wife. Spreading himself comfortably on the sofa, he would have the rest of the evening to himself, without her nagging presence. He lit his pipe. "So, young man, tell me, was there ever an independent Ukraine?"

Kulik was not in a talkative mood, but he forced a reply: "Ukraine has never been a sovereign state, except in the time of Bohdan Khmelnytsky. This was in the summer of 1657, before Belorussia and Russia existed." Feeling increasingly annoyed and impatient, he tried to change the subject. "Why talk about the past when there's no place for it in our lives anymore? These are new times and we must learn to cope with what lies ahead."

Just then Marusia came into the room. How radiant she is, Kulik thought, that glowing complexion, those moist lips. He felt a wave of excitement. All he wanted at that moment was for the old man to stop his incessant chattering and go off to bed.

But Valentyn, refilling his pipe, went on more loudly. "All in all, I'd say life under the Czar was better than it is now. In fact, the officers in the Czar's army don't even begin to compare to today's NKVD men. There used to be more respect for the individual, wouldn't you say?"

Kulik answered, "And what about the *moujiks*? Do you think they also were more respected in the days of the Czar?"

Valentyn gave this question serious consideration. He was delighted to have the undivided attention of such a fine and learned visitor. "*Moujiks*, since the beginning of time, have been destined to live lives of poverty and degradation," he said. "However, if and when they resettled into the cities and acquainted themselves with the finer things in life they were able to think differently. Take me, for example. I was born in a village—in other words, I was born a *moujik*, and then I became a cabinetmaker. When I lived under the Poles, I took it upon myself to learn Polish, and now that the Russians have taken over I taught myself to speak Russian. And learning Russian was the best thing I could have done for myself and my family. Life became easier. Today when I walk out in the street my neighbors call out: there goes Valentyn Nikodimovich. See how it is, now people always address me by my patronymic, even people I barely know. Villagers live in the dark, they hardly even know what *patronymic* means! I don't talk like a *moujik* anymore, no, I talk like a Russian. I've become accepted wherever I go, and people look up to me." He said to Kulik, "You talk of the new times we live in and how we must learn to cope with them, but why do you resist everything that's going on around you? How do you singlehandedly propose to fight the established new law? You'll only lose. It's better to join them than to fight them."

Having spoken these words, the old man's manner changed; he appeared troubled and confused. He scratched his chin. "Hmm . . . about these Russians, I've been giving them some extra thought lately. I have to admit, my mind's not totally made up. They seem to have some very peculiar ways about them. It's as though they're not always what they seem. To be honest, it's becoming harder and harder to make sense of anything. Innocent people are being pulled out of their homes and vanishing to God knows where. I'm not so sure that things will come to a good end."

Valentyn paused; his own words seemed to cause him uneasiness, even trepidation. "Yes," he said, "there's uncertainty everywhere, and there are many things happening that we don't like or understand, but in the end, as difficult as it may be, it will be for our own good. That's what we're being told and that's what we must accept. I say it's better to talk in Russian than in a language of a republic, especially in the cities. I say, leave Ukrainian to the *moujiks*! The laws of survival have changed and as painful as it may be, we have no choice but to change with them. As you said earlier, we must learn to cope with what lies ahead."

To Kulik it was obvious that Valentyn knew quite well everything that was going on around him but chose not to understand it. The words *motherland, nation, patriotism* had lost their meaning for him. He was accepting the fact that the Ukrainian people, their language and culture, were being annihilated before his eyes. Kulik felt alone, fearfully alone, like a solitary tree in the vast steppe.

A clock on the wall struck ten. Kulik glanced briefly at Marusia, who stood at the window, partially shaded by the muslin curtains. Her face looked different, blank and unmoving, like a mask, and her body seemed almost wooden. Like her father, she had all too readily succumbed to the new laws of the land, a new Russian patriotism, an attitude representative of the petty bourgeoisie in her neighborhood and in neighborhoods like hers all across the republic. Kulik thought, What good is the Ukrainian language when only Russian is being recognized? Let Ukrainian remain in the villages where it belongs with the dull and unenlightened *moujik*. It has no place in the schools, the government, or public offices.

These thoughts further dampened Kulik's spirit; his head grew heavy with fatigue. He murmured gloomily, "But how can things be any other way?" Ukraine had never had self-government, and for centuries control over all aspects of life had come from outside its borders, namely, from Russia. In the end, he thought, Ukraine had suffered a loss of national identity and developed deep-rooted feelings of inferiority. Consequently, they were a people who forever looked outside themselves for political and cultural survival. The very foundation of the country's existence, repeatedly wrecked by these outside forces, had fallen into moral decay. He asked himself, How can the people start fighting now and against such overwhelming odds, when they know they will only lose, as they always have? Soviet ways have now been imposed, with their intensified campaign to destroy all that is non-Russian. Forever lost in this terrible anomaly, who are Ukrainians really?

Kulik no longer listened to the old man who was jabbering away. The room was stuffy; he drew a white handkerchief from his pocket to wipe the sweat from his brow, but he felt cold. He had to get away from this house, from these people, as far away as possible. He got up and announced, "Well, it's quite late. I'd better be off."

"And where might you be off to?" Valentyn looked inquisitively at him.

"To Katia Street. I usually board there when I'm in Pinsk. I'm sure there's something available. Good night and thanks for a pleasant evening."

Picking up his satchel, Kulik made for the door. Marusia hurried after him, and clutching his arm, looked urgently into his eyes. She was very upset. "Ivan, please stay with us tonight. I'm afraid for you. You mustn't go out there."

Kulik looked at her steadily without moving or drawing away. He couldn't help but be affected by her sincere concern for him. He felt an outpouring of love and his heart throbbed. He threw his arms around her, and covered her face with kisses. Gently stroking her hair, he whispered, "Don't worry about me. I'll be fine."

But as he spoke these words, he felt a sensation of terror that he had never felt before. It was as if he had no more freedom even to think, and everything in his life was suddenly and irreversibly decided. Marusia looked really alarmed; he had never seen her like this. Putting his lips to hers, he pressed her trembling body against his as if for the last time. Then releasing her, he had a burning impatience to be off. But where could he go?

There was something frightful in the air tonight and it was approaching quickly. He believed his days were numbered. He knew he had to muster the strength to go on, but was there any place left for him to go? Giving Marusia one final embrace, he found his way onto the sidewalk, and stumbled into the night.

CHAPTER 29

The next morning Kulik left his room on Katia Street and walked quickly toward the city center. The sun was rising over the houses, and the dark lines of the rooftops were just beginning to take on a brilliant orange hue. There was an odd breathlessness in the air, and although the sky was blue and clear, to the south it was obscured by a thin veil of dust and smoke. The streets were empty. Kulik hastened toward the Gosbank. Undoubtedly the queue had already begun to form, and the sooner he got there the better chance he would have of getting his money. He had just turned onto Karalyna and crossed over to the other side, when he heard a rumbling sound from somewhere around the corner; with each second it grew louder and louder. It was coming from directly behind him. When he turned to look, his heart gave a thump and he stood rooted to the spot. A big black car was creeping along, almost hitting against the curb, getting closer and closer. He was frightened and pained by the beating of his own pulse.

"It's the Black Crow!" he cried aloud.

The car came to a full stop a few meters away, the back doors flew open and two men jumped out onto the sidewalk, one in civilian clothes, the other in NKVD uniform.

"Get into the car!" the one in NKVD uniform shouted and grabbed his arm.

Kulik pulled back, but his knees seemed to have turned to water. The one in civilian clothes took him by the shoulders and pushed him toward the car with such force that he almost fell. He scrambled into the far corner of the back seat, his heart racing. The

313

street was completely deserted. It occurred to Kulik that this was usual NKVD practice: they almost always did their work in the early hours of the morning or in the dead of night, without witnesses or the possibility of interference of any kind. The car made a sharp turn and entered Sovietskaya Street, and it was only then that he realized where he was being taken: to the Zovty Prison! "Finally my turn has come," he repeated to himself over and over. He began to experience a profound sense of fear and helplessness. Everything around him was so unreal it was almost surreal.

Then he became angry with himself, angry for having so recklessly and stupidly fallen into their trap. Why hadn't he stayed away from Marusia? Why did he have to look for her yesterday evening after work and walk her home? And why didn't he just go to Katia Street right away as he had originally intended? Why? Why? Why? All these questions piled up inside him and he tormented himself with them. Staring out the window without seeing anything, he was hit by a cold reality:

Sobakin! It was Sobakin who was behind this!

He knew that he was now completely penned in without any hope of escape.

The main gates of the prison were open, as if expecting them. The car drove into the courtyard and stopped at the side of the building with its motor running. A young guard in army uniform holding a rifle, immediately came to the car and opened the back door. Signaling to Kulik with his head, he poked the barrel of his rifle between his shoulders, and prodded him toward a side door. Kulik took a deep breath, and tried to strengthen himself to face whatever pain and humiliation awaited him there.

Walking down a broad, darkened corridor, Kulik could feel wafts of cold air seep through the stone floor. Odors of mold mixed with rust and mildew filled his nostrils. At a rickety wooden table pushed against the hallway wall, a snub-nosed officer with a shaved head, perhaps twenty-five or thirty years old, sat writing in a notebook. When he noticed the men standing there, he rose and pulling a Nagant revolver from his holster, announced to the guard, "I'll take over from here." Then pointing to a staircase at the end of the corridor, he gave Kulik a shove and ordered, "Hands behind your back! Get going! That way!"

Kulik started up the steps, not daring to turn his head or look back. The walls, black and roughly plastered, exuded a damp, pungent smell. He felt as though he was in a long, dark, endless tunnel. When finally he reached the second floor, the guard kicked him to one side and commanded, "To your left!"

Passing door after door, all painted the same drab, musty brown, they came to the end of the corridor, where there was a door much the same as the others, but with an iron gate in front of it. Both the door and gate were ajar and Kulik was shoved inside. He saw a bookcase, several wooden chairs, a desk and various other pieces of government furniture. At the back of the room was a closed door, undoubtedly leading to other rooms. A balding NKVD man of about forty-five was standing at his desk talking on the phone. Kulik could hear the words *da, nyet* spoken alternately, and it struck him at once that the man was taking orders from some higher-up. Upon seeing Kulik, the man quickly ended his conversation and hung up. He offered Kulik a seat opposite his desk, dismissed the guard and closed the door. Opening a small tin box on his desk, he pulled out a *makhorka* cigarette, lit it and handed it to Kulik, who realized this was a calculated gesture, one commonly used at the start of most interrogations. He took the cigarette, and inhaling the smoke deep into his lungs, felt a brief moment of relief.

The interrogator tapped his fingers on his desk and drilled his eyes into Kulik. "We're detaining you today because we need to get a few things clarified."

Kulik tried to remain calm. He thought, "This is how it almost always starts. First they begin with something inconsequential, then before you know it, they've got you pinned on some trumped-up charge." Trying his best to stay in control, clearing his throat, he said, "This morning I was on my way to the Gosbank to collect wages for the teachers of the Hlaby Village Soviet, when for some reason I was intercepted by your men on the street."

The interrogator examined some papers on his desk and appeared not to be listening. Without looking up, he started coldly on a line of questioning.

"With whose money did you obtain your education in Vilno?"

"My own. I worked as a laborer and paid my tuition from my wages."

"What about when you were in the *gymnasium*, whose money did you use?"

"I completed my classes at the *gymnasium* by night, and by day I repaired houses and did odd jobs around town. Later it was the same with university."

There was a long pause as the interrogator thumbed through some files. He kept this up for several minutes. Kulik knew this was just another tactic intended to fray his nerves.

"Did you belong to the Polish fascist organization, Legion of Youth?"

"No organization ever interested me. I kept mostly to myself."

As he carefully recorded these answers in a notebook, the interrogator's tone grew more menacing. "Did you belong to the Ukrainian National Student Movement in Vilno?"

Kulik froze. He struggled with himself to find something to say. After a moment, he blurted out the first thing that came to his mind. "A moment ago you asked if I belonged to the Polish Legion of Youth and now you ask if I belonged to some Ukrainian student movement. Asking me these questions, well, you might as well be mixing oil with fire."

"How so?" The interrogator didn't seem to understand.

"Well, first of all, there would have been no sense in starting a Ukrainian movement in Vilno, because, as you know, Vilno is a Lithuanian city and was under Polish occupation with a very limited Ukrainian population. Secondly, the Poles have always sought out and persecuted Ukrainians, and to support one of their organizations would be sheer treachery on my part."

The interrogator bent his head over his notebook. He was obviously ignorant of the goings-on in Vilno, especially between

Ukrainians and Poles. But it did not take him long to fire more questions.

"Can you give me a guarantee that when you were in Vilno you did not belong to a Ukrainian movement of any kind?"

"The only guarantee I can give you is my word. I lived a very quiet and peaceful life. I was interested only in my studies."

"Did you keep company with other Ukrainian students?"

"As I've already mentioned, there weren't many of them. The few that were there were studying medicine or law or engineering, and because my major was in history, we weren't in any of the same classes. So we didn't get to know one another. I only knew several by name or in passing."

"Do you know what became of any of them?"

"No."

"How did you come to live in Vilno? Did you move there with your parents?"

"No, when I was a boy, at the age of nine, I had a few run-ins with the police, the Polish police, that is, and they sentenced me to a reform school, which happened to be in Vilno. That's how I came to live there."

"What about your parents?"

"They remained in the village. The police never told them where I was. I never saw my parents again until I was twenty."

The interrogator raised his eyebrows, and a thin smile strayed onto his lips. "So, in other words, you rebelled against Polish oppression, and from such an early age! And even after being sent to a reform school at the age of nine, you decided to earn your living and make something of yourself. Commendable, very commendable." Then slapping his hand against his thigh, as if having just thought of it, "Hah! Why, your life almost sounds like the life of our great, most revered writer, Maxim Gorky!"

Kulik, startled by the comparison, looked at his interrogator in astonishment. He said, "I suppose you could look at it that way. From a very early age, like Gorky, I had to overcome a harsh life and fight overwhelming odds."

The interrogator rose from behind his desk, and paced the room. Pausing to look the window, he asked without turning around, "Are you familiar with out Soviet literature?"

Kulik was determined not to say too much; he thought this was the best course for someone in his position. But he could not resist the challenge. Literature was his forte, all literature, and in between his studies he had in fact taken a keen interest in Soviet writing. He started to mention all the names he could think of, taking care, however, not to let slip those who had fallen into political disfavor: Zoshchenko was the greatest satirist of all times; Mayakovsky was unparalleled as a poet, and his "Ode to Revolution" had great mass appeal; and Alexsei Tolstoy, with *The Road to Calvary*, was a true spokesman of his times.

The interrogator stared at him, and asked curiously, "Where, may I ask, did you come to learn about these authors?"

"Mostly in Vilno when I lived under Polish occupation. Some of them I read legally and others illegally."

The official walked back to his desk, and looked sternly at Kulik. Two hours of questioning had gotten him nowhere. Time was running out. His sole aim now was to discredit Kulik, break his spirit and produce a confession of some kind. He needed something, anything to take back to his superiors. He began another line of questioning: Why was Kulik promoting Ukrainian in his school? Did he belong to the Organization of Ukrainian Nationalists? Was he anti-Semitic? Why did he allow the incident involving the Jewish schoolteacher, Haya Fifkina, to get out of hand? Barely waiting for answers, he started in on Kulik's personal life: How old was he? Who were his parents? How many siblings did he have?

As Kulik answered question after question, he had a strong premonition of worse things to come. This was all just the beginning, a prologue to the drama. Before long he would be in the hands of more sophisticated interrogators, with more elaborate cross-examination methods, who would try to link him to some ludicrous crime and, without a scrap of real evidence, convict him. A cascade of lies would soon descend upon him and he would have to find a way to ward them off and stay on top of things. He needed to muster his moral strength and prove himself capable of enduring the impending physical and psychological torture.

After several more hours of grilling, the interrogator reached for his notes, read them aloud, and told Kulik to sign them. When Kulik readily complied, the interrogator pressed a button on the wall beside his desk.

Almost instantly the same guard appeared on the threshold, this time wearing a blue government overcoat, his shaved head covered by a black cap with a visor. From his insignia Kulik noticed he was a sergeant-major. As Kulik was escorted down the same flight of stairs they had come up, he indulged in a wild hope. "Maybe they'll spare me. Maybe this guard with the holstered Nagant will show mercy and lead me into the courtyard, and out the gates."

They reached the landing, then the corridor, and there to the left was the door that led outside. Kulik felt his body being pulled in that direction as if by a magnet. With all his heart he had to believe he was about to be released. Then from behind him the stiff, harsh voice of the guard, "Keep moving! To your right!"

In one flash all hope died, and he found himself being prodded into another wing of the building. It was completely empty, and except for the clicking of the guard's boot heels against the hard concrete floor, there was silence. A few more steps and he came upon a double doorway guarded by a young sentinel armed with a rifle. The sentinel flung the door open, then snapping his fingers three times, signaled Kulik with his head to move forward. A steep narrow staircase shot straight downward, to the underground. Kulik descended, bracing himself to face the worst.

"My time has finally come. It's over."

At the bottom of the staircase, several paces to the right he was ordered to stop before a huge steel door. There was the grinding of a key, and the creaking of rusted hinges. He was pushed into a large, square room with a bare cement floor and slimy green walls, permeated with the stench of sweat and urine. The only light came from a tiny barred window.

About a dozen men in tattered, dirty clothes, were huddled in a corner, staring vacantly before them. Every few minutes the silence was broken by terrible fits of coughing. Kulik found his way to a narrow makeshift bench against the far wall and sat down. After a while, he began to feel the chill of the cold, damp air. As he shivered, he felt something warm and comforting fall around him. Someone had slipped a coarse prison blanket over his shoulders and had even tucked it in at the sides. When he looked up he saw one of the prisoners standing over him. The man pointed to the tiny window.

"It's probably a fine sunny day out there," he said, "the kind that makes you want to jump into the Stryy River and go for a swim."

Kulik was struck by his strange accent, and his broken Ukrainian. He listened to him, trying to guess where he was from. The man said he had been in this cell for eight days. His eyes shifting from side to side, he leaned forward and whispered, "These men are afraid of me because I speak my mind. I'm not one to make propaganda speeches, no, I say what I feel. At first the prisoners thought I was an informer; as a matter of fact, some of them still do. But I'm no informer, no, not I. I am Aristotle Kasparidos, the Greek! I was born on the great Greek peninsula, where with a lot of hard work, I became a man of means. Ah, the Aegean and Ionian Seas, to bathe in them just once more!"

Kulik listened in astonishment. A Greek? In a Soviet prison? "How on earth did you ever land here?"

"A very good question, young man. I like people who are interested in the stories of others. We Greeks like to talk, we like to talk more than we like to listen. The southern temperament, it can't be helped."

He said that he was a very shrewd businessman, "but hopeless when it comes to politics. And for this I paid a very high price. I'm a calculator, not a strategist. It all started a few years back when I was in London looking around to invest in wilderness property. I was urged by my colleagues to go to the Canadian embassy, but the Devil took me to the Polish one instead. And it was there that I found out about your Pinsk Marshes."

Kasparidos told about his life in painstaking detail, for nearly an hour. His story ended with the Bolshevik invasion. "One night the NKVD came and arrested me. And now here I am with no hope of ever getting out. They made me confess to some ridiculous charge. I'm not even sure what it was. Then they threw me into this cell."

He turned and walked away. He kept circling the cell, repeating his story, half to himself, half to the other men. He started with London, then the Polish embassy, how he met his wife, his villa in the Pinsk Marshes and finally, his arrest. He repeated himself again and again. The prisoners paid no attention; he might have been talking to the four walls.

The long day was finally beginning to take its toll on Kulik. He slid to the floor from exhaustion. Fragments of thoughts and images floated through his mind. For the next hour or so he dozed off and on. Suddenly someone was kicking him in the back and tugging at his arm. A uniformed warder was standing over him, signaling for him to get up. Before he knew it he found himself outside the cell door being prodded up the same staircase he had come down hours before. He passed the first floor, the second, all the way to the top. Scarcely conscious of where he was, he stumbled down one corridor, then another, making his way more and more deeply into the belly of the prison.

In the administrative wing, from behind one of the doors came a series of painful, despairing cries. Muffled noises followed, then more cries. Kulik fell into a state of panic; his nerves were completely frayed. The sound of someone being tortured was more than he could bear; it tore at his very core. He continued down the halls, barely able to move his feet.

Finally they stopped at a door marked "Tarnovetsky, Major-General" in bold black letters. The warder gave several vigorous knocks and almost immediately a man of about fifty appeared, heavy-set, with dark blue eyes and a bulging forehead. He was dressed in full uniform with high leather boots and decorations on his chest. He summoned Kulik inside and ordered him to sit on a wooden stool opposite his desk. Kulik did as he was told; he was sure that this Major-General would finish him off in just a few minutes.

Tarnovetsky put on his glasses and carefully scanned Kulik's deposition papers. Shaking his head, making notes, he muttered under his breath. Kulik tried to prepare himself for a hopeless conflict. When finally Tarnovetsky began, Kulik was surprised that he did not initiate a sophisticated line of questioning, one that might trip him up and push him into corners from which he could not escape. Tarnovetsky proceeded to reel off routine questions almost identical to those Kulik had been asked that morning. What was his date of birth? Who were his parents? How many siblings did he have? Did he belong to any subversive organizations?

Kulik dared to believe that his fate had not yet been sealed after all. He listened for what was to follow, holding his breath.

Tarnovetsky rose and paced the room with his hands behind his back. "We've verified your social origin and naturally it's to your advantage. We also know you spent five years in a reformatory for boys under Polish occupation and that later, without help from anyone, you earned a university degree in Vilno. I must admit, that's all good, very good. But what concerns us is your anti-Soviet behavior. Yes, some serious accusations have been building against you. Our sources tell us you've been making unwise choices in direct conflict with the regime. To date, we're aware of everything." A crafty look came to his eye. "You'll be happy to know we're in the position of giving you another chance because we're confident your behavior will improve and in time you'll correct these mistakes. In short, we're willing to overlook everything, for now."

Kulik was completely at a loss. The words *for now* spun around in his head. What did Tarnovetsky mean by them? Did he really intend to release him? Or did he intend to release him only to arrest him again, tomorrow or the day after ? Was he trying to further jangle his nerves, to wear him down completely? And where did this charge of anti-Soviet behavior come from, and how was he in conflict with the regime? The accusations against

322

him were so vague that a part of him felt they were laughable. This could not really be happening. But it *was* really happening and it was happening to him. Tarnovetsky was tricking him, testing him, and he was sure that any minute now the Major General would abruptly change his mind and accuse him of some serious crime. His heart sank, and he knew he could not possibly hope to be released, never in a million years.

Only the creaking of the floor broke the silence in the oppressive room. Several minutes went by: it must have been well past midnight. Almost in a feverish state, Kulik waited for Tarnovetsky to at last finish him off. But, incredibly, Tarnovetsky seemed to have another purpose. An unexpected glimmer came to his eye and his face softened; for a brief moment he seemed to betray a kind of humanity. Handing Kulik a cigarette, he said in a low voice, "In future, comrade, I don't advise you to get into conflict with us. You'll only lose."

Kulik swallowed hard. All this was pure madness; this last remark was meaningless. He knew he must not fall into their trap. Determined not to say the wrong thing, almost without being aware of what he was doing, he began spewing political platitudes:

"There's no reason why I should even think of getting into conflict with the regime. After all, I'm a citizen of the great Soviet Empire and my job as a teacher is to educate the young about our exciting new system and everything it has to offer. Glory to the October Revolution! Glory to Stalin!"

Tarnovetsky applauded enthusiastically. "Very well said! Yes, you have a formidable job ahead of you. You must set a precedent for others and your behavior must be exemplary. A Soviet teacher has to be a model citizen. Socialism is the goal of all workers' movements, and it will succeed only when we stand united and work toward the common goal. Long live the World Communist Revolution!"

He walked back to sit down at his desk, opened a dossier on top of a stack of files and studied it intently.

Kulik clenched his fists and kept very quiet for fear of irritating him. An endless stream of thoughts rushed at him: was his prosecutor going to come up with some wild accusation and charge him with it? Was he going to throw him back into the dungeon? Was he intending to finish him off right then and there? Tarnovetsky was behaving as if he had already made a decision. In a flash Kulik understood that there was a plan for him, a plan that had been in the works from the very beginning. It was just a matter of time before his nerves snapped.

Tarnovetsky rose slowly from behind his desk. Incredibly, he closed the dossier and said, "I'm done with you for today. We'll call upon you again soon. But you have nothing to worry about. When we do, it will be just a formality as it was today. You're free to go."

Kulik sat, dumbstruck. The investigation was over. He was free to go. Free to go! He felt like a man condemned to death who was suddenly pardoned. Escorted down to the first floor, to the exit doors, he was handed several documents and some personal items. A uniformed official led him along the cobblestone courtyard to the main gate, where he unlocked it, and set him free, like a bird from a cage

Stunned and bewildered, still trying to make sense of what had just happened, Kulik walked swiftly along the road, and then quickening his pace, broke into a run. His freedom was nothing short of a miracle.

He made his way through the dark streets, past large stone houses, and a stretch of warehouses and factories. When at last he caught sight of the Roman Catholic church tower, he realized that he was just moments away from Market Square. He had to keep moving, running away from everything, and there was no time to lose. The NKVD had let him go just to hunt him down again. They might already be on his trail and moving in on him. He must get off the streets and out of sight as fast as possible. He decided the best place for him to go would be the Park of Culture and Rest. He ran for ten or fifteen minutes. At last, entering the park gates, within seconds he found himself lost in the depths of the park's thick pine forest. Groping his way through the dark, he could hardly discern the objects around him. Twigs and dried leaves snapped and rustled beneath his feet, and every now and then he could see long black shadows with their random outlines stretching and disappearing into the emptiness. He listened for the sound of the river. Just at that moment came the whistling of an engine, then the clanking of chains. A freighter was sailing down the great Pina, probably on its way to Kiev or Dnepropetrovsk. And at that moment he made a decision. He would follow the river, then move along its tributary, Stryy, go south, in the direction of the Carpathian Mountains, then over the mountains, to the west. It would be a long journey, some five hundred kilometers, and it would be almost entirely on foot.

As he scrambled up onto the edge of the embankment, he paused to catch his breath. Thoughts whirled through his head and he couldn't think straight. Yesterday he was headmaster of School Number Seven and today he was a man on the run. Everything was unreal, strange and incomprehensible. The darkness bore down on him like a mass of lead and his mind became even more tangled.

As he was listening to the swirling of the river beneath him, it was only then that he became overcome with despair. He cried aloud: "Sergei! Sergei, I must go and get Sergei and take him with me. They'll show him no mercy!"

But soon he realized it would be too dangerous, it would only result in disaster for them both. Then he thought of Marusia, of Zena, of Ohrimko. . . . He was leaving them all behind, never to see them again. They would stay in a land with no future, a land forever at the mercy of a ruthless despot up to his elbows in blood.

The uncertainty and sense of loss were unbearable. Feverishly, trembling all over, he burst into bitter tears, and as much as he tried, could not stop sobbing.

At last the Stryy! Kulik inhaled deeply and looked around. The sun was already starting to creep over the eastern horizon and it was just a matter of time before everything would be drenched in sunshine. He started along the shore, quickly and vigorously. He had to keep moving, staying one step ahead of the secret police. Listening to the sound of the water, his spirit lifted. He was filled with hope. He believed that his life was not over.